# Rooted & Remembered

by Melody K. Smith

ISBN: 979-8-9990074-3-8

For my friends who acted like 'the moss is misbehaving again' was a completely normal sentence.

And for the strangers who picked up this book, read the back, and thought, *"Sure, why not?"*

You took a chance.

You stayed for the weird magic.

You're now partially responsible for the emotional consequences.

Thank you. Truly.

*Remembrance restores possibility to the past, making what happened incomplete and completing what never was. Remembrance is neither what happened nor what did not happen but, rather, their potentialization, their becoming possible once again.* "

— Giorgio Agamben

# Preface

I knew the moment I wrote the final words of *Stirred & Spellbound* that Cassie's story—and Emerdeen's—wasn't truly finished. Sure, the page said, "The End," but the threads kept tugging. Quietly at first, but then louder. The kind of insistent magical nudge you pretend not to notice until it starts rerouting your grocery lists and whispering through your dreams.

I didn't know where the next chapter would take me. I thought perhaps I'd rest, let the dust settle, maybe finally clean the glitter off my desk. But, as is often the case with matters of magic and memory, I wasn't the one steering. A force, vague but persuasive, stepped in. Maybe it was ancestral magic. Maybe a benevolent spirit. Maybe just a very determined, slightly chaotic fairy with a flair for plot twists and unexpected roots.

Either way, the path unfurled before me.

Through the arches.
Into the roots.
Dancing between the blooms.

What came next was not just a continuation, but a deepening. Of story…of self…of the magic that asked not to be cast but remembered.

And so, dear reader, whether you've come with soil on your hands or stardust in your shoes, I'm grateful you've arrived.

There's something waiting for you here.

— *melody*

# Chapter One: The Wrong Kind of Silence

Morgan had always loved silence.

Not the forced hush of expectation or the strained quiet of people waiting to speak. They meant the other kind. The sacred kind. The stillness that draped itself across a room after a spell had landed just right. The quiet between two good friends who didn't need words to understand one another. The weightless pause in the forest just before the dawn chorus began.

But this silence wasn't like any of those. It was the wrong kind.

It had a density to it, a sort of breathless thickness that pressed in around the edges of Morgan's awareness like fog wrapped too tightly around the lungs. It didn't muffle the world, it erased it. Just a little, just enough to make them second-guess whether it had ever been there at all.

They stood by the riverbank behind Stirred & Spellbound, watching the current hesitate. That was the only word for it—hesitate. The surface quivered in place, neither rushing nor resting. It looked as if the water itself was trying to remember what it meant to flow.

Morgan tilted their head, squinting slightly. They'd been out here before sunrise, drawn not by need or habit, but by that quiet itch behind their ribs. The one that came when magic wanted to say something it didn't yet know how to phrase.

They weren't sure what they expected. Some secret shimmer in the undergrowth, maybe, or a spellbird tangled in the thorns again? But what they found instead was… this. The silence. The hesitation.

The not-quite-rightness of the world.

Morgan reached into the leather pouch slung across their chest and pulled out their thread journal, bound in twilight-blue hide and stitched with silver moss. They thumbed it open to a blank page. Or what should have been a blank page.

Thread laced the parchment with faint, silken strands of copper and charcoal, weaving together in an unfamiliar pattern. Not words or glyphs. It was something older. They hadn't put it there. They were certain of that.

As they leaned closer, the threads pulsed once, like breath or heartbeat. Then they vanished.

Not unwound. Not burned away. Just gone.

Morgan's stomach sank. They looked up again, scanning the horizon. The greenhouse loomed nearby, a mosaic of glass panels catching the first rays of morning like a prism, casting rainbow freckles across the earth. Inside, they could just make out movement. Cassie, probably, arranging the day's supplies for her morning workshop. If Morgan had to guess, it was either *Boundary Setting Through Broomwork* or *Feral Herbs and the People Who Love Them*.

Cassie had taken to naming her workshops with a kind of chaos that could only be described as inspirational. They suited her. So did this place, truth be told. Stirred & Spellbound had become more than a crafting sanctuary; it was a tether point. A breath. A haven.

Morgan smiled faintly and closed the journal.

They should go inside. There were chores to be done, appointments to prep for, a quiet consultation later with one of the newer Makers who couldn't quite get her enchanted ink to stop narrating her insecurities aloud. But Morgan didn't move. Not yet.

Because in the corner of their mind, uninvited but oddly welcome, drifted a name.

Gabe.

It shouldn't have meant anything. And yet it snagged on their thoughts like burrs on wool.

They hadn't heard that name in years. Not in conversation. Not in dreams. It belonged to a thread they'd long since set down and never dared to pick up again. A possibility that had never been woven.

And now, without warning, it was back.

Inside, the greenhouse buzzed with the familiar energy of enchanted chaos.

Cassie stood near the central table, brow furrowed, surrounded by a collection of broomsticks all mid-dispute. One refused to stop shedding pine needles. Another had grown a mustache. A third spun in lazy circles on the floor like it was trying to summon a dust devil from boredom alone.

Morgan slipped in quietly, their steps barely brushing the mosaic tile floor. Cassie looked up, the corner of her mouth twitching into a crooked grin.

"Ah, the strong and silent type," she said, waving a hand in mock greeting. "Come to save me from my aggressive cleaning tools?"

Morgan arched a brow. "I thought you said they were blessed for energetic alignment."

"They were," Cassie said. "Then one of them found out it was made from leftover hedge wood and took offense."

Morgan walked over and eyed the spinning broom. "Do you want me to...?"

"Please. If it flings one more acorn at my head, I'm invoking an exorcism by sarcasm."

Morgan knelt, whispered a grounding charm, and laid one hand on the broom's bristled base. It stilled immediately, releasing a sigh that was far too dramatic for an inanimate object.

Cassie clapped. "Your magic touch, as always."

"I think it just wanted to be seen," Morgan said softly, standing again.

"Don't we all." Cassie's voice held more depth than the joke warranted, but she waved it off. "You look like you didn't sleep."

"I didn't."

"Trouble, or the usual 'dreams have teeth' thing?"

Morgan hesitated. "Something's... stirring. Quietly. But it doesn't feel like it wants to be found yet."

Cassie nodded, her expression shifting to something thoughtful. "Like waiting for the next sentence in a story you forgot you were telling?"

"Exactly that."

Cassie placed a steady hand on Morgan's shoulder. "You'll find it. Or it'll find you. Either way, I'd bet the broom stash that it's yours to weave."

Later that afternoon, while the workshop hummed with laughter and mossy glamour, Morgan sat beneath the shade of the willow tree beside the river. They opened the journal again. This time the page was truly blank.

But they didn't need the thread to appear again. They could feel it now, somewhere deeper. A presence in the quiet. A calling.

Not a threat. Not yet. But not a memory, either.

4

Something… becoming.

And somewhere inside that strange, persistent stillness, the name echoed once more. Gabe.

Morgan closed their eyes as the river flowed again. But the silence remained.

## Chapter Two: Brooms, Boundaries & Blunt Instruments

"Remember," Cassie called, "you don't control the broom. You invite cooperation. Preferably without threats."

A broom launched itself across the room and slammed into a shelving unit.

Cassie winced. "That's more of a suggestion than a requirement."

The workshop was in full, unhinged swing.

Sunlight streamed through the greenhouse panes, casting rainbows over the chaos unfolding inside Stirred & Spellbound. Six participants stood in a semi-circle, each paired with a stubbornly enchanted broom. Most of the tools were still upright. A few were sulking. One had developed an attitude so pungent it now shed lavender oil aggressively whenever touched.

Cassie, in her apron that read *"Witch, Please"* and a ribbon-wrapped braid that dared you to underestimate her, moved with the calm of someone long since past the threshold of controlling the room. She'd surrendered to the mayhem hours ago. Now she was simply… facilitating.

"Let's try it again," she said, grinning through the madness. "Ground yourself. Connect. Establish emotional boundaries. Communicate with confidence."

A younger woman named Eliza, who had just finished a month of break-up candles and psychic cord-cutting baths, took a deep breath, extended her hand toward her broom, and said in her best therapist voice, "I respect your need for autonomy, but this is a collaborative sweep."

The broom twitched. Then shot twenty feet into the air, hitting the rafters with a clatter and showering the group in dried rosemary.

Cassie clapped politely. "Honestly, better than I expected."

Bram leaned over from where he was painting protective sigils onto the workbench in shimmering indigo. "This is why I don't enchant cleaning supplies. Too much inherited trauma."

"Your enchanted ladle tried to start a union last week," Cassie pointed out.

"And I supported it. Even gave it a lunch break."

Morgan watched from a perch near the potting shelf, arms crossed, lips pressed in a half-smile. Cassie had noticed their restlessness since that morning. They were quieter than usual, more inward facing. The kind of silence that meant something was coming but hadn't yet arrived.

She filed that observation away. For now, the brooms needed wrangling, and her tea timer had just exploded for the third time today.

By the end of the first hour, two brooms had been gently dismantled, one participant had accidentally invoked a small windstorm that now lived in a pickle jar, and Cassie had started writing a new workshop proposal:

*"Magical Conflict Resolution for Inanimate Objects with Feelings."*

As the group took a break with tea and peach scones laid out like offerings to the gods of household management, Cassie drifted over to Morgan.

"Thoughts on today's triumphs?"

Morgan gave a small shrug. "No one burst into flames."

"Low bar."

7

"It's Monday."

Cassie snorted. "True."

They stood in companionable silence, watching the breeze scatter herb petals across the greenhouse floor.

"Did the thread show up again?" Cassie asked quietly.

Morgan didn't answer right away. "No. But the quiet hasn't left."

Cassie nodded. "You ever think silence might just be the universe trying to find the right words?"

Morgan gave a soft, sideways glance. "Do you always turn my existential dread into a greeting card?"

"Not always. Sometimes it's a bumper sticker." She bumped her shoulder gently against theirs. "Let me know when you're ready to unravel it. I'll bring wine and morally flexible candles."

They were about to reply when the front bell chimed. And for a moment, everything stopped. Not dramatically. Not with fear. Just... quiet. A pause so subtle even the broom with commitment issues seemed to sit straighter.

The man who entered didn't look magical. He looked like he might yell at a cloud for being "inefficient." Tall, lean, khaki'd to death, and holding a clipboard with the same reverence one might hold a sacred tome. He glanced around with clinical interest.

Cassie gave Morgan a look that could only mean: Uh oh.

"Hello!" she called out, bright and terrible. "Welcome to Stirred & Spellbound. We're currently in a sacred session involving trauma-informed broom diplomacy. Do you have an appointment or are you just spiritually lost?"

The man blinked. "I'm Dr. Everett Shaw. I've been asked by the Alden's Landing Preservation Board to conduct a community compliance audit of mixed-use properties involving botanical and mystical practices."

Cassie's smile widened. "Ah. So spiritually lost, then."

Dr. Shaw made a note on his clipboard.

Cassie turned to Morgan and whispered, "I give him three days before the compost bin eats him."

Morgan, expression unreadable, replied, "Two. If Bram adds cinnamon."

Dr. Everett Shaw walked the length of the greenhouse with the meticulous caution of a man afraid of stepping in something he couldn't quantify. His eyes scanned every surface, every herbal bundle, every charm-woven windcatcher spinning lazily above the potting station. The clipboard in his hands clicked with alarming frequency, each tick of his pen like a mosquito buzzing in the middle of a moon ritual.

Cassie tracked him like a cat watching an overly confident pigeon.

"So," she said brightly, "what exactly does a community compliance audit of a mystical botanical site entail? Are you measuring the spiritual density of the oregano or checking to see if the chamomile is plotting sedition?"

Shaw frowned. "The Preservation Board has received several complaints."

"Let me guess," Bram said, appearing at her side like summoned sass. "Too many wisteria vines climbing civic buildings, or perhaps a haunted weathervane reciting town bylaws at midnight?"

"There are reports," Shaw continued, unbothered, "of unlicensed enchantments, undocumented use of energy manipulation, irregular zoning of magical structures, and…" he squinted at his notes, "…a rumor about sentient moss."

"That's not a rumor," Wren called from the back, arranging drying bundles of dreamroot. "That moss pays rent."

"Name's Barry, short for Mildew Barrymore," Bram added. "Very punctual. Bit judgy."

Morgan, still watching from the edges, let the corners of their mouth twitch. The Coven's chemistry never failed. Their humor was more than habit, it was armor. Against grief. Against the mundane. Against people like Shaw who mistook structure for safety.

Shaw sniffed, visibly unamused. "I am here to ensure the residents and businesses of Alden's Landing operate in accordance with town law. All structures and practices must align with Section 8.3 of the Public Harmony and Sustainability Charter."

Cassie tilted her head. "Public Harmony?"

"Yes."

Her smile was slow and dangerous. "I'd argue harmony is exactly what we're offering. Emotional regulation through creative practice. Conflict resolution with organic glitter. Tea-based trauma healing. We're basically public health with better lighting."

"This is not a joke, Miss Merrin."

Cassie's expression turned sharply sweet. "It rarely is, Dr. Shaw. But that doesn't mean it has to be joyless."

He checked another box. "I'll be reviewing your permits, safety protocols, and any spell craft certifications by week's end."

"Wonderful," she said, voice like honey stirred into a storm. "In the meantime, feel free to browse the gift nook. We've got hex-neutral candles, boundary-boosting bath salts, and our bestselling book: *Manifesting Through Mild Petty Revenge*."

Dr. Shaw paused, looked over at a display of hand-lettered affirmations carved into reclaimed birch bark, one of which read *"You're not difficult, you're just divine with opinions"*, and made a sound like a man trying to digest unsanctioned joy.

He turned toward the door. "I'll return tomorrow."

Cassie waited until he was out of earshot, then clapped her hands. "Alright, team. We've officially met the antagonist."

"Do we hex his clipboard?" Wren asked.

"Too obvious," Bram replied. "We charm it to rephrase all his notes into love poems. Extremely confusing. Marginally romantic."

"Or" Cassie mused, "we say nothing. We continue as usual. With just enough enchantment in the herb bins to make his hair stand on end every time he walks by. Very subtle. Extremely municipal."

Morgan leaned in. "He'll file a complaint."

"Of course," Cassie said. "And we'll respond with hand-lettered correspondence on enchanted stationery that smells faintly of judgment and sage."

Wren offered a slow clap. "Masterful."

Cassie gave Morgan a sideways glance. "Still feeling the weird magic shift?"

Morgan nodded slowly. "Yes. And now I'm starting to think he's part of it."

11

"He's got the vibe of a cursed fountain pen."

"Or someone who once lost an argument to a willow tree and never recovered."

Cassie's humor slipped just slightly as her eyes narrowed in thought. "Still. People like him don't just show up. Someone sent him. And whoever that is, whether mundane or magical, they want something."

Morgan's gaze drifted to the place where Shaw had stood.

Something was off. Not just with him, but with the way the threads in the air had trembled when he walked in. As if the weave of the space had hiccupped. That almost never happened. Not without reason.

They made a mental note to check the river again. Soon.

That night, after the brooms had been tamed and the workshop cleaned, Cassie found a note in the spell nook. It was folded carefully, tucked between two bundles of eucalyptus and witchgrass.

It read: *"Your structures are beautiful. But something underneath them is shifting. Ask the one who remembers. Ask the silent one."*

No signature.

Cassie turned the parchment over. It was lined with a faint shimmer of copper thread. She didn't need to ask who it was meant for.

Morgan was already watching the night sky, listening for the next silence that didn't feel like rest.

## Chapter Three: The Stillness That Waited

The river was never quiet for long. Even in the deepest parts of winter, when the banks lay blanketed in frost and the trees whispered in bare, brittle voices, the water moved. It always moved.

Until now.

Morgan returned to the river the following morning, drawn again by that same hollow note in the air, a dissonance in the weave. The sunlight filtered through the trees in soft angles, catching on dew-heavy branches and illuminating the path with a dreamlike haze. But the beauty didn't soothe them.

It unsettled.

They paused at the edge, boots crunching softly over the damp, rooted trail. The river still looked like a river. Still wound the same slow path behind Stirred & Spellbound. Still reflected the leaves overhead in glimmering mosaic.

But it wasn't moving. At least not in any way that made sense. It shimmered with the idea of movement. Like it was performing, playing at being itself.

Morgan crouched, reaching out with a tentative thread of magic—subtle, woven from memory and tone, not force. They whispered something soft and shapeless into the current. The water responded, but not with a ripple. With a silence. A reply in the same still language that had haunted them for days.

Morgan's fingers twitched. Something beneath the surface of the river was waiting. Not a creature. Not even necessarily a force, but a presence. One they hadn't touched in years.

They opened their thread journal again, half expecting to find another apparition of copper and charcoal winding through the page. But this time, there was something different.

In the center of the parchment: a single name.

*Gabe.*

Not written in ink. Not even woven. Just… there. Like the page remembered it for them.

Morgan closed the journal slowly, heart thudding not with fear, but recognition. A knowing that settled deeper than thought.

This wasn't a haunting.

It was a return.

They sat by the river for a long time, letting the weight of the name settle in their body. They hadn't spoken it aloud since the Hollowing. Since Emerdeen was nearly unraveled by grief and fracture. Since choices had been made, not wrong ones, but definitive ones. Ones that carved paths into permanence.

They had walked away from that thread before it could be spun. Now, it was calling back. Not with accusation. Not even with hope. Just presence.

Morgan took a breath, slow and measured, and reached out, not with magic, but with memory. They let themselves remember Gabe.

Not as someone, exactly, but as something, a thread that could have been part of them. A voice they'd almost grown into. A shadow-self they'd chosen not to become or perhaps hadn't been ready for yet.

And in that remembering, the silence shifted. Not completely, but enough.

The river gave a ripple. Just one. It moved like breath returning to a long-sleeping body.

Later, they would try to explain it to Cassie. How it felt like the world had been holding its breath, and now, with the whisper of a name, it had exhaled. Cassie would nod thoughtfully, then offer them a mug of rosemary-citrus tea and a sarcastic, "Congratulations, you've emotionally dislodged a river."

But for now, Morgan stayed. They took off their boots and socks and stepped into the water.

It wasn't cold. It was expectant.

They stood there, up to their ankles in something that felt older than memory. And as they stood, they closed their eyes, let their thoughts drift into the current, and whispered again. Not a spell, not a request, just a truth.

"I remember you."

The water rippled again. And this time, it sang.

Not in notes. Not even in words, but in something just as real.

Possibility.

# Chapter Four: Threadshock & Tea Breaks

The first sign that something had shifted came when Bram's measuring spoons began reciting poetry.

Not just any poetry, prophetic poetry. And not even the broody kind that Morgan sometimes scribbled into margins or Baz coaxed from stonework. No, this was rhyme-heavy, full of aggressive enjambment, and delivered with the cadence of a bard on too much mint tea.

Bram, who had been trying to measure cinnamon for his *Clarity & Clapback* candles, squinted at the spoon. "Did you just say, 'the thread returns, but not as one, stitched in shadow, sun undone'?"

The spoon jangled in reply, smug as silver could be.

Cassie glanced up from her nearby workbench, where she was layering petals and finely chopped rowan bark into charm sachets. "That's either a premonition or a failed workshop slogan."

"Could be both," Baz added. He was stringing together floating stones and sigil-marked shells in a spiral formation. "Did you feel it earlier? That thrum in the air?"

"I felt it," Wren called from across the greenhouse. "It knocked over my tincture shelf. Lavender and emotional repression all over the floor."

"It was Morgan," Cassie said quietly, dusting her hands free of herbs. "Something changed."

They all fell silent for a beat, the usual coven banter giving way to the reverent hush that only true magic commanded. Not chaos-magic. Not craft-magic. Core magic. The kind that rewrote blueprints with a whisper and left the bones of the world humming.

Baz looked up, his sea-glass eyes serious. "What do you think they touched?"

"Something old," Cassie replied. "Something waiting."

An hour later, the Coven assembled in the main gathering hall of Stirred & Spellbound (half greenhouse, half cottagecore dreamscape) with mugs in hand and a spell circle unfurled across the floor in lazy spirals of chalk and fern.

Cassie stood at its center, arms crossed, mind already spinning.

"We've got echoes in the air," she began. "Runes smudging without cause, tools twitching, and an uptick in unspoken weirdness."

"The spoons," Bram added helpfully.

"Yes, the spoons," Cassie deadpanned. "But also... the land is listening again. The Tree's roots are tense. And I don't think Morgan's just sensing it, they're part of it."

Baz nodded. "It started this morning, didn't it? That's when the thread spiked."

"I was making peace tea," Wren murmured, "and it tried to transform into anti-anxiety soup. Which would've been fine, except it summoned a salt golem. In a mug."

Bram looked delighted. "Did it have a name?"

Wren deadpanned. "Greg."

Cassie stifled a laugh. "Okay, so: Morgan's magic is stirring something deeper. That's not unexpected, considering what they carry. But if Emerdeen's balance is responding... we need to be ahead of it."

Baz's fingers drummed against his ceramic cup. "I'll check the ley maps tonight. See if the threads are drifting."

"I'll restock the ward kits," Bram said. "And give the spoons a time-out."

Cassie moved to the tall wooden cabinet at the far wall and pulled open the drawer marked *'For When It Gets Weird'*. Inside were sigil-binders, enchanted maps, a scrying locket shaped like a teardrop, and a small tin labeled *"Nope Mints."*

She popped one in her mouth and turned to the group. "If we're heading into another unraveling, let's at least do it with snacks, sass, and solid magical infrastructure."

Just then, the front door swung open, slamming far harder than it should have, and a gust of cold wind spiraled through the room, carrying a strange scent: river mist and scorched memory.

Every candle flickered out.

No one spoke.

Then from the darkness, a voice cut the tension.

"Well. That's new."

## Chapter Five: Threadlines and Thornroots

Morgan returned barefoot. Not out of ritual, or even forgetfulness, just a quiet instinct. The river still clung to their skin, and something about putting shoes back on felt… false. They wanted to feel the earth under their feet, the leaf-damp path like a thread running beneath them, stitching one breath to the next.

The walk back to Stirred & Spellbound felt longer than it should have. Not in distance, but in density. Like each step had to part the air, which now shimmered with barely veiled attention. The wind whispered in syncopated hushes. The stones hummed, faint and rhythmic. Even the light filtering through the trees seemed to carry weight.

Morgan wasn't sure if they were returning from something or stepping into it. When they reached the greenhouse, the door was already open. That was the first sign something was off.

The second was the smell: damp cedar, singed mint, and oddly, rosemary tea with an identity crisis. They stepped inside.

Cassie was standing near the ward table, sleeves rolled, runes glowing faintly along her knuckles. Baz leaned over a shimmer-map hovering in midair, eyes narrowed, hair full of stardust and tension. Bram, Wren, and two newer Makers were doing a half-circle triage with the enchanted spoon drawer, which appeared to be attempting a dramatic escape.

Cassie looked up the moment Morgan stepped through the threshold. "There you are," she said. Not accusatory. Not surprised. Just deeply aware that something had shifted. "Let me guess. You took a walk, and the river told you a secret it wasn't supposed to."

Morgan gave a small, dry smile. "It didn't tell me anything. It just remembered me."

Baz turned, wiping a smear of chalk from his wrist. "Something's moved in the ley flow. The World Tree's aura is shedding bark."

"Metaphorically," Wren added quickly. "So far, but that energy flow is strong."

Morgan stepped farther in. "I think the threads are waking up again. Not the ones we saved. The ones we left behind."

Cassie raised a brow. "That's comforting. Do they want tea? Closure? To file a class-action suit for magical abandonment?"

"They want… form. Voice." Morgan hesitated. "They're not angry. Just unfinished."

The room stilled.

Baz muttered, "The Threadless."

Cassie sighed and leaned against the worktable. "Of course. Because it's been, what, two years since our last magical existential reckoning?"

"Almost three," Bram offered helpfully.

She shot him a look. "Don't help."

Morgan approached the spell map on the table. Threads of colored light shifted gently above it, representing known magical tethers in Emerdeen. Most glowed with steady brightness, stable. Some flickered, as if reconsidering their decisions.

One, near the heart of the World Tree's root system, pulsed irregularly. Copper and shadow, with an echo of something Morgan couldn't name.

"I don't think this is just magic," they said. "It's memory. Possibility. A shape that was never allowed to settle."

"Unmade?" Baz asked.

"Unspoken," Morgan said softly. "But not gone."

Cassie exhaled slowly. "Alright. We'll anchor the space. Boost containment wards. I'll reinforce the threshold tethers and put out the 'Do Not Disturb Unless You Are a Well-Behaved Spiritual Being' sign."

"Should I charm the spoons to stop prophesying?" Bram asked.

"No," Cassie replied. "I want to know how it ends."

Later, after the chaos calmed and the map quieted, Morgan sat alone in the center of the spell circle, barefoot, journal open. The page was blank again. Waiting.

They could feel the pull now, not just under their skin, but in the room itself. A low, insistent vibration, like a loom in motion somewhere out of sight, just beyond the veil.

Their fingers moved on instinct. This time, they didn't write a word. They wove a name.

Not Gabe. Not yet. Just the first thread.

## Chapter Six: The One You Could Have Been

Morgan didn't dream so much as remember sideways. Sleep didn't offer rest anymore. Not with the threads stirring. Instead, it unfolded like a loom, and Morgan, whether they wanted to or not, became part of the pattern.

It began with a hum. Low. Continuous. A vibration deep in their chest, as if someone was tuning an old harp inside their ribcage. Not unpleasant. Just... inevitable.

Then the dream-shadows came. Half-formed spaces without edges, memories made of suggestion instead of substance. Morgan stood in a room they didn't recognize but somehow knew. Wood-paneled walls. A river-colored rug. A single chair facing the window. And someone in it.

They couldn't see his face, not fully. The air shimmered around him, obscuring detail. But he felt familiar. Not like family or a lover.

Like an echo. Like an almost.

The figure looked out the window, where the sky bled gold and gray.

"I didn't expect you to come back," he said. His voice was quiet but sure. "You left so carefully."

Morgan tried to respond but couldn't. Their mouth moved, but no sound came. The dream wasn't built for speech. Only witnessing.

The figure stood, still faceless but defined now by posture - graceful, reserved, resolute.

"Do you remember the choice?" he asked.

Morgan didn't need to ask which one. The memory flared unbidden: the Hollowing, the fractures in Emerdeen, the desperate weaving of light and dark to keep the world from unraveling. They remembered standing at a fork in their own spirit, one thread of them reaching forward, one folding away.

And choosing to stay rooted and remain quiet. It was to give form to others, not themselves.

The figure stepped closer. Not threatening. Not demanding. Just present.

"I was the one who kept walking," he said. "Not forward. Not backward. Just... between."

Morgan's heart thudded. The dream shivered at the sound.

"I'm not here to haunt you," the figure added. "You never harmed me. I'm still part of you. Just not a part you ever named."

Then he reached out a hand, not to touch, but to offer.

And finally, Morgan heard a name, not from his mouth, but from the space between them. The echo of it sang in the threads woven under their skin.

Gabe.

Morgan woke with a gasp. They were still in the greenhouse. Still seated in the spell circle. The air was warm with night magic and the lingering scent of lemon balm. Somewhere nearby, Wren muttered in their sleep and turned over on the reading couch.

Morgan's heart raced. The vision had been clear, not dreamlike, not metaphorical. It was memory. Not of something that happened, but of something that could have. And now it wanted voice.

They rose slowly, grounding themselves with breath. One step, then another, toward the potion sink to splash water on their face.

In the warped mirror above the basin, their reflection shimmered just slightly. Not distorted. Just... double-exposed. For a moment, another shape stood beside theirs. Same height. Same build. But held differently. Straighter. Quieter.

The mirror flickered. Then settled.

Morgan stared at themselves for a long time. And for the first time in years, they asked the question they'd carefully avoided:

What would I have become if I hadn't stopped becoming?

# Chapter Seven: Ghosts That Never Were

The first sign came from the old post office. Not that anyone in the Coven used it regularly, unless you counted the enchanted parcel pigeon Cassie had trained to deliver spell kits and handwritten affirmations (usually with a glitter seal and a slightly passive-aggressive tea blend).

But that morning, the postmaster, Mrs. Norwood, who believed in punctuality, practical shoes, and exactly zero magical nonsense, stormed into Stirred & Spellbound with a scowl sharp enough to cut thread.

"I would like to know," she said, brandishing a crisp manila envelope like a curse tablet, "why your little group of moss-scented troublemakers is interfering with my mail."

Cassie looked up from her jar of calendula paste. "We haven't even hexed the post office this month."

Mrs. Norwood slammed the envelope onto the counter. Inside was a letter and it was addressed in Morgan's handwriting to someone named Elias, at a house that hadn't existed in Alden's Landing in over seventy years.

Baz, hovering nearby, went pale.

Wren took one look and whispered, "Oh no."

Cassie lifted the letter gently. It was sealed with golden thread, frayed at the edges, and bore the faint scent of rosemary and… regret.

"Morgan didn't write this," Cassie said. "Not recently."

"No," Baz agreed. "But I think they might have, once."

Mrs. Norwood snorted. "Well, tell them to keep their imaginary pen pals out of my mail routes. And while you're at it, explain the ceramic frog in my lobby that keeps singing opera."

She turned and left in a huff. The door slammed behind her.

Cassie exhaled and held up the envelope. "Okay. So, memory is manifesting now."

By midday, the rest of the town had joined in.

A retired schoolteacher reported finding a stack of hand-drawn maps in his attic, none of which matched any known geography, but all of which were signed in Morgan's careful cursive.

A child claimed that her imaginary friend had "finally come back" and was "made of leftover stories and starlight."

Even the ley line crystal at the town's crossroads shimmered with flickering scenes from unlived days. Alternate paths. Forgotten wishes. Old choices, caught in magical stasis.

Cassie met the Coven in the greenhouse just after sunset, lit with storm lanterns and tension. "It's not just echoes anymore," she said. "We're seeing full bleed-through."

Baz ran a hand through his hair. "The veil's gone soft."

"Memory magic doesn't usually do this," Wren added, pacing. "It archives; it doesn't perform."

"It does if it's Threadless," Bram said softly. "These aren't ghosts. They're maybes. Might've-beens."

"And they're latching on to real space," Cassie murmured, "because something or someone is pulling at the weave from the other side."

26

Morgan entered the room, silent as ever, eyes shadowed but steady. "It's not someone," they said. "It's me."

The room went still. Morgan stepped into the circle of candlelight, holding the golden-threaded envelope.

"I didn't write this," they said. "But I could have before the Hollowing. Before I chose to stay quiet."

Cassie moved to their side. "And now?"

Morgan's voice was soft, but sure. "Now I think I need to remember what I chose not to become."

Wren leaned forward. "Do you think these are warnings?"

"No," Morgan said. "I think they're invitations."

Outside, the wind picked up. And far below, beneath the roots of the World Tree, something opened. A door made of not-quite-light and the sound of a loom drawing breath.

## Chapter Eight: Wardwork & Whisperfolk

Cassie called it a "containment picnic." Mostly because the word "containment" sounded too grim by itself, and "picnic" was the only way to get Wren to bring snacks.

The Coven had spread out over the southeastern edge of Alden's Landing, where the threadlines had begun fraying the worst. Just past the overgrown rail fence near the orchard, where the veil between memory and form was now so thin that time sometimes hiccupped.

Cassie stood in the center, directing magical traffic with a wand shaped like a watercolor brush and a spell map scribbled on the back of an old scone recipe.

"Bram, you're on shimmer-traps," she said. "Set one by the walnut grove and another near Mrs. Norwood's hydrangeas. But not too close. The hydrangeas bite."

"On it," Bram replied, already stringing fine copper wire between two wind-bent fence posts.

"Wren, I need a perimeter charm that doesn't attract moths this time."

"No promises," Wren muttered, grinding up lemon balm and honeysuckle resin with a mortar that looked suspiciously like a coffee mug.

Baz, sitting cross-legged at the heart of the makeshift field grid, was humming softly under his breath, coaxing invisible leyline energy into harmonic alignment. The air around him shimmered faintly with golden light, like heat rising from old parchment.

Cassie dipped a finger into the soil and whispered a grounding phrase under her breath. A line of ivy curled up in response, wrapping gently around the base of a stone rune she'd planted like a stake.

"This is all very comforting," she muttered. "Which naturally means something weird's about to happen."

It did. Three minutes later.

It began as a flicker. Just a shimmer in the air between two willow trees. At first, Cassie thought it was heat mirage or leftover magic from Baz's leywork.

But then it spoke. Not in language, in memory.

A feeling swept across the field: a rush of breathless joy, followed by the taste of apples, the scent of autumn, the weight of a decision not made.

Cassie staggered back.

Wren dropped her mortar.

Baz froze mid-hum.

The shimmer stretched.

And then they saw it.

A figure. Blurred, shifting, genderless. It shimmered like thread caught in light. There, not-there, full of outlines that changed with every blink. A cloak that might have been moss, hair that might have been stormlight. And eyes that mirrored nothing and everything all at once.

It didn't step forward. It unfolded.

"Threadless," Bram whispered.

Cassie stepped in front of them instinctively, a protective sigil flaring to life on her wrist.

The figure didn't approach. Didn't threaten. It simply existed.

And with it, the air vibrated with the echo of a hundred near truths, i.e. unwritten letters, unnamed feelings, paths not taken and still waiting to be chosen.

Cassie swallowed. "I get it," she said softly, mostly to herself. "They're not here to destroy anything. They just want to be real."

The figure tilted its head, then vanished like it had never been there at all.

Except... the grass was pressed in a faint circle where it had stood. The air still shimmered with unfinished thoughts. And the wind carried the ghost of a voice:

"Almost."

That night, as the Coven gathered around the bonfire at Stirred & Spellbound to recalibrate wards and process what they'd seen, Cassie stood slightly apart, a spoonful of honeyed tea held loosely in her hand.

Morgan joined her quietly. "They're starting to step through," she said.

Cassie didn't flinch. "We met one today. Not hostile. Just... yearning."

Morgan's gaze stayed on the fire. "They were never angry. They were only ever paused."

Cassie turned, watching their face in the flickering light. "Can you guide them? Anchor them, somehow?"

Morgan nodded slowly. "Maybe. But not from here."

Cassie's eyes narrowed gently. "You're going below."

"Yes."

She reached out, squeezing their shoulder. "Then take what you need. And come back whole."

Morgan looked up, the firelight catching in their eyes. "I don't think wholeness is the goal anymore."

Cassie smiled, weary and proud. "Then come back true."

# Chapter Nine: The Echo Between

The dream didn't begin; it returned.

Morgan stood in the greenhouse again, but not the one that existed now. This was the version from three years ago, before the Hollowing, before the river shifted, before Cassie and Baz had poured so much of their magic into its restoration that it pulsed with shared breath.

This version was quieter and smaller. It smelled of cedar oil and unshed grief.

The worktables were bare. The shelves half-stocked. The air buzzed not with energy, but possibility.

Morgan stood at the threshold, barefoot, again. Across the room, someone was assembling a loom. Slowly and carefully. Like they were coaxing it into being rather than building it.

The someone was Gabe.

Not the shimmering outline from their dreams. Not a faceless echo.

This time, Morgan could see him clearly.

His features weren't sharp; they didn't need to be. It was the feeling that landed first: grounded presence, measured thoughtfulness, a sense of potential contained in skin and shadow. His hair was dark, curling slightly at the edges. His clothes were simple, timeless, softly layered. And when he looked up, his eyes were not quite Morgan's, but close.

He didn't smile. But his gaze held recognition. Like they'd left mid-conversation and were only just now returning.

"You almost didn't come," he said, his voice warm and quiet, like dusk made audible.

Morgan stepped forward. "You're not real."

Gabe tilted his head. "Neither are you. Not the version of you that stayed still. But we're both becoming, aren't we?"

Morgan's chest tightened. "You're the path I didn't take."

"I'm the shape you let go. The part that kept walking." He gestured around the unfinished greenhouse. "You left something behind here. And not just potential. Memory. Form. The world remembers us both, even if you didn't."

Morgan looked down at their hands. "You feel real."

"I am." Gabe walked toward them. "Because the threads are waking. The Archive remembers what wasn't woven. And I'm part of it. Just like you are."

Morgan's breath came unevenly. "Are you angry?"

"No," Gabe said simply. "I'm lonely. There's a difference."

Silence bloomed between them soft, rich, like fertile soil. Then Gabe reached into the air between them, and it rippled.

He plucked something invisible, a threadlight, and twisted it into a tiny, glowing spiral between his fingers. "The Threadless aren't coming to undo you. They're trying to become. But they don't know how. Not without someone to remember them into shape."

Morgan's hands trembled. "I don't know how to do that," they said.

"You do," Gabe said gently. "You just have to stop believing that remembering is the same as regretting."

Morgan looked up.

Gabe took a step closer and pressed the glowing spiral into Morgan's palm. It pulsed once like breath and melted into their skin.

And just before the dream began to fall away like ash on wind, Gabe whispered:

"Come find me. I'll be where you almost were."

Morgan woke with a start. This time, they didn't hesitate. They packed only what they needed: a notebook, a bundle of anchoring thread, three runes stitched with Cassie's wardwork, and a candle that had never gone out.

At the base of the World Tree, the earth split quietly. Not with violence, but invitation.

Morgan stepped into the Archive Beneath.

Not to retrieve what was lost, but to remember what had never been.

# Chapter Ten: The Archive Beneath

The descent wasn't vertical. It wasn't even physical, exactly. It felt more like unraveling.

One moment, Morgan was beneath the World Tree, fingers brushing bark older than language, and the next, they were walking through a space that didn't begin so much as recognize them.

The Archive Beneath wasn't underground. It was underneath - beneath time, beneath memory, beneath all the threads they hadn't pulled.

The path was barely a path at all, stitched together from steppingstones of unfinished thoughts. Morgan's feet moved without direction, guided not by will, but by resonance. Each step hummed beneath them, vibrating with fragments of almost. The walls shifted.

At first glance, there were no walls. Just infinite space, quiet and glowing. But as Morgan moved, memories took shape: a childhood bedroom that never quite existed, a mirror that reflected not their face but the feeling of being twelve and wanting to disappear. Shelves grew out of fog, holding books whose titles changed mid-sentence, all written in Morgan's handwriting.

They passed a window hanging in midair, unattached to any wall. Through it, they saw a younger version of themselves, seated in a classroom that never was, answering a question they were never asked: What would you be if you weren't afraid?

Morgan didn't stop walking.

The Archive pulsed with ambient memory. Not memories they'd made, but memories that had almost been theirs. They recognized none of the furniture, but all the feelings.

Ahead, the path forked. To the left: a corridor of music. Faint strains of a lullaby Morgan didn't remember learning but could hum by instinct. The walls there shimmered with spectral outlines of faces, familiar but unlived.

To the right: a staircase made of threadlight. Each step held a name, some forgotten, some never spoken aloud. The air smelled of ink, river fog, and quiet hope.

Morgan hesitated, then turned left.

The corridor opened into a vast chamber where the walls breathed. Literally.

They moved in and out like lungs, lined with soft, glowing sigils. Floating globes of memory drifted past, glimpses of love never pursued, fights never started, ideas abandoned too soon. One brushed Morgan's shoulder, and a flash of emotion hit them like a storm: longing for a name that had never been given.

The air here was heavier. Not oppressive. Just full. Alive with the tension of all the might-have-beens.

Morgan touched one of the sigils. It vibrated beneath their palm. For a moment, they saw Gabe, not in front of them, but around them. Like he'd been stitched into the very breath of the Archive. Not haunting. Just… present. Waiting.

Morgan exhaled, pressing both hands to the wall, letting their magic sync with the room's rhythm. "I'm here," they whispered.

And the Archive responded. Not in sound, but in opening.

A seam split down the center of the chamber, revealing a staircase that led deeper, not down, but inward.

Morgan stepped through and the door closed behind them.

## Chapter Eleven: The Name That Never Settled

The chamber smelled like childhood dreams left too long in the sun. Not sweet. Not bitter. Just faded, like something once important, now fragile.

Morgan stepped into a space that pulsed not with energy, but anticipation. The walls here no longer breathed. They shimmered. As if watching.

Ahead stood a figure. Not quite human, but not quite not.

They had the outline of a body, tall and lean, wrapped in layers of translucent fabric that shifted with every flicker of thought. Their face blurred at the edges, like a sketch unfinished. Their presence pressed lightly against the air, like fog on a windowpane.

Morgan didn't move.

The figure turned, slow and careful.

Their eyes were... vacant, but not hollow. Like they hadn't been filled in yet. Their gaze skimmed across Morgan, pausing not in recognition, but curiosity.

The silence deepened.

Then: "You know me," the Threadless soul said. Their voice echoed not in Morgan's ears, but in the space behind their sternum.

Morgan swallowed. "No. But I think I could."

The soul tilted their head. "Is that permission?"

Morgan hesitated. "To become?"

"To be," the Threadless replied, voice fraying around the syllables. "I remember wind. Books. A garden that might have been mine. But no name held."

Morgan took a breath, slow and grounded. "Then let's find one."

The soul flickered and the room responded.

The walls began to fill, not with writing, but moments. Floating images and impressions surrounded them: a wooden swing under a rain-heavy sky. A stack of letters never sent. A hand reaching for a candle, unsure whether to light it.

Morgan moved among the memories like they were shelves, each one humming with intent but no anchor.

They reached for one: a moment of shared laughter between two children, one who might have been Morgan, the other shadowed in light. The feeling of I know you wrapped around their hand like thread.

The memory whispered a word: "Lem."

Morgan turned back to the soul. "Lem."

The figure paused, then smiled. It was the first true shape they had taken. The form settled, just slightly more defined: limbs more solid, edges clearer. Still in flux, but calmer.

Lem nodded once. "Thank you."

"Who were you supposed to be?" Morgan asked softly.

Lem shrugged. "A friend. A rival. A question." They looked down at their hands, watching them become. "I didn't need to be remembered perfectly," Lem said. "Only believed into being."

Morgan placed a hand over their chest. "Then you're here."

The Archive hummed in response.

Around them, more flickers moved in the fog. More souls not yet named, each carrying a resonance, a breath of self not yet spoken. They drifted closer. Not converging. Just noticing.

Morgan looked around. "I think I know what I'm here to do," they said.

# Chapter Twelve: Woven of Echo and Intention

Morgan didn't expect the naming to feel like grief, but it did.

Not sharp or painful, just weighty. Like a song long forgotten, returned in the voice of someone you've never met but somehow miss. Each time they named a soul, it felt like making space in their own chest. Like sacrificing a little certainty for the sake of creation.

Lem stayed close, their shape more stable now, though still shimmering at the edges. They walked alongside Morgan through the Archive's newer layers. Corridors made of impression rather than structure. Shelves hovered midair, trailing ink that never dried. Lamps flickered with memorylight - soft, flickering beams born from laughter, hesitation, and half-held dreams.

The Threadless came slowly. Some peeked out from between dream-doors and faded into corners. Others arrived with stories trailing behind them like cloaks. Stories that never got to be told but longed to be true.

Morgan didn't ask them to define themselves. They asked them what they loved. What they feared. What they remembered that no one else could.

And with each whisper, each hesitant answer, a thread caught in the air and began to spin.

The second to take shape was Una.

She appeared in a cloud of feathers and whispered lullabies, her voice like dandelion seeds in wind. Her form was older than Lem's, weathered with patience, as though she'd waited a long time to be noticed. She held a book in one hand, its pages blank.

Morgan asked gently, "What do you want to write?"

Una looked down at the book, fingers trailing across the leather. "My silence."

Morgan blinked. "You remember silence?"

Una nodded. "All the ones I kept. For others. For peace. For fear."

Morgan didn't speak. Just extended a palm.

Una placed the book in it and a single word bloomed across the first page: *Witness*.

Her body solidified slightly. Her breath deepened. The book remained blank, but now, the pages turned with purpose.

She had been woven.


The third was a whisper in color, barely more than shape: a fluid soul who shimmered between forms. They spoke in gesture, not language. Drawing images in the air that shifted depending on who watched.

When Morgan tried to speak to them, they only drew one thing over and over: a tangle. Lines, loops, overlaps. No center.

"I don't know how to help you," Morgan admitted, the words catching in their throat. "You're too many things."

The being shimmered again, this time forming not a body, but a single thread, hovering before them. It was deep violet. Warm and unfinished.

Morgan touched it and whispered, "Not one thing. Not one thread. But valid."

The thread glowed and the soul pulsed with clarity. Their name was not spoken, but it was understood.

By the end of the third day, Morgan had helped seven Threadless find names. Not names in the traditional sense, but anchors. Memories. Intentions. A wish spoken aloud.

And each time, the Archive responded with walls unfolding, passages unlocking, breath returning to forgotten spaces. They were no longer just a visitor. They were becoming part of the weave.

Lem approached quietly as Morgan rested by a spiral of threadlight, hands covered in lingering shimmer.

"You're unraveling," Lem said softly.

Morgan gave a tired smile. "Not unraveling. Opening."

"You're carrying too much," Lem warned.

Morgan looked out across the horizonless space of the Archive at all the souls still flickering, waiting, wondering if they could be. "I'm not carrying them," Morgan said. "They're carrying me."

Lem nodded and then reached into the air and pulled down a thread of their own. It was copper and blue, singing softly. "For you," they said. "From all of us."

Morgan took it, hand trembling. The thread wound around their wrist and vanished into skin.

A gift. A tether. A promise.

## Chapter Thirteen: The Roots Begin to Sing

Cassie woke with threadlight on her fingertips. She blinked at the ceiling of her loft, bleary and disoriented, before realizing she hadn't cast anything the night before. No dream spells, no protective glyphs, yet the residual shimmer on her hands thrummed with magic. Old magic. Quiet magic.

Morgan's magic.

She sat up slowly, brushing a hand over the soft knit blanket Baz had enchanted to smell like safety. It hummed under her touch.

Beside the bed, her bedside tea mug had refilled itself with rosemary and river mint. That hadn't happened in three years.

Cassie swung her legs over the edge and stood barefoot in the center of her room, feeling a gentle pull in the air, like gravity had suddenly remembered it could be emotional.

She padded downstairs, where Baz was already up and standing in the center of the greenhouse, staring at the ceiling like it was trying to whisper a prophecy.

"Let me guess," she said, voice still husky with sleep. "You felt it too."

Baz looked over, his expression half-wonder, half-concern. "Something's threading through the leylines. Not surging. Weaving."

"Threadless?"

"More like… Threadfound," he said, voice reverent. "Morgan's not just calling them. They're naming them. One by one."

Cassie stepped up beside him. "So, we're not unraveling?"

Baz shook his head. "No. But we are changing."

That morning, the greenhouse came alive in ways it hadn't since the Hollowing. Spell tools levitated gently from their shelves, rotating in subtle patterns as if tuning themselves to a new song. The scent of lavender thickened in the air, mingling with citrus and something wilder, less cultivated.

The vine wall hummed with a new growth pattern: spirals over spirals, mimicking the resonance of a loom in motion.

Cassie reached for a broom and found it already sweeping. She looked at Baz. "Okay. That's unsettling."

He nodded, eyes wide. "But also, impressive."

The magic didn't stop at Stirred & Spellbound. Reports trickled in throughout the day.

Mrs. Norwood's garden bloomed in precise geometric patterns. Mandalas that no one had planted.

At the apothecary, jars began to rearrange themselves, alphabetizing by emotional resonance rather than name.

A toddler drew a sigil in fingerpaint on her wall. When her mother copied it onto paper, her chronic migraines stopped for two days.

The magic wasn't chaotic. It was revelatory.

Wren returned from the market looking stunned. "Someone dreamed a spell and woke up speaking it aloud. In hexameter."

Bram laughed. "Are we finally hitting the poetry apocalypse?"

Cassie didn't smile. Well, not fully. Because she recognized this kind of magic. She'd felt it only once before when she, Baz, and

Morgan had rewoven the World Tree. When desperation met memory and turned into a miracle.

But this time, it wasn't desperation driving it. It was becoming. And it was everywhere.

By evening, the air shimmered with pressure like the world had taken a deep inhale and was holding it, waiting for the exhale to arrive.

Cassie stood under the willow tree behind the greenhouse, watching fireflies drift like punctuation across the dusk.

Baz joined her, silent for a long moment. Then: "Do you think they'll come back different?"

Cassie didn't answer immediately. She touched the bark of the willow, feeling the pulse beneath it. The way the roots reached toward something distant. Something… between. "They'll come back truer," she said softly.

Baz looked down at his hands. "I think we all will."

Far beneath their feet, the Archive pulsed. Not in chaos, but in cadence.

A loom turning. A breath being woven. And somewhere in the weave, Morgan whispered a new name.

And the world rippled in response.

## Chapter Fourteen: The Mirror in the Thread

The room was quiet. Too quiet.

Morgan had grown used to the Archive's ambient magic. The hum of memory-light, the soft shuffle of unformed steps, the quiet ache of longing folded into every corridor.

But this chamber? It didn't breathe. It watched.

It was octagonal, rimmed with walls that shimmered not with light, but with shadow—cool-toned and velvety, like being wrapped in twilight. There was no door, no exit. Just a threadline at the center, suspended like a pendulum above a silver basin.

As Morgan approached slowly, the pendulum moved. Not toward them, around them. Weaving. Drawing a circle.

Then, with no sound at all, the thread dipped into the basin and from the water rose a reflection in the space.

It stepped forward as if summoned. As if it had been waiting.

The figure looked exactly like Morgan. Same eyes. Same gait. Same impossible softness edged with purpose.

But this Morgan wore different threads. Robes of unfinished sigils, gloves that pulsed with held-back magic; their presence was bolder, calmer, rooted in choice, not reaction.

Morgan stared.

Their double met their gaze, head tilted slightly.

"You're the one who stayed quiet," the reflection said.

Morgan swallowed. "You're the one who didn't."

"I kept walking," the other said. "You held the loom. I held the blade."

Morgan stiffened. "I didn't come here for a battle."

"No," the reflection said. "You came here to remember. But remembering isn't enough."

They circled one another now, two echoes in orbit.

"You made peace with silence," the other Morgan continued. "I made form. I chose to become without permission. Without waiting to be named."

Morgan flinched.

"That's what you fear, isn't it?" the echo said. "That you're not weaving magic, you're weaving comfort. That you're building sanctuary while the world remakes itself in echoes."

Morgan's voice was low. "You think I've hidden."

"I think you've hesitated," the reflection said. "And hesitation is a spell all its own."

The chamber pulsed. Threads wound tighter.

The mirror-Morgan raised a hand. Between their fingers appeared a thread of dark gold, sparking with both shadow and truth.

"This isn't about who you were," they said. "It's about whether you're brave enough to carry who you could have been."

Morgan took the thread. It burned, but they didn't drop it. Instead, they held it to their heart. And with their other hand, they reached out to join it.

The Archive rippled. The figures merged, not into one, not into symmetry, but into intention.

The thread sealed itself into Morgan's wrist like ink soaked through skin. Their breath came faster. Their thoughts didn't race; they harmonized.

Because the truth wasn't either/or. It never had been.

They weren't the Weaver or the Walker. They were both.

The chamber softened. The light returned and a new door appeared. And for the first time, Morgan stepped through without hesitation. Because they were no longer searching for themselves.

They were themselves. Even the parts they hadn't chosen.

## Chapter Fifteen: Something New in the Weave

Cassie woke to the sound of her tea kettle singing a lullaby. Not whistling. Singing. In three-part harmony.

She blinked twice, sat up, and looked over at her kitchen shelf, where the kettle had rearranged itself with the rest of the mugs into a formation that looked suspiciously like a spiral. "Alright," she muttered, rubbing her eyes, "either I'm dreaming, or Morgan's almost home."

Downstairs, Baz was already awake, barefoot and cross-legged in the center of the workshop floor, surrounded by bowls of starlit ink and cedar-scented ward powder. A sheet of glass floated in front of him, reflecting not his face, but a glow that pulsed from deep below the greenhouse.

Cassie stepped into the space, wrapping her cardigan around her like armor. "Tell me this is a peaceful pulse and not a magical pressure cooker moment."

Baz didn't look away from the floating glass. "The roots are humming. The leylines are soft. The magic is stretching, but it's not breaking."

Cassie tilted her head. "Stretching how?"

"Like the weave is making room."

She sat beside him, watching as the glass shimmered, showing glimpses of the Threadless, not fully formed, but closer. More cohesive. One of them smiled in the reflection, as if noticing they were being seen for the first time.

Cassie exhaled slowly. "They're becoming real."

"They're becoming true," Baz murmured.

Wren arrived shortly after sunrise, eyes bleary, arms full of wildflowers that had grown overnight in spirals around her cabin. Bram followed an hour later with a tray of lemon shortbread and a handful of enchanted silver threads that wouldn't stop vibrating in perfect rhythm.

None of them said it aloud, but they all knew.

Morgan was coming back. And they would not be the same.

Cassie moved through the greenhouse in reverent silence. She touched the loom at the back wall, Morgan's loom, and felt it breathe beneath her palm. Not literally, of course. But energetically. It pulsed with potential.

The threads on it shimmered in a way she didn't recognize. Not glowing or sparkling, just alive.

"Morgan's changed," she whispered.

Baz came up beside her, his hand slipping into hers. "So have we."

Behind them, Wren layered protective sigils around the perimeter, whispering soft spells that bent time in spirals. Bram placed tiny mirrors between the potted herbs each angled to catch not light, but memory.

The Coven moved like one body, preparing a space not just for a return, but for a reentry. Because Morgan wasn't just bringing stories. They were bringing threads that had never existed. Names that had never been spoken. And the world would have to make space.

As dusk approached, the sky above Alden's Landing began to change.

The clouds curled in woven layers. The wind shifted to match an unseen rhythm. Even the birds paused their flight as if sensing something sacred drawing near.

Cassie lit a candle at the doorway of Stirred & Spellbound. She didn't speak a spell. She just waited. Not with worry or fear, but with the calm certainty of a thread about to meet its needle.

## Chapter Sixteen: Threads Come Home

The air shifted before Morgan appeared.

Cassie felt it first. Not in her bones, not in her skin, but in the spell-thread she kept tucked behind her ear. It flickered like a heartbeat and then stilled, as if pausing mid-breath.

She stood at the threshold of Stirred & Spellbound, watching the willow leaves tremble without wind, the air thickening like dusk before a storm.

Baz came up behind her, gaze already distant, attuned to something he couldn't yet name. "She's close," he said.

Cassie gave him a sidelong look. "You know they don't care for 'she,' right?"

Baz winced. "Force of habit. Sorry."

"You're fine," Cassie said, then turned back toward the path. "But you're right."

Morgan was coming and they weren't alone.

When Morgan stepped through the veil at the edge of the greenhouse garden, the world noticed.

The plants shifted toward them, as if aligning to a song only they could hear. The leyline crystals embedded in the workshop windows sparked with resonance. Even the enchanted wind chimes, which normally played a whimsical loop of forest tones, dropped into silence.

Morgan stood at the path's edge, barefoot with golden thread wrapped loosely around their hands. And at their side, taller than expected, cloaked in soft shadow and possibility, stood Gabe.

Cassie blinked. She wasn't sure what she'd expected. A glow? A triumph? A well-timed gust of thematic wind?

But not this. Not someone so steady. So real.

Gabe looked like the memory of a forest at dusk - quiet, rooted, impossible not to feel. His eyes mirrored Morgan's, but not their shape, their intent. Deep. Reflective. Alive with the echo of something new.

Morgan didn't speak right away. They simply stepped forward, one slow pace after another, until they crossed the garden threshold and exhaled.

Cassie met them halfway. Her voice broke the hush like thread slicing clean through silk. "You brought company."

Morgan's mouth curled, equal parts exhausted and luminous. "They weren't a fragment anymore. They were a choice. I just... named them."

Cassie looked past them, into Gabe's face. "You've got good taste in alternate selves."

Gabe offered a smile. "I've always liked the way she says things."

Morgan arched a brow. "You're not supposed to say 'she' either."

"I'm new. I'll learn."

Cassie chuckled softly. "That's fair."

Baz approached, slow and measured. "Is he Threadless?"

Morgan looked down at the thread coiled in their palm.

"No," they said. "He's Threadfound."

The wind picked up and the ground beneath their feet vibrated, ever so faintly, as if welcoming something into its weave.

Cassie felt the moment like a tether catching. Morgan wasn't just back; they were anchored with a name on their lips and a new soul at their side.

And the magic of Emerdeen would never flow the same way again.

## Chapter Seventeen: The Collector of Moments

Gabe didn't speak much the first two days. It wasn't out of shyness, though his silence often read as stillness, but because he preferred to watch. Not with the intensity of someone who hadn't seen the world before, but like someone who remembered it differently and wanted to see if it was still true.

He spent most of the first morning walking the grounds of Stirred & Spellbound with slow, thoughtful steps. He stopped to feel the curve of a doorknob, the texture of lichen on the greenhouse bricks, the sound of spoons rattling in their drawer (now fully possessed again, Bram swore).

And then he started collecting. Not souvenirs, moments.

Cassie found the first one under her tea mug:

"Bram laughing so hard at his own pun that he accidentally enchanted a butter knife. 8:46am. Slightly dangerous joy."

Written on a narrow slip of parchment-thin thread-paper, rolled tight and bound with a copper filament. She unfolded it like a fortune cookie, smiled, and tucked it into her pocket without comment.

By midday, there were ten more. Slipped under potted herbs, in the folds of the welcome mat, even hanging from the tail of a willow frond outside the front porch.

Baz found one on his workbench:

"Cassie hummed a spell into existence without knowing. Wren pretended not to notice. It was kind."

Wren discovered hers tucked in a jar of dried rosehips:

"Morgan touched the doorframe like it was a memory. No one else saw."

When asked about it, Gabe only shrugged.

"They're just small truths," he said. "Little anchors. If the world starts to blur again, I want to know what was real."

The townsfolk had opinions.

Mrs. Norwood eyed him with suspicion, particularly after her garden hedge rearranged itself into a shape that resembled a musical staff and then refused to grow in straight lines.

"He's polite," she admitted to Wren one morning at the market, "but he looks like a haiku waiting to happen. And my begonias are acting weird."

Bram thought Gabe was "quietly hilarious" and spent one afternoon trying to get him to admit whether he could shapeshift or not.

Gabe responded by slipping him a thread-paper note that read: "You've already imagined five versions of me. Pick your favorite. I'll do my best."

Baz, more sensitive to magic than most, said that Gabe's presence was like standing near a low-tuned harp. You could feel it, even when it wasn't being played.

And Cassie? Cassie watched Morgan.

Not because she didn't trust Gabe. On the contrary, she trusted him instinctively. But she knew that becoming changed people. And Morgan had become something more than they were before.

So had Gabe.

Which meant the town would, too.

On the third evening, Gabe helped Morgan plant a circle of new spellflowers behind the greenhouse, each one grown from

56

threadlight and Archive soil. He paused mid-dig and pulled a slip of thread-paper from his sleeve. He passed it to Morgan without a word.

Morgan read it aloud.

"You hesitated today. Before telling Wren the truth. But you told her anyway. That counts."

They looked at him.

He didn't explain. He didn't need to.

They tucked it into the soil beside the seeds.

Cassie watched from the porch, arms folded, heart tugging sideways. "I think," she whispered to Baz, "that he might be the most dangerous kind of magic."

Baz glanced over. "How so?"

She smiled softly. "He sees everything. And he chooses to keep it."

## Chapter Eighteen: The Ones Who Remember You Back

Gabe woke before the light changed. Not before dawn, before light itself decided it would be dawn. Before the sky chose a color and before the birds cleared their throats.

He dressed in silence, pocketing a fresh roll of threadpaper and a thin graphite wand Morgan had enchanted to write thoughts before they formed.

The cottage door creaked open with a familiar sigh and he stepped out into morning-still Alden's Landing. Mist curled low over the river, and the edges of town hadn't quite committed to existing yet.

Gabe liked thresholds. And today, he was walking toward one.

He felt the Threadless presence before he saw it. It wasn't a sound, or a shape, or a shift in wind. It was attention.

A sudden sharpness in the world like a sentence that didn't finish because someone remembered you mid-thought.

He followed the thread of it through the apple grove beyond Wren's garden, where the trees leaned too knowingly and time sometimes frayed at the edges.

There, standing beside a bench that hadn't been there yesterday, was a figure made of dusk-colored light.

Even though gender flickered with the breeze, she stood still, arms folded, head tilted, as if listening to music that hadn't begun.

Gabe didn't speak.

The Threadless soul turned. Their face wasn't defined, but their recognition was. "You were the first one," she said. "The first to leave."

Gabe exhaled. "I stayed."

"You became." Her voice was made of ribbon and wind, threaded with old knowing.

He stepped forward, slowly. "I didn't forget you."

"No," she said. "You left because of us. Because of what wasn't chosen. You were made from the silence between names." She stepped closer. "I remember you," she whispered. "Even when I didn't know what remembering meant."

Gabe felt his chest ache, not with pain, but memory too large for bone. He reached into his coat pocket and pulled out a slip of threadpaper.

*"A soul without a shape still casts a shadow."*

He held it out to her, and she took it, and in that instant, something seemed to settle. Not fully, not yet, but like the first note of a song remembering how to be sung.

Morgan found him hours later, seated on the grass, back against the new bench, a fresh spiral of threadlight blooming around his boots.

"They're still here," Gabe said quietly.

Morgan sat beside him. "Who?"

"The part of me that didn't come back alone."

Morgan smiled. "You always had more than one thread."

Gabe reached out, brushing his fingers across the mist where the Threadless had stood. "They're starting to surface."

Morgan nodded. "We'll make space." They turned to Gabe. "Are you ready for that?"

Gabe didn't hesitate. "I remember them," he said. "And they remember me."

## Chapter Nineteen: Spell Circles and Soft Openings

Cassie stood at the head of the town square, arms crossed, hair braided with tiny wards, and a clipboard charmed to take notes by emotional priority.

The last time Alden's Landing had gathered like this, it was to vote on whether the enchanted wishing well should be relocated after it developed a tendency to demand increasingly abstract metaphors for spare change.

This was slightly more serious.

Behind her, the Crafting Coven buzzed in controlled chaos: Wren laying down memory-safe glyphs along the cobblestones; Bram arguing with a talking lantern over the ethics of hosting liminal beings in municipal spaces; Baz murmuring to the leyline crystal that marked the town's energy center, coaxing it into a new harmonic pattern.

Cassie, meanwhile, addressed the curious and moderately anxious townsfolk now seated in rows of magically sturdy folding chairs.

"So," she said, flashing a smile that suggested she'd already won an argument no one had started, "you're probably wondering why there's a faint shimmer to the air, a rise in ambient empathy, and why your begonias have started humming elegies."

Mrs. Norwood narrowed her eyes. "Are we under magical siege?"

Cassie grinned. "Only in the emotional sense."

She stepped down from the fountain steps and paced the circle. "Morgan has returned. Gabe is with them. And with that return comes a shift in Emerdeen's magic. It's not breaking. It's expanding. The Archive is reaching outward. And the Threadless souls who were never given shape are coming through."

Someone gasped.

Cassie raised a calming hand. "They're not monsters. They're not ghosts. They're potential. Unspoken stories. They've never harmed us. They just want form."

Mr. Ellis, who ran the candle shop and rarely trusted anything unlit, stood and asked: "And how do we know they won't take form by stealing ours?"

Baz responded gently from the edge of the circle. "Because Morgan didn't anchor them by command. They anchored them by invitation. And now, we're doing the same."

The preparation wasn't just magical, it was personal.

Wren created welcome bundles of charm-touched herbs that encouraged grounding and clarity of self.

Bram hand-stitched thread bracelets to help townsfolk remain attuned to their core memories. "Think of it as an anti-inspiration charm," he said cheerfully. "Keeps your sense of self from being overwritten by ambient existential magic."

Cassie herself distributed a new pamphlet:

*Hosting the Threadless: A Guide to Ethical Hospitality and Minimizing Unexpected Poetry*

It included:

- Tips for identifying a Threadless presence (Hint: soft shimmer, emotional déjà vu, a faint scent of something you've never smelled but instantly recognize).

- Common misunderstandings (They don't want to possess you. They want to be themselves, they just don't know how yet).

- Recommended offerings (Warm tea, space to speak, patience, and anything woven by hand).

By sunset, the town square was encircled with hand-drawn sigils of soft welcome and intentional boundaries. The veil shimmered at the edges of perception, like the sky was remembering how to blink.

Cassie stood back and surveyed it all. The spell lines, the stones warmed by meaning, and the lanterns now flickering with resonance instead of fear.

Baz stepped beside her. "You did it," he said. "You prepared a town for souls that never learned how to arrive."

Cassie smiled, bittersweet and bright. "We all did." Then she whispered, just loud enough for the night to hear: "Let them come home."

## Chapter Twenty: The First Thread Walks

No one saw the Threadless arrive. They felt it first.

A ripple in the morning air, like reality exhaled through velvet. The wind curled through Alden's Landing in spirals, tugging at curtains and setting wind chimes into soft dissonance. The birds paused mid-song. Even the leyline crystal at the edge of the square turned a slow, deliberate shade of amber.

Cassie was in the middle of explaining the subtle difference between "welcoming presence" sigils and "please do not emotionally imprint on me" glyphs when it happened.

She felt it like a hand resting gently on her spine. And then, across the green, between the herb stand and the weaving table, a shimmer took shape.

No burst of light. No dramatic wind. Just… presence.

A figure began emerging, half-seen, half-felt, then slowly, irrevocably, real.

They were androgynous, wrapped in layers of dusk-hued thread that moved like light through water. Their hair shimmered like old ink, eyes wide and luminous, unsure whether they were afraid or just overwhelmed by the weight of becoming.

A hush fell over the entire square. Children stopped mid-game. Shopkeepers leaned forward. Someone dropped a spoon, and no one even blinked.

The Threadless soul took one step forward and gasped. Not from fear, from feeling.

Cassie moved first. She didn't reach for a weapon or a ward. She extended a cup of tea. It was still warm.

The Threadless hesitated, then took it. Their fingers were solid now. Shaking, but real. "My name," they said softly, "is waiting."

Wren stepped up, eyes soft. "Then we'll help you find it."

The entire town didn't crowd them. Instead, they gave space, offered space. A gentle ring of awareness and welcome. The spell-etched stones shimmered once in confirmation, then went still.

Bram placed a slip of thread-paper on the nearby bench, a message written in looping script:

*"You are not too late. You are right on time."*

The soul read it and smiled. It was their first.


Later, as the sun shifted higher, the spellline at the edge of town pulsed again. Just once. Another shimmer blinked in, too brief to form. Not yet ready but watching.

The town now had a rhythm, a threshold, and a pulse.

Cassie turned to Baz, eyes damp, breath steady. "That," she whispered, "was the first one."

Baz nodded, lips parted in awe. "And not the last."

## Chapter Twenty-One: Thread, Tea, and Trouble

Morgan had never built a sanctuary from scratch before. They'd reforged one, restored one, and even reimagined one using the bones of old magic and Cassie's tendency to manifest sarcasm into structural spells.

But this? This was different.

The Hollow of Becoming wasn't rooted in stone or story. It needed to be flexible, alive, and capable of holding contradiction without collapsing. Which is probably why the first blueprint tried to turn itself into a topiary.

Morgan frowned at the enchanted scroll now sprouting tiny leaves. "It's resisting logic again."

Gabe looked up from where he was braiding threads of potential into a lattice of warm light and cool shadow. "Maybe it needs emotional validation."

"It's a floor plan, not a poet."

"Tell that to the chandelier," Gabe said, nodding toward the ceiling, where a floating cluster of moss-light had grown legs and was now attempting interpretive dance.

Morgan rubbed their temples. "Why did I think weaving an entire liminal haven between worlds would be linear?"

"Because you're hopeful," Gabe said. "And a little reckless."

Morgan narrowed their eyes. "Says the man who stuffed thirty-three moments into one boot."

Gabe shrugged. "It was a meaningful morning."

The Hollow had begun to take shape in a pocket between dimensions. Not hidden, just gently folded. Walls woven from translucent memory-vines and anchored with rune-stones that pulsed when a soul drew near.

The entrance was not a door, but a decision.

And the interior? Ever-shifting, on purpose.

A central hearth that burned with warmth drawn from accepted truths. A corridor of reflection where names whispered themselves into being.

And the Looming Tree, a sapling born from the roots of the World Tree and Morgan's own threadmark, now standing at the Hollow's center, leaves shimmering with names not yet spoken aloud.

Today's task: finalize the binding threads to seal the Hollow's perimeter.

Morgan held up a spool of golden potential-thread.

Gabe, beside them, held one of... glittering fishbone?

Morgan frowned. "That's not thread."

"It wants to be," Gabe said cheerfully. "It was caught between a metaphor and a discarded enchantment about shimmering identity. I'm giving it a chance."

Morgan blinked. "You're trying to make the boundaries of the Hollow inclusive by letting magical conceptual fishbones help stabilize reality?"

Gabe grinned. "Is that... not the assignment?"

Morgan stared at him and then laughed. Loud. Uncontrolled. A hiccup of pure, real joy that echoed off the memory-walls like the first chord of a brand-new song. "All right," they said, wiping their eyes. "Let's anchor this place with magic, compassion, and whatever strange, sparkling nonsense we are."

As they worked, Morgan whispered threads into the framework:

Room for the names not yet spoken.
A resting place for the echoing heart.
A path that welcomes the unsure and unready.

Gabe added:

A bench for the confused, with snacks.
A window that shows you not where you're going, but where you paused and why.
A small closet for dancing in private, no questions asked.

By the time the boundary shimmered into completion, the Hollow pulsed with something more than magic. It pulsed with permission…to exist, to evolve, to arrive before you're ready, and leave when you're whole.

Morgan sat at the base of the Looming Tree, threadmap spread across their lap.

Gabe sat beside them, biting into a honey apple conjured from memory and mischief.

"Do you think they'll come?" Gabe asked.

Morgan smiled softly. "They're already on their way."

## Chapter Twenty-Two: A Name with No Hurry

They didn't know where the path began. Only that it unfolded for them. One moment they were wandering the edge of Alden's Landing, held together by hesitation and half-memory, a shimmer tucked inside the thrum of the wind. The next, a thread tugged softly at their chest, not forceful, just welcoming.

So, they followed. Not out of certainty. Out of hope.

The Hollow of Becoming revealed itself like a breath exhaled slowly in reverse. There was no gate. No gatekeeper. Only the sense of yes brushing against their edges.

Their first step was met with warmth, not heat, not light. Something quieter. Like moss remembering sunlight. Like kindness that didn't ask for thanks.

The path wound inward through memory-veined stone and soft, shifting wilds. There were no straight lines. Only spirals. Only space.

They passed a window in midair showing a childhood they had almost lived.

A lantern hummed softly with the sound of their nearly named laughter.

A corridor of vines whispered thoughts they'd nearly spoken aloud in dreams.

But it was the tree that stopped them. The Looming Tree. Its leaves shimmered with intention. Each one bore not a name, but the feeling of one. Some glowed softly. Others pulsed like sleeping stars.

At its roots sat two figures. One they recognized.

Morgan.

Weaver of silence. Stitcher of story. Anchor of the thread-path.

The other was unfamiliar and yet somehow echoed.

Gabe.

Memory-braided. Shadow-steadied. Smiling like someone who knew what it meant to exist sideways and still choose forward.

They didn't speak. They just looked. And it was enough.

The Threadless soul stepped into the circle of tree-light.

Morgan rose and approached slowly. "You don't have to become all at once," they said.

"I don't know what I am," the soul whispered.

Morgan reached out, offering a slip of thread-paper. It was blank. "You're here," they said. "That's enough."

The soul took it, held it, and pressed it to their chest, and for the first time since flickering into the world, they breathed fully.

Later, the Hollow wrapped itself around them like a bed of soft dreams and tea-warmed air, a gentle hum at the edge of every heartbeat.

And the soul, still unnamed, still unfolding, wrote their first word onto the page:

Almost.

The page shimmered. And so did they.

# Chapter Twenty-Three: After the Becoming

It was one of those evenings where time moved sideways. The kind where the sun didn't so much set as stretch out in warm gold across the garden, reluctant to leave. The wind carried the scent of lemon balm and loam, and somewhere a bird kept forgetting how its song ended.

Cassie sat on the back porch of Stirred & Spellbound, her bare feet tucked beneath her, a mug of something too herbal to be comforting and too honest to be ignored warming her hands. She didn't look up when Morgan approached. Just tilted her mug slightly in offering.

Morgan took the spot beside her without hesitation, folding into the rhythm of Cassie's silence like someone who'd been part of it for years.

They sat there for a while, saying nothing. Which, between them, was practically a declaration of affection.

Eventually, Cassie asked, "So… what now?"

Morgan didn't answer right away. They watched the leaves stir in a pattern that almost felt intentional.

"I thought the becoming would be the end," Morgan said softly. "That once the Threadless had form, it would all settle."

Cassie huffed a laugh. "Nothing ever settles. Especially not people."

Morgan smiled. "They're not people. Not exactly."

"No," she agreed. "But they're learning how to be."

She sipped her tea, made a face, and added a spoonful of honey from the jar enchanted to whisper affirmations while stirring. "I guess I thought the world would snap back to normal," Morgan said. "But this…this is the new normal, isn't it?"

Cassie stretched her legs out, her feet glowing faintly from proximity to a charm circle she'd forgotten she drew. "Morgan, we live in a greenhouse full of sentient embroidery floss and emotionally unstable brooms. Normal left us years ago."

They both laughed quietly, from somewhere near the ribs.

"But yes," Cassie said, more gently now, "this is the shape of the world going forward. Threadless becoming Threadfound. New stories joining the weave."

Morgan nodded slowly. "It's beautiful. But…"

Cassie arched a brow. "But?"

"It's going to get complicated."

Cassie shrugged. "What doesn't?" She glanced sideways at them. "You worried?"

"I'm… aware," Morgan said.

Cassie considered that. "Good. Stay aware. But also stay weird. That's our only real advantage."

Morgan leaned their head back against the porch post, eyes half-lidded. "The Hollow is stable now. It's ready."

Cassie looked at them, her smile soft but sure. "And so are you."

A pause.

Then: "You came back different."

Morgan didn't deny it. "I am different."

Cassie bumped her shoulder lightly against theirs. "Good. We don't grow things just to keep them the same."

As the stars arrived, gentle and slow like applause after a soft-spoken performance, the two of them sat in a silence that asked nothing.

Eventually, Cassie said, "What if they want more?"

Morgan blinked. "More than becoming?"

"More than just… shape. What if they want meaning? Purpose? Bad poetry and disastrous love affairs and opinions about how we organize the spice shelf?"

Morgan smiled faintly. "Then we teach them."

Cassie nodded, satisfied. "We'll start with cinnamon. Always start with cinnamon."

They didn't stay up late that night. But they did stay long enough to see the first Threadfound soul walk the garden path under moonlight, barefoot, eyes wide, humming something uncertain.

Cassie raised her mug in greeting. Morgan simply said, "Welcome."

And the world kept weaving.

# Chapter Twenty-Four: The Audit Returns

The wind picked up before he appeared. Not a stormy wind, just brisk. Intentional. Like the kind of breeze that preceded bad ideas dressed in good suits.

Cassie was elbow-deep in a batch of cauldron biscuits (her term for spell-kissed scones) when the front door of Stirred & Spellbound creaked open.

She didn't look up; she didn't have to. She knew that clipboard anywhere.

"Well, well," she drawled. "If it isn't the ghost of red tape past."

Dr. Everett Shaw stepped inside, impeccably pressed, offensively punctual, and exuding the smug scent of sandalwood and policy. "I'm here to complete the compliance audit," he said.

Cassie wiped her hands on a dish towel enchanted to hum in passive-aggressive protest. "I thought you were devoured by the compost heap," she said sweetly.

"I was briefly detained."

Baz poked his head in from the hall. "Is that what we're calling spiritual digestion now?"

Dr. Shaw ignored them, already scanning the greenhouse like it was a crime scene that had failed to respect local zoning ordinances. "Let's begin," he said crisply, flipping open his clipboard. "I understand this facility is now housing undocumented entities."

"You mean souls?" Cassie said.

"I mean persons, if you can call them that, without origin records, assigned purpose, or recognized civic status."

Cassie narrowed her eyes. "They're not property. They're people."

Shaw made a note. "Unregistered people."

From the back room, a broom launched itself off the shelf and dive-bombed Shaw's shoes.

Cassie sighed. "Gerald. We've talked about this."

Morgan entered then, all calm certainty and wind-woven grace, Gabe at their side.

"Dr. Shaw," Morgan said.

He didn't turn. "I assume you're behind the reality bending."

"I guided it," Morgan said. "They did the rest."

Shaw finally looked up. "They?"

As if on cue, one of the Threadfound wandered in from the garden, holding a small ceramic owl and a cup of tea labeled *Emotional Stability (Mostly)*. They smiled gently at Shaw. "Do you smell moss?" they asked.

He blinked. "What are you?"

They thought about it. Then shrugged. "Happy."

Shaw bristled. "You can't regulate happiness."

Gabe leaned in. "You've tried, haven't you?"

By midday, Shaw had drafted a proposed ordinance to categorize Threadfound as "magical anomalies under observation."

Cassie countered with a petition titled:

*"We Don't Need Your Filing System to Exist: A Polite Rebuttal with Cookies."*

Morgan suggested a town circle be held to listen to the Threadfound before assigning definitions. Shaw called it "dangerously interpretive." Bram offered to enchant his clipboard to scream every time he made a reductive note. It screamed seven times in the next hour.

But beneath the humor, tension coiled. Because Shaw wasn't just a nuisance anymore. He represented something older, the fear that stories must be neat to be valid. That becoming had to follow rules. That existence required permission.

And the Threadfound?

They weren't asking for permission. They were asking to stay.

## Chapter Twenty-Five: Containment, Compliance, and Controlled Chaos

Dr. Shaw's first mistake was attempting to catalogue the Threadfound alphabetically. His second was trying to assign them provisional registration numbers.

By the time he'd reached "TF-008: Provisional Name - Juniper Echo," Juniper had already reorganized the town's bus stop into a memory garden and spontaneously learned to knit regret into wearable scarves.

Cassie stood at the edge of the square with a cup of coffee and a stack of re-labeled files. Each one bore a sticky note that read: *"Not yours."*

Shaw was undeterred. He paced the cobbled square like an auditor in search of an infraction, muttering about liability exposure and metaphysical trespassing clauses. Everywhere he turned, the town shimmered with magic that refused to be boxed.

One Threadfound helped Wren charm the bakery oven to rise only when someone believed in themselves. Another spent the morning asking townsfolk, "What part of yourself have you forgotten?" and then offering small, woven tokens stitched from the answers.

And still, Shaw scribbled.

*"Emotional disruption: widespread."*
*"Nonlinear identity expression: unregulated."*
*"Civic infrastructure compromised by philosophical ambiguity."*

Baz caught sight of the last line and laughed so hard he nearly fell into a pot of glow-thyme.

At a hastily arranged town meeting (held in the tea garden because the town hall had been temporarily occupied by a Threadfound orchestra experimenting with wind), Shaw presented his case.

"These entities pose a risk," he said. "Their origins are undocumented. Their boundaries are unclear. Their presence destabilizes the social fabric."

Cassie raised an eyebrow. "And yet crime is down, community engagement is up, and we had our first spontaneous moonlight poetry potluck last night."

"Exactly," Shaw snapped. "Chaos masquerading as charm."

Morgan stood. "It's not chaos. It's becoming."

Shaw turned on them. "You've blurred the line between reality and imagination."

"No," Morgan said. "We've stitched them together."

A murmur of agreement rippled through the crowd of makers, bakers, healers, curious neighbors, and one toddler currently trying to feed a constellation-shaped biscuit to a very patient Threadfound.

Shaw's jaw tightened. "Then I'll be escalating this to the regional council."

Cassie clapped her hands. "Fantastic! I've always wanted to test whether enchanted court transcripts can also serve as dramatic one-woman shows."

Wren added, "We'll serve snacks."

The meeting dissolved into something between a garden party and a spell-circle.

Shaw stormed off toward the inn, flanked by floating clipboards and a small hex-immune umbrella that Cassie had definitely not charmed to follow him whispering "loosen up" on the wind.

But beneath the laughter, the town felt it: This wasn't over. Shaw was a ripple. Something older, colder, was moving behind him.

And while the Threadfound weren't dangerous…the people who feared their freedom might be.

## Chapter Twenty-Six: A Soft Thread, Pulled

Dr. Shaw liked routines. Routines were proof that the world could be folded neatly. A life built from clipboards and calendars, borders and bullet points. Nothing frayed. Nothing improvised.

Which is why he ate the same breakfast every morning: black tea, two eggs, toast, and half a grapefruit. No sugar.

That morning, he found a hand-written note beneath his grapefruit spoon:

*"If everything must fit, what do you do with the sky?"*

He blinked at it. Then looked up. Across from him sat Thimble.

Not the Thimble. Just... Thimble.

That was the name they'd chosen. No surname. No fanfare.

Just Thimble, wearing a cardigan that looked like it had been knit from the feeling of being slightly overwhelmed and quietly optimistic.

"Morning," Thimble said, cheerful but not loud. "Your routine was... too quiet. I wanted to say hi."

Shaw blinked again. "You're not permitted to just appear in dining establishments uninvited."

"I didn't appear. I walked in," Thimble said, sipping their tea which glowed slightly and smelled like library dust and rosehips. "Also, I brought jam. It's emotionally stabilizing. Plum and self-compassion."

They slid a small jar across the table.

Shaw stared at it like it might erupt into interpretive dance. "I don't need jam."

"Most people don't," Thimble agreed. "But we're not most people, are we?"

Shaw narrowed his eyes. "I am a licensed human."

Thimble tilted their head. "Oh, I never doubted that." They smiled, soft and unbothered. "What do you think is going to happen?"

"To what?"

"To all of this," Thimble gestured vaguely out the window toward the marketplace where a woman was bartering tomatoes using haiku, and a Threadfound child was learning hopscotch by practicing the stages of metamorphosis in chalk outlines.

Shaw frowned. "It's unsustainable. Emotional logic does not scale. Societies require structure."

Thimble nodded. "I like structure. It's like knitting. You need tension and shape, or it all falls apart."

Shaw seemed slightly mollified.

Thimble stirred their tea. "But sometimes," they said, voice softening, "a dropped stitch makes something accidental and beautiful. Not wrong. Just… new."

There was silence. Not because Shaw agreed. But because for once, he didn't know how to disagree.

They sat there for nearly an hour. Shaw didn't speak much. Thimble didn't push. They talked about weather and the strange satisfaction of reorganizing a drawer. And the fact that Thimble had once tried to become a lighthouse, emotionally, but decided that welcoming people in was more useful than just blinking warnings at them.

When they finally rose to leave, Thimble paused. "I don't think you're a villain," they said gently. "I just think you're afraid that if the world isn't tidy, it might forget how to hold you."

Shaw didn't answer. Not right away. But that night, back at his room, he found himself staring at the jam jar on his nightstand. He didn't open it. But he didn't throw it away either.

## Chapter Twenty-Seven: How Do You Solve a Problem Like Bureaucracy?

By week's end, Dr. Everett Shaw had declared war on:

- Improvised spellcasting within fifty feet of a municipal structure
- Spontaneous reality shimmer
- "Unlicensed metaphysical bonding rituals" (which apparently included tea circles)
- The enchanted crow that had begun delivering unsolicited affirmations to grumpy shopkeepers

He'd also posted Twelve Notices of Infraction around town, rewritten the welcome sign to include the phrase "Subject to Inspection", and tried to rename the greenhouse district "Zone B: Magical Activity Under Review."

Cassie stood in the center of the square reading the latest bulletin. She didn't laugh. She blinked twice, sipped her coffee, and said, "We're going to have to remove him."

Wren, standing beside her with a charm-woven basket of emotional recalibration muffins, said gently, "Cass. That's murder talk."

"No," Cassie said. "It's municipal stewardship."

Bram leaned around the wishing well, holding a sign that read *Manifesting Calm, Do Not Approach.* "What if we compost him again?"

Baz sighed. "Too soon. The compost hasn't forgiven us."

By the end of the day, Shaw had personally reprimanded a Threadfound child for altering the hue of public roses to match their feelings and ordered the temporary shutdown of the tea garden on the grounds that its ambient empathy field was "disruptive to objective thought." The tea garden was shut down.

That was the line.

The town met that night under the gazebo, which had gently grown wings after the last full moon and was now affectionately called The Floof. Everyone brought snacks. A few brought pitchforks. Mostly symbolic.

Cassie stood on the bench, hands on hips, gaze blazing. "Okay, friends. I'm not saying we stage a coup. I'm just saying accidental dimensional misplacement is technically not illegal."

Gabe raised a hand. "We could distract him with a folder of minor contradictions and then quietly hex the edges of reality until he forgets his name."

Morgan smiled. "We'd have to do it gently. He's more tightly wound than a regret spiral."

Mrs. Norwood (formerly Team Shaw) muttered, "He banned my begonias for 'emotional unpredictability.' He can burn."

Wren suggested a spell of subtle misdirection that would cause his compass to always point to the nearest unresolved childhood insecurity.

Bram proposed a decoy Shaw made of animated parchment, constantly filing itself.

Baz quietly enchanted Shaw's clipboard to change every note he wrote to an increasingly revealing diary entry.

*June 4th: I fear I may be wrong. The tea smells like a better life. What if they're not lost? What if I am?*

Cassie's response? "Perfect. Let's see if he can audit that."

The next morning, Shaw found his office (the inn's small back parlor) filled with potted plants bearing placards:

*"We are unregulated joy."*
*"I exist. Therefore, I defy."*
*"Try filing this, Everett."*

On his desk sat a biscuit that radiated mild annoyance and cinnamon. And beneath it, a note in Morgan's threadmark:

*Some things can't be quantified. But they can be welcomed.*

# Chapter Twenty-Eight: The Fray at the Edge of Order

By day ten, Dr. Shaw had stopped using doors. Not metaphorically, literally.

He no longer trusted them. Too many had started leading him to inconvenient places: spiral staircases that went nowhere, enchanted glens that whispered affirmations, one unusually pushy closet full of community theater costumes.

He now entered buildings through windows. Wren's bakery window. Bram's attic. Cassie's herb nook, which responded by politely vanishing for forty-eight hours.

The townsfolk were done. Even the most even-tempered Threadfound like Juniper, who had taught herself embroidery using wind and hope, glared when he passed.

The leylines around Alden's Landing pulsed with quiet warning.

And still, Shaw marched on.

That morning, he stood in the square with a bullhorn charmed against whimsy, holding aloft a document titled:

"Mandate for Magical Normalization and Reversal of Non-Civic Entities."

It hummed with restrained bureaucratic aggression.

Cassie stepped forward, arms crossed, hair practically crackling with indignation. "You can't reverse what never fit your form to begin with."

Shaw's voice rang out over the crowd. "You have invited instability. You've built a sanctuary on sentiment. This place was governable! And now it's a glorified fairy tale!"

"Fairy tales," Morgan said, appearing from the garden's edge, "are how people survived history."

Shaw whirled. "This is not survival! This is collapse disguised as compassion! And you"

He pointed at Morgan, voice rising. "…you started this. With your soft words and open doors and Threadfound naming parties. You unraveled everything."

Morgan didn't flinch. They simply stepped forward and said, calmly: "I reminded the world it was more than your margins."

Shaw's voice broke then. Not in volume, but in tone. It cracked like a brittle bone of belief. "Magic should obey," he hissed. "It should be contained. Labeled. Safe."

Cassie's voice sliced through the air like silk over steel. "Magic isn't safe, Everett. Neither is love. Or identity. Or becoming."

The crowd had stilled. The leylines pulsed once.

And then finally Shaw snapped. He raised the document like a weapon, and the air around him convulsed. Spells flared. Runes activated without consent. He reached into something old and tight and angry.

The ley crystal at the square's center turned red. The sky shifted shade. And then the ground opened.

Not violently. Just… deeply. Like something was tired of being restrained.

A hush fell and from the Hollow, a single Threadfound stepped into the square quiet, radiant, real.

They walked straight to Shaw and held out a hand. And said: "You don't have to fear what won't hold shape."

Shaw stared at them, his chest rising, his breath shallow, the clipboard shaking in his hands. And then he screamed—not with rage, but with collapse and grief, with the terrible ache of a man who had bent his life around control because no one had ever taught him how to be soft. He dropped the clipboard, dropped the spell, and fell to his knees.

## Chapter Twenty-Nine: After the Undoing

Morgan felt it before they knew it. A pulse, gentle, but sure, moving outward from the center of Alden's Landing like a sigh exhaled by the land itself. Not sorrow. Not relief. Something older.

Permission.

They stood in the heart of the Hollow, hands buried wrist-deep in thread-soil, coaxing the Looming Tree into a new season of growth, when the magic stuttered then shifted.

Gabe straightened from his work beside the entry path. "You felt that too," he said.

Morgan nodded. "Something unknotted."

They stepped back from the Tree, watching its leaves flutter in new patterns. Not letters. Not names. Questions.

Gabe tilted his head, reading their movement like wind-stirred language. "The weave is asking."

Morgan didn't answer right away. Instead, they stepped into the center of the Hollow and whispered, "What are you now?"

The air shimmered. A new threadline arched above the doorway. Not closed, not open. Folded. A spiral, like a path beginning again.

Gabe moved beside them, brushing his fingers against a nearby sigil. "Shaw's collapsed."

Morgan blinked. "Literally?"

"Knees, screaming, dropped his clipboard. Very dramatic."

After a pause, they: "I didn't want him to break."

"You didn't break him," Gabe said gently. "The shape he clung to broke. Because the world grew past it."

Morgan swallowed. "He was trying to stop what he didn't understand."

"And now," Gabe added, "he can begin to."

Outside the Hollow, the Threadfound stirred. They didn't flinch at the shift in the air. They leaned into it, sensing, perhaps, that magic was no longer trying to be understood but met halfway.

Inside, the walls of the Hollow pulsed. The central hearth shifted hue: soft gold to thread-deep green. The Looming Tree rustled despite no wind. A new platform unfolded near its roots. A place not meant for naming or remembering. But for imagining.

Gabe stepped up onto it, expression uncharacteristically unsure. Morgan joined him.

"Do you think the Hollow is evolving?" Gabe asked.

Morgan smiled. "I think we are. And the Hollow is just listening."

They reached into the air; fingers brushing an unformed thread of possibility and wove the first circle not shaped by past or pain but play. It shimmered around them, full of laughter not yet lived, mistakes not yet made, and a thousand futures choosing where to begin.

Far away, under the starlit porch of Stirred & Spellbound, Cassie felt a tug in her threadmark and looked up.

The stars above Alden's Landing had rearranged themselves ever so slightly. Not into a message, but a spiral.

# Chapter Thirty: The Unbinding of Everett Shaw

Shaw didn't remember falling. Not entirely. He remembered the heat in his chest, the tremor in his hands, the unbearable pressure of everything slipping out of his carefully labeled boxes. He remembered the Threadfound standing before him, open and unafraid. And he remembered letting go.

Now, he sat alone in the reading room of the inn. The windows were open, the curtains breathing in and out like lungs learning how. Sunlight pooled in the corners, hesitant and golden.

And he was… quiet. No clipboard. No charts. No words.

The room was silent in a way that invited rather than accused.

Across from him sat a cup of tea someone had placed there while he was too undone to object. The tag on the bag read:

*Infusion for Softening: contains lemon balm, gentian, and uncomfortable truths.*

He didn't drink it, but he didn't throw it out either.

The door creaked open. Cassie stepped inside, not striding but drifting, like someone who respected the air around broken things.

She held no clipboard, only a chair, which she turned backwards and straddled with casual defiance. "Want to talk about it?" she asked.

Shaw stared at the floor. "I don't even know what it is."

Cassie tilted her head. "It's the part where the world stopped pretending you were in charge of it."

A silence passed like a long sigh. Shaw said, "You were always against me."

"No," Cassie replied. "I was always against the idea that you were the only one who knew what was best."

She leaned forward. "You weren't wrong to want order. You were just wrong to think only control could keep you safe."

He swallowed. "I thought... if I could just contain it..."

Cassie's voice softened. "You wouldn't be left behind."

His throat tightened. "Do you have any idea what it's like to see everyone else become something beautiful while you're still holding a rulebook?"

Cassie gave a small, sad smile. "Everett, we're all making it up as we go. Some of us are just doing it with sequins."

He stared at the teacup again and finally lifted it. But he didn't drink. Not yet.

Cassie stood.

"No one's asking you to become anything you're not," she said. "But if you're tired of only being what you were told, there's room here."

At the door, she turned back. "You're allowed to change. Even if the forms don't have a section for it."

Then she was gone.

Shaw sat in that chair long after the tea cooled.

He didn't speak or stand, but when the sun shifted, it caught the glint of a single scrap of paper he'd pulled from his pocket.

A Threadfound had given it to him days ago. He hadn't read it.

He opened it now. It said:

*The first form you file doesn't have to be final.*

His eyes burned…and for the first time in his life, Dr. Everett Shaw did not file a response.

He simply breathed.

## Chapter Thirty-One: When Magic Learns to Laugh

The Hollow was humming. Not like before. Not with the subtle pulse of spellwork or the low resonance of memory-weft magic.

This was new. It was bright, unpredictable, and alive.

Morgan stood at the edge of the spiral grove, where the Looming Tree had recently unfurled a branch in the exact shape of a question mark, and watched as color drifted through the air like pollen from a dream.

Gabe approached from the side path; hair dusted in glitter that he swore was an accident. "Someone sneezed and summoned a constellation," he said.

Morgan raised an eyebrow. "Health hazard?"

"Hope hazard," Gabe replied, brushing off his sleeve. "It spelled a haiku in the air. Something about breadcrumbs and stars."

They both looked toward the center of the Hollow where a Threadfound was currently levitating six inches off the ground while arguing with a sentient quilt about the ethics of emotional nap scheduling.

Nearby, another Threadfound coaxed a patch of soil into growing "maybe-plants": blossoms that bloomed only when someone nearby admitted they didn't have all the answers.

And over by the hearth?

Two more had begun shaping something entirely new:

Magic that wasn't inherited. Magic that didn't come from the world before. Magic that was born now.

Morgan exhaled slowly, watching the sparks catch in the air…intent made visible. "I think they're making their own system," they whispered.

Gabe nodded. "Not replacing what was. Just… layering."

One of the Threadfound, the same one who once called themself "Almost", approached with a handful of ribbon-thoughts gathered from the Reflection Corridor. "We don't want to just be real," they said, voice quiet but steady. "We want to create."

Morgan knelt before them. "Then you can."

"We don't know the rules."

Morgan smiled. "Neither did we. That's how this place happened."

The Looming Tree dropped a single leaf. It shimmered, split mid-vein between gold and green.

Gabe caught it before it hit the ground. "Dual-threaded magic," he said softly. "Born and becoming. Memory and imagination."

He passed it to Morgan.

Morgan tucked it behind their ear. "I think the Hollow is evolving again."

"No," Gabe said. "I think you are."

Morgan didn't answer right away.

They just stood, watching as a Threadfound painted laughter into the air with a brush made of kindness, and thought…This isn't the end of becoming. This is what happens after.

## Chapter Thirty-Two: Resistance in Soft Focus

Dr. Everett Shaw was no longer screaming, but that didn't mean he wasn't still causing problems. If anything, the new quiet Shaw was worse.

No more declarations in the square. No more magical audits with screaming clipboards.

Instead, he'd taken to "documenting anomalies" in what he now referred to as his Reflection Log: a notebook bound in spell-quieted leather that he carried everywhere like a holy text.

And the entries?

They were getting... weirder.

> June 17th, 7:42 AM
> *Observed a child teaching a pinecone to apologize. Possibly effective. Pinecone now radiates mild remorse.*
>
> June 18th, 3:03 PM
> *Morgan's presence causes measurable reductions in ambient dread. Uncertain if replicable or just... them.*
>
> June 19th, 10:12 AM
> *I may have been offered friendship. Unsure if accidental.*

Despite it all, Shaw kept refusing to name the Threadfound as citizens. He claimed they lacked fixed identity. He argued they had no birth records. He tried, however unsuccessfully, to ban metaphors in council meetings.

And when Wren opened her bakery for a Threadfound apprentice named Mallow (who had a gift for turning emotional growth into literal, edible pastries), Shaw filed a thirty-seven-point complaint citing "psychospiritual intoxication of the public via confection."

Cassie read the complaint. Then, in her most polite voice, announced that the next town meeting would be held in a circle, on a hill, under the full moon, and that all minutes would be interpreted through dance.

Privately, Baz was worried. "Shaw's not malicious anymore," he said one evening to Morgan. "But he's stuck. And stuck people, in a place this alive... they can start to pull against the weave."

Morgan didn't disagree. "He doesn't understand how to be part of something changing."

"Do you think he ever will?"

"I think," Morgan said, "he's still trying to be right. And what we're asking him to be is real. That's harder."

That same day, Shaw attempted to initiate a formal review of the Hollow by posting a notice on the greenhouse gate:

*NOTICE OF PROPOSED INSPECTION: Unregulated Liminal Facility, Subject to Review Under Provisional Reality Integrity Guidelines*

Cassie found it and she promptly added a second notice underneath:

*NOPE.*

Wren taped a muffin to the post with a sticky note:

*Contain this.*

And Bram, never one to waste a moment of surrealism, turned the whole gate into a slow-moving philosophical riddle. To enter, one had to answer a question posed by a mossy stone about whether time could be kind.

Shaw stood outside it for two hours. He did not answer, did not enter and eventually left looking, just slightly, unmoored.

That night, one of the Threadfound left a folded note on his windowsill. It read:

*You can come in when you're ready. We won't be waiting, but we'll still be here.*

He read it twice. Then, with a sigh, logged a new entry.

> June 20th, 11:13 PM
> *I don't understand them.*
> *And they haven't made me go away.*

## Chapter Thirty-Three: The Magic of Maybe

It started small. Just a gentle shift. A sense that reality had begun listening more closely, not just to spells or rituals, but to intention and curiosity…and to hope.

Mrs. Norwood was the first to accidentally manifest a weather charm. She hadn't meant to. She'd simply been muttering to her roses about "a little more sun, and fewer metaphysical side effects, thank you", when the clouds parted like a curtain and the flowerbeds turned their faces skyward in what could only be described as polite applause. She insisted it was a fluke, but it wasn't.

Across town, Ellis from the candle shop began crafting wicks that shifted scent depending on what the person nearby needed to hear:

- Lavender and cinnamon for courage
- Peppermint and old paper for clarity
- Fresh rain and cedar for grief without language

He called them Threadlights and pretended he didn't notice when one flickered teal and citrus whenever Cassie was nearby.

"Shut up," she told it one afternoon.

It flickered back: Absolutely not.

The children caught on quickest. They started making Possibility Pouches - little sewn bags of fabric dreams and hopeful objects. Most were nonsense. But occasionally, when opened at the right moment, the pouch would whisper something useful:

"Don't say it. Listen."
"Take the red path today."
"Apologize before it's too late."

No one could figure out how the messages appeared, but no one wanted them to stop.

The Threadfound didn't force the changes, they just lived. They opened doors without knocking and rearranged the town's sense of pace. Some set up circles of story-sharing at dawn; others wandered the market asking, "What do you wish you'd been told sooner?"

They weren't always graceful. One Threadfound turned the fountain into a memory loop for three days, and everyone had to relive their most embarrassing moment while ordering coffee.

But even that became... part of it. Part of becoming.

Cassie noticed it first. The spell circles had grown gentler, not weaker, but more adaptive. They pulsed with breath instead of barriers. "Emerdeen's listening," she told Baz one evening while placing teacups that now brewed themselves based on emotional resonance.

Baz smiled. "Do you think we're changing the town?"

"No," Cassie said. "I think the town is changing with us."

By the end of the week, a new kind of sign appeared beneath the old ones at the square's entrance. Painted by hand, thread-stamped by Morgan, and pinned with a charm that sparkled when spoken aloud:

*Welcome to Alden's Landing.*
*Come as you are.*
*Leave what you don't need.*
*And if you don't know who you are yet...*
*That's okay. We'll make space.*

## Chapter Thirty-Four: Miriam and the Magic That Waited

Miriam Wrenhart didn't consider herself particularly magical. She made tea like a ritual, sure. She knew her way around a broom, and once in her twenties she'd convinced a stubborn shadow to leave her hallway by sheer force of will and chamomile.

But that was decades ago. She was seventy now, give or take a year - she liked to round down when asked.

She had her routines. Her cardigan rotation. Her soap carved with her initials. Her notebooks of *Things to Say at Important Moments*, which were always blank when she needed them most.

So, when the world began to shimmer, when children walked with dream-painted palms and the breeze carried laughter shaped like lanterns, Miriam mostly stayed out of it.

Mostly.

She first noticed it in her garden. The marigolds began whispering in the late afternoons. Not urgently. Just… gently. Like they were checking in.

"Do you still like the sunlight here?" they asked.

She responded out loud, felt silly, and then admitted, "Yes, but the soil feels tired."

The next morning, the roots had shifted themselves to richer ground.

Miriam didn't tell anyone. She just brought the marigolds an extra saucer of honey water and said, "Thank you," like it was the most natural thing in the world.

The second thing was the book.

It had been on her shelf for years, untouched. A gift from a niece who meant well but assumed Miriam was more poetic than she was. *The Language of Threads and Other Quiet Magics.*

Miriam opened it one rainy afternoon out of boredom and found a note on the first page that hadn't been there before:

"It's not too late."

She closed the book immediately. Then opened it again.

Same words. Different feeling.

By the end of the week, her knitting had started finishing her thoughts. The scarf she was working on shifted colors mid-row, becoming the exact shade of sky she'd always imagined in a memory that didn't have one.

She cried a little, then kept knitting.

It was Morgan who found her one morning sitting by the well, notebook in her lap, hands gently glowing with light not her own, but not borrowed, either. "Miriam?" they asked.

She looked up, startled, but not afraid. "I think I'm... remembering things I never did," she said softly. "And I don't know what to do with them."

Morgan smiled. "Maybe you don't have to do anything. Maybe it's enough to hold them."

They sat together for a long while. The wind wrapped around them like a shawl. And when Miriam finally looked down at her hands, the light had quieted, but it was still there.

Soft. Warm. Waiting.

She returned home that night and wrote her first poem in the blank notebook she'd been carrying for thirty years.

It wasn't perfect, but it was hers. And that, she thought, must be its own kind of magic.

# Chapter Thirty-Five: The Grace of Small Magic

Miriam started baking again. She hadn't touched the old recipes since her sister passed, since the family fractured into polite holiday cards and occasional regrets. But now, with the marigolds humming softly outside her kitchen window and a Threadfound named Fen gently tending her herb beds with silver-painted fingernails, it felt... possible.

The bread rose faster these days. Not unnaturally fast, just right. Like it remembered what it was supposed to become. Miriam found she did, too.

At the market, she surprised herself. She bought cinnamon she didn't need. Told Ellis the candle maker that she missed the scent of first snow, and he handed her a wick that flickered blue and said, "Then let it remind you."

She left a loaf of rosemary bread on Dr. Shaw's porch with no note or explanation, just warmth. She told herself it was to make sure he didn't starve while brooding himself into an ideological coma. But the truth was simpler: she had more now, and enough meant she could give some away.

She began attending the story circles in the square. At first, she sat at the edge, knitting memories into scarves no one asked for and telling herself she was only there to listen. Then, one evening, someone asked, "What was the first thing you ever believed in?"

And Miriam said, without thinking, "A moth. I thought it might be my mother, come back to remind me not to marry Henry."

There was laughter. Not mocking but understanding. And someone said, "Did you marry him?"

"No," Miriam replied. "But I dated someone worse. Just to be sure."

And just like that, she was in.

Fen visited more often. They didn't speak much, just wandered her kitchen, touching the walls like they were feeling the house's pulse.

Miriam found herself asking, one evening, "What does becoming feel like to you?"

Fen smiled. "Like a coat I never realized I was allowed to wear. Not heavy. Just mine."

Miriam nodded. Then, softly, "I think I've been living in someone else's jacket for a long time."

"You can take it off," Fen said. "Or add sleeves. Or turn it into a kite."

Miriam smiled. "A kite sounds good."


She started dreaming in color again. Not bold, crashing palettes, but soft tones: tea-soaked gold, frost-pale blue, the exact green of the mint she'd once grown for someone who never came back.

She wrote the dreams down, then stitched them into small squares of cloth, and began leaving them in unexpected places:

- A dream of dancing on a rooftop, tucked into the lining of Cassie's coat.
- A dream of apology shaped like moonlight, under Shaw's clipboard.
- A dream of forgiveness (her own) tied to the branch of the Looming Tree with a silver ribbon.

She didn't tell anyone, but the Hollow noticed.

And when Morgan next visited her kitchen, the teacups had already set themselves out. "Have you been practicing?" they asked.

Miriam smiled and poured. "No. Just remembering differently."

## Chapter Thirty-Six: The Thread That Listens

The Threadfound was named Lilt, and they were barely a week into form, still trailing stardust in their hair and sometimes forgetting how walking worked on corners. Their eyes carried entire symphonies, most of them unfinished. Their voice had not yet decided on a pitch, and they could not sit still. Not even in sleep, which Lilt insisted was "a vibrating state of conceptual pause."

Miriam watched them flit around the edges of the town square, pockets full of buttons and loose thoughts, trying to collect stories the way one might chase lightning bugs. Eventually, she stopped them with a question. "What do you want to do with the stories?"

Lilt blinked. "Tell them!"

"Why?"

Lilt hesitated. "Because… they're beautiful?"

Miriam smiled softly. "Then let them breathe first."

They began meeting on the sun-warmed bench behind the greenhouse. At first, Lilt jittered, fiddling with ribbon scraps, humming under their breath, attempting to sketch people's memories from across the garden using only guesses and color-coded wax.

Miriam said nothing. She just sat with hands folded, feet still, and tea cooling in its cup.

After a few days, Lilt started arriving early. Still moving, but less frantically. They brought Miriam a spool of thread they'd found near the Hollow and a question folded into a leaf:

*"What happens to stories when no one listens?"*

Miriam answered with a quiet truth: "They get louder. Or smaller. Or strange. Sometimes they turn into riddles and live in spoons."

Lilt blinked, then laughed and sat down.

The first story Miriam taught them wasn't hers. It belonged to the wind. They listened together, heads tilted just slightly, as the late afternoon breeze rustled the pages of her notebook and carried the scent of something too old to name. "It's not about collecting," Miriam said. "It's about keeping. Letting it stay long enough to matter."

Lilt wrote that down in purple ink on their forearm and it glowed for the rest of the day.

Soon, they began recording stories together but not with parchment and quill, with presence. They listened to the silence after a joke. They noticed which sighs meant "I'm okay" and which ones meant "ask again." They followed the threads of memory woven into tea rituals, half-finished embroidery, and the way Wren always paused at the door before stepping into her shop.

They began weaving these moments into small books, binding them with thread made from Lilt's stardust and Miriam's quiet. They were not published or shelved. Just...offered in the Hollow and sometimes in town.

One book read:

*"Here is a story that changed no laws, no maps, and no destinies. But it made someone breathe deeper. That's enough."*

One day, Lilt asked, "Is this becoming?"

Miriam considered. "No," she said. "This is being."

Lilt nodded slowly, then took her hand. And together, they sat in stillness that wasn't empty, but full of everything no one else had thought to keep.

## Chapter Thirty-Seven: The Naming Circle

The Hollow shimmered with quiet anticipation. Its threads were woven from memory and had begun to hum in a harmony too complex to be called a song and too kind to be called power.

Morgan stood beneath the Looming Tree, their hands open, palms glowing faintly with threadlight. Around them, the air had thickened into possibility...soft, golden, and strange.

Tonight, the Threadfound would gather. Not to be named, but to name themselves.

They arrived in silence. One by one. Some barefoot, some cloaked in fabric made of woven pasts, some trailing ideas that hadn't quite settled into words.

Lilt came first, carrying a book stitched with Miriam's patience and stitched in stardust. They nodded once to Morgan and took their place beneath a branch that curled gently downward, like a gesture of welcome.

Una followed, wrapped in wind and lullabies, her name now threaded through the ribbons of her sleeves. She brought a lantern that pulsed with the heartbeat of stories untold.

Then Lem, ever watchful, ever becoming, stood beside the central stone. They placed a silver thread across the circle's edge, offering a bridge for those still unsure.

By moonrise, the Hollow was full.

Morgan stepped into the center and did not speak. They simply began to weave. Not a physical loom, but one made of intention.

They lifted a strand of laughter. A thread of doubt. A sliver of memory from a soul who had once been a whisper and now stood as a name.

As Morgan worked, the others joined. Not all at once and not in unison, but with rhythm, reverence, and truth. The circle grew, not in size, but in depth.

Each Threadfound stepped forward and offered something:

- A color that had followed them since their first glimpse of the world
- A sound they couldn't describe until they heard it in someone else's voice
- A word that made them flinch once, but sing now
- A silence they had turned into shelter

These became names - not fixed or final, but true.

Morgan gathered them all, threaded them into the air, into the roots of the Looming Tree, into the pathways of the Hollow itself.

Each name became a light, and each light became a place. And the Hollow… held them all.

At the end, Morgan stepped back, breath slow, arms heavy with what had been offered.

Gabe approached, quiet and steady. "That was beautiful," he said.

"It was theirs," Morgan whispered.

"And yours," Gabe added, placing a hand over their heart. "You gave them the thread."

Morgan looked at the glowing weave, now drifting gently through the Hollow like starlight unbound. "No," they said. "They chose to pull it."

Far above, the sky blinked in quiet wonder. And beneath it, in the world stitched from maybe and memory, names hung like lanterns.

## Chapter Thirty-Eight: The Echo Beyond the Hill

It began with a door that wasn't supposed to be there. A plain wooden one, painted teal and humming softly with unread stories. It appeared in the back room of a city library three towns east of Alden's Landing.

The custodian found it first. She opened it, expecting a closet. Instead, she found silence. A silence so gentle it asked who she was and didn't demand an answer.

She didn't step through, just yet. But she whispered her middle name, one she'd never liked, and the silence whispered it back like a promise.

When she returned the next day, the door was gone. But her name felt different... chosen.

In a mountain village two days north, a weathered path reappeared. It had been lost to landslide. Along its edges bloomed wildflowers never catalogued, petals bearing runes no one could quite read.

A child wandered off the path and came back hours later with a stick that sang their dreams back to them. They now carry it everywhere. It hums most when they're afraid.

A stranger in a coastal town found a pebble on their windowsill with the word "stay" etched into it. They hadn't told anyone they were planning to leave, but they stayed.

In pockets of the world, people began dreaming in new colors. Not vivid, but honest shades that had no name in language but pulsed with the feeling of "I am still here."

A shopkeeper woke remembering a song she hadn't written and found sheet music on her nightstand.

A lost letter arrived two decades late with a single word added in the margin: *remember.*

A teacher began noticing their students describing themselves differently. Not louder. But truer.

It wasn't chaos. It wasn't a flood. It was permission. Not granted by Morgan or the Threadfound, but by the weave itself.

Wherever a truth had been silenced… Wherever a self had been forgotten…

The magic of naming whispered:

You are not too late.
You are not unfinished.
You are not alone.


Back in Alden's Landing, Cassie sat on her porch, sipping tea that now tasted faintly like early mornings and second chances. She looked out at the world beyond the hills and felt it pull, not in distance, but in invitation. "They're hearing us," she murmured.

Baz joined her with a book that had rewritten its title overnight. It now read: *Becoming Is Not a Closed Loop.* He smiled. "Or maybe we're hearing them."

## Chapter Forty: The Language Lilt Invented

Lilt didn't wake up the next morning. They emerged. From sleep, yes, but more from a night full of whispers that weren't dreams, and dreams that weren't quite memories. The world had tilted in a new direction, and they had tilted with it.

Their hands hummed with threadlight, but it wasn't Miriam's soft golden warmth. This was something different. Less complete and more curious. Not yet known, but already true.

They didn't tell Miriam at first. Not out of secrecy, but reverence. It felt like speaking too soon would jar it loose, like naming a creature before it had finished becoming.

So, they walked. They wandered the edges of the Hollow with a satchel full of loose pages, feathers, pressed leaves, words that had once been wept, and six polished stones that smelled like ink and dawn.

They began leaving marks. Not symbols. Not spells. Just... gestures.

A pressed palm on a stone wall. A ribbon tied where silence had once hidden too long. A page tucked inside the Looming Tree's hollow trunk that read:

*Not all stories begin with once. Some begin with almost.*

The Threadfound began noticing. They'd pause mid-conversation, mid-breath, mid-becoming. Then turn. Then know.

Something had changed. Lilt didn't call it a spell. They called it a reminder. A magic that didn't cast or bind or shape. It simply said: You're still here. And I see you.

Their favorite place became the in-between paths. Those corners of the Hollow where the world folded in subtle spirals, not hidden but unspoken.

There, Lilt began their real work. They built a listening post, not with wood or stone, but with layered questions:

- What did you almost say?
- What does your silence want to become?
- Who would you be if you believed you were never too late?

Visitors began to find their way there. Not because they were told, but because they needed. And when they sat within the circle, Lilt didn't ask them to speak.

They simply offered a square of fabric, a piece of chalk, or a blank note. And people filled them with things they hadn't yet dared say aloud.

One day, Miriam came and sat in the circle, eyes steady, hands quiet.

Lilt didn't speak. But they placed a square of woven thread between them, stitched in two directions: Miriam's soft golden truth, and Lilt's wild silver wondering.

It shimmered gently. Miriam picked it up, smiled, and said, "You've made a language."

Lilt beamed. "Only the beginning."

That evening, they returned to their corner of the Hollow, thread dust in their sleeves and pages full of names that hadn't needed words. They wrote in the margin of their own book:

*Magic doesn't always change the world.*
*Sometimes it just remembers it differently.*

And that, too, is becoming.

## Chapter Forty-One: The Magic He Never Learned to Name

Shaw first heard of the listening circle from a Threadfound with glitter in their hair and a talent for planting doubt with the same care one plants herbs.

"It's not a spell," they said, brushing a pearlescent vine off their shoulder. "It's a space. For what wasn't said."

Shaw frowned. "That's not magic. That's… therapy in a costume."

The Threadfound smiled. "You say that like it's not the same thing."

He didn't go right away. He told himself he was observing. Monitoring the ripple effects of communal introspection.

In reality, he watched from a distance through the shimmered edge of the Hollow's far path, where the world blurred into potential and boots didn't scuff the ground so much as ask permission.

He saw people enter the circle carrying silence and leave with their posture realigned. Not taller, but truer.

He saw Lilt hand out fabric and chalk, receive nothing in return but breath and gratitude.

He saw Miriam speak only three words to a crying man, and those words fold into his hands like a cloak.

He didn't understand it. But worse, part of him did.

The night he finally stepped into the Hollow, he didn't bring his clipboard. He brought a note that was folded six times, tucked in the inner pocket of his coat. It wasn't addressed to anyone; it was a line he hadn't said aloud in over twenty years:

*I didn't know how to stay when I couldn't fix it.*

He stood at the edge of the circle, but didn't step in. He just watched.

Lilt noticed him. They didn't smile or beckon. They simply tilted their head in that way of theirs that said - if you're here, it matters.

Shaw stepped forward one pace, then froze.

Miriam, seated at the far end of the circle, looked up and met his gaze. She didn't challenge him or attempt to comfort. She just saw him. Fully.

For what he had been. For what he wasn't yet. For what might still be possible.

It undid him like a single stitch pulled loose from a too-tight collar. And suddenly, he could breathe.

He left the circle without speaking, leaving the note too.

Lilt found it later, opened it, and smiled. They didn't need to write anything in return. The Hollow had already received it.

Back at his room, Shaw didn't write a report. He made tea.

Not perfectly or precisely, but with care. And when the steam rose, it smelled faintly of remembering.

## Chapter Forty-Two: The Questions He Didn't File

Shaw returned three days later. He wore the same coat and still didn't carry a clipboard. But he had a pencil behind one ear, and the unmistakable posture of a man who wanted to understand more than he wanted to be right.

The listening circle wasn't full that morning, it was just Lilt sketching air with their fingertips and Miriam humming softly over a piece of threadlight she hadn't yet decided to keep.

Shaw paused at the threshold. The Hollow recognized him. It didn't flinch, didn't shimmer. It simply made room.

Miriam didn't speak.

Lilt did. "You came back."

Shaw nodded. "I... think I have questions."

Lilt smiled gently. "That's what this place is for."

He didn't sit right away. Instead, he circled the edge of the grove, pacing like a man measuring possibility against protocol. Finally, he asked, "What exactly do you do here?"

Miriam raised one eyebrow. "What do you think we do?"

Shaw exhaled. "You gather feelings and silence. People's forgotten selves." He hesitated. "You don't fix them."

"No," Lilt said. "We just witness."

Shaw was quiet for a long time. Then: "How is that magic?"

Miriam's answer was a whisper. "Because when something is witnessed without judgment, it begins to believe in itself again."

He sat then, however stiffly and uncomfortably. Like the earth might decide it wasn't ready to hold him. But it did.

The moment he lowered himself into the ring of softened ground, the air around him warmed. Not with fire, but with attention.

Lilt handed him a blank square of fabric.

He looked at it like it was a test. "What am I supposed to put here?"

"Something unfinished," Lilt said. "A thought. A word. A truth you haven't looked at yet."

"I don't know if I have any."

Miriam smiled. "Everyone does."

He held the fabric. Long enough that his fingers left a trace of warmth. He didn't write anything. But after a while, he whispered something under his breath too low for them to hear. Then folded the square and placed it in the center of the circle.

Lilt didn't open it. They didn't need to.

The Hollow pulsed once, like a ripple beneath the soil.

Shaw cleared his throat. "Will anyone… answer it?"

Miriam's voice was calm. "Maybe. Maybe not. But now it's not just yours."

He stayed until the light shifted into gold. When he finally stood, Lilt offered him a soft gray and sea-glass green thread, the color of edges softened by time. "A thread for questions," they said.

He tucked it into his pocket. And for the first time in a long time, he didn't walk away like a man who needed to know everything. He walked like someone who had just been heard.

## Chapter Forty-Three: The Shape of Listening

Lilt stayed long after Shaw left. The fabric square he'd folded remained in the center of the circle, untouched but not unacknowledged. It shimmered faintly like a pebble in water, still sending ripples long after it had landed. They didn't move it or store it. They just sat beside it and breathed.

Because sometimes that's what guidance meant: not answering, not solving, just being still enough for someone else to feel their shape return.

Later, Lilt walked the path Miriam called The Spine. A narrow trail that traced the Hollow's oldest memory-lines. It was where they often came to think. They didn't bring their sketchbook, but a pouch of threadmarks they hadn't yet sewn into anything, and a question they'd been carrying in their chest since Shaw had looked them in the eye and not asked to be fixed.

What does it mean to hold space for someone you don't understand? In the early days of becoming, Lilt had assumed guidance was like light: bright, directional, certain. But Miriam had taught them otherwise. That sometimes being a guide meant becoming a frame, not the painting, not the painter, just the boundary that let someone else know they belonged.

And now... Lilt wondered what shape their frame would take.

Not everyone needed silence. Not everyone needed softness. Some people needed play. Some people needed fire.

Some, like Shaw, needed to be startled into stillness. Could Lilt do that? Could they stretch themselves without disappearing?

A Threadfound named Corin joined them on the trail, without speaking. He carried a broken compass and a jar full of rainwater memories. They walked for a while, the two of them, exchanging no words. Then Corin asked, "Do you ever feel too soft to lead?"

Lilt didn't answer right away. But eventually they said: "Softness isn't the opposite of strength. It's what strength looks like when it isn't performing."

Corin nodded. Placed a stone at the path's edge and kept walking.

Later that night, Lilt returned to the circle alone. They knelt beside the square Shaw had left and added one of their own. Blank but bordered in thread. A frame. A silent invitation.

And between the two of them, something shimmered. It wasn't a spell or a shape. Just a promise:

*You don't have to know how to lead to begin holding light.*

## Chapter Forty-Four: When the Hollow Turns Toward the World

Morgan felt the change before it reached the roots. Not with their eyes. Not even with magic, but with their body.

The Hollow had always been a living thing, breathing in stories, exhaling permission, but now it was no longer simply a place to receive. Something had shifted in the weave.

It wanted to move. Not vanish. Not close. Open.

They stood beneath the Looming Tree at dawn, hands trailing over bark that felt warmer than before. The tree pulsed gently, leaves stirring in a rhythm that didn't match the wind. "Are you ready?" Morgan whispered.

The tree answered by dropping a single leaf. A spiral of silver and green.

Morgan caught it and felt the pulse of a message:

*What has been found must now return.*

They called a quiet gathering. Not everyone came. Just those who knew the Threadfound, who had begun shaping magic of their own, the ones who felt the outside world's pulse rising like a tide.

Cassie arrived with crumbs on her coat and that particular look in her eyes that meant she was trying not to be too sentimental.

Lilt sat beside Miriam, their fingers tracing a new pattern in their lap.

Gabe stood near the edge, arms crossed, watching the Hollow like it was an old friend preparing to leave the room without saying goodbye.

Morgan didn't make a speech. They simply stepped into the center of the Grove and said, "The Hollow is no longer just a haven. It's becoming a bridge."

A murmur ran through the circle.

"A bridge to what?" someone asked.

Morgan's voice was soft. Steady. "To everywhere that needs remembering."

That night, the Hollow cracked. Not like glass, but like shell.

The spiral paths began to echo in wider rings. Memory-vines unfurled past the edges of the glade, weaving into doorways that didn't exist the day before. The Looming Tree stretched, not taller, but deeper, its roots threading toward thresholds waiting to be touched.

A pond appeared near the northern edge, its surface reflecting other skies. A door blinked into being in the Hollow's southern field. No handle. No hinges. Just the sense that it was waiting for someone who hadn't yet arrived.

Morgan stood in the middle of it all, heart full, soul bare, hands open. "This was never meant to stay hidden," they said.

Gabe stepped forward. "And you?"

Morgan looked to the stars that now shimmered just a little differently above them.

"I don't know if I lead it anymore," they said. "Maybe I just… accompanied it to its next becoming."

Cassie chuckled, wiping something suspiciously tear-like from her cheek. "Well," she said, "you're still the best damn midwife to a liminal shift I've ever met."

As the Hollow began to weave outward into the world, into dreampaths and unnamed doorways and memory-marked corners of forgotten places, Morgan stepped to the edge. Not to close it. Not to guard it. But to leave a message, stitched into the bark of the Looming Tree:

*The way forward is not away from who you were.*
*It's toward who you're willing to remember.*

## Chapter Forty-Five: The Path That Called Her Name

The door didn't appear in the usual way. There was no glow, no gust of warm wind, no whispered invitation woven into birdsong. It was just... there.

Set into the side of an overgrown garden shed behind a boarding house in a city that didn't believe in magic anymore. The door had no knob. No hinges. Just a soft spiral carved into the wood, and an edge that shimmered only when she looked away.

Her name was Naomi, and she hadn't believed in portals since she was nine years old and her grandmother's mirror stopped showing her reflections that weren't real.

She stood before the door now, one hand wrapped around a cold cup of tea, the other gripping a letter she hadn't had the courage to open for three years. She had dreamed of this door before. In those dreams, it had always whispered one word: Begin.

She didn't know what made her step through. Only that she'd been standing still for too long. And when her foot touched the threshold, she didn't fall. She folded like breath into air, like light into morning. And the next thing she knew, she was somewhere else.

The Hollow was quiet when she arrived. It wasn't empty, it was listening. The ground beneath her feet was soft, woven with moss and meaning. The sky above was the color of old maps and new ink.

She took one breath, then another. The letter in her hand vanished. And in its place a ribbon of thread, wrapped twice around her wrist. Silver and green. Unfamiliar and true.

She wandered the path for hours or maybe minutes, drawn by instinct more than reason. She passed a low stone etched with a question: *"What part of yourself have you misplaced?"*

She didn't answer out loud, but the Hollow heard her silence and offered space anyway.

Eventually, she reached a clearing. And there, at its center, sat a figure waiting. Young. Bright-eyed. Hands marked with stitches and stars. "Welcome," said Lilt, without surprise.

Naomi blinked. "I don't think I was invited."

Lilt tilted their head. "You weren't. You were remembered." They held out a small square of fabric and a threadless needle.

Naomi stared. "I don't know what to do with this."

Lilt smiled. "Perfect. That's the only way to begin."

Naomi sat down. For the first time in years, she didn't reach for answers. She reached for the thread and started to stitch.

## Chapter Forty-Six: The Road That Shouldn't Exist

Wes wasn't lost. Not exactly.

But his GPS had frozen three towns back, his phone kept suggesting he "try again later," and the gas station attendant had said, "If you get to the place with the blue bridge and the dandelions that don't blink, you've gone too far."

He hadn't asked for clarification. Somehow, it felt like he wasn't supposed to.

Now, the road had narrowed into a two-lane curve of tree-shadow and sky. The air had a softness to it like it remembered rain that hadn't fallen yet. There was music on the wind. It sounded like someone humming while stirring a pot. And just when he was about to turn around…A sign appeared. It was hand-carved and faded.

**Welcome to Alden's Landing.**
*Come as you are. Leave what you don't need.*

He slowed down and turned off the car. And sat very still.

The town looked like something out of a forgotten storybook, if that book had been dog-eared, rewritten in the margins, and left in a sunlit attic for twenty years.

There were shops with signs that pulsed faintly in your peripheral vision. Wind chimes that harmonized with people's laughter. A child skipping stones that bounced twice then disappeared entirely.

Wes started walking, and with every step, the strange sensation grew. The air here was listening. Not watching - listening.

He passed a tea shop where the door opened before he reached it.

Passed a market stall where the vendor handed him a peach without asking. "It looked like something you'd lost," she said.

He took it and said thank you and kept walking.

By the time he reached the town square, he felt the weight of something he hadn't realized he was carrying begin to lift.

A woman with quick eyes and a smudge of flour on her cheek watched him from a bench. She raised a brow. "First time?" she asked.

Wes nodded slowly. "I don't know why I'm here."

She grinned. "That's the best reason." She handed him a paper pamphlet titled:

*Threadfound Things to Know (Whether You Know You Are or Not)*

He flipped it open, and the first line read:

*If you've found your way here, you've already begun.*

As he sat on the edge of the square, peach in hand, warmth in his chest, Wes realized that this wasn't a destination. It was a return. Not to a place, but to a possibility.

## Chapter Forty-Seven: Threads Meet Hands

Wes hadn't meant to follow the smell of cinnamon and lavender through the crooked iron gate. But it was magnetic. It pulled him past flowering hedges and a greenhouse with steam-kissed windows, through a back garden where herbs hummed and the soil looked like it had secrets to tell. And then he was standing in a sun-drenched kitchen filled with the Crafting Coven.

Not robed or haloed or shimmering with theatrical power, just alive with that quiet, self-assured energy of people who knew exactly how to stitch reality into something softer.

Cassie turned first. She was dusted in flour, her hair pinned up with something that sparkled faintly (maybe salt, maybe starlight), and her eyes sharpened like she'd already read his name on a spool somewhere. "You brought peach," she said.

Wes blinked. "I...what?"

She plucked the fruit from his hand, took a bite, and nodded. "Good start."

The others began filtering in.

Wren, all serene precision and thousand-yard empathy, offered him tea before he asked. She didn't say welcome, just "we've been expecting someone you didn't know you were."

Bram popped out of a pantry with a bundle of thread and a grin. "We haven't had a Wes before. That's a good name. Feels grounded. Like a step you meant to take."

Baz said nothing at first, just handed him a square of fabric with three question marks stitched into it. "You'll need this later," he murmured.

Wes opened his mouth to speak, but Morgan appeared in the doorway then looking radiant, grounded, and with eyes like open pages. Every question he had uncoiled.

Morgan didn't speak. Just nodded once. As if to say: You've been seen.

They brought him into the greenhouse. Not to explain things, but to ask.

"What kind of magic do you remember by accident?" Wren asked.

"What doesn't let you sleep?" Cassie followed.

"If you could undo one silence, which would it be?" Bram added, handing him a pen that glowed when he hesitated.

Wes didn't know how to answer. So, he didn't. He just stood there, overwhelmed, mouth full of words he hadn't yet sorted into truth.

Cassie smiled. "Don't worry. We start with stitching long before we start with sense."

By sunset, he'd helped Morgan rearrange the sigil stones along the eastern path. They didn't talk much, but as he placed the last stone, it pulsed once under his fingers.

Morgan looked at him, not with surprise, with recognition. "You're not here to remember what you lost," they said. "You're here to name what you almost became."

Wes blinked. And for the first time in years, felt something click into place that didn't have to make sense to be real.

That night, back in the guest room above the greenhouse, he found a folded note on his pillow:

*We don't need to know why you came.*
*We just need you to stay long enough to find out.*

It was signed only with a stitched symbol: Three threads in a spiral.

The mark of the Coven.

## Chapter Forty-Eight: The Pattern That Isn't Obvious (Yet)

They gathered in the greenroom. Not because it was formal, but because it was where the spell-stitched chairs adjusted for mood, and the tea cart had started brewing on its own whenever someone had a dilemma.

Cassie arrived first, carrying a biscuit and a theory. "He's either here to repair something no one remembers is broken," she said, "or he's the kind of soul who teaches reality how to laugh again."

Baz arched a brow. "That's a lot of pressure for someone who still flinches when the sugar bowl blinks."

"It shouldn't blink," Bram muttered.

"It's learning boundaries," Wren said soothingly, cradling a cup of Clarity Blend. "Give it time."

Morgan entered last. They didn't sit. They stood near the window, fingers trailing over the rune-carved sill, eyes turned toward the Hollow. "He doesn't resonate with old threads," Morgan said. "He doesn't echo anyone who's come before."

Cassie leaned back in her chair. "So, he's not Threadfound?"

"No," Morgan said. "He's something... adjacent. A listener, maybe. Or a reframer."

"Disruptor?" Baz offered.

"Restorer," Wren countered.

"Instigator of biscuit-related prophecy," Bram added with a grin.

Cassie snapped her fingers. "He did bring that peach."

"That peach," Wren said, half-smiling. "Which tested as 87% memory."

Morgan nodded slowly. "It's possible he's a bridge."

"To what?" Baz asked.

"Not to where we've been," Morgan murmured. "To what we haven't built yet."

The Coven fell quiet.

Not with doubt, but with recognition. That hush that came when magic leaned in just a little closer to listen.

Cassie tapped her fingers on the rim of her mug. "Maybe he's here to challenge us."

"To do what?" Bram asked. "Change?"

"No," she said. "To stay changed."

A vine slipped through the window then, carrying a folded piece of parchment, as if the greenhouse itself had decided to submit testimony.

Wren opened it and read aloud.

*He's not a thread.*
*He's the thimble.*

Morgan smiled faintly. "Not a weaver. Not the cloth. The thing that lets the work be done without breaking us open."

"That's... poetic," Bram said. "And also, very Alden's Landing."

As they returned to their tea, the chairs shifted slightly, and the sugar bowl gave Wes a tiny nod of approval from the shelf.

## Chapter Forty-Nine: The Echo Under His Fingertips

It started with buttons. Not glowing buttons. Not enchanted buttons. Just… misplaced buttons.

Wes had offered to help Bram organize the old drawer of "useful miscellany" in the greenhouse workshop, a drawer that squeaked like it held secrets and, as it turned out, did.

Bram handed him a tin. "Sort these by vibe, not color. Cassie's system."

Wes blinked. "I'm sorry… vibe?"

"Joyful, haunted, or questioning," Bram said, completely serious. "You'll know when you know."

Wes didn't know. At least not at first. But as he sat cross-legged on the floor, hands sifting through buttons made of bone, shell, and memory-soaked resin, something shifted. Every time his fingers brushed a certain kind of button, the air changed. It became softer. Like the moment before someone tells you a truth.

And when he held one—an opalescent disc with a chip on its edge— he heard a sound. Not aloud. Inside.

A laugh. A familiar laugh. From a voice he hadn't heard in ten years. His sister's.

He dropped the button and stared at his hands.

Bram looked up. "You okay?"

Wes nodded, slowly. "I think I just… heard something that shouldn't be here."

Bram grinned. "Congrats. You're haunted."

"No," Wes said, still stunned. "It wasn't bad. It was… mine."

Over the next few hours, more moments came.

A humming hum from a ceramic bead.

A heartbeat echo in a shard of threadspool.

And in the bottom of the drawer was a brass brooch that made the entire room pause when he touched it.

Cassie stepped in and nearly dropped her tea. "Wes," she said, voice low. "That brooch hasn't spoken since Morgan first arrived."

"It spoke?"

"No," she said. "It listened."

Later, Morgan sat with him in the garden.

Wes turned the button over in his hand, the one with the chipped edge and the echo of his sister's laugh. "I didn't cast anything," he said.

Morgan smiled. "You didn't have to."

"So, what is this?"

"You're a resonator," they said. "Your presence wakes things. Not by force. By… familiarity. You reflect things people forgot they remembered."

Wes blinked. "That sounds… intense."

"It's gentle," Morgan said. "But that doesn't mean it isn't powerful."

Wes went to bed with three objects in his pocket:

- The chipped button
- The whispering brooch
- And a small spool of silver thread that hadn't glowed for anyone else in over a decade

He didn't know what they meant, but he knew they belonged to someone.

And for the first time since arriving, he felt like maybe he did, too.

## Chapter Fifty: The Stories That Stirred

It started with Wren. She was arranging a tray of tea jars. Nothing out of the ordinary, when one tin she hadn't touched in years rolled off the shelf and landed in her hands.

A blend she'd made once and hidden away: rosehips, bay leaf, ginger root, and grief.

She hadn't labeled it because she hadn't needed to. Now, it whispered her mother's lullaby as she lifted the lid.

And standing ten feet away, not touching a thing, was Wes. He didn't notice right away or do anything.

But Wren smiled as her fingers tightened on the tin. "Interesting," she murmured.

At the bakery, a Threadfound named Fen was shaping memory-scones that were ordinary until they touched Wes's hand. Then they bloomed into swirls of flavor Fen didn't recognize. He took a bite and blinked back tears. "This tastes like... the day I first laughed."

Wes stared. "What?"

"It was cloudy," Fen said, voice shaky. "And someone had drawn a smiley face in the fog on a window. I thought it was magic. Turns out, I was right."

At the market, Cassie held up a bolt of old fabric, unused for years. She'd once intended it for a spell that never quite knew what it was.

Wes walked by. He didn't touch it. He didn't even see it. But the weave shimmered and then realigned.

Cassie blinked. "Well. Someone's got a field around them."

Baz, watching from the herb stall, just smirked. "Told you he was a thimble."

The real shift came when Miriam paused mid-stitch during her morning ritual. She held a thread that had refused to behave for weeks. And the moment Wes was passing by on his way to return a library book, the thread pulled itself smooth. Then formed a shape.

A story symbol. One that hadn't been used since the earliest days of the Hollow.

She didn't say anything to him then. But that evening, she stitched a small patch and left it on his windowsill. It read:

*You are waking the stories we didn't know we still carried.*

Wes couldn't explain any of it, but he felt it in the subtle way people looked at him. Not with awe, but with recognition. As if they'd misplaced something long ago and only now realized it had returned. Not tangibly, but to their memory.

He asked Morgan about it. "Is this… safe?" Wes said. "What if I stir things people aren't ready to remember?"

Morgan studied him. "You're not unlocking anything that isn't already asking to be heard. You're just... answering."

They paused, then added: "You don't rewrite stories. You remind them where they started."

That night, Wes stood in the greenhouse, surrounded by old tools, thread scraps, and dream-salted herbs. He didn't cast a spell. He didn't chant. He just breathed.

And the wind picked up slightly, circling once, carrying with it the sound of pages turning.

## Chapter Fifty-One: The Room That Holds What We Couldn't

Morgan had walked the Hollow a thousand times. They knew its thresholds like their own pulse: the Naming Grove, the Echo Paths, the Listening Circle stitched together by Lilt's gentle insistence. Every space had its own resonance.

And yet this corridor was new.

Tucked behind a spiraled column of moss-stone and memory root, the doorway pulsed softly. Morgan stepped through. The temperature changed. So did the air.

Heavier, but not oppressive. Like a place that understood grief and grace in equal measure.

The room beyond was dim, not dark. A place designed for what wasn't ready to be seen but couldn't be buried. It wasn't lined with shelves, but with small alcoves and each glowing faintly with a pulse of something held but not owned.

Morgan walked slowly, the way one walks through sacred ruins or someone else's dream. They paused before a shallow bowl that shimmered with salt and breath. The placard beneath it read:

*Untended Regret: Age 7*
*Felt but never spoken. Released midwinter, carried by hands that shook too quietly to be seen.*

Morgan swallowed. The next alcove held a folded scarf, frayed at the edges.

*Affection Not Returned.*
*Still warm. Still waiting. Not ashamed.*

They turned the corner. And there, seated on the floor, was Gabe.

Not surprised. Just… aware. Like someone who had been expecting this moment, eventually.

"You found it," Gabe said softly, not rising.

Morgan knelt beside him. "What is this?"

Gabe rested a hand on a glowing stone shaped like a palm turned upward.

"It's where the Hollow sends what people let go of too quietly. Not names. Not stories. Just… feelings. The ones that didn't get held."

Morgan traced a thread between two alcoves. One full of frustration, the other of peace that had come too late. "And you've been tending this?"

Gabe nodded. "Someone has to."

For a moment, neither of them spoke. Then Morgan asked, "How long?"

Gabe's fingers flexed against the floor. "Since before I came to Alden's Landing. Since I was a boy, really. I've always... felt where feelings go. Even when no one names them."

Morgan looked at him differently then. Surprise? No. Reverence. "You're not just grounding us," they said. "You're holding the weight we forget to name."

Gabe's voice dropped, almost embarrassed. "It's not magic like yours. It's not... visible."

"It's sacred," Morgan replied. "And it's yours."

They stood together. Morgan placed a hand over an alcove labeled *Unspoken Apology (Offered Too Late)*. It pulsed once, then dimmed, as if comforted by company.

Morgan turned to Gabe. "Let me help you tend it."

Gabe smiled. "Then I'll show you where we keep the joy no one believed they deserved. It sings when someone walks past who does."

# Chapter Fifty-Two: The Ground Beneath Us

It started with static. Not electrical, but emotional.

Small things at first - tea over brewing itself, charms igniting prematurely, Lilt's chalk lines bleeding off the walls and into doorframes. The Hollow pulsed too fast, too hot, like it was outgrowing its own skin.

Cassie was the first to say it aloud. "The air's thick with everyone else's becoming."

Morgan nodded. "The magic's not settling. It's... skipping."

By sunset, Wren reported the Threadfound couldn't sleep. Too many dreams and not enough anchors.

The town gathered near the Looming Tree that evening, restless and buzzing. Even the coven's spells began to fray.

One of Cassie's grounding teas produced spontaneous tears.

A threadline re-stitched itself into the shape of a broken promise.

Morgan's voice caught mid-ritual and wouldn't come back down.

It was Gabe who walked into the center. Not with a spell or tools, but with salt and soil.

With the soft, unshowy weight of presence, he knelt and pressed both palms to the ground. Then whispered.

The words were not in common speech. Nor were they Threadbound. They were old earth-and-memory words. Rootworker words. They weren't for shaping spells, but for stitching safety through the marrow of the land.

The soil rippled around him, as though sighing. As if tension itself was being welcomed home.

Morgan felt it first: the drop. A slow settling of the weave.

Lilt slumped into stillness for the first time in days.

Wren exhaled like she'd been holding everyone's breath but her own.

The Hollow softened.

The lights dimmed.

And the noise of becoming was no longer clamor.

It was song.

Gabe stood slowly. The back of his hands streaked with mud and something older.

"Where did you learn that?" Morgan asked, breathless.

Gabe looked up. Eyes glowing faintly, not with light, but lineage. "My great-grandmother," he said. "She was a rootworker. Keeper of house-spirits and hush. Said every grief had a shape, and every shape had a place to be planted."

Cassie approached, arms folded, expression soft. "You've been carrying this all along?"

"Didn't seem like the kind of magic people made room for," Gabe said.

Morgan smiled. "Then we make room now."

That night, under a blanket of soothed sky, Gabe built a ring of soil, salt, and threadlight around the Looming Tree. This grounding circle wasn't to contain magic, but to remind it of home.

It didn't sparkle. It didn't pulse, but for the first time in weeks, the air inside Alden's Landing stilled.

And held.

## Chapter Fifty-Three: When the Map Forgot to Say No

The road did not change so much as it shifted, as if the land itself were exhaling. What had once been familiar routes blurred at the edges, twisting just slightly to make room for something new.

Dead ends softened, their finality loosening, and paths that had never quite held their names pulsed faintly with recognition, as though the earth remembered something long forgotten.

That was how they came. Not in sudden droves, not in clamor or chaos, but in a quiet, deliberate alignment as though every step had been waiting for its own place in the pattern.

The first to arrive was a violinist from the coast, a woman whose hands had not touched strings in years. She had dreamed of a place where each note reverberated with the weight of words she had never spoken. At dawn she walked into Alden's Landing, the sea-worn case slung across her back, her fingers already humming a melody she could not recall writing. She asked for no directions. Instead, her voice was clear and certain as she inquired, "Where does the air sing the clearest?" Bram, without hesitation, pointed her toward the Hollow.

The second arrival came from the north, a tattooist carrying a weathered sketchbook filled with symbols that had never made sense. As she crossed by the greenhouse, the stones near the porch stirred, shifting into sigils that answered her drawings with a language she had longed to hear. Tears fell freely. Wren pressed a warm cup of tea into her hands, a blend called Recognition. Its flavor carried the impossible ache of her mother's handwriting.

A gardener followed, though they could recall nothing of their own childhood. A flower had drawn them, lowing relentlessly outside their window, refusing to be ignored. When their steps finally carried them into Alden's Landing, the vines curling along the porch rail of Stirred & Spellbound rustled in greeting. No words were written, none spoken, but the sound conveyed one truth, carried directly into their bones: Welcome.

The town adjusted in its own way. Slowly, like a body learning to breathe deeper than before, it widened to make space.

Wes bent the spiral pathways into gentler arcs, so the Threadfound could walk alongside the newcomers without tangling in the thrum of memory.

Miriam carved out a second Listening Circle near the bakery, a place intended for those who were not yet ready to speak but still needed to be held.

Cassie doubled her biscuit production, muttering with mock severity that sometimes what people needed most were "emotional carbs."

Morgan, with Lilt shadowing at their side, inscribed a new threadline along the edge of the Hollow. Its shimmer was quiet but certain, carrying the promise: You belong, even if you do not yet know why.

One evening, Gabe lingered at the circle of the Looming Tree. He listened to the laughter threading with uncertainty, to the confusion mingling with relief, to the ache that softened under the cadence of community. He smiled at the sound of it all, the music of something becoming. "Looks like we're not just a town anymore," he said softly.

Morgan's gaze slid toward him. "No?"

Gabe shook his head. "No. We're a threshold."

## Chapter Fifty-Four: The Space Between Familiar and Becoming

Bram was the first to say it out loud.

"This place used to be weird," he said, stirring his tea with a cinnamon stick that occasionally blinked. "Now it's... organized weird. Like intentional weird."

Cassie smirked. "That's what happens when you put a system in your serendipity."

Baz arched an eyebrow. "Or people in your poetry."

"I'm just saying," Bram huffed, "when three different people ask where the gift shop is, something's shifted."

"Did you tell them it's the corner of Morgan's soul where memory rests on purpose?" Cassie asked innocently.

"Of course I did," Bram said. "One of them gave me a tip."

Elsewhere, Wren found herself dodging a spontaneous book club forming in the corner of her tea shop hosted entirely by newcomers who had interpreted her silence as "an invitation to begin." They discussed a novella that didn't exist in any official archive but had apparently appeared in multiple dreams.

By the end of the week, it was being performed in shadow-puppet form in the square.

"Do I resist or publish it?" Wren asked, watching a paper lantern do an interpretive monologue about longing.

Miriam patted her arm. "You steep it and see what flavor rises."

At the apothecary, a new arrival named Ora politely asked if the herbs could be interviewed before being harvested.

The rosemary approved.

The thyme was "considering its narrative arc."

"Perfect," Cassie muttered. "Now the plants want editorial rights."

In the greenhouse, a group of Threadfound had gently claimed one of the outer sheds and turned it into a "room for identities that haven't picked a shape yet."

Gabe nodded with approval.

Baz squinted. "Does it have plumbing?"

"It has purpose," Gabe said, like that was the same thing.

Mr. Linton from the edge of town insisted on calling the Hollow "that sparkly moss pit."

He built a wooden sign in his front yard that read:

*NO VISIONS, VIBES, OR FLOATING SCONES.*

By the weekend, the sign itself had gently levitated and was being used as a serving tray at Wren's tea lounge.

No one mentioned it to him. But even amid the confusion and adjustment, something else pulsed underneath: Belonging.

Not just for the new arrivals. For the original ones.

Cassie sat one night on the porch beside Morgan, sipping tea that tasted like her first-ever "maybe."

"Does it scare you?" Morgan asked. "That we're not just ours anymore?"

Cassie watched the Threadfound laugh with a violinist in the street, lanterns blinking gently overhead.

"No," she said. "It means we did something right. We built something so true, it didn't want to stay small."

She grinned. "Besides. More people to help clean up when the sugar bowl mutinies."

It did, at that exact moment.

Morgan didn't flinch, just smiled.

## Chapter Fifty-Five: The Festival of Almost

It started with a single banner, hand-stitched by Lilt and hung (without permission) across the town square.

THE FESTIVAL OF ALMOST
*Celebrating everything that nearly happened and the magic that came anyway.*

Below it, someone (probably Bram) had added:

*Open to all identities, near-misses, and brave mistakes. Glitter optional. Laughter encouraged.*

No one remembered agreeing to it, but by midmorning, everyone was involved.

Wes built an impromptu Resonance Tent, where visitors placed objects that hummed with memory. A cracked spoon that spontaneously composed a lullaby when held near a Threadfound named Faye.

Cassie offered "failure pastries," filled with combinations that shouldn't have worked but somehow did, i.e. lemon and sage, raspberry and burnt sugar, apology and almond.

"I call this one *'Didn't Get the Job but Realized I'm Free,'*" she said, handing it to Gabe.

He bit in and cried a little. Approved.

Children ran wild with chalk spells, doodling enchantments that made the sidewalks sing compliments to passersby.

Miriam hosted a "Not Quite Poem Exchange," where anyone could trade an unfinished thought for someone else's almost-truth.

One read:

*I was nearly enough once.*
*Now I'm just trying again on purpose.*

She placed it under her shawl and whispered, "That'll do."

In the Hollow, Morgan opened the southern path and released a slow swirl of threadlight into the square.

It didn't land. It danced.

One by one, people joined it. Twirling, weaving, some with grace, some with comedic wobble, all with wonder.

No one led. But somehow… no one was left out.

Wren poured tea for strangers who were no longer strangers.

Baz played a soft rhythm on a three-stringed instrument he hadn't touched in years.

And Lilt stood beside Gabe, watching the lights float like echoes that had finally been heard.

"Do you think we made this happen?" they asked.

Gabe didn't answer. He just smiled. As if to say:

You didn't make it happen. You remembered how.

At sunset, everyone gathered in the square for the "Lantern Lighting of Near Misses."

Each person lit a small floating lantern and whispered something that almost was…a dream that didn't manifest, a goodbye never said, a life not lived… but never forgotten.

The sky shimmered with their truths.

No sorrow. No shame. Just the shared light of what might have been and the warmth of what had become instead.

And in that glow, Alden's Landing exhaled.

Not to rest. To receive whatever came next.

## Chapter Fifty-Six: Afterlight

The morning after the festival arrived like a secret that had already been forgiven. Mist curled low across Alden's Landing, not hiding anything, just tucking it in.

The square was quiet. Threadlight shimmered faintly in the air like the magic hadn't quite settled, and the cobblestones hummed underfoot with the memory of laughter, music, and almosts finally given shape.

Cassie brewed coffee outside the greenhouse. It was strong, slightly chaotic, definitely infused with joy. She handed mugs to Baz, Morgan, and Gabe without asking.

They sat around the garden table with mismatched chairs, half-washed dishes still piled in a bin nearby, flower petals stuck to Baz's sleeve.

No one spoke for a long time. They just drank. Breathed. Watched the steam rise and the Hollow slowly uncoil from celebration.

Morgan was the first to break the silence. "Did last night feel… final?"

Baz shook his head. "Not final. Just… named."

Gabe nodded, setting his mug down carefully. "It felt like a chord that's been waiting to resolve."

Cassie stretched her legs, sighing deeply. "It felt like a town that finally figured out it doesn't have to shrink to stay safe."

They all sat with that and let it settle.

Gabe reached into his coat pocket and pulled out a scrap of parchment. A list. Not a to-do list. A letting-go list. Words written by townsfolk and Threadfound the night before. Collected gently, anonymously. Meant to be burned. But he'd kept one.

*I thought I had to be small to be loved.*
*Turns out, I only had to be true.*
*– Unknown*

He passed it around. Nobody said a word until it reached Cassie. She smiled softly. "That one's going in the cookbook."

Baz leaned forward, resting his elbows on the table. "So. What now?"

Morgan swirled the last of their coffee and watched a drop spin in circles. "We keep the path open," they said. "But not just the Hollow. Ourselves. We let the world show up and we show up back."

Cassie snorted. "That's the most poetic way I've ever heard someone say brace yourself."

"Would you prefer 'get your magical shit together'?" Morgan asked.

"Much more my tempo", Cassie laughed.

Gabe looked out toward the edge of the garden, where the Hollow's newest threadline pulsed like a heartbeat waiting to become a road.

"I think it's not about what we become next," he said. "It's who we're willing to become with."

Baz raised his mug. "To that."

They all clinked their cups. Softly. No grand ritual. No spell. Just shared breath, shared ground, and a feeling that was more than magic.

## Chapter Fifty-Seven: The Thread Between Us

The Hollow was still. Not silent. Just… held.

It was late and most of the town slept, lulled by the residual magic of the festival and the comfort of knowing they belonged, even if they hadn't yet found the words for why.

Morgan stood beneath the Looming Tree, fingers trailing its bark, which pulsed faintly with a magic they could now hear more than see. Soft. Low. Like a promise still unfolding.

Behind them, footsteps. Unhurried. Familiar.

Gabe.

"You always end up here after everything," he said gently, stepping beside them.

Morgan smiled, not looking away from the tree. "It listens. Even when I don't know what I'm saying."

Gabe nodded. "So do I."

They were quiet for a moment. Not uncomfortable. Just letting the space settle around them.

Then Morgan asked, "Do you ever wonder… if you were meant to be more than the anchor?"

Gabe tilted his head. "I used to."

"And now?"

"Now I think anchoring isn't being still. It's being steady while everything grows."

Morgan turned to him, eyes soft. "And does that feel like enough?"

Gabe hesitated. Then reached into his pocket and pulled out a silver and green thread.

One they'd found together, months ago, in a part of the Hollow that hadn't existed until Morgan opened it and Gabe grounded it.

"I didn't tie it," he said. "Didn't know if it was a thread to pull or a bond to keep."

Morgan took it from his hand, holding it between their fingers like breath.

"It's both," they said. "It always has been."

They sat at the base of the tree, the thread between them. No declaration. No ritual.

Just the quiet knowing that there was a future neither of them had dared imagine until the other made it feel safe to hope.

Gabe rested his head lightly on Morgan's shoulder.

Morgan laced their fingers with his.

The Hollow exhaled.

And for the first time in its long, listening life, it felt witnessed in return.

# Chapter Fifty-Eight: Misfires & Maybes (The Education of Lilt)

Lilt had been assured more than once that magic would eventually "settle with practice." This, however, had proven to be nothing short of a lie. Miriam, with her steady kindness, had offered a gentler interpretation: "Magic grows sideways before it roots." Unfortunately, Lilt's magic seemed to have taken that statement as a personal challenge, refusing to grow in any predictable direction at all.

The most recent example of this came in the form of the Truth Tap embroidery circle. It had been intended as a calm and accessible gathering, a memory-stitching workshop where both Threadfound and newcomers could sit together and ease into shared creation. The concept was simple enough: thread a needle, recall a memory one was ready to hold without fear, and stitch a small symbol onto a piece of linen. The exercise was meant to soothe, a practice of gentle remembrance.

Instead, the workshop spiraled almost immediately. Unbeknownst to anyone, Lilt had enchanted the embroidery thread with a charm of emotional amplification. Within minutes, the circle dissolved into tears. Participants were no longer quietly sewing clouds and stars but were sobbing into one another's shoulders, confessing secrets from past lives, and embracing tree stumps as if they were long-lost kin. By the time Cassie arrived to check on the gathering, the entire space resembled an impromptu confessional.

"I only wanted to stitch a cloud," one trembling newcomer sniffled, "but now I remember the summer I let a friendship die over mismatched handwriting!"

Cassie stood in the doorway for a long moment before blinking slowly. "All right," she said carefully. "We're just going to... call that cathartic."

Lilt could only nod with solemn gravity. "The thread was a little too receptive."

"You think?" Cassie replied, already detangling another participant from the lower branches of a weeping willow.

The embroidery mishap might have been forgiven quickly if it had been an isolated incident, but soon after came the debacle of the Listening Lantern. The idea had been charming lanterns that glowed brighter in the presence of someone who longed to be heard. Yet in their excitement, Lilt had forgotten to limit the number of voices each lantern could carry. The test lantern, affectionately but uneasily nicknamed Clive, absorbed far more than it was ever meant to hold. By the end of its second evening, Clive had developed a mild form of sentience and an alarming tendency to recite half-remembered arguments in seven distinct accents.

Morgan discovered it one afternoon floating menacingly above the herb garden, bellowing in a voice not quite its own: "You never said you liked the hat, Jeremy! YOU NEVER SAID!"

"Lilt," Morgan said flatly, "your lantern is traumatizing the parsley."

Horrified, Lilt rushed over, whispered a panicked "sshhh," and tucked the still-muttering lantern into a drawer now labeled *apologies in progress.*

For all the chaos, though, something meaningful had begun to take root in Lilt's experiments. The Listening Circle they co-created with Miriam attracted a steady flow of visitors. Guests stitched their quiet requests into ribbons and pinned them to what had come to be known as the "Maybe Wall." The words written there varied—one read, *I don't know who I am when no one needs me,* while another confessed, *Can I be real if I'm still shifting?*

Through every tangle of thread, every backwards-drawn symbol, and every chalkboard that mischievously spelled rude words in Old Spellscript during otherwise solemn ceremonies, Lilt kept showing up. They held the space, sometimes awkwardly, sometimes brilliantly. They laughed at their own blunders, apologized in whatever form felt most fitting - once with scones still steaming from the oven, another time with a haiku scrawled onto parchment and delivered by a goat, and kept trying.

By the end of the week, Miriam found Lilt sitting cross-legged outside the Hollow, streaks of thread dye marking their cheeks in bright lines of fatigue and pride. Their eyes sparkled as they looked up at her.

"Did you know one of the lanterns started humming lullabies?" they asked breathlessly.

Miriam tilted her head. "Did you mean for it to?"

"No," Lilt admitted, a grin tugging at their mouth. "But I think it wanted to."

She smiled and held out a small gift: a thimble that shimmered faintly with quiet magic. "For when you want to try something new," she told them, "or for when you want to fix something old."

Lilt studied it for a long moment, then looked down at their ink-stained fingers, across to the Hollow waiting in the twilight, and finally back to Miriam. A mischievous grin spread fully across their face.

"Let's break reality gently."

## Chapter Fifty-Nine: Threadlines and Thorns

Lilt believed in being prepared. The canopy was hung with charm-dampening silks (just in case the thread got... emotive again). The chairs were arranged in a perfect spiral. Not a circle, too predictable. Each seat had a square of enchanted cloth that vibrated gently when you told the truth near it.

They called the class:

"Stitching the Story: A Gentle Weaving of Memory and Almosts." (Subtitled: *You Don't Have to Cry but It's Okay if You Do.*)

Twelve people had signed up and three brought snacks.

One brought a quill that snored.

Lilt stood at the front, hands clasped nervously, smiling wide. "This workshop is about naming what we didn't know we carried," they began. "Using thread as translation."

And for a moment, it all felt right. Until...

"Or," came a voice from the edge of the glade, "we could discuss the neural encoding of autobiographical memory and its unreliable narrative structure."

Heads turned to find Dr. Shaw, hands in his coat pockets, brow furrowed like the sky had offended him, had arrived.

Uninvited. Unapologetic.

And currently standing inside the spiral, which every Threadfound in the workshop noticed immediately.

Lilt blinked. "Dr. Shaw. Hello. I... didn't know you were interested in textile storytelling."

"I'm not," he replied flatly. "But I heard a rumor a lantern called me passive aggressive, and I want to address the issue at the source."

Cassie, seated with a scone in hand, whispered, "It's true. The lantern was Harold."

Lilt cleared their throat. "We're focusing on soft magic, Dr. Shaw. Not psychological diagnosis."

Shaw stepped around a threadcircle that sparked in protest. "Memory is unreliable. Narrative is biased. You're basically building spell-based projection therapy."

An elderly gentleman who had sewn a leaf into his shirt and called it "emotionally brave" raised a hand. "Is he allowed to say words like that here?"

"No," Lilt said brightly. "But we don't expel people for being inconvenient."

Shaw muttered, "Convenient delusion is still delusion."

Cassie loudly crunched her scone.

The workshop devolved slightly after that.

A spell-quilt misfired and wrapped itself around someone's ankles. A threadline began spelling "RUDE" on the grass every time Shaw opened his mouth. One of the enchanted cushions wept gently into someone's lap and had to be comforted.

And yet, Lilt stood tall. "Even when truth interrupts," they said, "you can still choose the thread you hold."

They looked directly at Shaw and handed him a needle. And a blank square.

"Care to stitch your projections?"

To everyone's surprise, Shaw didn't leave. He sat. Grumbling. But he stitched.

And when he stood an hour later, he handed Lilt a square of cloth. No design.

Just one word:

Restraint.

He didn't explain or wait. He just walked away.

The threadline beneath him winked.

Afterward, Miriam patted Lilt's shoulder. "You didn't lose the thread," she said. "You let it tangle long enough to find its own knot."

Lilt looked at the stitched square in their hands and smiled. "I'm adding 'navigating interruptions by intellectually insecure skeptics' to the syllabus."

Cassie raised her scone. "To Harold!"

# Chapter Sixty: The Man Who Didn't Leave

Shaw hadn't meant to stay. Not after the first few weeks. Not after the Hollow opened. Not after the sugar bowl began muttering evaluations of his emotional intelligence. And especially not after he cried during that Listening Circle and pretended it was allergies.

But stay he did.

First in the inn. Then, slowly, at the edges of things. Wandering the Spiral Path. Sitting near the Looming Tree when no one was looking. Writing notes in his journal with the urgency of a man trying to document something he didn't fully believe in.

And now?

He was still here. He sat alone in the old apothecary garden that morning, watching the sun catch the dew on the edges of spell-kissed herbs. Someone (probably Lilt) had tied threadmarks to the fence posts. They fluttered like waiting thoughts.

He opened his notebook and wrote:

*Day 119*
*I have yet to confirm whether this place is a functioning model of collective metaphysics or a dangerously well-organized delusion made compassionate through craft.*

He paused, then added: I'm beginning to prefer the second option. And I do not know what that means for me.

Gabe passed him that morning. Didn't say a word. Just nodded like someone acknowledging a difficult truth without inviting it to tea.

Shaw was used to being measured. He wasn't used to being seen. And it unnerved him. He opened a second notebook that no one knew he carried. This one wasn't for observations. It was for fragments. Not facts.

- *I remember when control was easier than kindness.*
- *The first time I told the truth, I apologized.*
- *Do they know what it cost me not to stay angry?*

He didn't answer those questions. Just closed the notebook, as if silence could press the pages flat.

Cassie found him near the vine wall later, arms crossed, staring at the way it had grown into the word welcome entirely on its own.

"I don't trust words that grow without roots," he said.

She shrugged. "Then follow them back. That's what the rest of us are doing."

He didn't argue. Didn't agree. But he didn't walk away, either.

Later that evening, he stood at the edge of the Hollow, watching the new arrivals filter through with awe in their eyes and sorrow on their backs. He whispered, "They'll break this place."

Morgan, who had appeared silently beside him, replied without flinching. "Or they'll make it strong enough to bend."

Shaw turned. "You still trust me being here?"

Morgan smiled. Not kindly. Not cruelly. Just honestly. "I trust that you haven't left."

He returned to the inn that night and opened his journal to a blank page and wrote only one line:

*I think I am the question this place hasn't answered yet.*

And for the first time, he didn't try to finish the sentence. He just let it hang. Like a thread that might become something true.

Or not.

# Chapter Sixty-One: Watchers and Threads Unspooled

The one who trusted Shaw, however tentatively and hesitantly, was Una.

Threadfound. Once a whisper barely held together, now nearly whole, but still moving with the cautious grace of someone who remembered what it was like to be formless.

She still wore that same humming thread around her wrist, the one Lilt had stitched for her when her voice first cracked through the Hollow's quiet. Her hands, ever warm, still smelled of cedar and honeyed parchment, like pages waiting to be turned.

Her magic was built around presence: noticing what stayed when everyone else had stopped looking.

She found Shaw one morning repairing a crooked bench near the spiral walk. He didn't know it, but this was where she'd first come apart. Back when she didn't yet know her name would hold. The symmetry made her stay.

He didn't see her at first. Didn't posture. Just worked, slow and precise, like order was the one truth he still believed in.

When he stood to leave, she spoke. "You don't like chaos. But you haven't tried to erase it."

Shaw froze. Then turned. "I don't believe in pretending it isn't there," he said. "I just… prefer it contain itself."

Una smiled faintly. "Even when it's trying to become?"

He didn't answer, but he stayed.

Over the next few days, Una returned. Not always to speak. Sometimes just to walk parallel to him. To hand him tea without asking how he liked it. To offer him a length of unbound thread, humming with hesitation.

He never asked what it was for. He just tucked it in his coat.

And for Una, that was enough.

But someone else watched.

Rhett.

Not a Threadfound. Not entirely from Alden's Landing either.

Rhett was a quiet archivist of the Hollow's deeper spells. He was unofficially assigned to track pattern shifts and root disturbances in the weave.

They didn't trust easily. And they didn't trust Shaw at all. Not his restraint. Not his silence. Not the notebook he carried like a talisman. Rhett had seen what order looked like when it became doctrine. They didn't want it repeated here.

That evening, Rhett followed Shaw as he walked the edge of the Hollow. Saw the way the threads bent slightly around him. Saw the way the spelllights dimmed, not from fear, but recognition. Saw how Shaw paused by the old tree where Lilt had buried a bundle of regret-stitching.

And how he left a folded page beneath the roots.

Rhett's eyes narrowed.

Later that night, Una lit a candle near the edge of the tea circle and waited.

Shaw arrived.

She offered him a seat.

He took it.

Rhett, hidden by spell-blurred shadow, watched them both.

And whispered into their threadjournal:

*He doesn't bend the Hollow.*
*He leans on it.*
*And it holds him.*
*But for how long?*

## Chapter Sixty-Two: When the Hollow Holds Its Breath

It began with silence. Not the gentle quiet of a Listening Circle or the reverent stillness of story keeping. This was a pause in the weave.

As if the Hollow, after so long attuned to memory, restoration, and remembering, had stopped responding. The spellthreads held, but they didn't sing. The wind moved, but it didn't whisper. And across Alden's Landing, the townsfolk noticed.

Not with panic, with posture. The kind of hush people instinctively fall into before a storm they aren't sure they're meant to run from.

Lilt was the first to feel the change underfoot. Chalk lines from their latest workshop curled into unfamiliar runes overnight. Not hostile. Not legible. Just...forward-facing.

They brought one to Morgan, who stared at it for a long time. Then said, "This isn't remembering. This is arrival."

At the edge of the Hollow, Gabe found a section of the ground that wouldn't accept grounding. He tried all three rootworker rites. The soil responded with flickers of unformed energy. Familiar to him, but wrong. Like someone humming a song they'd never heard and somehow, it was in his key.

He pressed his hand flat and whispered, "What are you becoming?"

The ground warmed but didn't answer.

Cassie's kitchen pots boiled over three times in one morning, even though she hadn't turned on the stove.

Wes walked past a mirror and caught a glimpse of a person he didn't know, but who looked at him like they knew him.

And in the apothecary, a shelf of unfinished elixirs reassembled themselves into a pattern Baz had only seen once before. Right before he lost someone he'd never met.

The Hollow pulsed once that night. Not visibly. Existentially.

And just like that, two new arches appeared on the southern edge. Not doors. Not gates.

Just frames of light and bark and threadless magic, humming with one intent:

*We are coming not to remember.*
*We are coming to choose.*

Morgan gathered the Coven at dawn. No speeches. Just this:

"We've prepared for what was lost.
We've held what was forgotten.
Now we must receive what has never been here before."

Cassie muttered, "Great. We've officially entered the 'mystical dread' chapter."

Baz offered her coffee.

Wren started setting up tea for twenty... then changed it to forty.

Lilt, quiet, traced a symbol in the dirt. It shimmered. And didn't stay still.

Whatever was coming wasn't just a seeker. It was something the Hollow had no name for.

Yet.

## Chapter Sixty-Three: Stitching the Threshold

The Hollow no longer vibrated with restless energy; instead, it had gone utterly still, listening with the kind of attentive silence that carried weight. That silence meant it was time to act.

Cassie, in typical Cassie fashion, decided that preparation began in the apothecary kitchen. She reorganized every enchanted jar, setting them in careful rows according to threat level and flavor. "Nothing says hospitality like labeled spells and prepped defenses," she declared as she tapped the lid of one particularly irritable jar, its label reading: *Stubborn Hope, Lightly Toasted.*

Morgan called the gathering inside the greenhouse. There was no ceremony in the summons, no elaborate ritual, only necessity. Standing before the tall spiral window, they spoke plainly. "These arrivals won't resemble the Threadfound," they said, their voice carrying into the leafy air. "They aren't fractured souls searching for a place to be held."

"They're choosing to come," Gabe added, his tone steady but edged. "And choice, as we all know, can be dangerous."

Baz's voice dropped into the quiet. "They might not even want to belong," he said. "They might come to reshape what we've built."

The Coven leaned closer, the weight of his words settling over them. Cassie broke the tension with a brisk clap of her hands and a sharp inhale. "Alright," she said, "roll call. Shields? Thresholds? Emergency anti-spiral cookies?"

"Baked," Wren answered promptly, lifting a basket. "Two dozen. Each labeled: *Eat me if reality frays.*"

Lilt stepped forward next, volunteering to inscribe soft barriers around the arches. Magic designed not to stop but to slow, forcing intention into every step across the threshold. "It's not to keep them out," they explained, "only to make sure they arrive aware."

Bram offered the Spiral Bell, a relic usually reserved for announcing resonance shifts in the Hollow. This time, it would rest beside the arches, a quiet sentinel. "If it rings without touch," he said, his hand lingering on the bell's silver curve, "we'll know the visitor carries magic the Hollow itself doesn't recognize." His words landed with weight. The bell had rung only once before, during Morgan's first Becoming.

To the surprise of many, Rhett joined in. They unrolled maps and notebooks, their meticulous records spilling onto the greenhouse table. "I know where the town strains under emotional overload," they said. "I can reinforce those places."

Cassie raised an eyebrow, lips curling into a sly grin. "So, you're working with us now?"

"I'm working against catastrophe," Rhett replied coolly. "You're just convenient."

"That's the nicest thing anyone's said to me all week," Cassie quipped, pressing a pastry into Rhett's hand as if sealing an agreement.

Even Shaw appeared, wordless, at the southern ridge. He carried with him a grounding compass and a small set of iron markers, tools not seen in the Hollow for decades. As he pressed one marker into the earth, Gabe glanced at him, startled. "You're aligning root energy," he said.

Shaw didn't look up. "I'm not here to convert anyone," he muttered. "I just want to keep the town from fracturing if the newcomers arrive with destabilized memory fields."

Cassie smirked. "You're adorable when you pretend you're not invested."

By the time the sun slipped below the horizon, Alden's Landing appeared unchanged to any casual onlooker. Yet beneath the cobbled

169

stones, behind the forest line, and along every spiraling path, preparations thrummed. Spells had been woven into the roots of trees, barriers had been softened to catch rather than repel, and threadlines shimmered faintly, ready to reweave themselves at the slightest touch.

As the arches took on their subtle glow under the moonlight, Morgan stood before the Coven, shoulders squared, voice calm but resolute. "This town has become a welcome," they said. "But not every welcome is safe. Our strength will not be in closing ourselves off, but in remembering who we are—before they arrive."

The words lingered in the night air, and the wind itself seemed to carry them further, brushing against stone, leaf, and lantern. For a single breathless moment, even the Hollow seemed to brace for what was coming.

# Chapter Sixty-Four: The Pull of Unsettled Belonging

It began not with a pounding in the chest, but with something subtler, a flutter in the footsteps. Each time Irie crossed the square, their stride fell slightly out of rhythm, as if a hidden hand tugged them forward. A step lingered half a breath too long, the next landed half a pause too late. Beneath their boots the threadpath responded, humming faintly, not with welcome as it once had, but with direction, as though the ground itself was whispering, this way.

At first Irie dismissed the sensation. They blamed the disorientation on the swirl of festival lights and music, or perhaps the sigils shifting too quickly in Lilt's workshop. Another time they told themself it must be the cassia bark steeped too strongly in their tea. But none of the excuses held. The pull did not fade. If anything, with each passing day, it grew clearer, like the world was removing distractions to point them somewhere inevitable.

They had lived in Alden's Landing nearly a year, ever since their name cracked open in a dream and they abandoned the fragments of a self they no longer wished to remember. The town had received them gently. Wren showed them how to brew silence that settled in the bones. Morgan taught them the art of resting without apology. Lilt coaxed trembling words from their throat and reminded them that a voice deserved to exist even when it shook.

For all that kindness, though, Irie had never felt fully settled. Something within them still itched, as if their becoming carried an unfinished epilogue that had yet to be written.

Lately, each morning seemed to draw them nearer to the southern edge of town, where the new arches stood. They were not merely stonework, but presences in their own right, waiting like unclaimed choices. Cassie was the first to notice the change.

"You're walking like someone whose thread is already half caught in another story," she remarked one morning, sliding a plate of pastries across the counter.

Irie gave a faint smile. "Do you think that means I don't belong here?"

Cassie's gaze softened, her voice losing its usual sharp edge. "I think belonging can be real and still be temporary."

That evening, Irie found themself standing before the arches alone. The Spiral Bell remained silent, its stillness offering neither warning nor welcome. Yet a small curl of wind slipped into their coat sleeve like an exhale against their skin. Inside their pocket rested the charm Wren had pressed into their palm months before, a grounding stone etched with the sigil of stay. As they touched it, the mark shimmered faintly and began to fade. It did not vanish, but rather transformed, as though even the spell understood that permanence was not its truest form.

Irie did not step through. Not yet. Instead, they knelt beside the archway and pressed their palm to the rootlight that curled out from the earth beneath it. The glow warmed their hand as they whispered, "If I am meant to leave, then let me carry all who loved me here with me."

The Hollow pulsed once in response. It was not an answer, but an agreement, as if the land itself acknowledged their request.

Far off, Lilt froze in the middle of a sketch, their pencil stuttering on the page. Gabe, working near the ridge, lifted his head instinctively toward the south without knowing why. And Morgan, seated quietly beneath the Looming Tree, felt one thread in their own being loosen. It was not lost. It was simply ready to move.

## Chapter Sixty-Five: The Step That Didn't Echo

Irie did not pack a bag, nor did they leave behind a note. Instead, they lingered in the quiet of their space, whispering farewell to the cup that still carried the memory of their favorite tea. They pressed their hand briefly to the Listening Patch that Miriam had stitched for them months before, then folded it carefully into the lining of their coat, as if it might steady their heart on the journey ahead.

The Hollow greeted them with silence that morning, yet it was not the silence of emptiness. It was the kind of silence that listens, holding its breath in expectation. As Irie crossed the southern ridge, their boots pressed into the threadwoven soil, and each step seemed to vibrate with a hum of possibility, as though the ground itself wanted to remind them that it had carried many beginnings before this one.

The arches stood waiting at the ridge's edge, twin sentinels woven from bark and breath and something older that had never been named. No two souls had ever described them alike. To some, they looked like warmth, a hearthstone flame in tangible form. To others, they appeared as risk, the shimmer of a precipice. To still others, they became a mirror, reflecting the truths that one tried hardest not to see. To Irie, they were a door that had never been meant to close.

On the threshold, they caught sight of their own reflection, and it startled them. Not because it was strange, but because it was familiar in a way they had not expected. The reflection smiled back, older, steadier, already walking a few steps ahead as though urging Irie to follow.

The moment their foot crossed the inner ring of the arch, the shift arrived. It was not the world around them that changed, but something within, as if the gravity of who they had been no longer held the power to anchor in place. It felt as though the story itself had loosened its grip. Not to discard them, but to release them into the freedom of authorship, whispering: Now it is yours to write.

There was no sudden vanishing, no dramatic shimmer. Instead, the air behind them folded gently, the way a book page turns, not erased or lost, but marked and ready for what comes next.

Lilt reached the ridge only moments later, their breath catching as their eyes fell on the scene. They saw the footprints pressed into the soil, the faint spiral of threadlight winding forward, and the empty space where Irie had stood only heartbeats ago. Softly, almost reverently, Lilt whispered, "Become well."

The arches pulsed once in answer, and then they simply waited again, silent guardians of choice.

Far above the Hollow, near the Looming Tree, Gabe lifted his face into the wind as if he had heard something calling across the distance. Morgan, tracing a new threadline nearby, paused, their hand resting lightly on the glowing pattern. They nodded, slow and certain. "They did not leave," Morgan murmured. "They continued."

Cassie, leaning against a post with her ever-present mug of coffee, blew across its surface, took a sip, and let a smile curl at the corner of her mouth. "Then I hope wherever they're going," she said, "the pastries are at least decent."

And somewhere, not so far beyond the edge of the Hollow but just beyond the reach of its oldest threads, Irie walked forward. Not away, but into.

# Chapter Sixty-Six: The Space They Left Behind

It was Wren who sensed it first. She had been in the middle of an ordinary morning, her hands steadying the kettle as she poured, her thoughts drifting through the kind of quiet that only came with ritual. Yet in the space between one heartbeat and the next, something faltered. The kettle stuttered in her grip as a presence swept through the room. It was not wind, nor was it magic in the usual sense. It was movement threaded through her chest like a goodbye she did not remember consenting to.

She caught her breath, steadied the cup she had nearly spilled, and set it carefully upon the table. Her lips parted around words that came unbidden, soft enough that only the steam heard them. "They stepped through."

At Stirred & Spellbound, Cassie felt it too. She had been halfway through reshuffling a collection of stubborn charm jars that refused to fall into alphabetical order. Her hand hovered over one particular jar, labeled *Memory: Faint but Fond*. For a moment its glass walls glowed with a tender light, and then the glow receded into stillness. Cassie shut the cabinet slowly and let her back rest against its frame. The sigh that left her chest carried both loss and recognition. "They really did it," she murmured into the quiet shop. "That brave, beautiful little thread."

Across the room, Baz lifted his eyes from the ledger he had been balancing. His gaze was steady, but the question lingered unspoken until he gave it voice. "Regret?"

Cassie shook her head. Her mouth curved not in sorrow but in something gentler, more complicated. "No," she said softly. "Envy, perhaps. And more than that, pride."

Down in the Hollow, Morgan had taken their place beside the arches. They had not spoken since sunrise, only watched in silence. The air still shimmered faintly where Irie had passed, as though the space refused to settle, unwilling to erase the trace of their crossing.

Lilt approached quietly and stood at Morgan's side. Without a word they knelt, placing a small, stitched square into the soil where Irie had paused the night before. In delicate lettering it read: *You were never meant to stay small. But you stayed long enough to change us.* The earth seemed to receive the offering with quiet reverence. The arches themselves pulsed once in response, not in mourning, but in acknowledgment.

Elsewhere, the ripples continued in subtler ways. One of Wes's resonance buttons pulsed a second too long when brushed, holding an echo it had not carried before.

A lantern in the Listening Circle flickered briefly, its light curling into the whisper of Irie's laugh before dimming again.

Gabe's grounding thread shifted slightly, bending westward toward the place Irie had chosen to walk.

None of these changes carried panic or disruption. They were not fractures. They were small adjustments, the way a quilt shifts to fill the hollow when someone rises from the bed.

By nightfall, a handful of townsfolk had gathered quietly at the southern ridge. None crossed, but they stood at the edge where the arches glowed faintly, holding the space where someone they had loved had found the courage to leave.

Rhett lingered farther back, their arms folded across their chest. They said nothing aloud, but when they returned home their journal bore a new page, written with firm strokes: *Departure is a kind of spell. And this place is learning how to cast it.*

## Chapter Sixty-Seven: The World That Waited

The ground felt different the moment Irie crossed through. Not unstable. Just... new. Like language in its first breath.

The air was warmer than Alden's Landing, warm with memory that hadn't settled yet. The trees here bent a little differently. Their leaves shimmered with colors Irie didn't have names for. Not unnatural, just undiscovered.

They paused on the other side of the arch. Not because they doubted, but because their bones felt watched. Not by eyes. By possibility.

The path ahead wasn't a path at all. Just a slow unfurling of moss and suggestion. Footprints appeared only after Irie had stepped. And when they looked back, they saw no trace of themselves.

"I guess this one doesn't run backward," they murmured. Their voice echoed faintly. Not back to them, but forward.

They walked for a long time, but not in minutes. In recognition.

The first thing they came across was a pool. It was glasslike, unbothered by wind, though the trees swayed above it. When Irie knelt beside it, their reflection didn't mimic. It watched and smiled first. "You always thought you had to fit," it said, without speaking. "Now you're in a world shaped to make room."

They stood. But they didn't run or cry. Something in their chest that had been coiled since the day they first heard the word "Threadfound", unwound.

The sky dimmed into a strange dusk, though the sun still hovered on the horizon. Irie came upon a small structure that was half-grown, half-built—like it had assembled itself from old stories no longer told.

A sign above the crooked doorway read:

*Rootlight Station*

Inside: cushions, blank books, and a single woven lantern that pulsed like a heartbeat waiting to sync with someone else's.

They sat and opened one of the books. Nothing was written, but a sentence formed as their fingers brushed the page:

*You are not the first to go.*
*But you may be the first to stay.*

They slept with their coat still on, hand resting over the Listening Patch. In their dream, Alden's Landing didn't call them back. It simply whispered:

*We're proud of you.*

## Chapter Sixty-Eight: Home, or Something Like It

The second morning in the Rootlight Station carried with it a stillness that unsettled Irie. It was not the emptiness of absence, but the disquiet of a place that lacked the comforting familiarity of home.

No clang of Cassie's charmed cookware drifted through the air, no rustling of Wes's resonance objects shifting restlessly in the night, no grounding presence of Gabe steadying the room simply by existing in it.

Irie folded the thin quilt that someone, or perhaps something, had left near their cushion, tucking it neatly under their arm before stepping outside. The moment they crossed the threshold, the world blinked. It did not blink with the warmth of sunlight, but with the sharp attentiveness of something vast and watchful.

The forest around them was not hostile, yet neither was it welcoming. It did not echo their name the way the Hollow always had, nor did it fold itself into shapes of recognition. Instead, it simply observed, unconvinced of what to make of them, waiting for proof.

Undeterred, Irie walked. Their steps carried them sometimes forward with certainty, and other times in quiet circles as though the path beneath their feet was deciding whether or not to hold. They came upon a stone spiral etched carefully into the moss, where the wind gathered in a way that felt like breath suspended in the throat of the world.

Later, they followed a bird whose feathers shimmered with starlight, a living fragment of the night sky. Yet at the edge of a stream that refused to hold reflections, the bird vanished, leaving only ripples that revealed nothing of themselves.

Everywhere Irie looked, the world appeared unfinished, not broken but paused, waiting for a shape to emerge from their presence. They pressed a hand to the bark of a nearby tree, where the peeling layers revealed patterns that almost resembled names. The touch loosened a question from their lips, a whisper more to the forest than to themself. "Is this how a home is built?"

A voice, neither near nor far, answered with quiet certainty. "Not built. Grown."

Irie turned sharply, scanning the trees, but saw no one. What they did find was a ring of toadstools glowing faintly in the undergrowth, humming with a rhythm that matched the pulse of their own chest. The circle enclosed a patch of bare soil that had not been there the day before, raw and expectant.

Kneeling, Irie pressed their palm to the earth, and warmth spread upward through their skin. In their mind, the world itself spoke, its words resonating more as feeling than as sound: If you plant something honest, you will find the door you were meant to open.

They stayed there for a long time, considering what might be asked of them. Then, reaching into the pocket of their coat, their fingers closed around a small object. A single button they had once meant to return to Wes but never had. It carried a faint resonance, a thread of his magic mingled with theirs, and woven through it all, the quiet blessing of Alden's Landing.

With steady hands, Irie pressed the button into the soil, covering it gently with earth. Their voice trembled, but their words were certain. "I do not know what I am making," they whispered, "but I am ready to grow it."

When dawn came again, they returned to find the soil transformed. From the place where the button had been buried, a small arch had formed, woven from root and thread. It was not yet wide enough to pass through, but it stood tall enough to mark a space, to promise that beginnings could take many shapes.

That night, when Irie returned to the quiet of the Rootlight Station, they found that a second cushion had been placed beside their own. There was no note, no explanation, only the silent presence of an invitation. To begin again, not alone.

## Chapter Sixty-Nine: The Thread Pulled Tight

The arches stirred just after dusk, their quiet resonance carrying through the trees like a low breath exhaled from the earth itself. Irie felt the shift before she heard it. A faint ripple moved across the threadlight etched along the forest floor, and her chest tightened as though someone had spoken her name aloud without ever using a voice.

She stepped out of the Rootlight Station, her pulse rising, half expecting the air to shape itself into a message. Instead, her eyes caught the outline of a figure waiting just beyond the new arch. The silhouette was familiar. It was Lilt.

They stood a little apart, their coat dusted with travel shimmer, curls more unruly than usual, and boots still carrying Hollow soil. Yet it was not their appearance that struck Irie most. It was the urgency in their eyes, a brightness that seemed to press forward faster than their words.

"Irie," they said, stopping just short of the threshold. They had not yet crossed the space that marked visitor from seeker.

Irie's lips curved in a soft smile. "You found me."

But Lilt did not return the smile. They took a step closer, their voice low and sure. "I wasn't looking. The Hollow sent me."

The air between them vibrated, not with hostility but with a tautness that felt like two notes straining toward harmony, each nearly aligned yet still held apart by a single heartbeat.

"You have been gone for thirteen days," Lilt said. "The rootlight in your old quarters refuses to settle. The charm jars drifted off their shelves. And Wes cried."

A small, fond sadness touched Irie's expression. "He does cry," she answered gently.

"Not where people can see," Lilt added.

Then, with deliberate steps, they crossed the threshold. No magic carried them forward, only purpose. "Irie… we do not know what this place is. You stepped through something untested, untethered. We believed we were making space, not losing you."

Irie turned toward the arch, letting her fingers trail across the living frame of root and thread that had grown from the soil. "Do I seem lost to you?" she asked softly.

Lilt did not answer with words, but the tension in their jaw betrayed the conflict pressing inside them. At last, they spoke quietly. "I came to bring you back."

The silence that followed was not sharp with pain but heavy with weight, as though the forest itself leaned in to listen. Irie did not move toward Lilt, nor did she retreat. She simply asked the question that mattered. "Back to what?"

Lilt blinked, their breath unsteady. "Back to the town. Back to the people. Back to us."

"I carry them with me," Irie said, her hand still resting on the arch. "I did not abandon them. I expanded."

Beneath their feet, the threadlight flickered, shifting in recognition of the tension, preparing for whatever change might come next.

"Are you saying you will not come home?" Lilt's voice was barely more than a whisper, fragile in the space between them.

Irie stepped forward until their hands found each other. Her voice was steady, carrying both assurance and invitation. "I am saying this is home. It grew from me, and now you are standing in it."

For a long moment, Lilt did not respond. Their silence stretched like held breath. Then at last they exhaled and said simply, "I brought tea."

The words loosened something in Irie, and her smile deepened. This time, Lilt's lips curved to match her own.

"You always bring tea when you are about to rethink everything," she teased gently.

"I hate rethinking things," Lilt admitted.

"I know," Irie said with quiet warmth.

Together they sat beneath the arch that had not existed a week before. Two cushions waited for them, side by side, as though anticipating this very moment. They poured the tea neither of them remembered packing and shared its warmth in silence, knowing the conversation would continue long after the cups were empty.

## Chapter Seventy: A Town Meant to Let Go

The arches didn't stop glowing; they pulsed softly but constantly. Not in a demanding manner, just available.

And that, it turned out, was somehow harder.

Cassie had reorganized the protective herbs twice in one week. Not because they were needed. Because it gave her something to do. "They're not portals," she muttered, tying a fresh ribbon of rosemary at the southern path. "They're invitations. Rude ones."

Baz didn't argue. Just handed her a lemon balm infusion labeled: For softening the ache of acceptance.

She scowled but drank it.

Wren started keeping extra chairs by the Listening Circle in case someone wanted to say goodbye before they knew they were leaving.

Only two had been used so far, but every morning, the dew clung to them like tears that hadn't found their speaker.

Gabe stood by the Looming Tree for hours each day, hand pressed to its trunk. "I can feel the weave stretching," he said once to Morgan. "Not tearing. Not even thinning. Just… changing direction."

Morgan nodded. "We were never meant to hold everyone forever."

"No," Gabe replied. "But we weren't told it would feel like pride and loss braided together."

Children began drawing the arches in chalk. Not as gateways, but as characters.

They gave them names: "Wander," "Wish," and "When."

No one told them to stop. Somehow, it helped.

Rhett doubled their notetaking.

They tracked who lingered near the arches too long, who looked at them with longing, who deliberately walked away, and who avoided them entirely. They told themselves it was research.

But each night, they stood at the edge of the spiral path and whispered, "Not yet," like a spell against change.

Even Harold the talking lantern grew quiet one afternoon and murmured, "They're not leaving us. They're fulfilling something."

No one knew if he meant Irie, or the town, or the future. Possibly all three.

By week's end, a new threadline began to sketch itself from the base of the arches to the heart of the square. Unbidden and unclaimed. Just… becoming.

And everyone saw it, everyone felt it. Even the Hollow adjusted. The soil shifted. The wind changed key. And no one knows who, but someone left a sign at the southern gate:

We are not a town with walls.
We are a story that opens its next chapter willingly.

## Chapter Seventy-One: The One Who Returned Differently

The arches had not shimmered for hours. Instead, they had settled into a low hum, a sound that was less noise and more vibration carried through the ground and into the body of anyone listening closely enough. Morgan felt it first, the subtle shift in resonance that tugged at the edge of awareness. Gabe felt it next, his hand stilling mid-task. Then Wren, halfway through pouring her tea, froze. She set the cup gently on the table and whispered into the quiet, "Something is coming back."

It was not Irie. It was not Lilt.

What approached was someone the town had not spoken of in weeks. Someone who had not left with ceremony or ritual, had not said goodbye, had not even whispered farewell. They had simply vanished as though swallowed by the air. Una.

She stepped through the arches just before dusk, her bare feet touching the soil with the certainty of one who had walked too far to turn back. Her hair was longer than it had been, braided with strands that caught the fading light like dust shaken from the sky and threads pulled from living roots. Her eyes glittered with constellations that did not belong to any map the town had ever known. Across her palms spiraled markings that shimmered softly. They were neither scars nor tattoos, but something entirely different, something new.

The arches did not pulse in greeting as they had for others. Instead, they bowed. Their shape curved almost imperceptibly, as if acknowledging her return with reverence.

Cassie saw her first. She dropped the spoon she had been using to stir a charm mixture, the sound clattering into the silence. Her lips parted in disbelief before she muttered, "You have got to be kidding me."

Una tilted her head, her expression unreadable, and then said in a voice that was calm but edged with familiarity, "Your rosemary still thinks too loud."

Cassie blinked and let out a breath somewhere between exasperation and relief. "So, you disappeared into the unknown and returned with an attitude. Good to know some things never change."

Gabe approached more carefully, his steps deliberate, as though he was moving toward a wild creature that might vanish if startled. He did not reach out to touch her. Instead, his voice carried the weight of the question that had been waiting since her absence. "Did you find what you were looking for?"

A smile curved across Una's lips. "No," she replied softly. "But I found what was looking for me."

She lifted her hand and opened her fingers. Resting just above her palm hovered a shard of light, delicate yet unyielding, threaded through with strands of memory. The glow carried whispers, not from the Hollow, but from something deeper, older, and wider than anything they had known.

Morgan's breath caught as they stared at the fragment. Their voice was low, but the words carried. "That is not our magic."

Una nodded, the starlight still reflected in her gaze. "No. It is what comes next."

The town seemed to pause as if the arches, the air, and every stone beneath their feet held their breath. They watched. They waited. And slowly, they began to understand. This was no longer only about who would leave through the arches, carrying pieces of the Hollow into the unknown. It was also about who might return. And what they might bring back with them.

# Chapter Seventy-Two: What She Didn't Say

They didn't hold a town meeting. But they might as well have.

By sundown, half of Alden's Landing had found a reason to "accidentally" pass by the greenhouse, where Una had taken up quiet residence beneath the ancient silverleaf vine.

Some brought offerings. Some brought questions. All brought expectation.

Una met them with soft smiles, cryptic nods, and silences so deep they hummed.

Cassie was the first to ask outright. "Did you go somewhere dangerous?"

Una tilted her head. "Define dangerous."

"Were there teeth?"

"There was choice."

Cassie narrowed her eyes. "You've gotten slippery."

"I've gotten wide."

Cassie blinked. "Well," she said, "that's upsettingly poetic."

Rhett came next with a notebook and seventeen carefully crafted questions.

Una answered none.

She simply looked at them and said, "You won't find the pattern you're chasing. The map hasn't been drawn yet."

Rhett's quill snapped in frustration. They stormed off muttering about epistemological boundaries and narrative contagion.

Una watched them go and whispered, "Not everything is meant to be diagrammed."

Wren brought tea. She didn't ask questions.

Una took the cup, held it to her lips, and closed her eyes. "This tastes like a memory that was forgiven without an apology."

Wren smiled. "I call it quiet return."

When Morgan approached, they didn't speak. They just sat beside Una on the bench, their hand resting palm-up between them.

Una placed her fingers lightly on top. And finally said, "It wasn't a place. It was a thread I had to follow until it let me become more than I'd been holding. Somewhere between forgetting and forming, I stopped being small. But I didn't stop being me."

Morgan didn't nod. Didn't agree. They simply said, "You came back."

And that was enough.

That night, as the stars settled into unfamiliar constellations above the Hollow, a new threadline stitched itself across the square.

It shimmered not with invitation, but with witness.

The town didn't know what Una had brought back. But they understood this:

She hadn't returned to explain. She'd returned to remind.

## Chapter Seventy-Three: Closer Than They Admit

No one expected it to be Bram who faltered first. He had always been the solid one, the cornerstone figure whose skepticism was as reliable as his scones. His presence anchored rooms the way stone anchors a foundation: unyielding, steady, predictable. His magic reflected that nature—tangible, sharp-edged, tidy in its boundaries, charming in execution but never allowed to wander beyond his control.

Threadlight made his skin crawl, crawling under his ribs like an itch he could never quite scratch. Prophecy drew only derisive snorts, muttered comments about "dreams dressed up as riddles." Nothing seemed likely to crack him. Nothing, until Una.

Una unsettled him, not because of the faint radiance that clung to her skin, but because she wore it as casually as breath. She seemed unconcerned that she glowed, as though light belonged to her as naturally as silence belonged to the night. Bram hated that. He hated that she seemed untouched by self-consciousness, that she moved through Alden's Landing like a star someone had forgotten to extinguish.

He told himself it was coincidence that his evening rounds always carried him by the silverleaf arbor after dusk. He repeated excuses to himself with every pass, calling it vigilance, professionalism, routine. When Cassie arched an eyebrow and asked why he had circled the vine six times already, he answered without pause, "Checking root flare integrity."

Cassie, who was stirring something thick and golden that smelled faintly of protective custard, didn't bother to disguise her disbelief. "Root flare my ass, Bram," she said dryly.

He grumbled about the importance of vigilance, about preventative measures, about anything that could disguise the fact that his feet were not following reason, but compulsion. And then, predictably, he went again.

Una never greeted him directly. She did not wave or meet his stare. Yet once, as he passed, her voice floated out toward the night. "The ones who fear the new magic often carry the seed of it." She did not turn. Her hand lingered against a bloom on the vine, a flower that had remained stubbornly closed for everyone else but unfurled in her presence as though waiting only for her touch.

Bram stopped short. His fingers clenched hard around the leather cover of the ledger he had not written in for days. His throat burned with words he would not release. He did not answer, but something inside him had already shifted, cracking along lines he did not wish to name.

That night, his sleep betrayed him. He dreamed in colors he had never planted in his garden—hues that burned bright and unfamiliar, shades that bled into each other like living fire. He woke with sweat dampening his collar, only to discover faint traces of threadlight clinging to his boots. His chest tightened. He had not walked in the Hollow recently.

The days that followed betrayed him further. He began to notice things that should not have been there. The air near Una moved strangely, breezes curling against their natural current as if reshaping themselves to brush her sleeve. His tools no longer whispered their usual commands of *prune here* or *water now*. Instead, they sang different invitations: *use me differently, dare me to grow something new*. One of his oldest tea jars, a plain vessel that had sat quiet for years, began to refill itself—not with leaves or herbs, but with the scents of his own childhood, captured moments he thought he had forgotten.

He told no one. But he stopped locking the doors to his workshop, leaving the night free to enter if it wished. Some part of him, the part he refused to acknowledge, was curious about what might choose to walk through.

It was late one night when his resolve gave out. He found himself at the arbor again, standing rigidly in the dark as though the vines themselves had summoned him. He cleared his throat with forced volume, an announcement that said, *I am not here by accident.*

Una did not turn immediately. Her gaze was still fixed on the leaves, her fingers brushing patterns into the silver light shimmer of their surface. "Would you like to ask me something?" she said at last, her voice calm, not unkind, but edged with the certainty that she already knew the answer.

"No," Bram muttered. Then, before he could stop himself, "Yes."

Una waited, her silence patient.

He hesitated, jaw working, until finally the words slipped free in a whisper, cracked and raw. "How did you let yourself leave the version of you everyone loved?"

For the first time, Una turned to face him fully. Her eyes reflected starlight, and yet her smile was gentle. "I loved that version, too," she said softly. "But I did not come back to live there."

The words struck him deeper than he wanted to admit. He looked away, unable to meet her gaze again. He said nothing, but something inside him bent under the weight of possibility.

By morning, his garden no longer looked the same. The gate stood wide open, its hinges creaking as if a wind had passed through in the night. And in the center of his carefully ordered plot, a new vine had taken root. Its leaves shimmered faintly, not with the restless burn of threadlight, but with the subtler gleam of something more dangerous.

It shimmered with possibility.

## Chapter Seventy-Four: Something Soft Took Root

Bram had always liked things that stayed where they were put. Well-labeled jars. Straight rows in the garden. Conversations that didn't require emotional spelunking.

Magic? He could handle it, so long as it behaved. And for the most part, it had.

Until Una came back with hands that hummed, eyes like dusk-before-dreaming, and that vine. That vine that only bloomed when no one watched. Now the world was wobbling in quiet, personal ways.

And Bram? He was starting to wonder if wobbling might not be the worst thing.

It began with the tea. Not the drinking. The blending. He reached for lemon balm and accidentally touched marigold and a whisper curled behind his ear like a memory: This one holds the truth you won't say aloud.

He dropped it, muttered "nonsense," and tried again. Same result.

So, he made the blend and served it to Wren the next day.

She cried halfway through her cup and said, "I think I've been missing my sister longer than I realized."

Bram didn't say a word, just refilled her mug with quiet.

Then came the journals. He'd always kept a meticulous log of crop cycles and weather shifts.

But one morning, he found a page he hadn't written. It was curved handwriting, not his own, detailing a dream he'd forgotten from childhood.

It ended with: You were brave then. You still can be.

He checked the ink, and it was still wet.

He tried to ignore it. Tried, too, to ignore the way the stones near his garden gate began to hum when he walked barefoot at night.

Or how one of his rosemary plants leaned east every time he thought of Una's words:
"I didn't come back to live there."

One evening, Cassie cornered him. Not with questions. With biscuits.

"You smell like threshold," she said, handing him one with lavender and lemon rind.

Bram scowled. "I smell like mulch and tea."

"You've started listening," she said, eyes twinkling. "It shows."

He didn't argue, which was suspicious.

Cassie arched a brow. "You thinking of stepping through?"

He shook his head. "Not yet."

Pause.

Then: "But I might build something that does."

That night, Bram returned to the garden and stood in front of the new vine. It shimmered softly under the moon.

He knelt, not to harvest or control. Just to be there while it grew.
And when he touched the soil, he whispered:

"Alright, then. You can stay. Let's see who we both become."

## Chapter Seventy-Five: The Vine That Wrote Back

Bram had spoken its name aloud only once, and even then, it was not with reverence but with the practicality of inventory. His voice had been steady, clinical, as he wrote it into the margin of a garden ledger: *"Uncatalogued vine, iridescent, east-leaning, root-harmonic, responsive to emotional presence."*

Cassie had immediately called it *Moody Bloom,* a name Bram dismissed with a scowl though it clung to him longer than he admitted.

Morgan suggested *Threadspin,* spoken with their usual curiosity, as if they expected the plant itself might one day approve or deny the title. Gabe, in his calm and deliberate way, simply asked, "Has it introduced itself yet?" Bram grunted at that, refusing to answer.

Yet in his private journal, the one he never left lying about, he had devoted an entire page to a single heading: *The Becoming Vine.*

It was unlike anything else in his garden. While his other plants followed the rhythms of soil and sun, this vine leaned toward something more ephemeral. Its tendrils shifted not toward light but toward questions. When Bram sat near it with a thought too heavy to contain, the vine seemed to respond. If he dwelled on sorrow, its curling arms stretched toward his knee as though to anchor him. When he closed his eyes and let himself remember the weight of someone he had once failed, a single silver leaf unfurled overnight, its veins tracing delicate spirals shaped like listening ears.

One night, alone with the cool hush of soil and stars, he whispered into its silence: "Why didn't I go after her?"

The vine did not move. It did not bloom. Yet the next morning, Bram found a soft petal pressed against his door. Its scent lingered with uncanny clarity—unfinished apologies mingled with thyme.

From that moment, he began to test it. He spoke regrets into the soil as though confessing to the roots. He played an old wooden flute, letting silence linger in the pauses as much as in the notes. He wrote journal entries by hand, folded them carefully, and buried them beneath the twisting roots.

The vine responded. Not always in ways that could be measured or recorded, but undeniably.

Sometimes the soil around it held impressions when he returned— spirals, arrows, once even the unmistakable outline of what could only be described as a judgmental shrug. Another morning, he discovered a pebble balanced on the rim of his teacup. When he picked it up, his breath caught. Tiny lines carved into its surface formed words: *Try again. Not smaller. Just gentler.* He nearly choked on his scone in surprise, but he did what it asked.

Word spread slowly, as word always did in Alden's Landing. Soon the garden was no longer a place sought out for vegetables or herbs but for something far stranger. Wren arrived first, a thread of grief tied visibly to her sleeve. She sat quietly for hours, and when she rose, her eyes were damp but lighter, her steps surer.

Baz followed, leaving behind a jar of echo-honey. "It's listening," he told Bram in a low voice. "I swear it hummed back."

Lilt came carrying a question they could not shape into words for anyone else. The vine bloomed deep violet that day, a color no one had seen before. They did not know what it meant, but all who witnessed it felt as though truth itself had expanded, making room where there had been none.

Bram did not share all that he experienced. He never told them about the way the vine bent almost imperceptibly whenever he laughed, or how its tendrils stretched toward the sky when he whispered the word *possibility*. He especially did not mention the night it pressed a single leaf against his palm. Woven through its veins, in root-thread so fine it shimmered, was one word: *Ready?*

Bram had not answered. He still did not know what the question meant, not fully. Yet that night, for the first time in years, he closed his eyes and let himself sleep with the garden gate unlocked, the door unbarred, and the air moving freely between the world and himself.

And in the silence that followed, the vine grew a little taller.

## Chapter Seventy-Six: When the Vine Stilled

The first sign was quiet. Not the warm hush of dawn, or the thoughtful pause between two questions. This quiet had weight. It pressed, waited, and watched.

Bram noticed it the morning the vine didn't move. Not when he greeted it. Not when he touched the soil. Not even when he whispered, "Good morning, you enigmatic little weirdo," like he had every day for a week.

It just… sat. Still. Colorless. Listening, maybe. But not responding.

He checked the soil. It was healthy. Then he checked the root temperature, and it was steady.

Tried speaking aloud, in rhyme, in recipe form. Nothing.

Cassie stopped by later with tea and a theory. "Maybe it's sulking. You've been asking questions; maybe it wants answers."

Bram grunted. "It's a plant, not a therapist."

Cassie winked. "Tell that to my basil. It judges me daily."

By midafternoon, the vine had begun to lean, but not toward anyone. It was towards the southern ridge. Towards the arches.

Morgan arrived with Lilt, both holding unfinished spellthreads.

The vine twisted as they approached. One coil pointing sharply to the sky, another looping low, forming a shape that none of them recognized.

Not quite a spiral. Not quite a glyph. Almost a question mark curled into a spiral, like a curiosity being tugged outward.

Gabe knelt beside the vine, pressed both palms to the soil, and closed his eyes. He breathed in. Let the root-magic come. And whispered, "It's looking for something."

"Or someone," Morgan added.

"No," Gabe said quietly. "Not someone who's gone."

He opened his eyes. "Someone who's coming."

That night, the vine bloomed once—brief and bright, gold-edged and humming.

No one touched it, but the next morning, a new sprout had formed at the base.

This one pointed inward. Not to the arches. Not to the Hollow. To the town itself.

And in the very center of Bram's garden, a single stone had surfaced from the soil. It was carved with a symbol none of them had seen before. Except for Una.

She arrived just as the light shifted and knelt beside the stone. Her face went still. "This," she whispered, "was etched into the first path I followed beyond the arches."

Morgan stepped forward. "What does it mean?"

Una looked at them all. Bram last. Then said, quietly: "It means we're no longer the only ones watching."

# Chapter Seventy-Seven: The Root That Led Inward

Baz did not hurry. He never did. His pace was steady, measured, deliberate, the kind of rhythm that reminded others to breathe. Yet that morning, as he stood beside Bram's strange vine and watched its newest sprout curl into itself rather than reaching outward, something shifted deep in his bones. The sensation was subtle at first, like a note struck slightly off pitch, but it deepened into a quiet dissonance. It was as though the Hollow itself was holding its breath, unwilling to say why.

He lowered himself to a crouch and reached toward the vine, his fingers brushing lightly against the tip of the spiral. The warmth that met his skin was not the shimmer of magic but the concentrated weight of attention. It did not hum as so many living things did. Instead, it pulsed, slow and deliberate, as if echoing his own heartbeat back to him.

Baz followed where it led. He traced the spiral's curve across the soil, his boots finding a path that wound steadily toward the old cobblestone walk near the greenhouse. Most avoided that path. Not because it was cursed or dangerous, but because it seemed to end nowhere. That was what people believed. Baz saw something else.

The signs revealed themselves in subtle layers. Rootlight overlapped faintly, crossing itself in patterns too precise to be random. Threadlines quivered as though trying to align with something hidden beneath the surface. Even the bricks shimmered faintly, as if the story they carried was struggling to take form.

He stepped carefully off the cobblestone path and lowered his palm to the ground. The threads below shifted at once, curling toward his hand like a creature recognizing touch. They were not guiding him. They were responding. Someone else had already passed this way. Someone had left traces that had not yet faded.

He followed. His steps carried him beyond the greenhouse, past the bakery with its warm scent of sugar and flour, past the small circle of benches where townsfolk lingered, past the great Listening Tree whose branches always seemed to bend nearer to the secrets carried beneath it. At every point, the thread beneath the ground curled tighter, the energy concentrating as though he was being drawn toward a center.

It brought him to the old well at the edge of the square. It had been sealed long ago, abandoned when the new water line was enchanted and the town no longer needed its depth. Children no longer played near it, and no one paused at its rim. Yet the vine's energy pointed here, unmistakably.

Baz stepped closer. The stones thrummed beneath his boots, faint but undeniable. It was not a call of welcome, nor was it warning. It was the quiet acknowledgment of discovery, as though the stones themselves whispered: *You have found the door, but not the key.*

He knelt at the rim, both palms pressed against the cool surface. His voice dropped into the well's silence, carrying the weight of a question he rarely allowed himself to ask aloud. "What am I not seeing?"

For a long moment, nothing stirred. Then a sudden gust of wind swept across the square. It caught hold of something hidden, a strand of rootlight that flared only when moved. It flickered, caught against the stone, and then formed a shape pressed into the wall. A handprint.

It was smaller than his own. Familiar, though not recent.

Baz laid his palm against it. The well exhaled at his touch, not with the breath of air but with the weight of recognition. A shudder passed through him. He stepped back quickly, not in fear, but in the sharp clarity of knowing. Someone had come this way. Someone had crossed into the town without touching the arches.

They had not entered from above. They had come through the roots.

Baz straightened, his composure outwardly calm, but his heart thrummed with urgency. He walked swiftly back across the square, his steps longer than usual, his focus narrowing to the faces he needed to find. When at last he reached Morgan and Gabe, his words carried none of his usual measured tone.

"We have been watching the arches," he told them, his voice firm. "But the next one did not need them. They are already here. They came in through the roots."

## Chapter Seventy-Eight: Beneath the Well, the Story Waited

They met just before twilight. Baz, Morgan, Cassie, Gabe, Lilt, and Bram—who insisted on coming "just to keep the plants from lying."

The well pulsed softly under the fading light, the root-spell Baz had traced earlier now fully visible spiraling out from the base like a sigil that had been waiting for the right hands.

Cassie squinted at it. "Tell me again how long this has been here?"

"Centuries, probably," Baz replied.

"And we never noticed it?"

Gabe pressed a palm to the well. "We noticed. We just didn't understand what we were feeling."

Morgan stepped forward, eyes half-closed, attuning to the threadlines in the stone. "This isn't a portal," they said. "It's an archive. A memory tunnel. Whoever came through didn't break in, they were called."

Cassie blinked. "By what, exactly?"

No one answered. The well began to glow. Baz touched the center of the spiral, and it opened. Not with force, but with invitation.

The stones uncoiled downward, revealing a narrow passage bathed in low, bioluminescent moss and flickering rootlight. A gentle breeze rose from below carrying not air, but story. Half-formed. Untranslated. Waiting.

They descended together.

Cassie muttered all the way down. "If we die in a glowing hole under a forgotten town, I just want it on record that I opposed this with full sarcasm."

Lilt offered her a glowing thread-charm shaped like a grin.

Cassie took it. Grumbled. "Fine. It's pretty."

The tunnel curved, twisted, and then opened. Not into the expected cavern, but a library. Not one built with wood and shelves. A living one.

The walls were made of layered bark etched with symbols that shimmered when breathed upon. The ceiling bloomed with fungal constellations that pulsed in patterns. And in the center stood a pedestal of stone with a bowl of waterlight - glowing, fluid memory that moved like silk across its surface.

Morgan stepped toward it. "It's a witnessing pool," they said softly. "It shows what the place remembers, if the place believes you can hold it."

Cassie folded her arms. "And what if it decides we can't?"

Lilt shrugged. "Then it probably shows us our worst haircut."

Baz stepped forward first. He reached into the pool. It didn't resist. Instead, it poured upward curling around his wrist, his forearm, his temple before settling into a single image that hovered in the air.

It showed:

- A figure.
- Small.
- Alone.
- Standing in the Hollow... before the Hollow was ever named.

Cassie whispered, "That's not Irie."

Morgan murmured, "That's not anyone we know."

The image shifted. It showed the same figure walking down the spiral steps, carrying a shard of something that pulsed in time with the Hollow's roots. Then it showed them turning with eyes glowing.

Not hostile, but unclaimed.

Gabe stepped closer. "They didn't come here to be found," he said. "They came here to remember something we've forgotten."

The pool dimmed and the rootlight flared as if answering the call. And from deep within the archive, farther than any of them could see, a footstep echoed back.

Not forward. Toward them.

# Chapter Seventy-Nine: The Thread That Walked Back

The air shifted. Not colder, not heavier. Just... aware, as if the Hollow itself had leaned in.

The waterlight in the pool shimmered once then went still. And from the far end of the archive tunnel, the sound returned. Not hurried. Not hesitant. Just a steady, rhythmic footstep on soil that remembered.

Bram instinctively took a half step in front of Lilt.

Cassie's fingers twitched toward a charm pouch.

Baz stood still, watching the darkness with the reverence of someone who understood not all arrivals come in peace, but not all danger wears a frown.

Morgan whispered, "Let them come."

And the footsteps did.

The figure came into view slowly, wrapped in a robe of dark thread and moss-laced cloth that shimmered like dusk caught in rain. Their face wasn't hidden, but it seemed to shift, not in form, but in familiarity. To each Coven member, the figure looked a little different.

To Baz: an echo of a long-lost teacher.

To Cassie: someone who reminded her of her mother's last dream.

To Gabe: a stranger... but whose rhythm of movement matched his own heartbeat.

Only Morgan saw them clearly. And whispered, "You're the Hollow's first echo."

The figure stepped into the full light of the pool. Their eyes held the shimmer of threadlight, but not from any known thread.

They looked at Morgan, and then to the pool. And spoke.

Their voice was low, layered, like many voices woven into one.

"You've called back the part of yourselves you buried. I am not from beyond. I am from beneath. I am the one the soil held in silence, waiting. You are the children of threads. I am the knot."

The pool flickered.

Gabe stepped forward slowly. "Were you... one of us?"

The figure tilted their head. "I am what was left behind when you chose to forget. I held the names no one spoke. I carried the magic no one claimed."

Cassie, mouth slightly open, whispered, "Why come now?"

The figure finally smiled. Not warm. Not cruel. "Because you are ready to remember what remembering cost."

And with that, they reached into the pool. Not to draw power. To return something. A single root-thread, glowing violet and silver, pulsed outward. The ground quaked.

Softly. Not in fear. In recognition.

And far above, in the town square, the arches flared once.

Then settled.

As if something long waiting had finally... arrived.

## Chapter Eighty: When the Ground Remembered

It began with the wind. It wasn't louder but tuned. The breeze that moved through Alden's Landing that morning carried a hum. A tone that made spoons vibrate in drawers and set wind chimes to harmonize in keys no one had taught them.

Wren's shop bell rang three times before anyone entered. Her tea leaves danced before they steeped.

In the garden, Bram's vine turned, not outward, not inward, but downward, as if acknowledging something beneath it with deference.

The Listening Tree dropped four perfectly symmetrical leaves onto the path where Irie had once walked. Each leaf bore a faint spiral mark. None of them decayed.

Cassie saw them. Whispered, "Oh no. The town's got opinions again."

In the apothecary, a bottle labeled *Dissolve Old Fears* uncorked itself and fizzed quietly, releasing a fog that smelled like thunder and burnt honey.

Baz took one look, tapped the shelf, and said, "We'll need containment wards."

Morgan replied, "No. We'll need understanding."

But not everyone responded with reverence. Some grew restless. Others… nostalgic.

A handful of townsfolk reported vivid dreams of people they'd never met. Dreams that felt like memories belonging to the soil beneath their homes.

Children began naming invisible animals they insisted were "made of breath and stories." And at least two chickens refused to return to their coop, choosing instead to sleep beneath the Spiral Bell.

Wes felt it in his bones. He woke up and instinctively touched a resonance charm only to find it had rearranged itself into the symbol Una had carried on her palm when she returned. He said nothing, but that day he avoided the arches. Even as they hummed, they seemed to be less like gates, more like receivers.

By dusk, the Hollow's central path began to shift. Literally. Spirals unwound and new ones formed. The land was not in danger, but it was no longer still.

Morgan stood at the Looming Tree, hand against the bark. They whispered, "We thought the thread was ours."

Beside them, Gabe murmured, "It is. But we're not the only ones weaving."

That night, Cassie couldn't sleep. She wandered through the garden, barefoot and muttering about "root-rattling ancestors and story ghosts." When she passed Bram's vine, it bowed toward her, just slightly. She stopped.

And for the first time in weeks, it spoke. Not out loud. In her.

It's time.

Cassie blinked. Then said, "For what?"

The vine answered: To remember where your magic began.

## Chapter Eighty-One: Beneath the Laughter, the Root

Cassie had always believed in inheritance, though never in the magical sense. The spoon collection she had received from her great-aunt? Certainly. Her mother's dry wit and devastating side-eye? Without a doubt. But ancestral magic? She had always assumed hers had skipped a generation, perhaps even a dozen.

That was why, when the vine near her greenhouse whispered, remember where your magic began, Cassie blinked at it, stared as if daring it to say more, and replied in her flat, unimpressed tone, "My magic began with caffeine and spite. Check your sources."

The vine said nothing further. Instead, it leaned toward the oak that grew behind her greenhouse. Cassie barely glanced at the tree in her daily life, because it had never seemed worth her time. It never bloomed, never whispered, never produced even a flicker of interest.

Until now.

As she approached, the bark shimmered faintly, catching the moonlight in a way that made her stop short. Cassie rolled her eyes. "Great. Now the plants are dramatic," she muttered.

Still, she reached out. The moment her fingers touched the trunk, warmth shot up her arm, followed by a rush of images that were not her own. She saw a woman in a cloak; her hands stained with ink and herb oil. She saw a small cottage beside a river she had never visited. She saw a child laughing as they drew sigils in the mud with the tip of a spoon.

The memories carried no names, only feelings, impressions carved into the roots of something old. Then her gaze shifted, and beneath the bark, faintly illuminated by the moonlight, she saw a word etched into the wood.

Caleen.

She whispered it aloud. The ground beneath her feet responded at once with a low hum, and the tree released a single acorn that fell into her hand. It pulsed faintly with threadlight, but it was not refined or polished. This was tangled, braided magic. It was rough, intimate, and ungoverned. Root-magic. Old, personal, and messy.

Inside her greenhouse, her shelves rattled as if caught in a sudden wind. Jars shifted and realigned, glass chiming softly against glass. One jar, long forgotten and coated in dust, rolled forward. Its label read: *Balm for the One Who Knows But Will Not Admit It.*

Cassie groaned and pressed her free hand against her forehead. "Alright, fine. I get it. I'm dramatic ancestry girl now. Hooray."

But her hands were trembling, because beneath her sarcasm something had taken root. This felt real in a way she could not laugh away.

She carried the acorn inside, sat before the hearth, and settled herself with the acorn in one hand and an old spoon in the other. She whispered the name again, "Caleen." The word did not feel comfortable, but it felt correct.

Beneath her feet, the stones of the floor responded. A low pulse shivered through them, and one tile lifted slightly. Cassie pried it loose with careful fingers. Hidden beneath was a cloth bundle. She unwrapped it slowly, her breath shallow. Inside was a folded letter written in delicate ink, a dried flower threaded with a strand of golden root, and a recipe written in faded script with the title: *For Returning What Was Left Behind.*

Cassie stared for a long while, her expression unreadable. At last, she leaned back, pressed the acorn against her chest, and muttered, "Alright, mystery relatives. Let's stir this cauldron."

Outside, the wind curled around the greenhouse, carrying with it the faintest of whispers. She begins again.

## Chapter Eighty-Two: The Root and the Loom

Morgan didn't knock. They didn't have to. The spellwork around Cassie's greenhouse recognized intention and Morgan's presence was never a question. The door opened before they touched it.

Inside, Cassie was standing barefoot in her kitchen, staring at a wooden spoon that had just stirred itself through a bowl of honey and crushed thyme.

She glanced up. "You're here to tell me this isn't normal, aren't you?"

Morgan looked at the bowl. Then the recipe on the counter. Then the threadlight tangled loosely around her ankles. They smiled softly. "It's your normal now."

Cassie groaned. "Unsubscribe."

Morgan approached the letter Cassie had found. It pulsed faintly. It was time-woven, not just handwritten. They reached toward it, and the ink shimmered as if reacting to their magic as well.

Cassie frowned. "It responds to you?"

Morgan nodded. "It's not just a recipe. It's a relay. This wasn't meant for one descendant. It's part of a rootline spell, a multi-generational enchantment."

Cassie blinked. "Like… magical chain mail?"

Morgan tilted their head. "Less spam. More sacred baton passing."

They sat on the floor; materials spread between them:

- The letter
- The dried flower
- The pulsing acorn

- The spoon (which had taken on a faint glow and absolutely knew things)

Cassie traced her fingers over the recipe. "It says, *'For Returning What Was Left Behind.'* I thought maybe it meant guilt, or an heirloom, or a magical casserole dish."

Morgan shook their head. "It's bigger. I think it's about a piece of your family's magic that was buried. Not metaphorically. Actually."

Morgan reached for the flower and held it close. The petals vibrated faintly with memory.

And then, just for a second, Morgan saw it.

A vision.

A forest clearing.

A younger version of Cassie. It wasn't her, but of her line. They were kneeling at the roots of a tree and placing a second acorn into a hollow in the earth. And whispering: *One day, when she's ready, let this call her back.*

Morgan blinked.

Cassie noticed. "You saw something."

Morgan nodded. "Your family didn't just pass down spells. They passed down a place."

Cassie looked at the acorn still resting in her hand. Its glow had deepened. It was no longer gold, but a warm copper laced with green. And in the space between her pulse and her breath, she heard it: Come home. Not where you lived. Where you began.

Morgan met her eyes.

"You need to plant it." Cassie smirked. "I swear, if a glowing ancestral cottage sprouts and starts offering me tea with ominous foreshadowing—"

Morgan smiled. "You'll drink it. And sass the teacup."

Cassie sighed. "Yeah. I will."

They stood together. Outside, the wind shifted.

As if somewhere, the land her lineage once held had already begun to stir.

## Chapter Eighty-Three: Where Her Magic Waited

Cassie had no idea how the grove found her. One minute, she and Morgan were standing behind her greenhouse near the silverleaf arbor, the acorn pulsing in her hand like a second heartbeat. The next, the wind twisted, the light dipped, and a path appeared - one that hadn't been there since ever.

Not paved. Not marked. Just… known.

The ground was soft underfoot, a carpet of moss and old story.

"Tell me again why I'm walking into a magical glade on the invitation of a root that glows like it knows too much?"

Morgan smiled. "Because it's your root."

Cassie sighed. "Gross." But she walked.

The grove was small and circular. Quiet in that thick, living way that made sound feel like it had to ask permission before speaking. At the center stood a single tree. It was twisted and wide-rooted. Older than the town and likely older than the arches. Its bark bore the faint shimmer of magic stored, not displayed.

Cassie stepped into the circle. The acorn in her palm flared, then stilled. And the earth in front of the tree parted. Just enough for her to understand: It's time.

She knelt and brushed aside the moss. Then whispered—not an incantation, not a spell—just a truth: "I didn't know I came from something ancient. But I know now. And I'm not afraid of the root anymore."

She placed the acorn into the hollow and pressed her palm to the soil.

Morgan stepped back, silent, but watching and witnessing.

The ground glowed. Threadlight, soft and amber, spiraled outward from the tree like old veins waking up. And behind her, walls appeared. Not stone. Not wood. Memory. Shaped into a cottage. It wasn't hers. But it was familiar. A place that felt like family humming in the walls.

The door opened by itself. Inside:

- Shelves of empty jars, labeled with names she hadn't heard in generations
- A kettle already warm
- A journal with handwriting nearly identical to her own, but older, slower, looping

Cassie picked it up and read the first line:

*To the one who laughs louder than her doubt:*
*You were always the one who would find your way back.*
*This place has been holding its breath.*
*Let it exhale.*

She sat in the doorway, blinking back something that wasn't quite tears.

Morgan leaned against the frame. "Well?"

Cassie exhaled. Grinned. "Guess I inherited real estate."

Morgan smirked. "Magical ancestral real estate."

Cassie nodded. "I suppose I'll need to dust."

Outside, the grove pulsed once and the Hollow, which was miles away, whispered her name in the roots.

# Chapter Eighty-Four: The Rooms She Already Knew

Cassie stood in the threshold for longer than she meant to.

The air inside the cottage didn't feel musty or old, it felt paused, like the place had been holding itself still for generations, waiting for the right hands to reach for its story. The scent was earthy and sharp, like crushed thyme and smoked sage. Her fingers brushed the frame of the door as she stepped through, half-expecting dust or cobwebs. But the surfaces were clean. Not polished. Just… respectfully untouched. Like the place had maintained itself out of stubborn pride.

She understood that.

The shelves along the far wall curved slightly which gave an intentional softness to their shape, like they'd been carved by someone who understood that magic, like memory, doesn't always grow in straight lines. Each jar bore a hand-inked label. Some with names like Caleen, Marta, Linnea and others with phrases like *"For Smoothing What Shakes"* and *"Held Breath, Third Harvest."* Cassie lifted one, heart thudding. Inside, a golden shimmer clung to the glass, swirling gently even though no one had touched it in what must have been decades.

She didn't open it.

The journal on the table drew her next. Its leather cover was cracked and warm beneath her hand, and when she flipped it open, she was surprised to find not spells, but letters. Dozens of them. Written from mother to daughter, mentor to apprentice, friend to future. One addressed "To the loud one with clever hands and coffee breath" made her laugh, loud enough to shake a few petals loose from the dried herb garland over the hearth.

And still, her throat tightened. They'd known she was coming. Maybe not her name. Maybe not her timeline. But the shape of her.

Her voice in the world. Her reluctance to be revered. Her craving for meaning without asking for it to be sacred.

In the back corner, a small loom stood under the window. Not ornate, but functional. Simple thread still wound through it, mid-weave, the last row unfinished. Cassie reached out, brushed the thread lightly, and immediately felt the tug behind her navel. Not painful. Not even magical in the usual sense. It felt like someone had just recognized her.

There were notes pinned to the loom's frame. She bent to read them.

*"This weave belongs to the one who can laugh in ritual and cry over bread."*
*"Finish only when you're no longer trying to prove you deserve to."*

Cassie let out a long breath, shaky and wry. "Well played, dead aunties."

There was a hearth, though it didn't burn with fire. Inside it, coals glowed softly, like embers that remembered warmth. She crouched, hand on the stone, and felt it pulse once beneath her palm. A drawer to the left clicked open, revealing a small collection of metal spoons, each with different handles: twisted, flat, spiral, leaf-shaped.

She laughed, despite herself. "So, it was hereditary."

At the far end of the cottage, a ladder led to a narrow loft. She climbed slowly, half-expecting a thunderclap or ancestral scolding. Instead, she found a bed tucked under the eaves, made with a quilt patterned in threadlines. It wasn't just decorative, but actual glowing threads woven through the fabric. They pulsed softly as she touched them, a rhythm she recognized but didn't understand.

Cassie sat on the edge of the bed and whispered, "You wanted me to feel safe."

The quilt warmed beneath her hands.

Downstairs, Morgan hadn't moved. They waited in the grove, patient, letting the space remain hers for now.

But as Cassie descended again, clutching the journal and one of the spoons, she didn't look startled or dazed. She looked steady and wiser. Like a doorway had opened inside her, not just around her.

She met Morgan's eyes and said, "This place doesn't just hold magic. It remembers intention."

Morgan nodded. "And now it remembers you."

Cassie tucked the journal under her arm. "Well. I guess I need to figure out what I'm meant to do with it."

Outside, the grove shifted, and the wind curled through the doorway like a welcome home.

## Chapter Eighty-Five: The Walk Back Changed Everything

Cassie did not rush as she left the grove. The path back had not shifted, yet it somehow seemed shorter, as though the trees themselves were gently nudging her onward. Not outward, but forward. She turned once, her hand brushing the threshold where the cottage rested beneath its canopy of ancient magic. The doorway did not close behind her. It no longer needed to. The place was part of her now. Perhaps it always had been.

Crossing the outer spiral and stepping into town, she felt the change immediately. The wind did not greet her. The cobblestones did not hum beneath her feet. The air did not ripple with approval or applause. Yet everything around her seemed to be watching. Not with suspicion. Not even with reverence. With recognition.

Cassie did not stride the way she often did, quick with humor and commentary. Instead, she settled with each step. Her usual sarcastic quips remained tucked in her chest, not gone but softened, as if even her wit knew this was a time to listen rather than to jest. She was carrying something new, and her very presence seemed heavier, fuller, almost resonant.

At Stirred & Spellbound, the wind chime above the door released a single, low tone as she passed beneath it. The sound reminded her of a long-held breath finally let go. Inside, Wren lifted her eyes from a teacup she was infusing. For a moment her expression widened, not in shock, but in a small, quiet awe.

"You smell like tree bark and thunder," Wren said matter-of-factly.

Cassie arched one eyebrow. "And here I was hoping for crushed lavender and metaphysical brilliance."

Wren's grin appeared slow and certain. "That is layered in, too. But there is no mistaking it. You have been claimed."

Cassie hesitated, then let her voice drop low. "I think I claimed back, too."

Baz waited for her near the greenhouse. He did not greet her right away. He simply looked at her with the kind of silence reserved for someone who had traveled both outward and inward and returned changed. "You are different," he said at last, his voice quiet but steady.

She held out the journal to him. "This is part of it. The rest is not written down."

He opened the first few pages, his expression unreadable as his eyes moved across the ink. Then he shut the cover and slid it into the crook of his arm as though it belonged to him as much as it did to her.

"Do we need to sit somewhere and unpack your emotional inheritance?" he asked, the corner of his mouth twitching toward mischief.

Cassie exhaled, a sound that balanced somewhere between a laugh and a low grief. "It doesn't unpack. It unfolds."

By sunset, word had already spread through the town. Not in the form of shouts or gossip, but like the hush before a storm, like threadlight tilting toward something not yet spoken.

Morgan met her in the square. Their eyes softened when they saw her. "You are carrying the anchor now."

Cassie shook her head. "No. I think I am carrying the invitation. The anchor is still rooted."

Morgan reached out and laid a hand lightly on her shoulder. "Then what do you want to do with it?"

Cassie looked toward the horizon, then back at the path that had led her here. Her answer came slowly, certain as the tide. "I want to open the door wider."

Above them, the arches did not blaze. Yet the light edging their curves began to weave together, faint threads braiding into something both familiar and new. It was no longer only an invitation. It was a return line, a thread of welcome for anyone who still had something worth coming back to.

## Chapter Eighty-Six: What She Made with Her Inheritance

Cassie did not tell anyone what she was planning. That was hardly unusual for her. She preferred her magic to arrive unannounced and her generosity to be disguised as inconvenience. Still, when the community board in the town square lit up on its own one morning and spelled out in slow, glowing threadlight, *Come to Stirred & Spellbound at dusk. Bring your emptiest cup,* everyone in town knew who was responsible.

Cassie groaned when she saw it. "Traitorous signage," she muttered toward the wind. The wind answered with a whistle that sounded suspiciously like laughter.

She spent the day in her kitchen, the windows flung wide to let in the shifting air. Her sleeves were rolled up and her hair tied back with a scarf that had once belonged to her grandmother. The fabric still held the faint scent of rosemary and ink, as if memory itself had been woven into the threads. On the counter stood a line of jars brought back from the ancestral cottage. On the stove a kettle pulsed with enchantment, heating water to the rhythm of her own heartbeat. In a heavy stone bowl, a spoon stirred itself slowly through petals, honey, and something older than either. It was not quite a potion and not entirely tea. It was something between the two. Something meant to restore what had grown thin and frayed.

By the time the sun slipped behind the ridge, people began arriving one by one. Wren carried a mug shaped like a shifting moon phase. Baz, quiet as always at first, held a vessel carved from petrified wood. Lilt came with a cup that curled in the form of a coiled question mark. Even Shaw appeared at the edge of the gathering, staying in the shadows with the air of someone who was curious but not yet willing to commit.

Cassie said nothing. She simply ladled the shimmering brew into each waiting cup, watching how it changed in the hands of the drinkers. Some mugs glowed brightly from within. Others dimmed, then re-lit as if remembering something forgotten. One cracked with a soft sound and healed itself after the first sip. When Wes drank, he let out a breath so deep it seemed to shift the very wind around him. When Rhett sipped, a new page unfurled across the surface of their journal as though it had been waiting. Morgan's cup filled before Cassie even touched it.

"It remembers me," Morgan said with a quiet smile.

Cassie, unimpressed with her own miracle, lifted a brow. "Of course it does. You practically breathe in root-language."

At last, someone asked the inevitable question. "What is this, exactly?"

Cassie paused, her ladle still hovering over the bowl. "It is called Hearththread," she said at last. "It is not a cure, and it is not a charm. It only reminds you of what has never left, even when you forgot it was still there."

A few people nodded. One person cried quietly into their cup. At the windows, the vines bloomed out of season, pale blossoms opening in the hush of twilight.

As night settled over the town, laughter rose again inside the shop. It was small at first, but genuine, carrying a weight of relief that no spell could have manufactured. Cassie sat at the counter with her own cup, the liquid within still swirling as if it resisted settling. Morgan joined her and leaned close.

"You just rewrote the concept of comfort," they said.

Cassie grinned. "Do not tell the spoon. It will get cocky."

They shared the silence that followed, letting the room hum around them. After a while Morgan asked, "Will you do this again?"

Cassie considered, staring into the slow whirl of her cup. "Maybe. If I remember how. Or if the wind reminds me."

Outside, the arches glowed faintly against the night. Just beyond them, the path back to the cottage pulsed—not as a summons to leave, but as a quiet acknowledgment. It seemed to whisper: We see what you made. And we remember her well.

## Chapter Eighty-Seven: What He Refused to Sip

Shaw never stepped inside Stirred & Spellbound. He lingered instead, keeping himself at the boundary where shadow met the greenhouse glow. He leaned against a wooden beam at the edge, his arms crossed, and his eyes narrowed, watching without joining. From where he stood, the light spilling outward was soft and golden, a warmth too perfect to be natural. The scent reached him even there, curling through the night air. It was Hearththread brew, sweet and spiced, but touched with something older and wilder that made his throat ache.

The ache was not thirst. It was memory.

One by one, he watched the others enter. Wren, Morgan, Baz, even Rhett, their voices rising in laughter, their shoulders easing as though something heavy had been lifted. They exhaled together in a rhythm that belonged to community, to belonging. The sound was invisible yet undeniable, a tether pulling them closer to one another.

When the vines along the windowsills bloomed out of season, Shaw flinched. The movement was subtle, but he felt it in his bones. The town had reached a secret consensus, a silent agreement that he was not part of. They had chosen to belong to something that did not need his permission, and he had not been invited.

Cassie's voice floated out through the glass panes, light and teasing, though it carried the unmistakable precision of someone who knew exactly what she was doing. "It is called Hearththread," she explained, her tone warm. "It just reminds you of what has never truly left you."

The crowd laughed, soft and gentle, as if the sound itself was a blessing. Someone whispered a prayer beneath the chorus. Shaw turned away, his jaw tight, his expression carved in restraint.

Later that night, long after the crowd had dispersed and the vines had withdrawn into their usual stillness, Shaw returned. He slipped quietly up to the greenhouse door and paused. Inside, the cauldron still shimmered with the remnants of the brew. The glow lingered in the corners of the room, faint but steady.

The place was empty. Yet on the counter, Cassie had left a single cup.

Shaw froze when he saw it. He knew immediately that it was meant for him, and the knowledge unsettled him. He hated that she assumed he would need it, hated that she was right.

He stepped forward, not close enough to touch, but near enough to feel the warmth radiating from the cup. The smell rose around him, sharp and intimate. It was the scent of air just before a storm breaks, heavy with promise, and of the paper his mother had once used for her letters. He closed his eyes against it.

"I do not need reminders," he muttered into the quiet.

But the spoon inside the cup shifted. It stirred once, gently, though no hand guided it. The sound was soft, deliberate, and carried a meaning he could not deny: You already carry them, whether you sip or not.

Shaw's breath tightened. He turned on his heel and left the greenhouse behind. His boots struck harder against the ground than usual as he made his way to the edge of the Hollow. He did not notice that the soil beneath him dimmed where he walked, or that the roots recoiled quietly from his steps. He did not hear the faint hush that passed through the arches as he crossed by, or see the vines draw themselves inward. The very air held its breath in his passing.

But it did.

Shaw still clung to the things he understood: order, structure, and control. He believed in them as firmly as he believed in stone walls and sealed doors. Cassie's magic was none of these things. It was a laugh breaking silence in a room that longed for quiet. It was a flower pushing through frost to prove winter could not hold everything still. It was the warmth of belonging that did not pause to ask permission.

And that frightened him more than any storm the Hollow had ever conjured.

# Chapter Eighty-Eight: The Grip That Slipped

Shaw woke before the first light touched the sky. The Hollow had not hummed for him in days, and the silence pressed against his ribs like a withheld breath. His workshop, once alive with small sympathetic magics, now sat inert. The tools were cool to the touch, as if they had chosen to withdraw their loyalty. The charmed instruments refused to respond, their strings slack and their runes dull. Even the ledgers, his most dependable companions, betrayed him; ink smeared at the edges of his neat handwriting and the pages curled defiantly, as though the books themselves resented being ordered.

Control had always been his closest ally, but even that was beginning to slip. So, Shaw did what Shaw always did when the ground shifted. He tightened the rules.

He began with schedules, rearranging the town circle into a new set of meeting times. He drafted protocols for Hollow interactions that read like sacred law. He designed regulations for the cultivation of magical plants near public structures, as though roots and vines might suddenly respect a perimeter if he simply declared it.

He printed each decree on thick parchment, crisp with clean fonts and precisely spaced bullet points. He nailed them outside Wren's shop, Baz's garden gate, and the entrance to Stirred & Spellbound. Each one bore the polished title: *Guidance for Community Harmony and Energetic Boundaries.*

Cassie laughed so hard she had to sit down on the cobblestones. Wren poured tea directly over one copy, the liquid soaking the ink into a blurred, unreadable wash. Morgan folded theirs into an origami frog that blinked when touched and hopped off the notice board entirely.

But Shaw did not stop there. If the magic would not stay still, then he would trap it in definition.

He tried to name the vine in Bram's garden using an outdated root-indexing system, writing and rewriting until the page was full of scratched-out guesses. He attempted to chart Una's shimmer magic across a color wheel, but the hues refused to hold shape and bled into one another like liquid light. He watched Gabe from a distance, sketching symbols in his ledger, only to have them rearrange themselves into forms he had not drawn.

The deeper he reached for clarity, the more his notes betrayed him. Pages curled at the corners, charts bent in on themselves, and the letters whispered things he had never written.

He turned to the Spiral Bell, determined to reclaim its order. He cleaned it until the bronze gleamed. He recalibrated its weight and rewrote its purpose in his ledgers as a *town stabilizer.* Yet the bell refused him. No matter how he struck it, the sound would not rise. Instead, it pulsed with a low hum, almost like a heartbeat, one that would not sync with his no matter how he tried to impose rhythm.

One afternoon, his efforts drove him back to the hidden well—the one Baz and the others had descended weeks before. Shaw stood at the edge, staring into the still darkness. His voice was steady but frayed when he whispered, "I never tried to stop it. I only ever wanted it understood."

The wind did not answer him. The ground did not shift. The well offered no pulse of light or thread of sound. For a long moment, there was only silence. Then, as if from far below, a whisper surfaced, a voice he did not know but could not dismiss. "You do not understand something by silencing it."

Shaw stumbled back, his fingers trembling. It was not fear that shook him, though it was close enough to taste. It was rage, hot and choking. And underneath the rage, sharper and more dangerous, was grief.

Because the town was moving on. Not past him, but around him. And it had stopped asking for his guidance.

## Chapter Eighty-Nine: The Mirror They Held Up

It was Wren who found him. Not by seeking him out, but by accident. She had gone to the well clearing for solitude, her arms filled with damp herbs and half-finished blessings. The Spiral Bell's energy had been restless all day, jittering in uneven waves, and the rootlight near her shop refused to settle into any recognizable pattern. She had hoped the quiet of the clearing might help her untangle it.

Instead, she saw Shaw standing at the lip of the forgotten well. She paused, not because she was afraid, but because she recognized the posture. It was the stance of someone unraveling under the weight of what they refused to name.

He did not turn when she approached. He did not speak when she set down her basket on the moss. But when she said, "You look like someone trying to tighten the knots around a story that doesn't belong to you anymore," he flinched, almost imperceptibly.

Still, his silence held.

Wren stepped closer, not invading, but making her presence undeniable. "I read your Harmony Guidelines," she said. "Very thorough. Very tidy. Entirely unrequested."

Shaw exhaled, the sound more like pressure escaping than relief. "This place needs order," he muttered. "You've all let yourselves be swept away. You're bending to a force that doesn't even ask who you are."

Wren tilted her head, her voice calm but edged with clarity. "No. We are finally becoming who we were before we forgot."

That struck. He winced, just slightly, and finally turned to face her. Exhaustion sat in his eyes, heavy and obvious, but beneath it something sharper lingered. Fear.

"They are losing themselves," he said quietly. "Cassie, Baz... Morgan. Even the land. It doesn't feel like home anymore."

"It isn't supposed to," Wren replied gently. "Home isn't a container. It is a current. And you have been damming the water for so long that you forgot you can float."

He looked away quickly, as though the ground itself might shield him. But she was not finished.

"You used to walk through the Hollow and feel it, Shaw. You didn't study it or chart it. You listened. You made space for other people's magic even when it contradicted your own. And now, you are the only one who hasn't shifted rhythm. That silence around you? It isn't control. It is disconnection."

His shoulders sank, not in surrender, but with the weight of recognition. The fight in him faltered.

"I didn't mean to step outside of it," he said, his voice directed more toward the wind than toward her. "I only wanted to stay grounded. I didn't want to lose the structure, the agreements we made."

Wren moved beside him and rested a hand lightly on his arm. "Structure doesn't mean locking the door. It means knowing when it is time to open a new one."

She turned her gaze on him fully, steady but kind. "So, I am asking you now, as someone who remembers who you used to be. Are you willing to come back?"

The clearing held its breath. Then, in the distance, the Spiral Bell rang once. The sound was low, mournful, and strangely inviting.

Shaw did not answer. But for the first time in days, the rootlight at his feet brightened.

## Chapter Ninety: The Slow Work of Returning

The day after Wren's words settled into his bones, Shaw woke before the sun and didn't reach for a ledger. Instead, he brewed a pot of plain, strong tea - the kind that didn't try to enchant anyone, didn't change flavor based on mood. Just tea.

He drank it in silence. Then put on his boots and stepped outside.

Not to lead. Not to enforce. To show up.

His first stop was Bram's garden. Not to lecture him about overactive soil rhythms or cross-pollinating intent threads, he just stood at the gate until Bram noticed him and gave a curt nod. "I brought compost," Shaw said, holding up the bucket awkwardly.

Bram arched a brow. "…You're volunteering?"

"I'm… attempting," Shaw replied.

Bram stepped aside and they worked in silence for an hour.

When Bram offered him a small trowel and didn't insult his technique, Shaw counted it as progress.

When the vine nearest the eastern plot turned ever so slightly in his direction, he didn't react, but his fingers trembled.

Later, he walked past the Spiral Bell and paused. Then carefully wrote a small note with no signature and tucked it between two stones.

Just five words: *I'm listening now. Not measuring.*

He didn't know if anyone would find it or believe it. But it felt right to leave something behind that didn't demand to be seen.

By midday, he found himself near Stirred & Spellbound, but he didn't go in. He left a small, wrapped bundle on the step. It was an old charm from his early days in town; one meant to soften the edges of held judgment.

Inside was a note:

*Cassie,*
*I fought the storm.*
*You offered tea.*
*I'm sorry I didn't know how to drink it.*

He walked away before she came to the door because he didn't need to be thanked or to be forgiven. Just... seen.

That evening, he returned to the well. Just to sit beside it. Palms open and listening.

The wind shifted once around him. It was cool, but not dismissive.

The rootlight under his boots didn't flare, but it didn't recede.

And for now, that was enough.

# Chapter Ninety-One: The Space Between the Leaves

Cassie didn't notice the bundle at first. She was elbow-deep in dried calendula blossoms and mulberry root, rearranging the spell shelves she had already fussed over twice that week. Order had always been her refuge. When the world pressed in too tightly, she tamed jars and lined up bottles, convinced herself that if she could sort magic into neat rows, perhaps her own restless thoughts would fall in line as well. It was an old ritual, one part habit and one part survival.

She had just stepped back to admire her work when the cottage grew too warm. With a sharp tug, she opened the front door to invite in the evening air, and that was when she saw it.

The package sat on the threshold, no bigger than her palm. A small wrap of oilcloth, worn at the edges and tied in a way that suggested more hope than skill. There was no flicker of enchantment stitched into the binding, no shimmer of protective glamour, no glowing sigil pulsing with smug superiority. Nothing announced itself as otherworldly. It was not magical in the slightest, which made it stand out even more. It looked plain. Human. Hesitant. Like an apology that wasn't certain of being received.

Cassie froze, staring at it for a long minute before crouching down to lift it with careful fingers. She turned it over as though it might speak if given the chance, and finally let out a long, weary sigh. "Oh no," she murmured. "He's trying to grow a soul again."

Back inside, she set the bundle on the counter beside the mortar and pestle that had not seen use since the last eclipse. The air in the cottage seemed to lean closer as she unwrapped the oilcloth, folding it back layer by layer. Inside lay a charm she recognized immediately, not because of any lingering power, but because of its clumsy sincerity.

One of Shaw's first attempts crafted long before the Spiral Bell, back when his hands had been unsteady and his belief in himself almost fragile. This was before he had tightened himself into rigid lines of order and rules, before the town had worn down his edges and convinced him that control was the only way to be useful.

The charm was rough in texture, the edges uneven where he had pressed the material too hard. It carried the unmistakable fingerprints of someone learning to shape meaning, someone earnest enough to risk failure. Cassie ran her thumb along its surface, her chest tightening with something that was not quite nostalgia and not quite forgiveness.

And then she noticed the note.

She unfolded the small scrap of paper and read it once quickly, then again more slowly, as though the second reading might soften the weight of the words.

*I fought the storm.*
*You offered tea.*
*I'm sorry I didn't know how to drink it.*

She did not cry, but she did sit down heavily, which for Cassie carried its own kind of significance. Her body, usually restless, had chosen stillness. The kettle in the corner seemed to recognize the moment, warming itself without her bidding. A spoon she had once carried back from her ancestral cottage began to stir an empty cup on its own, as though reminding her that she was not entirely alone in this silence.

Cassie looked from the quietly humming kettle to the charm in her hand. "Well," she muttered under her breath, "he still can't rhyme. But at least he's starting to listen."

She tucked the charm onto a high shelf behind jars labeled willingness, laughter at one's own expense, and simmered pride. She liked the idea of it resting near such companions. Close enough to be acknowledged but not given too much authority. Her heart, careful and still bruised, was not ready for absolution. Yet even as she arranged it there, she felt the faintest flicker of something - an acknowledgment of the reach, however clumsy it had been.

That night, when the square filled with lanternlight and the slow murmur of evening, Cassie stepped outside. Across the way, Shaw sat alone near the old well, his posture as rigid as the stone he leaned against. She did not cross the space between them, nor did she call out. Instead, she poured a second mug of Hearththread tea, carried it to the stone bench that lay halfway between their two places, and set it down. She did not linger. She simply walked away, her footsteps soft against the cobblestones.

The next morning, when she opened her door to sweep out the dust of the night, the mug was gone.

## Chapter Ninety-Two: When the Thread Twists Back

Morgan hadn't expected the loom to act up again. They were already behind on repairs after a week of subtle disturbances, i.e. threads shifting of their own accord, whispers in the warp that weren't theirs, and more than one charm snagging on stories that didn't belong to this plane. Still, they approached the Looming Tree that morning with their usual blend of reverence and irritation, sleeves rolled up, hair tied back with an herb-thread ribbon, and the quiet certainty that today, at least, the magic might behave.

They were wrong. Again.

The central loom, which is the one closest to the Hollow's heart, was weaving without input. Not frantically. Not in distress. Just slowly, insistently, pulling thread from a skein Morgan hadn't touched and moving it through the warp with careful precision.

At first, they thought it was a leftover spell. A misaligned intention maybe, or an echo of Gabe's recent ritual work. But no, this was deliberate.

The thread was knotting in a very specific place, over and over, forming a spiral that folded in on itself. It wasn't random. It wasn't decorative. It was a message. One that spoke in silence.

Morgan sat back on their heels and exhaled, pressing a palm to the bench as if to stabilize the ground beneath them. It wasn't the first time the loom had tried to tell them something. But it was the first time in weeks that the pattern refused to resolve.

As they leaned closer to examine the newest pass, footsteps thundered through the entrance to the Hollow.

Wren. Of course.

She rarely ran. Even in emergencies, she preferred to float in with a wind at her back and a teacup somehow still in hand.

So, the fact that she was breathless, cheeks flushed, and hair coming loose from her knot, was enough to make Morgan straighten immediately.

"There's a problem," she said, her voice low but urgent, "at the southern arch. And you're going to want to see it before the Threadkeepers do."

Morgan blinked. "Define 'problem.'"

Wren pressed a hand to her chest, catching her breath. "Not dangerous," she said. "Just... tense. And very, very visible."

Which was Wren-speak for it's about to get messy in public.

Morgan didn't ask for more. They stood, gave the loom one last wary glance, and followed.

The arches always seemed peaceful at first glance. To the average visitor, they appeared to be elegant, humming gateways strung with rootlight and intention. But Morgan knew better. The arches listened and they responded. And often, they reflected whatever energy passed through them.

Which meant that what they were walking into wasn't just a personal disagreement, it was an echo.

When they arrived, the tension was immediate. A semi-circle of townsfolk stood along the perimeter, whispering low and sharp behind fingers and scarves. The threadlight along the arch had dimmed slightly, a sure sign of spiritual resistance, and in the center of it all was Una, Irie, and Lilt.

All standing with varying degrees of anger, discomfort, and desperation.

Morgan's stomach tightened. This wasn't a scolding. It was a breach.

They moved without hesitation, their boots whispering against the soil as they stepped into the open circle, hands up in a show of neutrality.

"Alright," Morgan said, voice calm but firm, "let's use inside voices and outside honesty. Who wants to start?"

Una crossed her arms, expression smooth as glass but eyes sparking. "Irie's been guiding someone through the arches," she said without preamble. "Privately, repeatedly and without declaring it."

Gasps and murmurs rippled from the crowd like birds startled from a tree.

Morgan turned slowly to Irie, giving her time.

"I didn't break protocol," Irie said defensively. "The Hollow allowed it. The arches responded. I didn't sneak anyone in. I followed what the land asked."

"And yet," Una replied, "you didn't tell anyone what they brought back."

Lilt, standing between them, looked visibly torn like a thread pulled taut between two storylines. "It's not the crossings that are the issue," they said. "It's the consequences. We're all feeling the shift. Even the land is… off."

Morgan felt it too, of course. The Hollow had been whispering uneasily for days, and the loom's behavior this morning now made a chilling kind of sense. They turned to Irie, this time gently.

"What's coming through?" they asked. "Not in theory. In truth."

Irie's throat bobbed as she swallowed. Her eyes shimmered, not with guilt, but with something more complicated.

"Not who," she said. "What." She stepped forward, placing her hand on the ground near the arch. The threadlight around her palm flickered but did not reject her.

"It's a kind of magic," she continued. "From somewhere the arches barely recognize. It doesn't speak in language. It speaks in emotion. Pure sensation. It moves through people, and I couldn't let it be turned away."

Morgan was silent for a long moment. Then they turned to Una.

Una's face remained composed, but her voice betrayed steel beneath. "She's tampering with an untranslatable source of power. That's not reverence. That's recklessness."

"And what would you have done?" Morgan asked, still even. "Let it knock unanswered at the door until it cracked the hinges?"

Una didn't flinch. "I would've listened before inviting it in."

Morgan nodded once. "We don't all hear the same way."

Lilt let out a slow breath and dropped to sit on a flat stone at the edge of the clearing. They looked exhausted, their usually fluid expression dulled by conflict.

"I didn't want to keep secrets," they said. "But Irie… she didn't seem afraid. And that made me trust her. Even when I didn't understand."

Morgan crouched in front of them, placing a gentle hand over theirs. "You trusted connection over comprehension," they said. "That's not a failure. But it is a risk."

The ground beneath the arch shifted again. Not violently and not with anger, but with the weight of an unspoken warning.

Morgan stood slowly, threadlight rising around their form in fine, steady strand like light unfolding from within. They looked at all three of them, letting silence stretch just long enough to command stillness.

"I'll go to the Looming Tree," they said. "I'll speak with the Hollow. Tonight. Alone."

Una opened her mouth, likely to protest, but Morgan raised a hand. "No committees. No circle vote. Just me and the thread that started acting out before any of this came to light."

They turned toward Irie. "I believe you didn't mean harm."

To Una. "I believe you're trying to protect us."

To Lilt. "And I believe you still want to hold the story together."

They stepped back, gaze sweeping over the crowd. "But belief isn't enough right now. The Hollow needs an answer. And I think it already has one. It's just waiting for someone to ask the right way."

With that, Morgan turned. They walked the spiral path away from the arch, not with urgency but with deep, measured purpose.

They didn't need the crowd's approval. They needed truth.

And sometimes, that meant walking into the root of a storm without knowing who planted the tree.

# Chapter Ninety-Three: What the Tree Carried Back

The Hollow was quiet as Morgan walked its spiral path.

It wasn't silent or still, but quiet in the way a hearth is quiet after the last log has burned down and the warmth still holds. Quiet in the way the ocean is quiet when it's listening from far beneath the surface. It was the kind of quiet that made you realize you were being heard, even if no one answered yet.

Morgan moved without rush. Their footsteps softened against the moss-streaked stone, the path marked by the faint glow of threadlight that had faded and returned three times already that day. The arches were restless. The stories were shifting.

And the loom—oh, the loom—wasn't just weaving anymore. It was remembering things out of order.

Morgan could feel it. Not panic, not resistance. But a kind of internal tangle forming under the skin of the world. And now the Looming Tree was humming with a frequency that no one else had yet noticed.

It was time to listen.

The Looming Tree stood tall in the center of the Hollow, its roots draped in moss, bark carved with hundreds of tiny glyphs - some etched by hand, others formed over time by wind, water, and will.

Morgan approached it slowly, as they always did. They removed their boots at the edge of the spiral. They untied the thread-gloved wraps around their hands, letting the chill of earth and night settle into their palms.

Then they stepped inside the root-circle and knelt. Not with formality, but with willingness.

"Hello." Their breath formed a faint curl of fog. "I don't have demands. I don't have solutions. I'm not here to fix you."

They placed one hand flat against the roots. The other curled around the knot of unfinished thread they'd pulled from the loom earlier that morning - the one that refused to align. "I just need to know what's waking. And if we've forgotten something that wants to come home."

The tree didn't speak, exactly. But beneath Morgan's palm, a pulse began.

Slow. Steady. Ancient. A rhythm not of heartbeats, but of memory.

Morgan closed their eyes. Let the pulse travel up through their arm, down their spine, into the base of their skull.

And then they saw it. A vision, no, a sequence. Colors, sensations, textures of moments - some their own, some borrowed.

They saw Irie, younger, standing at the far side of the arches, her fingertips brushing a shimmer in the air that didn't come from any Hollow-thread.

They saw Una, years ago, sealing a memory inside her palm, then burying it beneath the spiral.

They saw Lilt—unsure, unformed—dancing on a thread they hadn't yet named, trailing laughter like breadcrumbs behind them.

And then…they saw themself.

Sitting beneath the Looming Tree during their first moon cycle in Alden's Landing, whispering stories into the roots with no magic, no titles, no role. Just hope. Just presence.

The vision shifted again.

Now they saw the arches as they had never seen them: from the inside.

From the root, where the arches weren't stone and thread but living bone, forged from a story older than even the Threadkeepers remembered.

And beneath that, far beneath that, a closed eye.

Sleeping, but restless. Turning slightly, like something that had dreamed too long and was beginning to remember how to wake.

Morgan's eyes flew open. They kept their hand on the root, breathing slowly through the tremble in their chest. "You're not just a gateway," they murmured. "You're a memory loop. And something is circling back."

The tree vibrated.

Not loud, but enough to rattle the unfinished thread in their other hand. It jumped once, twice, and then stilled.

The knot? It had come undone…on its own.

Morgan sat back on their heels, eyes wide in awe. They whispered, "You weren't showing me what's coming. You were showing me what we've forgotten to hold space for."

The Hollow had always bent toward connection. But connection without reflection became fray. And that's what had happened here. The magic Irie had welcomed, the power she didn't know how to name.

It wasn't foreign. It was familiar.

Just not recent. Just not comfortable.

They reached into their satchel and pulled out a single silver pin. It was one they had carried for years and never used. It was meant to anchor threads during threshold rituals, but Morgan had always sensed it was waiting for a bigger story.

They pressed it into the soil beside the root and the threadlight around the Looming Tree flared in a deep indigo pulse.

A knowing. A signal.

The Hollow had accepted the communion.

More than that, it had responded.

Morgan sat in the root circle for several minutes longer, breathing slowly, watching the threadlight settle.

They didn't feel triumphant. They felt humbled. Because the Hollow had never needed to be understood. It needed to be trusted.

And trust, it turned out, wasn't built through clarity. It was built through continuing to show up.

When they stood to leave, the roots didn't hum, and the Looming Tree didn't shimmer. But the unfinished loom-thread in their hand had rewoven itself into a circle.

A thread that had unraveled. And found its own way home.

Morgan whispered, "Thank you."

And the breeze that followed them out of the grove was warm, and quiet, and just barely touched with laughter.

## Chapter Ninety-Four: The Charm That Wouldn't Stop Complimenting Strangers

Cassie had one rule for her new line of enchanted pocket charms:

"No unsolicited poetry, no rhyming prophecies, and absolutely no kissing noises."

Simple enough.

She was aiming for whimsy-adjacent, not full-blown fae foolishness. Something folks could tuck into a coat pocket or satchel for a bit of encouragement during long walks or bad hair days. The kind of charm that would murmur something like "you've got this," or "your eyebrows are doing amazing things today," and then quietly power down until needed again.

She'd even tested the prototype herself. Once on a Tuesday with no major cosmic alignments, under the faint influence of leftover Hearththread and a mild caffeine buzz.

It had gone well. Too well, perhaps. Because by Thursday, the charms had taken on a life of their own.

It began with a quiet hum at the apothecary counter. Cassie had just placed a small copper dish of the finished charms near the register with a hand-lettered sign that read:

*Kind Words for Strange Times – 1 bloomroot each.*

The first buyer, old Mrs. Henders from the Spiral Garden District, tucked hers into her coat pocket, thanked Cassie, and left without incident.

Twenty minutes later, Cassie heard shouting from the street. Except it wasn't shouting. It was gushing.

"Your elbows are majestic!"
"I've never seen such a confidently curved nose!"
"Those boots scream inner peace!"

Cassie stepped outside to find Mrs. Henders blinking rapidly while the charm in her pocket chirped compliments at everyone within a ten-foot radius.

"Make it stop," the woman hissed, as a passing delivery boy received an unsolicited ode to his sock choices.

Cassie attempted a quieting spell. The charm winked at her and shouted, "Even your stern expression is oddly radiant!"

Cassie swore under her breath. "Fantastic. They're sentient and flirty."

By the following afternoon, ten charms had been sold and all ten had amplified. One had developed a taste for complimenting household furniture. Another insisted on rhyming compliments with vaguely threatening undertones:

"Your smile is bright, your step is strong,
I'll follow you all the day long…"

Wren tried to intervene with a sound-based binding spell. It failed.

Baz tried to recalibrate the sigils using grounding salt. It backfired. Now one charm whistled while it praised plants for their "gutsy photosynthesis."

Cassie finally shut the shop early and declared a charm recall. She posted a new sign:

**TEMPORARY CHARM MALFUNCTION. PLEASE RETURN IF YOUR POCKET IS FLIRTING WITH PASSERSBY.**

She poured herself a mug of her strongest cinnamon brew, laced it with a sigh and a shot of honesty tonic, and slumped behind the counter with a groan. "I was aiming for affirming," she muttered to the ceiling. "Not emotionally needy greeting cards with a superiority complex."

Morgan appeared in the doorway just before sunset, back from their communion with the Looming Tree. They stood there quietly for a moment, watching as one of the charms in the dish complimented their shoelaces with suspicious fervor.

Morgan raised a brow. "I leave the Hollow for twelve hours and your magic develops attachment issues?"

Cassie didn't look up. "Don't start. They're multiplying."

Morgan picked one up and it immediately trilled, "Your aura is so well-balanced I could hang curtains on it." They gently set it back down.

Cassie finally laughed, resting her forehead on the counter. "This is what I get for mixing ancestral voice thread with leftover Hearththread. It's like I gave my great-grandmother espresso and a megaphone."

By nightfall, the charms had mellowed slightly. Possibly from exhaustion, or perhaps because Cassie finally managed to rework the binding glyphs to include boundaries.

She left one on the counter, gently whittled down to a single, contained phrase: "You're doing your best. That's enough."

She smiled. Small. Tired. Genuine.

Even Morgan smiled at that one. "Still want to release them to the public?"

Cassie shrugged. "Maybe not as pocket charms."

Morgan tilted their head. "Fridge magnets?"

Cassie grinned. "Affirmation wind chimes that only whisper when you really need it."

Morgan leaned against the counter, the threadlight curling lazily around their wrist. "You always do this," they said.

"What?"

"Make magic feel less like a mystery and more like a warm, slightly unhinged hug."

Cassie raised her mug. "That's the brand."

As the town settled into evening, the charms tucked themselves into quiet slumber, each resting in bowls of moon-soaked salt.

No longer shouting. No longer praising furniture.

Just still. A little wiser.

And so was Cassie.

She made a mental note to rewrite her charm parameters.

No unsolicited poetry.
No flirty rhyming.
And maybe, just maybe, only enchant when fully caffeinated.

# Chapter Ninety-Five: The One That Got Away

Cassie had nearly wrestled the rogue charm situation into compliance. By Monday morning, most of the louder trinkets had been soothed, re-sigil'd, and tucked neatly into jars filled with lavender-dampened rice. A few still twitched when someone walked past, muttering half-hearted affirmations through clenched glyphs. "You radiate accessible wisdom!" one declared at Baz before collapsing into sleep again. For the most part, though, the chaos had been tamed.

She felt good about herself. Smug, even. Which was, naturally, the exact moment it unraveled.

"I'm missing one," she muttered, staring at her hand-labeled ledger titled *Cassie's Enchanted Charm Catastrophe (Do Not Laugh)*. She flipped a page and re-counted: thirteen made, twelve returned.

She frowned. Then frowned harder. "That's one too many loose compliments for a town this emotionally unprepared."

She re-traced her sales log, which was roughly half-ink, half coffee ring stains and featured a suspicious number of question marks. Apparently, someone had taken a charm and not logged it, not paid, and certainly not brought it back once the enchantments had gone haywire.

The worst part? She had no idea who had it.

And with a charm like this one (charged with unstable ancestral magic and a tendency to improvise), it wasn't just lost. It was out there. Doing things.

The first clue came from Mrs. Halbrook, who stormed into Stirred & Spellbound in a flurry of lace and righteous indignation. "Your charm made my cat cry," she announced.

Cassie blinked. "I'm sorry?"

Mrs. Halbrook thumped a tote bag on the counter. "It snuck into my greenhouse and started praising the azaleas for their 'spiritual resilience.' Next thing I know, my calico is weeping under the begonias and refusing to come down."

Cassie opened her mouth, closed it, and nodded solemnly. "I'll add emotional manipulation of pets to the disclaimer."

The second clue was harder to ignore.

Wes showed up around midday, holding an odd bouquet. "This was on my doorstep," he said, thrusting the arrangement forward.

Cassie examined it. Six sprigs of yarrow, two pinecones, a twist of cinnamon bark, and a single daffodil wrapped in what looked like... one of her charm tags.

"Oh no."

The handwriting was unmistakably hers. But the message?

*"Your grief hums in beautiful harmony. I would hug your shadow."*

Cassie stared at it. Then at Wes. Then at the bouquet again. "I didn't write that," she said.

"I figured," Wes replied. "But whatever's out there thinks it knows me."

Cassie spent the rest of the day hunting. She checked every shelf in her shop, every back pocket of every forgotten satchel, the hollow nook behind her herb grinder, and even the little crawlspace under the garden bench where magical misfires sometimes liked to hide.

Nothing. It was officially missing.

She drafted a town-wide notice.

*MISSING: One enchanted charm.*
*Appearance: Probably small. Definitely loud.*
*Behavior: Excessively affirming, emotionally perceptive, prone to*
*interpretive poetry.*
*If found, do NOT offer it tea. It thrives on attention. Please return to*
*Cassie. Gently.*

She posted it on the community board, tucked a few copies in tea shops, and gave one to Rhett, who was already compiling a spreadsheet titled *Wayward Magic Incidents, Ongoing and Avoidable.*

By twilight, the trail had gone cold.

Cassie sat on the edge of the Spiral Bell's stone base, legs stretched in front of her, one hand pressed to her temple, the other wrapped around a lukewarm mug of "Emergency Fix-It Tea" (a calming blend she'd renamed three times in the past week).

Morgan found her there. "I take it the rogue charm has not returned itself out of remorse?"

Cassie looked up. "It left a bouquet. It made a cat cry. It may be attempting a one-charm performance art piece about emotional intimacy."

Morgan didn't laugh. Not immediately.

"Let's find the little menace."

That night, they searched together.

Quiet streets. Back alleys. The wild herb patch near the outer arches where Cassie once swore a moon-blessed dandelion winked at her.

They followed faint glimmers of energy, places where the charm had clearly been. At the edge of the riverbank, they found words carved into the dirt:

*"Everyone leaves eventually,*
*but you -*
*you stayed.*
*Gold star."*

Cassie sighed, soft and tired. "It's affirming lonely people now."

Morgan tilted their head. "Maybe it's not broken."

Cassie didn't answer. She just looked toward the dark tree line, where the charm's glow was faintest.

They never found it that night. But the next morning, Cassie woke to a note on her windowsill.

*Dear Cassie,*
*I went where the ache was.*
*They needed me more than you did.*
*Thank you for making me messy.*
*— C.*

Cassie read it twice.

Then three more times.

She didn't cry, but she did brew a fresh cup of her strongest coffee, sip it slowly on the back step, and murmur to no one in particular,

"Well. I suppose not everything we make belongs to us forever."

## Chapter Ninety-Six: The Charm Found Her Anyway

Tamsin Lowell wasn't the kind of person who got swept up in magical mishaps. She lived at the farthest edge of Alden's Landing, in the small stone cottage with the mossy fence that even the Hollow seemed to politely avoid. It wasn't that she disliked magic. She just preferred it in measured doses, pressed between the pages of field guides or laced subtly in tea blends, not galloping through the village square shouting compliments at strangers.

So, when the charm arrived wrapped in a twist of daffodils and placed silently on her garden gate, her first instinct was to turn around, go back inside, and pretend she hadn't seen it.

She very nearly did. But something about the way it waited stopped her.

It wasn't glowing. It wasn't humming. It simply… was. Patient. Unassuming. And, somehow, a little sad.

She took it inside and set it on the windowsill above the sink. Tamsin ignored it for a full two days.

It didn't move. Didn't speak. Didn't sing about her cheekbones or her posture or the robust emotional maturity of her spice rack.

She thought it might be broken and that made her feel relieved. Mostly.

On the third morning, she poured water into the kettle, turned around, and jumped.

The charm was glowing faintly. Just enough to cast a pale threadlight onto the countertop.

She narrowed her eyes at it. "If you start rhyming at me, I swear to the Spiral I will drop you in the compost."

The charm stayed quiet. But then, in a soft, almost uncertain voice, it whispered:

"You've been alone so long, you forgot it wasn't a requirement."

Tamsin froze. Her hands tightened on the mug she hadn't realized she was holding. "…excuse me?"

The charm gave off a gentle pulse of light.

"You always say you're fine. But you never ask if you want to be."

She stared at it for a long time and then walked away.

That night, she dreamt of her mother's handwriting. Of paper lanterns floating across a river. Of laughter she hadn't heard in years.

When she woke, the charm was tucked beneath her pillow.

She didn't remember putting it there.

By the end of the week, she'd stopped trying to rationalize it.

The charm didn't follow her, exactly. It just… showed up. When she was pruning the lavender. When she forgot to eat lunch. When she hesitated at the threshold of the village square and told herself, not for the first time, that no one would notice if she didn't attend the market festival this year.

It never pressured her. Never chattered. Just whispered small, impossible things.

"You could speak and still be safe."
"You don't have to earn your belonging."
"You remember more joy than you allow yourself to admit."

Each time, the words unraveled something she hadn't realized she was holding tight.

On the eighth day, Tamsin stood in front of her mirror, brushing her hair, and found herself saying aloud: "…what would happen if I went?"

The charm that was perched quietly in a jar of calendula on her windowsill offered no answer. Just a faint warmth. As if to say: Try it and see.

She arrived late to the town gathering wearing a wide-brimmed hat and carrying her own tea, as she always did.

She stayed on the edges, but people saw her.

Baz gave her a nod. Wren offered a smile. Cassie was busy wrangling a bouquet of semi-enchanted spoons but flashed a thumbs up.

And Morgan?

Morgan met her eyes across the square, held her gaze, and dipped their head. Not in greeting, but in acknowledgment. As if to say: You were always welcome. We just didn't know how to wait long enough.

That night, Tamsin placed the charm back on the windowsill. "I suppose you can stay," she said softly.

The charm glowed once. Then whispered: "You let me in. That was the magic."

## Chapter Ninety-Seven: The Thread You Let Go

Cassie hadn't expected the charm to write back.

Especially not in so many words and not in literal script. But the note that had appeared on her windowsill days ago, folded just so, flecked with daffodil pollen and carrying her own signature twine, was unmistakably from the one that got away.

And it had said everything she didn't know she'd been hoping to hear.

*I went where the ache was.*
*They needed me more than you did.*
*Thank you for making me messy.*

She read it every morning now. Not in any ritualistic sense. She just… liked seeing it. The paper had begun to curl slightly at the edges. The ink shimmered faintly with the last of its attunement glow. But it was the message itself that lingered. Not in the way memory does, but in the way intention leaves a thumbprint.

It had become part of her mornings. Like coffee. Like breath.

Like the realization that not all magic is made to stay.

That afternoon, Cassie was in the workshop at the back of Stirred & Spellbound, surrounded by test vials, open journals, a plate of crumbling shortbread, and a semi-retired charm that had recently decided to hum Gregorian harmonies anytime someone mentioned their feelings.

She'd muted it with a cheesecloth and a stern glance.

Now, she sat at the center of it all, spoon stirring her tea with the steady rhythm of someone pretending they weren't processing something.

Wren had come and gone.

Morgan had offered a nod and a knowing smile earlier that day.

Even Baz had peeked in, dropped off a small packet of fennel seeds, and left with no questions.

And still, the charm's absence echoed louder than the charms that remained.

Cassie reached for her ledger. Not the one marked "Charm Catastrophe," though that one remained active and growing. This one was older, hand-bound in marbled paper with a button clasp and a smell like warm cedar and ink.

Inside: pages dedicated to enchantments that never quite became product lines.

Some scribbled half-spells. Some were doodles of concepts that made her laugh. Some, well, some were simply too tender to share.

She turned to a blank page, uncapped her pen, and paused.

Then, carefully, she wrote at the top:

*Magic that leaves you better than it found you.*

She didn't have a plan for this one. Didn't know if it would become anything other than a single page, or a whispered idea that settled between shelves. But it felt good to name it.

To admit that some things aren't meant to be sold. Some are just meant to find their way into someone's life and make it a little easier to be here.

That charm had done it. Not because Cassie had designed it to, but because it had grown into itself.

And maybe that was the real magic.

Unsupervised becoming.

A knock on the back door startled her. She opened it to find a small bundle wrapped in waxed cloth and tied with a ribbon the color of weathered bone. No note this time. Just a quiet presence.

Inside: a pressed daffodil. A sprig of lavender. And a hand-drawn sigil in pale green chalk on a smooth river stone.

Cassie ran her fingers over it and smiled. The sigil was hers. But the variation wasn't.

Someone had learned it. Modified it. Made it their own.

She laughed quietly.

The sound of being seen without needing to be named.

Later that night, she added one more line to the journal.

Below the heading, in smaller, messier script:

*Letting go doesn't end the thread.*
*It just stops you from holding both ends.*

She closed the book gently and let the quiet settle around her.

## Chapter Ninety-Eight: The Hollow Remembers Differently

Morgan was the first to notice the rhythm was off.

It wasn't obvious. The threads still moved, the roots still pulsed in their quiet, knowing way, and the looms responded to intention as they always had. But something beneath all of that had shifted.

At first, they thought it was fatigue. They'd been holding too much lately. Mediating between Irie and Una, reconciling arcane inconsistencies in the Threadkeeper archives, and watching Cassie's charming misfires unfold with equal parts delight and apprehension was tiring.

But this wasn't exhaustion.

It was echo.

The Hollow hummed, yes, as usual. But the hum had a signature, a familiar curve that Morgan could trace with their breath alone. Lately, though, that signature had... altered. The notes weren't wrong, exactly. Just remembered differently. A subtle stutter in the resonance. A pause where there had never been one. Like someone trying to recall a song from childhood but adding a new harmony they didn't know they knew.

Morgan stood in the central circle, barefoot, eyes closed, palms facing down.

They listened. They had always listened.

But today, the Hollow was speaking back in a voice that did not come from the branches or the stones or even the ancient loom embedded in the Looming Tree's bark.

It came from underneath.

They moved slowly through the spiraled grove, fingers brushing old knots in the tree roots, glyphs worn nearly smooth with time. The air felt denser today. Not heavy, just charged and expectant.

When they reached the western quadrant where the moss grew thicker and the ground always ran slightly warm, they paused. It wasn't a place most people lingered. Not cursed, not dangerous, just… forgotten. A quiet fold in the land.

Morgan knelt. The moment their palm touched the soil, everything stopped.

The birds.
The threadlight.
Even the distant pull of the arches.

For a breathless second, the world exhaled.

And beneath their skin, something responded.

A soundless, vibrational memory.
Not language.
Not imagery.

Texture.

Like the Hollow was remembering a version of itself that did not include them.

Morgan pulled their hand back slowly, heart beating faster than they liked. "Okay," they whispered. "So… you're not broken. You're remembering. But not like before."

They stood, brushing the earth from their knees.

This wasn't a thread from the past. It was a counter-thread—one that ran beneath everything they'd built, everything the Hollow had supported. It wasn't antagonistic. It didn't hum with challenge or defense.

But it was distinct.

Older, maybe. Or newer than time allowed.

Whatever it was, it didn't belong to the traditional pattern language. It didn't respond to root glyphs, or elemental invocations, or even ancestral sigils.

It resonated like a pre-story.

Morgan returned to the Looming Tree by nightfall. The looms were quiet. The air cool. The lanterns glowed with no assistance.

They didn't touch anything. Just walked in slow circles, tracing paths worn by those who had passed through before them - Cassie, Gabe, Lilt, so many unnamed.

But tonight, none of those echoes spoke.

Only the new one.

Subterranean. Subtle. Sure. And slowly rising.

That night, Morgan lit a single threadcandle and wrote one line in their private ledger:

*"The Hollow remembers differently when it's about to become something more."*

They didn't know what would follow, only that they needed to listen deeper than ever.

And not just to what they hoped to hear.

## Chapter Ninety-Nine: The Frequency Beneath the Thread

Morgan hadn't worked with crystals in years. Not because they didn't respect them. Quite the opposite. But in the Hollow, most people preferred the feel of things that grew, pulsed, twisted – the kind of magic you could coax with breath and intention and hands stained from roots and dye.

Crystals had always felt a little too… still. A little too tidy. Their vibration didn't sing; it waited.

But this new resonance with the humming beneath the arches and the loam, the one even the Looming Tree refused to shape, it wasn't responding to thread or story or song. Which meant it might just be waiting for something older…slower. More mineral than myth.

They began with the crystal jars in the southern alcove. They were dusty from disuse, labeled in Cassie's suspiciously dramatic calligraphy. "DO NOT STARE INTO THE LABRADORITE AFTER MIDNIGHT," one said. Another warned: "Moonstone is not a mirror, despite her confidence."

Morgan smiled as they sorted and then selected four:

- Smoky quartz, for grounding in the presence of instability.
- Lepidolite, for easing transition between inner and outer knowing.
- Selenite, to act as conduit.
- And, finally, blue kyanite. The harmonizer of unspoken language, often used for resonance reading in deep ley intersections.

They wrapped them in threadcloth, slipped them into the pockets of their vest, and walked into the forest alone.

The Hollow didn't resist, but it watched. Morgan could feel it in the way the wind folded itself around their ankles. In the hush of the undergrowth. In the rootlight that blinked slowly, like a cautious eye opening in sleep.

They found the grove again, the warm earth pocket where the resonance had first spoken. It was unchanged. Except now, the moss was… receding.

Just slightly. Revealing a patch of soil the color of cooled embers.

Morgan knelt and placed the smoky quartz first. Its surface fogged immediately, but then again, no surprise, and then it shimmered. Not glowing. Not reacting to them. Reacting to something else.

They laid the lepidolite next and the air temperature dropped.

The kyanite hummed softly before it even touched the ground.

And the selenite?

It refused to sit still.

It vibrated, then slid of its own accord into a shallow groove Morgan hadn't seen beneath the soil. A line, a vein.

They cleared the dirt gently with their hands and what they uncovered was unmistakable.

It wasn't root, it was rock.

It was a smooth, vein-like pathway running beneath the grove, faintly pulsing with light that didn't match any known color language. Something between violet and silver, between longing and beginning.

Morgan touched it.

Their breath caught.

It wasn't just magic. It was a frequency.

Images swelled in front of her. They weren't visions, or memories, but impressions:

People walking across thresholds that hadn't yet formed.
Names being chosen not for the past, but for possibility.
A shape - round, fluid, rooted - not a tower, not a gate, not a loom.

A seed.

Morgan pulled back, heart racing. This wasn't a memory resurfacing. It was a future forming.

Not foretold. Not channeled.

Just… responding.

To them.
To the Threadfound.
To Cassie and her offerings.
To every act of brave becoming that had rippled outward through the Hollow and into the world.

This frequency wasn't from something buried. It was from something germinating. The crystals around them hummed in harmony, softly and surely.

Morgan stood slowly, palms dusty, eyes wide. They whispered to the air, to the roots, to whatever was listening now:

"You're not a memory.
You're a calling."

And the Hollow, just for a breath, sang back.

# Chapter One Hundred: What Grows Beneath Us

Morgan didn't summon the Coven with urgency, only clarity.

They'd long since learned the difference between alarm and invitation, between reacting and responding. So, they sent word the usual way: folded notes tucked under the bellroot vines, a faint glimmer in the Hollow's rootlight at twilight, and a single phrase etched into the surface of the Spiral Bell itself:

*Come when you can hear the hum.*

By the time the sun dipped behind the western tree line, they'd gathered.

Cassie arrived first, still dusted with flour and lavender pollen, mug in one hand, crooked grin in place. Baz came not far behind her, the sleeves of his shirt still rolled and the faint scent of peat and thyme clinging to his collar. Wren followed, barefoot and already scribbling impressions in the air with a charmed fingertip that left trailing glyphs behind like mist.

Rhett arrived with the subtle dread of someone who'd accidentally agreed to participate in magic while half-asleep.

Morgan met them in the grove, where the moss had receded to reveal the vein of silvery-violet light beneath the soil. The crystals that still humming softly from the night before had been placed in a careful ring around the grove's edge.

No one spoke at first. Not because they didn't have questions. Because they could feel it.

That hum. That strange, almost tender resonance pulsing up from the ground, not through the threadlines they knew, but from something deeper.

Something that didn't echo memory or spell.

Something emerging.

Morgan cleared their throat. "I don't know what this is," they said plainly. "Only that it didn't come from the past." They picked up the kyanite crystal. It vibrated subtly against their palm.

"I tried sigils. I tried thread. I tried silence." A faint smile. "But it was the crystals that answered. Not as tools, but as translators."

Cassie tilted her head. "Translators for what?"

Morgan gestured toward the ground. "Something waking. Something that feels more like a frequency than a spell. It's not asking to be shaped. It's... becoming."

Baz crouched beside the crystal circle, hand hovering over the line where the moss had peeled back. "It's not just emergence," he murmured. "It's rooted emergence. Like it's grown from us. But not for us."

Wren nodded, eyes far away. "It's the Hollow responding. Not repeating. Not remembering. Responding."

Cassie sipped her coffee and gave a theatrical sigh. "So, what you're saying is that in our quest to weave together forgotten memories, rethread interdimensional grief, and birth a town-sized greenhouse full of emotionally intelligent looms, we accidentally inspired the land to... grow a feeling."

Morgan tilted their head. "More like... grow a starting point."

Cassie pointed with her mug. "Still on brand."

They stood together in the grove as the sky deepened to dusk, the crystals glowing faintly in resonance.

No one tried to catalog the energy.
No one tried to contain it.
They just listened.

Because this wasn't the kind of magic that came with instructions, it came with presence.

Finally, Morgan looked around the circle. "I think we're standing in the middle of a threshold," they said. "Not one we cross, but one that grows through us."

Wren murmured, "So the question is… are we willing to let it?"

There was no formal answer.

Just nods.
Stillness.
Shared breath.

And the certainty that whatever was coming next, they wouldn't meet it alone.

# Chapter One Hundred One: The First Bloom

It began with a shimmer. Not dramatic. Not theatrical. Just a shimmer across the soil near the Looming Tree like heat rising from stone, or breath fogging glass in a room that's just been made quiet.

Morgan was the first to notice. They were finishing a rootwork inscription along the perimeter of the resonance grove, checking the angles of the grounding crystals, when their hand passed over a stretch of moss that wasn't moss anymore.

It looked the same. But it pulsed. Not visibly, not in any way someone else might have caught, but under their fingers, the rhythm was unmistakable.

A heartbeat - not human. Not Hollow.

But present.

They knelt, brushing away a thin veil of lichen to reveal something new underneath. It wasn't plant, not entirely. But it had grown.

Where there had only been soil and softened root, something now pressed upward. A kind of bloom, half-unfurled, made of something between bark and petal. Its surface shimmered with threadlight that wasn't pulled from any known loom. The shape was unfamiliar. It was spiraling inward, not outward, and glowing with a soft iridescence that shifted color when you looked too long.

Morgan didn't speak. They simply witnessed.

And the bloom, which is what they decided to call it, responded to their stillness with a faint sigh, like air adjusting to space it hadn't occupied in years.

The next morning, the bloom was taller.

Cassie was the one who found it then, arriving early with her travel mug and a stubborn attempt to re-stabilize a charm that had started humming lullabies at bread.

She paused mid-step. Then tilted her head, squinting. "…Did the ground grow a fossilized tulip?"

Morgan, already nearby, cross-legged and deeply focused on a vibrating quartz grid, looked up. "It's a resonance bloom."

Cassie nodded slowly. "Sure. Of course it is. And let me guess. This one hums emotionally complex haikus and demands water blessed during a waxing crescent?"

Morgan grinned. "No. It hums nothing. It just… is."

Cassie crouched beside it, careful not to disturb the crystals. The bloom shifted faintly, responding to her nearness. Not completely opening but tilting. "Okay, that's unsettling," she muttered. "It likes me."

Morgan's grin widened. "It recognizes you."

By midweek, the bloom had grown again. More of them had appeared, always one at a time and never near paths or stones. Always slightly off-center. Always spiraling inward.

Wren called them "listening gardens."

Baz simply stood with his hand resting gently on one, whispering, "It's not a plant. It's an arrival."

No one touched them. Not with magic or with tools.

It became understood that these were not to be harvested.

They were not answers. They were beginnings.

The townsfolk took notice. First with curiosity, then with wonder. And then slowly, cautiously, with reverence. Not because they were told to, because the blooms never behaved the same way twice.

One pulsed when a grieving widower passed by, his silence breaking just long enough to hum.

One curled its spiral inward when a child tried to pick it, only to uncurl moments later with a low, forgiving light.

One, near the Spiral Bell, began glowing only at dawn.

They weren't just reacting.

They were responding.

And Morgan, watching from the Hollow's edge, felt a shift inside themselves they couldn't name yet. Not a change in power.

A deepening of presence.

That evening, Morgan sat near the first bloom, their hands resting on their knees, eyes half-closed. "You're not ours," they whispered. "But we're part of you now, aren't we?"

The bloom shimmered.

Not an answer.

A continuation.

# Chapter One Hundred Two: Things That Listen Back

At first, the townsfolk kept their distance. They tiptoed around the blooms as one might avoid an unexpected animal curled in the road, aware and uncertain. But then the listening began. It did not come from the blooms themselves, but from the people.

It started with the baker. Nara Bell was known for her sourdough loaves, which had a way of softening moods even on the hardest days. Yet she had not spoken to her brother in almost three years, and the silence between them had hardened like a crust left too long in the oven.

One morning, carrying a basket of rye, she passed the first bloom with her jaw set tight. The bloom tilted toward her. It did not flare or glow. It only turned, quiet and steady, as if acknowledging what she carried inside.

That evening, Nara sat down with ink and paper. She did not weave a charm into the words or call on any enchantment. She simply wrote. In the morning, she slipped the letter into the post box without a word to anyone. Days later, when she passed the bloom again, she set a small piece of bread on the moss at its base. The bloom bent slightly in return, its curve full of warmth, as though it understood the offering and received it with thanks.

Children began sitting near the blooms during their lesson breaks, whispering secrets they never shared with friends.

Older residents stopped to rest their hands on the mossy ground, not to siphon magic but to feel the hum that was neither sound nor silence.

Some brought offerings in tiny forms. A note. A button. A pressed flower. A joke scribbled in a child's hand.

One man laid down a photograph and walked away with tears he never explained. No one mocked him. By then everyone had seen it.

The blooms responded. Not dramatically, but in a way that was unique to each person, as if they were reading what had not been said and choosing whether to reflect it or to hold it quietly, like a secret placed gently in safe hands.

And then there was Shaw.

He did not approach a bloom for seven days. It was not fear that held him back, but principle. "I have worked with memory sigils since before half this town could spell threadkeeping," he muttered when asked. "I do not need moss with opinions."

Still, he watched them closely. He took notes when he thought no one noticed. He measured the spirals and tracked the shifts in hue. He observed how they responded to silence compared to sound.

He even, though he would not admit it, dropped a small, polished stone near one of them just to see what it would do. It did not move until he walked away. Then it glowed briefly.

On the eighth day, Shaw stood near the Looming Tree with papers in hand. He was intent on presenting his latest theory that the blooms were a misfired spell loop from the Loom's emotional memory core.

Cassie stood nearby with crossed arms and raised eyebrows. "Just say you are curious," she said.

"I am skeptical," Shaw replied stiffly. "Same hat, different feather." Before he could continue a child tripped while passing and tumbled headfirst into the moss. Shaw, of all people, caught them instinctively.

The child blinked up at him. "Oh. Thanks." The bloom beside them shimmered. It was not at the child but at Shaw. A soft ripple of faint silver and blue pulsed once and then breathed out.

A low warmth settled over him. Shaw did not move and did not speak. His papers slipped from his hand and landed on the moss. The

275

bloom turned toward the fallen notes. For the first time in weeks, Shaw laughed. The sound was short, sharp, but real. "Alright," he murmured. "Alright, you have my attention."

That evening Shaw passed Morgan outside the Hollow. He did not stop. Yet as he walked by, he said, "They are not remembering. They are noticing."

Morgan smiled. "So are we."

## Chapter One Hundred Three: Where No One Was Listening

The next bloom didn't grow near the Looming Tree. It didn't sprout from the resonance grove or spiral out beneath the arches. It didn't hum its way into being under someone's watchful eye.

It bloomed in the place no one had touched in months.

The old post office.

It had been closed since last autumn, ever since the roof began to sag and the town's delivery magic moved to the Hollow's shared archive room. Everyone assumed someone would eventually renovate it into an art space or a meditation nook or yet another tea annex.

But nothing happened. The windows dusted over. The charms on the door faded. And the building... waited.

Until one morning, when Maribelle from the bakery passed by and felt something tug at her apron hem. She turned and nothing was there at first, but when she saw the faintest glow through the cracked window.

It took three hours and a pair of very determined cats to confirm it.

Inside the old post office, nestled on the warped floorboards beneath a rusted sorting table, a bloom had begun to unfurl.

It was smaller than the others.

Delicate, dusky violet and coated in a shimmer of golden-gray dust like moonlight pressed into memory.

No one had planted anything there. No one had marked it with runes or threadlight.

But there it was. Spiraled inward. Humming soft.

And listening.

By nightfall, word had spread.

Morgan came first.
Then Baz.
Then Rhett.
Then, quietly, a cluster of townsfolk who hadn't set foot in the building in years.

They didn't enter at first.

They just stood at the open threshold, peering in through the cracked wood and filtered light, unsure of how to engage with something that had grown where neglect had settled.

Finally, Cassie stepped forward, boots creaking softly against forgotten floorboards, and sat cross-legged on the ground beside the bloom.

It didn't glow brighter. But the air grew warmer.

And somewhere behind her, someone exhaled a breath they didn't know they were holding.

"That space," Morgan whispered, "was once full of waiting."

Letters.
News.
Goodbyes.
Unspoken things that never arrived.

"And now," Baz murmured, "it holds a bloom."

They took turns entering, just to bear witness.

By the next morning, a small bench had been placed just inside the doorway.

Plain, no charm or plaque.

Just a place to sit. A place to listen.

No one could say why the bloom had appeared there.

Some said it was grief, finally given form. Others thought it was forgotten connection rethreading itself. Cassie said the bloom had good taste in dramatic metaphor.

But Morgan?

Morgan believed something simpler. "It appeared where no one was listening.
Until someone did."

## Chapter One Hundred Four: What She Left Unsent

The old post office had always made Maren uneasy. Not afraid, just… guilty.

It had nothing to do with the creaky floorboards or the charm-burnt walls or the faint scent of old lavender wax. It was what she had left there.

A letter. Folded once. Never sealed. Never sent.

She had written it five years ago, on a wind-heavy afternoon after too many days of silence. It had been to her sister. The one who'd left Alden's Landing with the storm and hadn't come back since.

They hadn't spoken since the Hollow first opened its doors.

That letter had been full of things she hadn't had the courage to say in person: apologies laced with vinegar, gratitude tangled in resentment, love that sounded like grief.

Maren had placed the envelope, unsigned and slightly wrinkled, on the post office counter.

And then she'd walked out.

She told herself she'd come back for it, but she never had.

So, when the bloom appeared under the sorting table, Maren knew. She didn't know how or why, but she just knew it was for her.

She waited until evening when the curious had come and gone, when the doorway had cleared and the bench was empty, and when the bloom's glow had quieted to a pulse so soft it barely showed through the floorboards. Then she stepped inside.

The air held dust and old promises.

She knelt in the same place where she had once stood, letter in hand, heart half-open. She didn't speak, but her hands trembled in her lap and the bloom turned. Just slightly. Just enough.

It didn't pulse. It didn't sing.

It listened.

For a long time, Maren sat in that silence. Then, carefully, she reached into her coat pocket and pulled out the letter. Still folded. Still unsigned. The paper soft with age.

She opened it and read the words. They were thinner than she remembered. Less sharp.

She smiled, small and weary. And then she did something she hadn't let herself do in five years.

She whispered, "I forgive you."

The bloom shimmered, not brightly, but deeply, as if the resonance itself had exhaled.

And for the first time in a long time, so did Maren.

She didn't burn the letter.
Didn't bury it.
Didn't send it.

She simply tucked it into the bloom's shadow and walked away.

Empty-handed and somehow more whole.

## Chapter One Hundred Five: Beneath the Floorboards

It started with a flicker beneath the floorboards. Not a glow. Not at first. Just a subtle warmth that rose through the planks of the old supply cottage tucked behind the greenhouse. It was the kind of warmth that didn't announce itself, but rather seeped in slowly, like the first touch of spring in bones that had grown used to cold.

The cottage itself had never asked for attention. It had always been a place of function rather than charm. Shelves sagged beneath the weight of half-used mulch sacks, rusted trowels, and long-forgotten bundles of dried herbs. Mismatched crates leaned against the walls, most of them labeled in Cassie's unmistakable script from one of her more theatrical days.

One crate bore the word "*Wyrmward*" in bold black ink. Another, "*Petal Justice*," which had never actually been explained. The one in the far corner simply read "*Not for You*," and no one had ever dared ask who that warning was meant for.

No one went there seeking stillness. No one lingered in the doorway hoping for inspiration or a moment of magical clarity. They went there to work, to rummage, to sigh over missing gloves and mismatched watering charms.

Perhaps that was why the bloom chose it.

Magic, after all, did not always settle in sacred groves or beneath full moons. Sometimes it grew where no one was looking, where no one had thought to guard their hearts too carefully. Sometimes, it bloomed in the forgotten corners. And when it did, it was quieter for it.

Wes was the first to feel it. He hadn't gone there for any reason other than to find the spade with the worn leather grip—the one that was slightly enchanted and warmed in his hand whenever a storm approached. He liked that spade. It didn't ask questions. It just knew what to do.

The moment he stepped over the threshold, something shifted in the air.

Not cold. Not menacing.

Simply aware.

It was the kind of feeling that stole into a room where someone had recently cried but had already wiped their face and tidied the cushions. The sorrow was gone, technically. But its impression lingered, settled deep in the walls.

Wes paused. He wasn't someone easily startled by energy. He'd spent enough time in Alden's Landing to understand that not all magic came with fireworks. But this was different. This was subtle.

He took a few steps farther in, slow and deliberate, eyes scanning the room. The afternoon sun slanted through a dusty windowpane, casting golden rectangles across the wooden floor. Dust motes danced lazily in the beams of light. The scent of cedar and dried thyme lingered, mingled with the faint metallic tang of aged spell-ink and worn copper tools.

Underneath all of that, something pulsed.

Not sound.

Resonance.

Low. Soft. Patient.

He followed it to the back corner of the cottage, where the floor dipped slightly. It was the same uneven patch everyone complained about, but no one had fixed. Near the wall, just past the crate labeled "*Unapologetically Unsorted*," the floorboards were warped with time and memory.

Wes crouched, placing his palm flat against the grain. It was warm. Not just sun-warmed wood. This heat felt different. It had a pulse. A quiet presence.

He leaned closer and then, just at the edge of one plank, he saw it. A soft violet shimmer glimmered faintly through a hairline crack.

He inhaled through his nose, slowly.

No panic. No summons.

He didn't call for Cassie. Or Baz. Or Morgan.

He simply reached for the old trowel propped against the wall and began to lift.

The board came up with little resistance. Too little, almost. As if it had been waiting to be moved. Beneath it, a hollow pocket had been carved into the earth, dry and carefully lined with threadbare cloth. The fabric looked as though it had once been used to wrap something for safekeeping, though time had frayed its edges and dulled its weave.

At the center, nestled like a secret too sacred for light:

A bloom.

Small. Hesitant.

Its petals curled inward, not tightly, but like a person pulling a shawl closer rather than reaching out. Its spiral was compact and full of depth. Color coiled from the base in indigo shades that darkened near the edges, streaked with fine, almost imperceptible veins of bronze.

It did not glow in the way other blooms had. There was no burst of radiant light or magical exclamation. Instead, the bloom murmured. It offered a kind of light that stayed close to the surface, like something it might share only if you stayed quiet long enough to listen.

Wes sat down cross-legged, elbows resting loosely on his knees.

He did not reach inside the cavity. He did not speak. He just sat there, hands resting in his lap, heart slowing to match the rhythm of whatever this was.

Something about the bloom felt different. Not threatening. Not even resistant. Just layered.

This was not a bloom to be studied or cataloged. It was not here to be used or understood.

It was here to keep company.

There was history here. Not his. But someone's.

Wes could feel it pressing at the air, not like weight, but like memory. Like the echo of footsteps on a staircase after the person has long since disappeared. This space had been used. Not for storage. Not for potions. Not for crafting.

Someone had once hidden here.

Not metaphorically. Literally.

And the bloom had grown in that stillness.

Not to reveal it. Not to expose it.

To witness it.

By the time Morgan arrived, drawn not by urgency but by the gentle call of something remembered, they found Wes still sitting in the same spot. His face was calm. His hands open.

Morgan stepped quietly inside, eyes flicking from Wes to the lifted floorboard.

They crossed the room and lowered themselves to the ground beside him. They didn't speak for a long moment. Only breathed with the room. Then Morgan said softly, "This one is holding."

Wes nodded. "It's different."

"Yes," Morgan agreed. "This one remembers what it meant to be safe. Once. Just once. And that was enough."

"It's not trying to tell us anything," Wes added. "It's just… being."

Morgan looked at him, the corners of their mouth lifting slightly. "Sometimes that's all a spell ever needed to be."

Later, Cassie would arrive. She would pause in the doorway for a heartbeat longer than usual. Then she would walk across the room, setting down a fresh mug of Hearththread for Wes and placing a honey-sage shortbread on the edge of the nearest crate, her only commentary a quiet, approving hum.

She would not ask what the bloom meant. She would not try to name it. She would simply sit beside them, palms resting on her thighs, gaze soft. Because not every bloom needed to mark a transformation. Not every hidden space needed to be cracked open for insight. Some were meant to hold.

To keep company with the forgotten.

To say, I see you, even if no one else ever did.

And in that moment, under the floor of a cluttered old supply shed behind a greenhouse, that was enough.

# Chapter One Hundred Six: The Hollow That Held Her

She had no name left when she arrived in Alden's Landing. Not the kind that clung to parchment or lived in family lines. Not the kind that passed easily from one mouth to another, catching in the throat like a song half-remembered. Whatever name she had once carried had long since been frayed by time.

Spoken once, years ago, in a season of life she no longer visited, it had become more silence than syllable. Not forgotten entirely, but too fragile to call out without unraveling.

What she carried instead was a thin satchel made of worn canvas, a bent spoon with a handle curved like a question mark, and the faint hum of something she had once called hope. It had dulled, yes, but it still lived somewhere in the hollow behind her ribs.

She did not mean to find the town. Or maybe she did. Perhaps the magic of Alden's Landing worked that way. Perhaps intention sometimes disguised itself as misdirection, letting people believe they were lost when in truth they were only being guided a quieter way.

Whatever the reason, when she stepped through the invisible edge of the town's border, Alden's Landing did not ask questions. It did not demand a name. It did not stop her to sort out her pieces or demand proof of belonging. Instead, it opened gently, like a gate that had not creaked in years and was grateful for the movement. The town let her pass through.

And then it let her stay.

She did not try to take up space. She moved lightly through the streets, careful not to wear down her welcome. She spoke little, offering only nods and soft thanks when kindness was shown. The townsfolk, for their part, offered distance—but not from coldness. It was a warmth that knew the weight of quiet. They had seen others arrive with eyes full of stories too heavy to tell. People who moved like they were borrowing time. Threadbare in spirit. Carrying too much memory in too small a body.

She worked during the early hours, often before the sky finished yawning into morning. The greenhouse saw her first. She would slip in before the glass caught the sun, pulling weeds, misting herbs, humming to the soil in tones no one else quite recognized.

Later, she could be found sweeping porches before shopkeepers lifted their shutters. She mended things without being asked. Buttons missing their matches. Hems with fraying thread. Habits that no longer held and needed a softer hand to guide them.

When the sky darkened too early and the wind turned the corners of the town into long, uncertain alleys, she would return to the supply cottage behind the greenhouse.

To the floor. To the hollow beneath it.

It had not been built for refuge. It was a flaw in the foundation, a dip in the earth that warped the boards. But time and repetition had shaped it into something else. A resting place. A forgetting place. A breathing space.

There was a gap near the back wall, soft with wear, just wide enough to slide through without splinters. She would curl there, folded in on herself, and let the day fall away like worn lace. In the quiet of that pocket, she did not have to be useful or articulate. She did not have to carry anything forward. She simply remembered how to breathe without bracing.

The creak of the wood above her became a lullaby. The wind against the shutters sounded less like intrusion and more like accompaniment. Her own heartbeat, once erratic and brittle, began to settle into a rhythm that no longer hurt to hear.

The hollow never asked questions. Not about where she had come from. Not about who she had left behind. Not about what she had lost or what she might still be holding.

It did not ask for a story. It did not ask for a name.

It only asked that she arrive.

And some days, that was all she could manage.

On one such evening, long after the sky had turned its darkest shade of indigo, she cried. Not with sobs. Not with shaking shoulders or heaving breaths. Just tears, slow and salt-sure, slipping down her face and into the earth below the floorboards. They soaked into the dirt without protest.

The ground did not shift beneath her. It did not rise to catch her grief or try to alchemize it into something brighter. It did not ask her to make it poetic. It just held her sorrow. Quietly. As if it had been waiting.

In the weeks that followed, she began to hum again. Not songs with lyrics, just melodies that rose from somewhere between memory and marrow. They were not beautiful in any conventional sense. But they were hers. They vibrated in her chest and passed through her lips like spells that only made sense when spoken into stillness.

And still, the hollow asked nothing more. It remained a place of witnessing. A space where being was enough.

Then, one day, she was gone.

There was no farewell left behind. No handprint on the glass. No rustle of spellwork in the corners. Only a clean teacup resting on the shelf. A bent spoon beside it. And a pressed sprig of rosemary tucked gently into the seam where the floorboards met.

The townsfolk noticed her absence in the way people feel a silence shift.

They did not speak of it loudly. They did not turn it into folklore.

They just felt it.

And then, as time passed, as seasons spun and names began to return to those who had once forgotten them, the cottage remained. So did the hollow.

And one day, long after her footsteps had faded from the path, the land remembered her name in the only way it could.

With a bloom.

It did not burst forth with color. It did not demand attention. It opened slowly. Steady. Purposeful.

A spiral of violet and bronze, nestled beneath the old board, pulsing softly in a rhythm that remembered not sorrow, but survival. It whispered of shelter that asked for nothing. Of silence that listened without agenda. Of magic that did not try to fix or claim. Only hold.

So, when Wes sat beside it, knees folded and head bowed, and Morgan arrived to kneel at its edge, the bloom stirred.

Not recognition. Not reunion.

But honor.

The kind that does not ask why you needed hiding.

Only says: You were here. And now, so is the magic that remembers.

## Chapter One Hundred Seven: The Shape Beneath the Spiral

They stayed longer than they meant to. Morgan and Wes, seated side by side on the weathered planks of the supply cottage floor, their legs tucked close, their conversation low and slow, like water finding its way around stone.

Outside, the sky had shifted through gold into blue. The air was soft with early evening and woodsmoke. The Hollow, for once, wasn't whispering back. It was just… holding them there.

Below, the bloom pulsed gently. Its spiral tighter now, as though folding into itself, protecting something that hadn't yet taken form.

"I didn't know magic could feel like this," Wes said eventually, voice low.

Morgan looked at him, not startled, just patient. "Like what?"

Wes hesitated. Then: "Like reverence without pressure. Like... something I didn't earn but am still allowed to witness."

Morgan turned their eyes to the floor, to the bloom glowing faintly beneath the gap in the boards. "It doesn't ask you to earn it," they said. "That's part of what makes it real. It just asks you to stay."

For a while, neither of them spoke.

The hum of the bloom wasn't sound, not exactly, but it vibrated through the wood, the air, the skin of their palms resting on the floor. Morgan reached out with their sensing hand, fingertips brushed the seam of the boards, where earth and memory had made a silent pact long before either of them arrived.

They exhaled. Slowly.

"There's something older here," Morgan said. "Not older in time. Older in design. This Hollow... it isn't just a repository for what was."

Wes tilted his head. "You think it's becoming something else?"

Morgan nodded. "I think it always was. We're only just learning to see it."

Wes traced a fingertip along the edge of a knot in the wood grain. "It reminds me of the first time I stepped into the archives. Back when I thought all this", he gestured vaguely toward the bloom, "was metaphor. Pretty folklore. I thought the Hollow was a memory engine."

Morgan smiled, faint and sideways. "A lot of people still do."

"But it's not," Wes said, softer now. "It's not about remembering anymore, is it?"

"No," Morgan agreed. "It's about becoming."

They sat in that truth together for a while. The kind of truth that doesn't demand action. Just acknowledgment.

The Hollow wasn't a vault, a shrine, or even a sanctuary. It was alive. Responsive. Listening. Not to control or guide or fix.

But to reflect.

The people. The grief. The beauty. The unsent letters. The things whispered into dirt and floorboards and air.

It grew not because it was told to, but because it was allowed to.

Wes finally broke the silence again. "I think I've been waiting for something like this my whole life," he said. "But I didn't know it had a shape."

Morgan leaned back on their palms, eyes tracing the ceiling beams above. "Maybe it doesn't," they said. "Maybe it just… spirals."

And beneath them, the bloom hummed its agreement, tucked in the quiet, spiral-shaped hollow of a place where someone had once asked for nothing more than space to survive.

Now it gave them something more: Belonging.

## Chapter One Hundred Eight: Not Exactly a Ritual (But Close Enough)

It started with a vague suggestion from Rhett.

"Should we… I don't know. Do something?" he asked one morning, standing near the old post office bloom with a mug of over steeped tea and his signature brand of mild discomfort.

Cassie, who was trying to coax a mildly enchanted broom out of someone's scarf basket at the time, glanced up.

"Do something?"

"Yeah. For the blooms. For the Hollow. For... all this becoming."

Cassie blinked. "You want to throw the magic a party?"

"Not a party," Rhett replied, with the wary tone of a man trying not to get assigned planning duties. "Just... something."

Morgan, passing by with a bundle of drying yarrow and a look of patient amusement, tilted their head. "Like a ritual?"

Rhett waved a hand. "Not a ritual. Not ceremonial. Just… a gesture. Communal. Improvised. Reverent-adjacent."

Cassie narrowed her eyes. "So, a town-wide offering with no coordination, no structure, and no idea what it's honoring?"

"Exactly," Rhett said.

Cassie sipped her coffee. "Fantastic. What could possibly go wrong."

Word spread, as it always did in Alden's Landing.

By that evening, half the town was preparing something for the "not-ritual."

Morgan declined to name it. Wren called it "a Resonance Response." Baz, more practical, referred to it simply as "That Thing on Saturday."

And so, That Thing on Saturday began to take form.

Cassie made charms.

Not the delicate kind, or the emotionally sensitive kind that had gotten loose before. These were small, ridiculous trinkets infused with good intentions and very little oversight. One congratulated you on finishing your tea. Another played a lute chord every time someone mentioned shadow work.

Morgan asked if she'd tested them.

"I test everything," Cassie replied confidently.

Three exploded into glitter by the end of the day.

Morgan said nothing.

Baz and a few garden-minded locals began constructing an enormous spiral path out of herbs, stones, and river-tumbled glass. It was beautiful. It was precise.

It was also, due to a particularly opinionated root system, crooked.

"It's not crooked," Baz insisted, arms crossed.

Cassie poked her head out of the shop. "It's spiral-adjacent."

Wes coughed discreetly and kept placing stones.

Meanwhile, the baking guild decided to contribute "symbolic bread."

No one knew what that meant.

Apparently, neither did they.

The resulting loaves included:

- A seven-plait challah that sang when sliced.
- A sourdough shaped like a blooming spiral (which briefly tried to levitate).
- And a cluster of miniature rolls stuffed with herbal intentions that confused everyone by giving wildly different affirmations depending on who bit into them.

One child claimed their roll told them to "reconsider their attachment to linear time."

By midday Saturday, the Hollow was buzzing. Not with formal energy, but with the kind of collective chaos that only comes from a community trying to express gratitude with crafts, baked goods, and completely unregulated magic.

And it worked.

Not because it was perfect.

But because everyone showed up.

They laid trinkets at the foot of blooms. They whispered names and offered buttons and hummed old lullabies with no known origin.

A group of teenagers spelled out a thank-you note in stones and pinecones on the overlook path.

Someone accidentally enchanted a bench to applaud everyone who sat on it.

Cassie decided to leave it. "It's earned the right to be supportive."

At dusk, as the last rays of sun bent around the arches, the Hollow responded with warmth. The blooms shimmered in unison, just once.

A shared breath. A quiet yes.

And somewhere, deeper than roots and older than language, the land smiled.

## Chapter One Hundred Nine: Just Us and the Crickets

The air still held laughter. Not loudly, just in the way the wind curled around corners, or how the spiral path of stones glimmered faintly with the last bits of spell-dust and sunset. The energy of the day had settled, warm and satisfied, like a collective exhale after a very long, very meaningful breath.

Cassie sat on the applause bench.

It had clapped three times when she first lowered herself onto it. She muttered "traitor" under her breath but didn't get up.

A moment later, Morgan joined her, easing down beside her with the tired grace of someone who'd spent the last three hours re-anchoring magically overconfident flower crowns and politely declining to interpret the sourdough's existential commentary.

The bench gave a polite, enthusiastic golf clap.

Cassie didn't even flinch this time. "Honestly, I've had worse fans."

Morgan huffed a quiet laugh, resting their hands on their knees. "Did you see the charm that wouldn't stop complimenting Wren's boots?"

"I made that one." Cassie grinned, smug and unrepentant. "It was supposed to promote self-esteem. Got a little... opinionated."

Morgan turned slightly to face her. "Did you mean for it to develop a foot-specific obsession?"

"Absolutely not. But in its defense, Wren's boots are fantastic."

They both laughed tired, full laughs that didn't need to go anywhere.

For a long time, they just sat. Crickets sang in the underbrush. Somewhere nearby, someone was playing a single note on a flute, repeatedly, trying to find the right breath.

298

Above them, the stars began to appear in soft, sleepy pairs.

Morgan finally spoke, voice softer now. "You know, this wasn't what I thought becoming would look like."

Cassie arched an eyebrow. "You mean it's not usually a mix of magical mishaps, emotionally sentient carbs, and symbolic moss spirals?"

"Not in the books, no."

They both smiled again. Smaller this time. More real.

Cassie leaned back, arms braced on the bench, staring up at the sky.

"I think the books always leave out the weird parts," she said. "Like how becoming doesn't always feel triumphant. Sometimes it feels like glitter in your bra and having a minor identity crisis because your charm fell in love with someone else's cardigan."

Morgan let out a delighted snort. "That's... alarmingly specific."

Cassie raised her mug. "I name no names."

Silence stretched again. But it was companionable now. Familiar. The kind of silence that didn't ask anything of them. The kind that let them simply be.

Morgan reached into their pocket and pulled out a thread-bound scrap of paper. It was folded carefully, edges softened by handling.

They passed it to Cassie without comment.

She opened it. A sketch. Just lines and loops. But it was unmistakably the shape of the resonance bloom. Not a replica - an echo.

It had grown from Morgan's hand like it had bloomed from the Hollow.

Cassie traced it with a fingertip, then looked up. "It's changing us."

Morgan nodded. "And we're letting it."

They both fell quiet again, this time not with exhaustion, but with something like reverence.

Or maybe just peace.

The crickets kept singing. The applause bench stayed mercifully silent. And beneath the floorboards, between the loam and the light, the Hollow listened.

# Chapter One Hundred Ten: After the Applause

Not everyone had stayed for the whole event. Some left early, overwhelmed by the laughter, the color, the sheer density of magic rippling through Alden's Landing like a tide that wouldn't stop rising. Some had errands. Some had excuses. And some, like Bram, just didn't know how to be visible in a crowd that was suddenly so good at being seen.

So, he had helped set out the rosemary bundles. He'd added a handful of charcoal chalk to the benches when no one was looking. He'd nodded at Wes. Smiled, sort of, at Cassie. And then, before the sun fully dipped below the western ridge, he'd quietly slipped away.

Now he sat behind the greenhouse, knees tucked to his chest, back against a pile of firewood that still smelled like pine and old spells. Above, the stars had come out. And beside him, planted between a crack in the stone, was a bloom.

It wasn't one of the main blooms. Not part of the spiral or any of the listening gardens. It hadn't been mentioned during the offering. It hadn't been admired or whispered to or even noticed.

But it was there. And it pulsed gently, with the kind of resonance that didn't ask for words. Just presence.

Bram let his head tip back against the woodpile. He hadn't always felt this disconnected.

There had been a time, years ago, before his mother left the town in search of something she never named, when he'd felt like part of the weft. His magic had been soft but steady. Mostly plant-based. Subtle. He'd been good at knowing when things needed replanting, when a bloom needed shadow instead of sun.

But over time, the edges of the town grew louder. Magic turned more visible, more vocal, more confident.

And Bram? He just... got quiet.

He exhaled slowly now, watching the bloom beside him shift its spiral, not toward him, but not away either. It shimmered once. Then again.

And that shimmer did something odd. It didn't speak. But it matched his breath.

One inhale.
One pulse.
One exhale.
Another pulse.

Like the bloom was saying, I see you even when you don't speak in magic.

Bram blinked, surprised by the sudden sting in his eyes. He thought of the others.

Cassie, lighting up every space she entered with laughter and a barely contained spell in her pocket.

Morgan, always so still and sure and shaped by the loom's rhythm.

Even Wes, who hadn't been here long, already seemed stitched into the fabric of the Hollow like he'd always belonged.

And Bram?

He had a vine in the windowsill that talked to him sometimes. He saved seeds from plants no one remembered. He knew how to make compost sing, but no one ever asked it to. He glanced down at the bloom. "You don't think that's nothing," he whispered.

It pulsed again. A little brighter.

"I don't know if I'm becoming," he added. "I think I might just be... staying."

The bloom shimmered once. Then stilled.

And somehow, that was an answer too.

He stayed there a long time after that. No ritual. No offering. Just him.

And the bloom.

And the quiet comfort of realizing that maybe, in this place of wild becoming and tangled magic and noisy joy, there was still space for someone who simply knew when to sit still, and listen as the world grew gently around him.

## Chapter One Hundred Eleven: The Bloom That Waited

Bram didn't expect the bloom to still be there the next morning. He hadn't marked the spot, hadn't told anyone about it. It felt private, somehow. Not secret but not meant for immediate sharing either. Just a small patch of glow nestled in the hairline crack between two old stones behind the greenhouse. A place where warmth seeped up from the earth like breath, and the hum of growth was more feeling than sound.

But when he stepped out at first light, wrapped in a cardigan that had seen better seasons, tea in hand, it was waiting for him.

Still. Subtle. Steady.

Bram smiled softly. Not wide. Just enough.

He knelt beside it, placed the mug gently to one side, and rested a hand on the stone nearest the bloom.

"Morning," he said.

And the bloom pulsed once in response.

It didn't grow larger. Didn't change color.

But it noticed.

And that noticing did something to him.

Because in all the wonder that had bloomed around Alden's Landing these past months—enchanted arches, story-looms, memory-lanterns and Threadfound souls—Bram had begun to wonder if his kind of magic had already passed.

If compost was still sacred.

If stillness was still enough.

But this bloom didn't want to be lit or spoken to or directed. It wasn't reacting to intentions, it was attuning. Matching him, slowly and surely, the way mycelium wraps itself into the roots of trees.

It had patience.

And so did he.

Each day that week, Bram returned. Sometimes just for a few minutes. Sometimes longer.

He brought little things. Not offerings, exactly. Just companions:

- A cracked pot full of lemon balm.
- A page from his planting journal with a sketch of an untested herbal braid.
- A handful of unsorted seeds too small to name.

He laid them beside the bloom. Didn't ask for a sign. Didn't expect change.

But by the third day, something shifted.

The stone near the bloom began to soften. Not crumble, not crack. Soften.

As though the mineral had decided it no longer needed to resist becoming something else.

Bram touched it. It wasn't warm, but it was no longer cold. The stone had taken on a texture more like bark than granite. And the bloom?

The bloom leaned slightly. Not outward. Toward him.

That evening, as the sun dipped below the greenhouse roof, Bram heard it.

A low, slow, rhythmic hum. Not a melody. A vibration. Like the ground was singing back to him in the same pitch he had been holding in silence for years.

He pressed his hand gently to the stone again and the hum deepened. For the first time in his life, Bram understood what it meant to root without reaching.

To offer presence as magic.

To grow not by becoming louder, but by becoming more himself.

And the bloom, small and spiraled and hidden in the crack, shimmered its approval.

## Chapter One Hundred Twelve: Tangled Threads and Tea Stains

The workshop had not been officially titled, but if pressed, Cassie would have called it "*So You Want to Bind a Blessing (Without Setting Anything on Fire)*." Baz, ever more diplomatic, had simply labeled the sign-up sheet "Threaded Intentions."

They split the duties the way they always did: Baz managed the setup, making sure the workstations were grounded, the tea was steeped, and no one had brought cursed string (again). Cassie handled the opening banter, charm demos, and ensuring everyone left with their eyebrows intact.

It worked. Mostly.

The space was already humming when Cassie entered, late, naturally, and trailed by three floating bundles of loose-leaf herbs she hadn't finished labeling.

Baz glanced up from the central table, where he'd just finished anchoring the spiral thread map. "You labeled that one '*Sleepy time but For Your Soul*.'"

Cassie dropped the herbs onto the sorting bench. "Because '*Astral Drift and Internal Soothing*' didn't fit on the tag."

Baz smiled. "It's nice to have you on-brand."

She winked. "Just keeping expectations low so we can wildly exceed them later."

The participants trickled in: a mix of familiar faces and a few new ones.

Rhett sat near the door, arms crossed, already regretting whatever charm he was about to befriend.

Maribelle brought a small locket to bless and a half-finished story about a goose with romantic inclinations.

One of the newer Threadfound, a shy teen named Liri, chose a spot closest to Baz's satchel of hand-dyed threads and refused to make eye contact with anything but the tea.

Cassie clapped her hands. "Alright, threadlings and spell-weavers, today's goal is to anchor an intention into a cloth-bound token. That means fabric, thread, some guided focus, and enough chaotic goodwill to bind a blessing without summoning anything with claws."

Someone in the back coughed nervously.

Cassie grinned. "Kidding. Mostly."

Baz demonstrated the binding loop, moving with the slow grace of someone who'd taught people how to knot intentions into thread for longer than anyone quite remembered. His tone was warm, even, grounded.

"This loop holds what you want to give," he said, guiding a shimmering cord around a soft talisman of folded linen. "And this one holds what you're ready to release."

Cassie whispered to a participant across the table, "And this one holds your misplaced confidence and seven questionable life choices, but don't worry, we don't tie that knot today."

By mid-workshop, the space was full of soft murmurs and the scent of sage, lemon balm, and something Cassie suspected was glitterroot gone mildly rogue.

Liri, still quiet, had produced a token that glowed faintly violet and only vibrated when approached with direct compliments.

Rhett's charm had accidentally looped itself into his sleeve cuff and was now attempting to bless his elbow.

Maribelle's goose story had become involved in a narrative loop with her locket, which now whispered mildly judgmental poetry.

And Baz?

Baz was moving through the tables with a soft smile, whispering affirmations into fraying fabric and reminding people that binding wasn't about perfection. It was about presence.

Cassie leaned on the worktable, watching it all unfold.

She didn't need to teach every spell. She didn't need to guide every hand. That wasn't the point anymore.

The point was this:

- The laughter.
- The slight panic when a charm hummed too loudly.
- The warmth of someone realizing they could make something that mattered.
- The accidental tea stain that made a talisman more personal, not less.

The point was connection.

After the workshop ended, as people filtered out with their wrapped bundles and unfinished stories, Cassie and Baz sat together near the back table. She looked over at him, brushing glitterroot from her sleeve. "Think we did, okay?"

Baz looked around at the quiet magic still hanging in the air, the threads that hadn't yet stilled.

"I think," he said, "we made something that will keep growing after we're done watching."

Cassie leaned her head against his shoulder, exhaled. "That's the goal, right?"

He nodded. "Every time."

## Chapter One Hundred Thirteen: Threads We Didn't Mean to Weave

The workshop space had gone still.

Chairs tucked in. Teacups abandoned in small half-crescent rings. The scent of scorched lemon balm still lingered faintly near the back table, and someone had left behind a charm that softly exhaled compliments every fifteen minutes, whether anyone was listening.

Cassie didn't rush to clean.

She sat with her legs curled up in one of the mismatched armchairs Baz had brought in last season, her hands wrapped around a chipped mug of something vaguely herbal and over steeped.

Baz moved with slower rhythms now, gathering stray threads and humming under his breath—a song that hadn't yet decided if it wanted to be a lullaby or a spell.

Eventually, he joined her, folding himself into the chair opposite hers, a matching mug in hand and a half-smile playing at his lips.

Cassie sipped. Grimaced. "This is terrible."

Baz grinned. "It's not the tea's fault. You overconfidently used the last of the grounding blend and then added mint like it wouldn't hold a grudge."

"Rude," she said. "Accurate, but rude."

They sat like that for a while.

Not in silence, just in the soft in-between that always followed a day full of weaving and intention-setting and accidental enchantments.

Cassie let her eyes drift across the room: the tables still glowing faintly where a participant's laughter had embedded itself into the woodgrain, a folded linen token resting where someone had forgotten it, the way the light caught the bits of thread scattered like constellations across the floor.

"It's funny," she said after a moment, "I used to think I'd teach workshops like these because I wanted to help people make things."

Baz raised an eyebrow. "And now?"

Cassie exhaled, long and slow. "Now I think I was just hoping someone would notice what I'd made. That I could offer a piece of myself, and it wouldn't just disappear into the air."

Baz nodded, quiet.

Then: "It doesn't disappear. You know that, right?"

She looked at him.

And he met her gaze, not intensely, not forcefully, just with the gentle steadiness of someone who had always chosen to see her. "It lives here," he said. "In the way people show up. In the way they thread what you've taught into what they need. In the way someone walks away with something they didn't know they were capable of."

Cassie blinked once. "Do you practice these speeches, or are you just naturally devastating?"

Baz chuckled. "I've had a lot of practice. You inspire reflection. And mild exasperation."

"I'm consistent," she said, shrugging.

The quiet stretched again. This time deeper. Wider.

The kind of quiet that settled not just around them, but in them. The kind that comes only after years of doing, of giving, of becoming, when you realize you're not just part of the magic…you're shaping it.

And it's shaping you back.

"I never planned for this," Cassie said.

"The Hollow?" Baz asked.

"All of it. The workshops. The town becoming something bigger. Us." She gestured between them, a small spiral with her fingers. "This rhythm we've fallen into."

Baz studied her for a long breath. Then reached across the space and tapped his finger gently against her mug. A spark flared. Her tea sweetened.

Cassie blinked. "Did you just sugar-spell my tea?"

"I did," he said. "And now you're obligated to admit it's drinkable."

She took a sip and smiled despite herself. "Fine," she said. "It's marginally redeemed."

Baz leaned back in his chair; one leg tucked under him.

"I didn't plan for this either," he admitted. "But I think," he paused, watching the last bits of dusk filter through the windows, "I think the best threads are the ones we didn't mean to weave."

Cassie tilted her head. "You're really leaning into the metaphor today."

"I'm surrounded by magic looms and emotionally volatile yarn. It's unavoidable."

They both laughed. And then they didn't speak, because there was nothing left to say.

Only this: A shared warmth. A deep knowing. And the gentle truth that neither of them needed to name what they were becoming. Only to honor that it was happening.

Together.

## Chapter One Hundred Fourteen: Threadbare and True

By the time they reached the cottage, the stars had softened into view overhead, pale and flickering like lanterns shy to announce themselves. The night air carried that hush that only came after a day full of people and spells and too much tea—not silence exactly, but the kind of stillness that offered permission to exhale.

Cassie kicked her boots off just inside the door. One of them made a noise that suggested it had held a grudge all day. She left it to sulk by the hearth and padded into the kitchen on socked feet.

Baz followed at a slower pace, closing the door gently behind them, hanging his satchel on the peg by instinct more than thought.

Neither of them spoke for a while.

They didn't need to.

The kitchen smelled like rosemary and yesterday's bread. There was still a faint shimmer in the corner where a charm had misfired earlier in the week and briefly decided to bless the soup pot every hour on the hour.

Cassie leaned on the counter, elbow propped up, watching Baz with soft eyes and a slight, crooked grin. "You know," she said, "we didn't technically set anything on fire today."

Baz raised an eyebrow. "That we know of."

"Progress," she replied. "We should celebrate."

"We should sleep."

She squinted at him. "You sound like someone who didn't spend three hours defusing a goose-themed locket loop."

He kissed the top of her head as he passed her. "And you sound like someone who needs foot rubs and a snack."

"Accurate."

In the soft light of the cottage, everything felt a little more real.

Cassie tossed her shawl over the back of a chair and flopped onto the couch with the grace of a toppled marionette. Baz moved easily through the space, lighting a few low-glow candles, fetching a tin of honeyed almonds, pulling down the comfort-knit blanket from the back of the chair.

They'd never really talked about what this was, this cohabitation, co-creation, co-everything, but it worked.

It felt like home.

Because it was.

Baz joined her on the couch; one arm draped casually over her shoulders. She leaned into it, letting her head drop to his chest with a tired sigh that carried more than just the weight of the day.

He ran his fingers gently along her arm, absent and soothing.

For a while, they listened to the faint creak of the house settling, to the tick of a charm-clock in the other room, to the wind brushing the glass like it had something tender to say but couldn't quite form the words.

"You ever think," Cassie murmured, eyes half-closed, "that we got here by accident?"

Baz didn't answer right away.

Then: "Not accident. Just not... intention in the way we thought."

She made a noncommittal noise. "I was aiming for peace and personal space. Instead, I got enchanted gardens, talking crafts, and a partner who sugar-charms tea when I'm not looking."

"You're welcome," he said.

She smiled against his chest. "It's not what I thought I wanted."

"And now?"

"It's better."

He shifted slightly, just enough to look at her. "Because of the magic?"

She met his gaze. "Because of you."

There was a pause then, small but weighty. Not dramatic. Just real.

Baz brushed a curl from her forehead. "We're building something here," he said quietly. "And I don't think it's just for the town."

"No," she agreed. "It's for us, too."

The words settled in the space between them like another thread in the loom.

Unrushed.
Unforced.
Woven.

Later, she fell asleep curled against him, mouth slightly open, a thread clinging to her sleeve and a faint hum of residual charmlight still pulsing at her wrist.

Baz stayed awake a little longer, watching the way her breathing matched the rhythm of the quiet house. Of the Hollow. Of this strange, beautiful life they hadn't meant to build, but had built anyway.

Together.

Threadbare.
True.
And whole.

# Chapter One Hundred Fifteen: A Town That Knows Your Name

Morgan walked the ridge at dawn, where Alden's Landing gave way to low mist and the scent of wild thyme clung to the air like memory. The mist gathered in the hollows of the land, catching the early light and turning the hills into drifting islands. This time of morning held something sacred, though no one had declared it so. The Hollow did not sleep exactly, but in these liminal hours, it rested. And when it rested, it listened.

Lately, Morgan had taken to walking before anything else stirred. Before the workshops unfurled their doors. Before the charms began their sleepy hums. Before Cassie brewed her first mug and left behind a trail of cinnamon-sweet spellwork that braided through the green. These walks were not about solitude, though they certainly brought it. They were about something else. Listening, maybe.

Or syncing. Or simply arriving again in their own skin before the day tried to shape it.

The Hollow was breathing. Not beneath them, not around them. With them. It had become a companion. It was not a tool, not a sanctuary, not even a secret. It was presence. Shared, aware, and impossibly patient.

The path curved along the outer edge of town, tracing what had once been the limits of the resonance spiral. In earlier days, those boundary stones had been clear markers—solid, unmoving, necessary. Now, when Morgan passed them, they flickered. Not in warning. In recognition. A pulse, slow and gentle, like a friend lifting their gaze in greeting but not needing to speak. The stones acknowledged them. That was new. That was everything.

Morgan did not answer aloud, but they smiled. A real one. Small and crooked. The kind that existed only for the moment that birthed it.

Below, the rooftops of Alden's Landing still held the soft shimmer of dew. Thin trails of smoke curled from a few early chimneys, signs that hearths had been stirred and homes were waking. One chimney in particular puffed with an unusual rhythm, and Morgan guessed. correctly that Rhett had already begun rearranging the spiral garden again, likely after some unsolicited critique from a charm that considered itself an expert in symmetry.

The town looked much the same as it always had. Cobblestone paths, crooked fences, the occasional flock of chickens that insisted on disregarding every magical ward in place to guide them. But it wasn't the same.

Not in shape.

In weight.

In presence.

Alden's Landing held itself differently now. It did not stand as a backdrop for the lives within it. It participated. It held you. It remembered. The stones hummed louder than they used to, especially when someone needed grounding. The trees leaned toward grief with a kind of quiet tenderness. The wind had learned the habit of replying—sometimes with song, sometimes with stillness, sometimes with a perfectly timed rustle of leaves that made you laugh when you didn't think you could.

Morgan had once been the quiet keeper of forgotten threads, content to work in the weave without being seen. But now… now they were something else. A guide, maybe. A weaver. A listener. Or simply a person who had helped open a door and then stood stunned when it opened them right back.

They made their way slowly down the hill, the soles of their boots brushing against dew-wet grass, the rhythm of their breath easy and slow. They passed the edge of the Hollow, past Wren's crooked fence where tiny charms dangled like chimes, each one singing a different spell of small encouragement. The old bloom by the post office caught their eye as they passed. It pulsed faintly, not demanding attention, but acknowledging it had been seen.

The town felt fully awake now, but not in the clattering, footstep-filled way of ordinary towns. This was a kind of waking that was felt before it was heard. A collective attentiveness. A sense that each breath was part of something larger, and that each person was being remembered back.

Morgan ducked into the greenhouse.

Bram stood near the far wall, murmuring to the vine that had made itself at home across the stonework. His hands moved gently as he spoke, offering no command, only conversation. The vine vibrated slightly, its leaves quivering in rhythm with his voice, as if in agreement. Bram lifted a hand when he saw Morgan and offered a smile that carried no need for words.

Morgan nodded and continued.

Their destination was the spiral chamber.

It was not consecrated. No sigils guarded the entrance. No incense marked the space. But whenever Morgan entered, the air stilled. As if the room itself understood the importance of pausing. As if it knew when to listen.

They stepped inside, letting the door settle softly behind them. The chamber was empty, the spiral at the center still etched deep into the stone floor. It glowed faintly in the morning light, just enough to remind them it was never entirely asleep.

Morgan sat. Cross-legged. Palms open. Nothing in their hands, nothing to offer, nothing to solve.

They breathed.

Not to meditate. Not to stir a spell or invoke a thread.

They simply breathed to be.

The silence was not hollow. It was full. Full of rhythm, of memory, of awareness that needed no name.

And in that stillness, it arrived.

The hum.

Not heard, exactly. Felt. It began in the bones, soft and sure, then traveled up the spine and settled at the base of the skull. It was not magic in the way they had once known it. It was more intimate than that. It was belonging.

Morgan did not speak.

They did not cry.

They did not shift.

They closed their eyes and let the moment hold them.

They did not need to do anything more.

Because sometimes, the deepest transformation does not arrive with fire or vision or a chorus of fate.

Sometimes, it arrives as a quiet town that remembers your name.

And whispers it back to you.

Not as a question.

Not as a command.

But as truth.

## Chapter One Hundred Sixteen: The Threads That Wove Themselves

It began the way most new magic did in Alden's Landing these days: with no announcement at all. No surge of light. No ritualized unveiling. No looms or glyphs or spells declared under full moons.

Just a thread. Spun across moss. So thin it might've been mistaken for dew.

Except it shimmered. And it moved.

Wren found the first one at dawn, unfolding itself along the footpath that ran from the greenhouse to the edge of the resonance grove. It hadn't been there the night before. She would've noticed. She always walked that path, always barefoot, always listening.

But this time, the ground felt different.

Not dangerous. Not humming with warning.

Curious.

She crouched, brushing a palm over the glimmer. The thread didn't disappear. Didn't fade or writhe or react. It simply lay there, gently pulsing with a rhythm that wasn't her own, but wasn't entirely foreign, either. It was like it had been waiting for someone to touch it.

When she did, the shimmer traveled, racing down the length of the threadline and branching like lightning made of memory.

By midday, five more had appeared.

All in different places. None in straight lines.

Each one spun not across roads, but between moments.

Between the threshold of the cottage Cassie had inherited and the old corner of the Hollow where her mother's name was still carved in faded sigils.

Between the overlook where Wes had first arrived and the bloom Bram had awakened behind the greenhouse.

Between Morgan's resting palm in the spiral chamber and the back wall of the supply cottage, where stone had softened to hold something sacred.

The town noticed.

Not all at once. But enough.

People began walking the new threads, not trampling, not out of curiosity alone, but with intention.

Some whispered to them. Others sang softly.

A few simply followed them, feet stepping gently on threadlines no one had placed, but which clearly led somewhere.

The threads didn't pulse for everyone.

But when they did, the light felt like breath—drawn up from the ground and into the chest, as if the land itself was reminding them:

You are connected.
You were always connected.
You just forgot how to walk the line.

Morgan traced one all the way to the river. It led not to the water, but to the fallen tree where they had once sat with Gabe, long before the blooms, before the Hollow fully opened itself.

The thread ended there. But the stillness did not.

324

They sat down, eyes half-lidded, and listened.

The wind pressed softly against the leaves. The ground pulsed once. And the thread beneath them stayed.

Waiting. Witnessing. Becoming.

Later, Cassie would joke that the Hollow had decided to redecorate.

Baz would counter that maybe the Hollow wasn't decorating so much as weaving back the things they hadn't meant to lose.

Wren would sketch the threadlines in her journal, being careful to map not just where they appeared, but how they felt.

Because the threadlines weren't roads.
Weren't spells.
Weren't instructions.

They were invitations.

From the Hollow.
To its people.

> Come remember what you've always known.
> Come follow what you've already become.

# Chapter One Hundred Seventeen: The Line Chose Her

Una didn't set out to follow the thread. She wasn't even looking for it.

She had gone out in search of silence. An increasingly rare commodity in Alden's Landing lately, between workshops that sang themselves open, charms that whispered affirmations from laundry lines, and blooms that occasionally exhaled just loud enough to startle the cat.

She'd taken the long way to the overlook, the one that looped behind the east garden wall and crossed the old dry creek bed. She liked the way it wrapped the town instead of cutting through it, how it offered enough space to not be needed for a little while.

But as she passed the far edge of the Hollow, just where the path narrowed between two old sycamores, she stopped.

Because there, lying across the footpath like a line drawn gently by hand and moonlight was a thread.

It shimmered faintly. Just a sliver of light, the color of brushed silver and something softer, maybe ash, maybe early morning fog.

She knelt.

Not to touch it. Just to see.

It didn't pulse. Didn't glow brighter. Didn't call to her.

But she felt it anyway.

That soft invitation. Like a question that wasn't urgent but was waiting.

She hesitated.

She had never considered herself part of the town's magic. Not really. Not in the way Morgan held threadlines in their palms or Cassie coaxed enchantments from teacups and glitter. Una observed, contributed when needed, offered resources and sense and strong tea.

But she had never followed until now.

She rose and stepped forward.

The threadline accepted the movement, not with light or fanfare, but with a deepening quiet. As if the path had exhaled. As if something had shifted, just a little, so that the ground beneath her feet felt more meant for her than it had a moment before.

She followed it.

Not far.

Not fast.

But steadily.

Through the sycamores.
Down a slope she hadn't noticed before.
Past an old stone marker she'd never read.
And into a part of the Hollow she didn't remember visiting, though it felt strangely familiar.

The threadline ended at a wall.

Not stone. Not wood.

Just thick, tangled vines, leafless but pulsing faintly with color beneath the bark, as if the whole thing had once been stitched with twilight.

In the center of the wall was a seam.

Narrow. Vertical. Faint.

The kind of mark that would vanish the moment you looked away, unless you were meant to see it.

Una reached out.

Laid her hand along the seam.

And the vines parted.

Behind them: a garden.

Not blooming.

Resting.

Beds of herbs with no names, plants with silver leaves that curled inward like they were protecting something, a circle of stones surrounding an old tree stump where someone had once placed a bowl—now filled with rain and three fallen petals.

It wasn't grand. It wasn't enchanted. But it was hers.

She didn't know how she knew that. She just did.

She stepped inside and sat.

Cross-legged, palms on her knees, just as Morgan had taught in earlier years, before she thought any of it would apply to her.

The threadline didn't follow.

But it didn't fade either.

It rested just outside the threshold.

As if waiting.

As if watching.

As if knowing she needed to find the rest of this alone.

Una exhaled. And for the first time in a long time, she wasn't thinking about what she was offering to others.

She was simply receiving.

The quiet.
The garden.
The fact that the Hollow had made a path—just for her.

## Chapter One Hundred Eighteen: What Grew in Her Absence

The garden didn't announce itself.

There were no sudden bursts of bloom.
No wind rushing to meet her.
No glowing sigils dancing across the stones.

Just quiet.

The kind of quiet that had been kept intentionally. Lovingly. Like a room someone prepared long ago, knowing that one day, she might return.

Una rose from the soft patch of moss she'd been sitting on and walked slowly through the space.

It was small. Contained. Not wild like the outer Hollow. Not ornamental like the spiral paths.

But shaped. Familiar.

She crouched near one of the beds.

The plants here weren't ones she saw every day. Some had no name she could place. A tall, spindly stalk with translucent leaves that turned ever so slightly toward her palm. Groundcover that shimmered when touched but dulled when ignored. A small tree that hummed faintly when she exhaled too close.

They weren't just unusual.

They were personal.

Una touched one gently.

A memory surfaced—not clear but felt.

A younger version of herself kneeling in a similar bed, digging with careful hands, speaking softly to the roots. Not casting spells. Just… tending.

The feeling landed in her chest with the weight of something she hadn't even realized she missed.

She had been here before.

Not in this exact form.
Not with these words.
But this place had been hers.

Or part of her.
Or shaped by her magic, long before she had the language for it.

She turned to the circle of stones near the center.

Twelve in total. Uneven in size but placed with intention.

And in the middle, the stump. Worn smooth, clearly touched by many hands over many seasons. On top of it sat a bowl—earthen, unglazed, and perfectly still.

Inside: three petals.

One deep violet.
One palest gold.
One a translucent gray that shimmered only when she wasn't looking directly at it.

They weren't fresh. Weren't enchanted.

Just waiting.

Una sat before the stump and didn't touch the bowl. She simply looked.

And in that stillness, more memory stirred—not with detail, but with feeling.

This had been a place where she came to leave things behind.

Not offerings. But emotions. Worries.

Exhaustions she hadn't wanted to burden others with.

Joy too fragile to share aloud.

She had placed them here in the garden's hush where the land would hold them, not to erase, but to compost. To make room.

For breath.

For clarity.

For return.

She stood slowly and moved toward the back edge of the garden. There, beneath an arched vine that hadn't yet bloomed, was a bench. A simple wooden seat, softened with age and time.

She brushed the surface with her hand. Etched into the wood, faint but still legible, were initials.

Her own.

Not just the ones people called her now.
But the old ones.
The full ones.
The ones she had abandoned when she reshaped herself into something simpler. Sharper.

Safer.

Her breath caught.

The garden didn't react.

It simply stayed.

Present. Patient.

Una sat.

Let her palms rest on her knees. And felt, for the first time in years, that she didn't have to earn stillness.

She could simply be held by it.

This wasn't a place she had forgotten.

This was a part of her that had waited to be remembered.

## Chapter One Hundred Nineteen: The Circle She Once Named

The light had changed again by the time Una stood. The shadows had lengthened, stretching like soft fingers across the stone path. A breeze whispered through the hanging vine above the bench. It was cool, weightless, as if brushing away the last of her hesitation. She walked slowly back toward the center of the garden, where the twelve stones still sat in their quiet ring around the stump.

They weren't arranged randomly. She saw that now.

There was symmetry to them, not geometric but felt as if each stone had been placed to hold space, not just shape. The moss between them had receded, ever so slightly, like the earth itself remembered the paths between one and the next.

She crouched by the first one, marked with a thin vertical line carved deep into its surface. It was old, that mark, worn, softened by weather, but still deliberate. Not a sigil. Not a rune. A tally? No, not a count. A marker. She reached out and placed her fingers along the stone's edge. It was cool beneath her skin, but not lifeless. There was memory there. Not the town's memory. Not the Hollow's.

Her own.

She moved clockwise.

The second stone had a faint curve carved across its top, not easily seen unless the light hit it at just the right angle. The third bore no mark at all, but her fingertips tingled the moment she touched it. She paused there, resting her hand fully atop it, and inhaled.

Something stirred.

Not a vision, not exactly. Just a sensation warmth behind her eyes, the echo of a voice long familiar and long gone. Her own voice.

Younger. Softer. Saying something like a promise, though the words themselves were gone.

She looked up at the stump in the center. The bowl still sat there, unmoved. The petals inside had not shifted, but somehow their presence felt more specific now, like they weren't just remnants, they were reminders.

One for presence. One for passage. One for protection.

And the stones?

They were the frame. The circle. The net.

A memory came, slow and careful:

Twelve nights. Twelve intentions. One for each turn of the moon. Not cast in ceremony but whispered during visits. One stone placed for each declaration of what she needed, what she longed to reclaim. She hadn't built the circle for spectacle or spellcraft. She'd built it for containment. For grounding what she was too afraid to speak aloud anywhere else.

Not a ritual. A return.

She'd been returning to herself, one stone at a time.

And she had forgotten.

Una stood and walked the circle now, slower, more reverent. As she moved from stone to stone, she felt the faint shift in resonance between them. This was not a structure for energy to be stored - it was a wheel. A map. A spiral meant to draw something inward: not power, but self-recognition.

One stone carried courage.
Another, grief.

A third, a promise of boundaries she hadn't known how to set at the time.

She reached the twelfth and final stone and paused.

This one was different. Not because of its shape or size, it was the most unassuming of the lot, but because as soon as she touched it, something beneath her ribs loosened. As if a thread that had been pulled taut for years suddenly released.

Una dropped to her knees beside it, breath caught in her chest, eyes prickling with heat she hadn't expected.

She remembered what this one had meant.

It wasn't an intention.

It was a question.

One she'd never answered.

Not aloud. Not even to herself.

"Who will I be when I am no longer hiding?"

The words came back like a wind—sweeping, gentle, unmistakably hers.

This was what she had left suspended.

Not her name. Not her magic.

But her becoming.

The breeze through the garden stilled. A hush settled over the stones.

And Una, older now, stronger, softer in different ways, pressed both palms to the twelfth stone and spoke aloud. "I think I'm ready to find out."

There was no response in light. No bloom sprang up from the dirt. No humming from the vines.

But the bowl on the stump trembled. Just slightly.

One of the petals shifted. And in the earth below her knees, something ancient and true aligned, like a thread that had found its place in the weave.

## Chapter One Hundred Twenty: Carried Back in Her Hands

The garden let her leave without ceremony. There was no flash of light, no closing of vines behind her. No magical gate clinking shut with finality. Just the hush of the path, the softened wind, and the steady presence of the threadline that waited like a companion rather than a guide.

Una stepped across it with new weight in her limbs.

Not burden.
Not fatigue.

Belonging.

It was subtle, but unmistakable. The difference between walking away from something and walking with it.

She made her way down the ridge trail, skirt brushing against grasses that leaned without resistance, the rhythm of her steps slower than usual. Not cautious. Just deliberate.

The town stirred ahead, quiet with morning but not asleep. She could hear the gentle clatter of someone arranging teacups at the café counter, the rise of a charm hum at the Loom's entrance, and Cassie's unmistakable voice laughing somewhere near the greenhouse.

Una's pace didn't quicken. She didn't rush to find them. She let the rhythm of the town fold around her, a blanket she hadn't realized she missed until she'd stepped into it again.

She found Morgan first, kneeling by a bloom that had grown half into a wall near the apothecary.

They looked up as she approached, sensing her before she spoke. Their expression didn't shift in surprise or concern. Just softened, recognition blooming across their face as if they already knew.

"You've been walking," Morgan said, standing.

Una nodded. "I found a place. Or maybe it found me."

Morgan studied her with eyes that always saw beneath the surface. "You brought something back."

Una hesitated. Her hands were empty, but she felt the truth of that statement settle in her chest.

"Yes," she said. "Something old. Something I made. A long time ago."

Morgan didn't press. Instead, they stepped forward and gently placed a hand to her shoulder, grounding her without anchoring her.

"Cassie's nearby," they said. "Come sit?"

The greenhouse was half-shadow, half-spelllight when they entered. Cassie stood by the long counter, scribbling notes on a charm tag and muttering about the ethics of enchantments that developed opinions about basil. She looked up when they arrived.

There was something in Una's stance—shoulders less guarded, the stillness in her eyes—that made Cassie immediately toss the pen aside and clear the bench with a sweep of her arm.

"I'm making tea," she said, not a question.

Una smiled. "I'm not arguing."

They settled in. Una on the stool nearest the counter, Morgan at the window ledge. Cassie moved with practiced ease, her magic curling gently around the kettle, the teacups, the small dish of lavender cookies she insisted she didn't bake for emotional reasons.

When the mugs had been passed and the silence had grown comfortably full, Una began.

She didn't tell them everything. Not all at once. But she spoke of the path. The thread. The garden. The twelve stones. The bowl on the stump.

The promise she'd left unanswered.

Cassie leaned in slowly as she listened, her expression uncharacteristically still. Morgan sipped their tea with both hands, eyes lowered, like they were reading the story between the words.

"I think," Una said at last, "that I made something sacred. Not for power. Not for protection. Just to hold space for becoming. For myself. For whom I might grow into."

Cassie reached across the table and squeezed her hand. "That's magic."

Una nodded. "I forgot it was mine."

Morgan looked up, meeting her eyes. "And now?"

"I remember."

They all sat with that for a moment.

The kettle clicked. The wind outside shifted. The greenhouse lights adjusted themselves slightly, catching the glint of Cassie's teacup charm and making it pulse like a heartbeat.

Cassie smiled. "You know what this means, don't you?"

Una raised an eyebrow. "You're going to make me host a workshop?"

Cassie smirked. "Absolutely not. I'm going to help you rebuild that garden. And then I'm going to convince the vines to behave."

"You won't," Morgan added.

"She never does," Una said dryly.

Cassie raised her mug. "But I try. And that counts for something."

The laughter came easy then. Familiar.

And underneath it, something even steadier:

Witnessing.

Because returning wasn't always about ceremony. Sometimes it was just telling the people who know how to hold you that you've remembered something precious.

And having them say, without hesitation—

Welcome back.

# Chapter One Hundred Twenty-One: Digging In

Cassie insisted on bringing tea. She tucked two mugs into a small woven basket, alongside a tin of ginger biscuits and a jar labeled *"Cleansing Salt (Possibly Lemon-Infused)*," scribbled in her usual loopy scrawl. The label had an optimistic question mark, as if even the salt wasn't entirely sure of its own identity.

Una, more measured in her preparation, brought her journal, a trowel, and something far rarer—cautious optimism. It had not walked beside her in years, but today, it had agreed to come along.

The morning air was crisp, and the sounds of Alden's Landing faded behind them, replaced by birdsong and the occasional whisper of wind through the trees.

The shimmer still arched gently between the old sycamores. It looked the same as it had before, humming softly between worlds. Una stepped through first. Her breath caught at the sight waiting beyond the veil.

The garden opened in front of her like an exhale. Everything was exactly as she had left it. And somehow, it was more. The light danced differently here, brushing the leaves in a way that felt deliberate. As if the place had been holding its breath, waiting for her return.

Cassie stepped through and let out a low whistle. "Well," she said, taking in the view, "you've been holding out on me."

Una's voice was barely above a whisper. "I didn't know I had this," she said, her eyes sweeping the space slowly. "Not really. Not until I came back to it."

Cassie moved forward, crouching near one of the outer stone markers. She ran her fingers along its edge, then let her palm rest on the cool surface. "It's still warm. Not magically warm, but emotionally. Like it remembers being loved."

Una knelt beside her and nodded. "It does. I think it remembers everything."

They began at the outer edges, where the garden had grown wild in their absence. Fallen twigs and weathered leaves had formed a patchwork over the paths, while ivy had crept across the threshold like it had been slowly reclaiming the space. The two women worked in a steady rhythm, brushing back the green veil and making room for light once more.

Cassie conjured a charm to gently clear the vines from the walkways, but the spell misinterpreted her intent. Instead of unraveling the vines, it tried to lull them to sleep. A particularly persistent vine curled lovingly around Cassie's wrist, sighing contentedly.

"This is why I never label things 'gentle unwind,'" she muttered, tugging half-heartedly. The vine clung tighter, as if comforted.

Una laughed. It came out sharp at first, surprised and almost startled, like it wasn't sure it had permission to exist. But then it rang out again, fuller this time, and the sound bounced gently off the garden's stone walls like it had been waiting there for years.

Cassie grinned without looking up. "That's better."

They continued toward the heart of the garden, to the ring of twelve stones. There was a hush in the center of the space, as if the garden itself was listening. Cassie circled the ring slowly, her hands hovering over each stone in turn. She tilted her head, thoughtful.

"They hum," she said after a moment. "Not like a spell would. Like they are waiting for something."

Una placed her hand on the old tree stump at the center of the circle. The carved bowl still rested in its hollow. The petals within it had dried and faded, but they had not moved.

"I think they are listening," Una said. "Not for instructions. For intention."

Cassie nodded, her brow furrowed in concentration. "Then let's give them something worth hearing."

They dug, not in large sweeping motions, but with the reverence of caretakers. The garden had gone untended for too long, and they knew better than to rush its return. Weeds that weren't entirely weeds were carefully pulled and set aside. Beds were unearthed and breathed into again. Herbs whispered their names as they were replanted, some of them ancient enough that even Cassie looked impressed.

Cassie found a stalk of shadowmint nestled between two stones. It smelled like dusk and resolve. She gently tucked it into her sleeve like a secret meant only for later.

Una unearthed a river pebble beneath one of the garden beds. Its surface was smooth, and a message had been etched faintly into it in her own handwriting - "boundaries are not barriers." She held it in both hands, feeling a quiet buzz travel up her arms. It was the warmth of a younger version of herself, now reintroduced through stone and soil.

By midday, they had cleared half the garden. Cassie declared it time for a break and spread a cloth over the old bench with theatrical flourish. She pulled out the mugs and biscuits as though she were summoning them from thin air and handed Una a steaming cup without asking how she took her tea. They sat beneath the gently arching vines. The leaves above them quivered slightly, as though stretching awake.

"You know," Cassie said between bites, brushing a few crumbs from her lap, "you could open this place up to others. Not immediately. But eventually."

Una sipped her tea and gave a quiet smile. "Maybe."

Cassie gave her a look over the rim of her mug. "You don't have to. But people would feel something here. This place has… permission in the soil."

Una's eyes wandered to the stones. Their alignment felt steady now, less like relics and more like allies. "I think it was never meant to be mine alone," she said. "It was just meant to be mine first."

Cassie leaned back with a satisfied grin. "That is a very wise and beautifully phrased way to say, 'I'll think about it.'"

"I learned from the best."

The light had shifted by the time they resumed their work. It had deepened into that golden hue that made everything look a little more alive. The garden felt different now. Awake. Not restless or impatient. Just ready.

Una, her knees dusted with soil and her fingers sore in a way that felt almost joyful, felt the rhythm of the place begin to move through her. This was not about restoring what once was. It was not about preserving the past or mending what had broken.

It was about presence. A re-entry into something ancient that had waited for her to notice.

They returned to work slowly, with the quiet ease of people who understood that transformation did not need a deadline.

One stone.

One breath.

One shared intention at a time.

## Chapter One Hundred Twenty-Two: Beneath the Garden, a Circuit

Cassie returned to the cottage late, hair full of dried rosemary and her boots half-soled with mud and moss. The sun had dipped behind the treetops in its usual sleepy glide, casting everything in that soft gold light Baz always said looked like forgiveness.

She pushed the door open with her hip, the herb basket in one hand, and paused to listen.

The house breathed back at her.

There was something grounding in coming home to a place Baz had tended while she'd been away. Even without words, the air felt different. Like someone had coaxed the space into stillness rather than just letting it sit idle.

Baz looked up from the worktable, where a half-assembled grounding array of copper coils and quartz discs glinted in the low light. He smiled when he saw her.

"You've been in the dirt," he said, warmly teasing.

Cassie dropped the basket onto the counter and plopped onto the couch with a dramatic sigh. "Una's garden."

"Una has a garden?"

Cassie grinned, pulled off her boots, and launched into the story. Threading it together with all the flair and momentum of someone reliving something precious. She told him about the hidden vines, the twelve stones, the bowl on the stump, the way the place had remembered Una's name even when she hadn't.

Baz listened in his usual way: not just with his ears, but with the quiet gravity of someone who understood that even the small details were sacred. He asked only once, gently, "Did she seem okay, being back in it?"

Cassie nodded. "Better than okay. She fit. Like the garden hadn't just waited, it had shaped itself around the space she left behind."

Baz was silent for a while after that. He stood, moved toward the window, and looked out toward the darker stretch of forest that guarded the Hollow's deeper edges.

"There's something in that," he said softly.

"In what?"

"In the idea of a place shaping itself to what's been absent. Not just what's present."

Cassie tilted her head. "Go on, darling inventor."

Baz turned, the edges of a smile playing at his lips. "If her garden still holds the residue of that memory, those emotional signatures, the intention of the twelve stones, then the energy beneath it isn't just old. It's layered."

Cassie nodded, catching his rhythm. "And?"

"And that means it might be possible to help it remember itself more clearly."

She raised an eyebrow. "Without overloading it?"

He grinned now, more fully. "Without altering anything at all."

Baz moved to the table and picked up one of the copper arcs he'd been working on. "I've been sketching out a low-impact harmonic loop. Something that resonates gently with latent memory frequencies. I was going to test it in the northern Spiral Grove, but now... I think it might be better served supporting places like Una's garden."

Cassie watched him, her eyes soft. "Not to amplify the magic," she said, "but to stabilize the story."

Baz nodded. "Exactly. Something like a net that doesn't catch, just... notices."

She stood and crossed to him, resting a hand on his shoulder. "You'd have to ask her."

"I will," Baz said. "If she's willing. I wouldn't install anything without her blessing."

Cassie leaned in, brushing a bit of moss from his hair. "Of course not. You're Baz. You ask permission before you enchant a doormat."

"It did say 'hello' a little too loudly after I charmed it," he said dryly.

She laughed.

Later that evening, while the kettle steeped and Baz added notes to his schematic in soft charcoal, Cassie sat nearby watching the light play across his focused face.

There was something beautiful about the way he made space for other people's magic. Never demanding, always offering. He didn't treat his craft like a fix. He treated it like an extension of memory. A conversation with things long buried and still breathing.

And now, somehow, he'd found a way to listen deeper.

# Chapter One Hundred Twenty-Three: The Gentle Ask

Baz took the long path through the trees, avoiding the more-traveled routes that wound near the bloom gardens and spell-touched benches. He liked the quieter paths. They hummed less, listened more. His satchel hung over one shoulder, not overfilled—just enough for a folded schematic, a few grounding coils wrapped in velvet, and a jar of sand that held memory better than most people did.

He hadn't made an appointment. It didn't feel like the kind of conversation you scheduled. You arrived softly, or not at all.

Fortunately, Una had left the vine arch open.

Baz took that as an invitation.

The garden was awake.

Not loud. Not blazing with new growth. But aware. As if the plants themselves had leaned in just slightly, curious. The stones at the garden's center glinted in the late morning sun, and he could feel, before he even stepped past the threshold, that something old had begun to stir again. It wasn't the kind of magic he usually worked with.

It was quieter. And it mattered.

Una knelt by one of the middle beds, her hands brushing soil from a cluster of silvery herbs Baz didn't immediately recognize. She looked up when she heard him, not startled, not guarded, just present.

"Hey," she said simply.

Baz smiled. "Hey. You have time?"

She nodded and gestured to the bench beneath the arching vine canopy. He joined her there, lowering himself onto the wood with the careful ease of someone who knew better than to rush reverent spaces.

They sat without speaking at first.

The garden filled in the silence for them: rustling leaves, a bloom opening with a sound like paper unfolding, the faint pulls of memory beneath their feet.

"I wanted to ask you something," Baz said eventually, resting his satchel across his knees.

Una turned to face him, curiosity flickering across her expression but no pressure in her gaze.

"I've been working on something," he continued. "A grounding array. It's not invasive. Doesn't push energy, doesn't pull it. It listens. Stabilizes resonance. Helps memory-holding places stay clear. Gentle, slow tech. No buzz. No enchantment unless you want it."

He paused.

Una didn't interrupt.

"I thought," he said, more softly now, "that it might help the garden remember itself. Not change it. Just… give it support. If that's something you want."

Una looked out over the circle of stones, the stump, the bowl that had once held petals and now held a small coil of moss like it had grown there for the sole purpose of anchoring a thought.

"Would it interfere with the way it remembers now?" she asked, tone calm but direct.

Baz shook his head. "No. It'd listen to what's already there. Amplify the clearest signals. Let the rest stay background, unless called forward. Think of it as a translator, not an interpreter."

She considered that. "And if the garden says no?"

"I take it apart before the tea cools."

Una smiled slightly at that; a warmth tucked beneath her usual reserve. She stood, walked to the center of the garden, and placed both hands on one of the stones.

The space stilled around her.

She stood there a moment listening, not asking. Then she turned back to him and nodded once. "One stone. You start with one."

Baz's eyes softened. "One is more than enough."

She gestured to the stone nearest the bench. "That one remembers patience."

He opened his satchel.

Carefully and reverently.

And the garden—blinking softly in the sunlight, vines rustling like laughter in the breeze—watched as something new and something ancient began, slowly, to learn each other's names.

## Chapter One Hundred Twenty-Four: Where Resonance Rests

Baz returned the next morning just after sunrise, before the town fully stirred, before the charm winds began to hum through the trees. He carried no more than his satchel which was lighter than usual, and a carefully bundled piece of copper-veined granite, already attuned, already listening.

The garden was waiting. Not with urgency, but with recognition. The vines had parted again, but this time they did not hang limp in greeting. They arched slightly above his head as he stepped through, almost like a bow. The scent of earth and crushed sage hung gently in the air, threaded with something fainter—metal, memory, and dew.

Una had left him a note tucked beneath a smooth stone near the bench. It read, simply: *"She's listening today. Speak softly."*

Baz smiled to himself, touched the edge of the note with reverence, and sat on the ground near the chosen stone, the one Una had said remembered patience.

He unpacked his tools one by one, laying them in a semicircle before him. No loud devices. No energy coils. Just his hands, a grounding needle carved from rosewood, and the copper array stone he'd infused with harmonic channels the night before. The copper wasn't loud. It didn't hum or flash. Baz had tuned it with stillness in mind, embedding the mineral lines with a resonance that moved like breath: inhale, hold, exhale, rest.

He pressed his palm to the garden floor and waited.

It wasn't something he rushed. He never did.

Magic, like soil, required presence more than pressure. And this garden, especially, didn't ask for action, it asked for acknowledgment.

For the first several minutes, he didn't move at all. Just sat in the rising light, listening. Beneath his palm, the earth held its own breath. Not resistant. Not closed. Just... cautious.

Then, slowly, gently, he whispered: "Not to bind. Not to change. Just to remember."

And something shifted.

It wasn't seismic. Not even magical in the way others would notice. But Baz felt it in the hairs on his arms, in the low thrum of the stone at his feet. The garden allowed him in.

He used his grounding needle to trace a slow spiral into the soil, just beside the original marker stone. The spiral didn't go deep, just enough to hold the stone in place, to create a point of reference the memory could orient to.

He placed the array stone at the center.

It clicked softly into the soil with the sound of something recognizing its match.

The air stilled.

Then pulsed.

Baz held his breath. Not out of fear. Out of reverence.

The pulse wasn't magic in the traditional sense. There were no glowing glyphs, no bursts of power. It was quieter than that. A soft wave that passed through the garden like wind through silk. A syncing.

He closed his eyes and pressed his fingers to the surface of the stone.

Yes.

The harmonic frequencies were taking root.

They weren't layering over the garden's memory; they were mirroring it.

Strengthening the weave.

Allowing the oldest threads—those thin and brittle from time—to hold firm again.

He sat there for another hour, not adjusting, not tweaking. Just breathing with the rhythm of the place.

As he did, he felt something else: a memory not his own brushing along the edge of his consciousness. A girl, younger than Una now, barefoot and wide-eyed, tracing the stones at dusk, whispering something about names she hadn't learned yet but knew belonged here.

It wasn't a vision.

It was a resonance. An echo.

And the garden shared it not as a message, but as a gift.

Baz blinked, heart full, and whispered, "Thank you."

The garden did not reply.

But the wind through the vines made a sound like someone humming - off-key, half-forgotten, and achingly familiar.

When he finally packed his tools away, the stone remained glowing faintly. Not with light, but with clarity.

The first thread had been restored.

Not claimed. Not commanded.

Just… remembered.

And now, the garden would breathe easier.

The circle would hold steadier.

And maybe, in time, more stones would follow.

But for now, Baz simply stood, touched the nearest vine in quiet gratitude, and stepped back through the arch, leaving behind something not built, but heard.

## Chapter One Hundred Twenty-Five: The Ground Beneath Her Breath

Una returned to the garden just before midday, her hands full of sage clippings and her thoughts pleasantly jumbled from a morning spent listening to Lilt describe the finer points of metaphorical weather. She hadn't planned to stay long—just a check-in, a trimming here or there, maybe another moment with the bowl on the stump. A familiar rhythm.

But the moment she stepped beneath the vine arch, she froze.

Something had shifted.

Not visibly. The leaves still swayed. The garden still wore its usual hush. The stones stood exactly where they had been, humble and listening.

But the air, the space itself, had changed its posture.

She didn't panic. Not exactly.

But her breath caught in her chest, and she placed a hand over her sternum as though trying to anchor something that had started to float upward without permission.

And then she realized, it wasn't something rising.

It was something settling.

She stepped forward.

Each footfall felt... certain. As if the garden knew the shape of her movement, remembered the pattern of her steps and had tuned itself accordingly.

There was a low vibration beneath her soles. It wasn't buzzing, or humming. Grounded. A sensation like leaning against a large, sleeping creature whose breathing rhythm syncs to yours whether you ask it to or not.

She walked slowly toward the ring of stones. And then she saw it.

Just beside the marker stone for patience, there was another. A small copper-veined stone resting in a shallow spiral traced into the earth. It didn't glow. Didn't pulse. But it felt warm, even from several feet away.

Baz's work. Of course.

She stepped closer, kneeling beside it, fingertips hovering just above the surface.

He hadn't altered the rhythm of the garden.

He had listened to it and helped it hold itself steady.

She could feel it in the air now. The way the resonance moved, not through the plants, but through the ground, like a heartbeat beneath the soil. As if the garden had been humming alone for years, and now someone had stepped in to sing harmony.

She placed her hand on the stone.

The response wasn't sound or light.

It was memory.

But not sharp-edged memories like pictures or pain. This was the memory of feeling. Like the echo of someone once sitting here under moonlight, trying to remember how to forgive themselves.

She didn't know if it was her own memory or one the garden held for her.

It didn't matter.

It felt real.

And it mattered.

As she stood and looked around, the garden seemed to breathe with her.

The plants didn't sway, but she could feel their attunement. Their calm.

The bowl on the stump no longer felt like an altar to a forgotten self.

It felt like a vessel being filled again, one breath at a time.

She knelt by it, her movements slow, and placed her hand above the water gathered from last night's light rain. It rippled once, not from wind, but from resonance.

She whispered, "I'm still here."

The water held the ripple longer this time.

As if replying, so am I.

When she left, she didn't look back. Not because she didn't want to, but because she no longer needed proof that the garden remained.

She could feel it now.

In the ground beneath her breath.

In the rhythm of her steps.

And in the knowledge that memory, once honored, becomes not a burden, but a resting place.

## Chapter One Hundred Twenty-Six: The Forgotten Thirteenth

The garden was settling.

That was the word Una kept returning to, repeatedly, like a mantra. Settling. The space no longer carried the raw energy of awakening or the jangling static of uncertainty. Instead, it had begun to breathe in a slower rhythm. Like an old book finally returned to its rightful shelf. Like warm soil pressed firm over freshly planted seeds. Baz's array stone had done exactly what he promised it would. There had been no flash of light, no shimmer, no tremor in the garden's pulse. Just a gentle alignment. A steadying hum that seemed to rise from the roots themselves, like the garden had exhaled after holding its breath for too long.

Una felt it in her bones. The garden was not just awake—it was at ease. So, when the unease came, it arrived like a quiet intrusion. No warning. No sound. Just a shift that made her breath catch.

It began as a whisper at the edge of her vision, a presence that did not demand attention but refused to be ignored. She was near the southern path, her hands gently brushing back a bed of lavender, checking for new buds beneath the overgrowth of moss. The morning had been calm, even joyful. But then, without cause or movement, something pressed against her awareness. A weight behind her—not like she was being watched, but as though something was waiting just beyond reach. Not a figure. A presence. Quiet. Insistent.

She turned slowly, careful not to jolt the moment. Nothing moved. The garden held its shape. But her eyes landed on a place that pulled at her chest. Just outside the ring of twelve stones, tucked between a stand of herbs and the soft curve of the moss bed, there was a bare patch of earth. It was small—no larger than a palm—but unmistakable. The moss that had crept over every other inch of the garden refused to touch this space. The soil there was pressed, not freshly disturbed, but settled in a way that felt deliberate. Like something had stood there once. And been removed.

Her breath stilled.

Only minutes earlier, the garden had felt like home. Now, something about the air had changed. It wasn't cold. It wasn't angry. But it had drawn inward, like a body preparing for a wound it remembered but could not stop.

Una stepped toward the bare patch, each footfall gentler than the last. As she approached, the breeze vanished. Not a single leaf moved. No birds called from the branches. Even the insects had gone silent, as if the entire garden had paused with her.

She crouched and extended her hand, letting her fingers rest lightly on the compacted earth.

The moment her skin met soil, a chill traveled up her arm. It was sharp and sudden, not painful, but intimate. Like a whisper curling backward into her thoughts.

And then it came.

Not a vision. Not exactly. More like a memory—but not hers.

It arrived in fragments. A pair of hands—older, worn—placing a stone into the earth. Not one of her stones. This one was jagged, dark, pitted with tiny veins of rust. There was no softness to it, no rounded edges from years of reverent touch. This stone had been placed with force. Not love. And behind the image, there was a voice, though it did not speak to her. It did not call her name. It watched. Not from now, but from long ago.

And the garden? The garden had not merely grown around that memory. It had wrapped it up like an old wound. It had folded the moment inward, tucked it deep beneath the ring of stones like someone hiding a broken thing beneath the floorboards.

Una pulled her hand back as if burned. The patch of earth remained still, quiet, and unassuming. But her pulse beat hard in her throat.

Twelve stones. Twelve intentions. She had placed them with care, listened to them, tended them. She had believed that was the whole of it.

But now, with a clarity that chilled her more than the memory itself, she knew.

There had been a thirteenth.

A stone not meant to guide or protect. Not meant to channel healing or help the garden remember joy. This stone had been placed to hold something in. To keep something out. And someone—someone not her—had removed it.

Not recently. That much she was certain of. The energy of the place bore the dust of time, not the heat of fresh tampering.

She stood slowly, her knees stiff from kneeling. She backed away from the bare patch and returned to the ring. The stones, usually so welcoming, now felt strange beneath her feet. They weren't changed. But her relationship with them had. She circled once, then again, her gaze darting from one to the next. Looking for signs she might have missed. But everything was in its place.

Everything but her certainty.

When she finally sat at the edge of the old stump, she did not place her hands on the bowl. She did not close her eyes or call upon the garden's rhythm. She simply sat, her shoulders tight, her breath short.

Her eyes remained on the bare patch of earth beyond the ring.

"Who did you keep out?" she asked softly.

The garden did not answer.

But the air shifted.

And the silence that followed did not feel empty. It felt like a story waiting to be told.

## Chapter One Hundred Twenty-Seven: What Was Buried with the Stone

Una didn't leave. She thought about it more than once, as the stillness lengthened and the garden seemed to pull ever-so-slightly inward, like it was holding a breath it didn't want her to notice. But leaving would've meant retreat. And retreat would've meant fear.

And if the memory she'd touched wanted her afraid, she wouldn't give it the satisfaction.

She sat instead, back straight, hands open on her knees, eyes trained on the bare patch of soil just outside the ring of twelve stones. The light shifted around her. Not darker. Just… denser. Like the air had grown thicker, woven through with threads too fine to see.

It began again without warning.

Not another vision. A feeling.

Something was reaching from beneath.

Not physically, there were no roots clawing their way toward the surface, no rumbles in the ground. But deep within her chest, behind the bone and between each breath, Una felt it:

A presence.

It did not come to greet. It came to observe.

And it already knew her.

The weight of its attention settled low and cold along her spine. It wasn't aggressive. Not yet. But it was intimate in the way a held breath in the dark becomes terrifying not because of what's seen, but because of what knows you're there.

Una closed her eyes.

She thought of the bowl.
The twelve stones.
The spiral Baz had laid just outside the circle, still humming low with gentle harmonics.

That was what held her steady.

Not protection. Recognition.

The garden still knew her.

But now, she suspected it remembered something else, too.

The impressions returned in pieces.

A hand that was not hers pressed into the soil from the outside. The shape of fingers calloused and strong, the edges of the nails blackened not from dirt, but from something darker. The stone they held was jagged, sharp, unnatural. Not a stone of intention, but of containment.

And it hadn't been placed as part of the circle.

It had been buried beneath it.

And she, in all her time tending and whispering and returning, had never felt it.

Because someone had wanted it forgotten.

A whisper unfurled then. Not into her ears, but along her skin.

It was not words.

Not a voice.

But it had meaning.

"I was not the first to find this garden."

The words weren't hers.

But they clung to her as if she'd once spoken them and then tried, desperately, to forget.

Her breath hitched.

Because with that meaning came an echo—a face. Brief. Fragmented. Eyes too pale, too wide, watching from behind a veil of leaves that didn't rustle when the wind passed. A presence that had not wanted the circle whole.

A presence that had benefited from what it concealed.

Una stood.

The movement broke the trance slightly. The air loosened its grip. The weight in her spine lifted by half.

But the knowing didn't leave.

It pressed behind her eyes. Sat beneath her ribs. It had seen her now, not just as caretaker, but as someone who might remember.

The garden didn't hush her.

But it didn't comfort her either.

Its silence had become... protective.

Like it, too, had only just begun to realize what it had been holding all these years.

Una stepped toward the bare patch again, slower this time.

The soil did not shift.
The vision did not return.

But the feeling—that watching—remained.

Still there.

Still waiting.

And now, she knew one thing for certain:

The thirteenth stone wasn't lost.

It had been removed.

Deliberately.

And someone, somewhere, might want it returned.

## Chapter One Hundred Twenty-Eight: What the Garden Hid

Cassie knew something was off the moment Una stepped through the cottage door. It was not anything obvious. There were no panicked eyes, no tears streaking her face, no singe marks of stray magic trailing across her sleeves. She did not come in wild-eyed with warnings about collapsing threadlines or ruptured spells. It was subtler than that—an undercurrent.

The way Una kept her arms close to her body, as though bracing against something invisible. The way her eyes didn't quite meet theirs, instead landing just past the far corner of the room, as if she was watching a memory still unfolding.

Baz, who had been seated by the window with a tea strainer in one hand and a loosely coiled length of copper wire in the other, looked up. His brow furrowed, and the small shift in his expression matched the tension that had crept into Cassie's own.

Una shut the door with a quiet finality. There was no urgency in the motion, but it wasn't casual either. It was careful, deliberate, the way someone closes a chapter they are not yet ready to reread.

"Where's Morgan?" she asked. Her voice was calm, but the calmness was stripped of its usual guarded humor. There was no hesitation in her tone, but it lacked its normal texture. It was smooth in a way that made Cassie instantly wary.

Cassie stood from the table. "Still down at the grove, I think," she replied. Her eyes searched Una's face. "What happened?"

Una didn't answer immediately. She pulled a chair closer to the hearth and lowered herself into it, palms flat against her thighs. The gesture looked like a tether, an attempt to ground herself. Her breathing was steady, but Cassie could tell that steadiness was being forced.

"It's the garden," Una said at last. Her voice was quiet, measured, but filled with unease. "Something feels wrong."

Baz leaned forward, placing his elbows on his knees. His movements were slow, as though giving Una time to speak at her own pace. "Wrong how?" he asked.

Cassie moved to crouch beside Una, offering a steady hand that just barely brushed her forearm in a silent gesture of encouragement.

"There's something I didn't see before," Una said. Her fingers flexed slightly against her legs. "A space I missed. A thirteenth space. I think there was a stone there once. Maybe it was buried. I'm not sure."

Cassie frowned. "You said there were twelve stones."

"I thought there were twelve," Una replied. Her words were sharper now, laced with frustration, not directed at anyone, but at herself. "But this place... the ground is different there. It's not just bare. It feels hollow. Emptied. Like something was there and has been removed."

She paused. Her voice caught on the next words, and for a moment she stared down at her hands as if they might offer her the courage to continue.

"When I touched it," she said, "something answered. But it wasn't mine. The memory didn't belong to me. It was... older."

Morgan arrived less than ten minutes later, summoned by one of Cassie's silver-thread charms. Cassie had released it into the air like a wisp of smoke, and the air itself had seemed to carry the message.

When Morgan stepped into the room, they took in the scene briefly. They did not ask what had happened. They simply lowered themselves into the empty chair beside Una and waited.

Una did not repeat everything. Not at first. But Cassie and Baz surrounded her with quiet questions, their tones soft and careful. Some were direct, others implied. Morgan remained silent throughout, listening with complete focus.

It wasn't until Una reached the part about the thirteenth space—about the feeling of a presence not born from her own memory, and the stone that had not been meant for guidance or growth but for containment that Morgan finally stirred.

"I've felt that before," they said quietly.

All three of them turned to look at Morgan.

"In the Hollow," they continued. "Long before the Threadfound arrived. Before the blooms. When I first came here, there was a pocket of space I couldn't read. It was dense. Quiet. Too quiet. I assumed it was damage. I thought it was trauma, like a scar in the land's memory. But now…"

Morgan turned to Una, their eyes steady.

"It feels the same."

Silence filled the room. Cassie folded her arms tightly and stared at the floorboards. Her jaw was set.

"All right," she said. Her voice was level, but there was a current of steel running beneath the words. "So, what we have is a garden that may have been designed to hold something in place. Maybe it was a memory. Maybe a spell. Or someone. And at some point, someone removed the seal. They didn't do it recently, and they didn't do it loudly. Just enough to make sure no one noticed."

Baz rubbed his hands together slowly, the copper wire now forgotten on the table beside him. "And we activated a harmonic array right on top of that forgotten place," he added.

Una shook her head. "The array didn't cause it," she said. "It just activated the resonance. Whatever was buried there… it had already been disturbed."

Morgan's eyes darkened slightly, their expression unreadable. "That means whatever had been sealed beneath the thirteenth stone has already had time to listen back. It might have already started remembering us."

For several long moments, no one moved. The room felt suspended, like it had drawn in its own breath.

Then Cassie stood and crossed to the window, pushing the curtain aside and squinting toward the horizon.

"You know," she said, her voice dry and overly light, "I kind of miss the days when our biggest problem was a sarcastic loaf of sourdough and a goose with a crush."

"You don't," Morgan replied gently.

Cassie sighed. "No. But I would gladly swap this creeping existential dread for a jealous barn animal and a rude baguette."

Baz reached for his notes again, flipping through the most recent pages. "We'll need to map the whole thing. Not just the garden. The resonance boundary around it. I can recalibrate the array to search for non-local memory patterns. If it flares, we will know the source did not come from Una or the original circle."

Cassie turned, her expression guarded. "And if it isn't just a flare? What if it's something older than the garden? Older than us?"

Morgan stood, shoulders squared. "Then we prepare to remember something the land was never meant to forget."

## Chapter One Hundred Twenty-Nine: The Weight Beneath the Thirteenth

The walk back to the garden unfolded in near silence. It was not tense in the traditional sense. No one was clenching their jaw or hurrying their steps. Yet there was a weight between them, a softness shaped like caution. It curled gently at the edges of their thoughts, brushing their ribs like the echo of a long-forgotten lullaby that somehow knew your name.

It was not fear exactly, but reverence. They were not marching toward danger. They were approaching a memory with teeth.

Cassie carried a basket looped over her arm, the contents rattling gently with each step. Inside were two mugs, a tin of ginger biscuits, and a few grounding threads tied in loops of rose and cedar twine. Cassie had no intention of facing ancient magical residue on an empty stomach.

Morgan walked beside her, hands open at their sides, fingers twitching now and then as if their body was trying to pluck a thread of resonance out of the air.

Una led the way, her stride steady, but her attention turned inward. She moved like someone who had become a needle herself, following the pull of thread she could no longer see but still trusted.

No one spoke until they crossed through the arch that shimmered between the sycamores.

The garden welcomed them with the same stillness it had held before. No rustling leaves, no sudden bloom of color or sound. The harmonic stone Baz had placed near the center still thrummed gently beneath the soil, the tone so subtle it could be mistaken for breath. Everything looked unchanged.

Except for the patch.

371

The space where the thirteenth stone should have been remained untouched. The soil there was dry and pale, resistant to growth. There was no moss, no herb sprouting defiantly through cracks. It was as if the land itself had decided nothing else should grow there.

And this time, the emptiness did not feel passive. It felt aware.

Not hostile, at least not yet. But watchful. As though whatever was beneath that patch of earth had taken note of their return and was waiting to see what they would do next.

Cassie stepped forward and knelt near the edge of the bare earth. She did not touch it. Instead, she hovered her hand just above the surface, palm down, her fingers curled slightly as if reaching for something just beyond her grasp. Her eyes narrowed, and her mouth pressed into a contemplative line.

"It's not trying to hide," she said eventually. Her voice was soft but certain. "But it is holding its breath."

Morgan nodded slowly, their eyes scanning the perimeter of the circle. "The boundary magic has been disturbed here. It hasn't been destroyed, just rerouted. Threaded through something else. Like someone stitched over an old wound instead of treating it."

Una knelt beside them both. Her voice dropped to a whisper. "I think I was the one who made that stitch."

The three of them remained that way for a while—seated in a triangle around the patch of earth, each facing inward. Their hands rested on their knees, fingers loose and open. None of them called on spells or sigils. There was no incantation, no invocation. This was not spellcraft. This was presence. This was witnessing.

Cassie broke the silence first. "What kind of magic do you bury like this?" she asked. Her question wasn't rhetorical, but it also wasn't aimed at anyone in particular.

The air responded before anyone else could. A cool breeze passed between them, brief and crisp, like a breath let out after a long pause.

Morgan tilted their head slightly. "Sometimes magic is sealed when it is dangerous. When it is too powerful or too broken to hold safely in the open. Or when it was never meant to be used in the first place."

Una shook her head gently. "This doesn't feel broken. It doesn't feel unfinished."

"No," Cassie agreed. "It feels like grief. Not the loud kind. The kind that gets buried because no one knows what else to do with it."

Morgan's eyes opened. "Then it's not just memory buried here," they said. "It's a decision. A choice someone made, maybe out of love, maybe out of fear."

The weight of the words settled around them. It did not accuse. It simply filled the space with a new understanding.

Una reached out and pressed her palm to the ground, just beside the bare patch. She did not touch the disturbed area directly, but the soil near it vibrated faintly beneath her hand.

"What if this wasn't meant to stay hidden forever?" she asked.

Cassie's gaze remained on the patch. "Then someone broke a promise."

Morgan inhaled slowly. "Or maybe the promise was never meant to be held by just one person. Maybe it was always meant to be shared."

No one moved. There were no dramatic revelations, no sudden flares of power. But something shifted all the same. They remained in that quiet triangle of breath and trust, three people who had become, without any grand announcement, caretakers of something ancient and unnamed.

After a time, Una finally spoke again. Her voice was steady but introspective. "When I created the original ring and placed the twelve stones, I did it to hold my own becoming. It was a circle of intention. It was for me."

She looked at both in turn.

"But this thirteenth space does not feel like mine. It never did."

Cassie reached out and rested her hand gently over Una's. "Maybe it belonged to someone else. Maybe someone else started to become something and never got the chance to finish it."

There was no tremor in the earth. No dramatic shift of power.

But the garden moved.

A single leaf turned on its stem, despite the air remaining still. A petal dropped from a bloom that had been closed since they arrived. It did not feel like warning.

It felt like recognition.

Beneath their hands, the earth warmed. Not in a rising, magical surge, but in a slow, grounding pulse. It was not asking to be solved. It was asking to be seen.

Each of them felt something different in that moment.

Cassie felt a name resting behind her tongue. It was a name she had never spoken aloud, but it nestled there as if it had been waiting in a dream.

Morgan felt a thread of emotional resonance hum through their chest, something ancient and unfinished. A song without an ending.

Una felt a heartbeat that was not her own but had once rested so close to hers that it had altered her rhythm without her knowing.

The three of them rose together, not with resolution, but with acknowledgment.

No choices had been made. No conclusions drawn.

But something had begun.

Cassie looked down at the bare patch. "It is not ready to speak," she said.

Morgan nodded. "But it is listening now."

Una exhaled and whispered the words as if making a promise.

"And we will be here when it does."

## Chapter One Hundred Thirty: The Memory That Knew Their Name

Morgan waited until well after dusk before returning to the garden. They weren't avoiding company, exactly, but there was a particular kind of magic that could only be heard in solitude. When the town quieted, when the last echo of laughter faded through the Hollow, and when even the wind stopped whispering long enough to let the old things speak. They left without charm or companion, just a low-burning lantern swinging gently in one hand and a thin woven shawl around their shoulders. It was cool tonight. The kind of cool that made the air feel clean, sharpened, and expectant.

The path to the garden was familiar underfoot, but not comfortable. Not tonight. The earth felt alert somehow, like it had turned slightly to face them. The trees leaned in closer than usual. Every step Morgan took felt noticed. Not judged. Just… registered. By the time they stepped beneath the vine-wrapped archway, they were already aware that whatever had stirred within the thirteenth space was no longer dormant.

The garden itself didn't react. The leaves didn't rustle. The stones didn't pulse. But the stillness had teeth. Morgan stood at the edge for a long moment, letting their eyes adjust to the dark, letting their breath slow until they could hear the threadlines beneath the surface begin to shift. They had always been good at sensing resonance— emotional energy layered in memory, held not just in places, but in objects, in people. And this space was full of it. But the thirteenth space… that was something else. It wasn't echoing past feeling. It was aware of the present.

They made their way to the stone circle without stepping inside. Instead, Morgan knelt just outside it, setting the lantern softly on the grass. Its golden light cast long shadows across the garden's beds, brushing the contours of each stone but never quite reaching the hollow patch of soil where the thirteenth stone had once been.

That space remained in shadow.

And it was in that shadow that the memory began to respond.

Not with images. Not yet. But with sensation. A sudden weight in Morgan's chest, familiar and wrong all at once. Like walking into a childhood room only to find it rearranged. Something in their ribs shifted, not in pain, but in recognition. They didn't gasp or retreat. They simply closed their eyes and placed both hands, palms down, on the earth.

The response was immediate.

Their name—not the one anyone used now, not the one they claimed or were given—rose in their mind like smoke from an old, forgotten fire. A name they hadn't spoken in years. One they thought had dissolved into the quiet of personal evolution.

But the memory hadn't forgotten.

It knew them.

Not just who they were now, but who they had been when they first came to the Hollow. Before the Threadfound. Before the Looming Tree. Before the weaving of stories and breath and roots.

It knew the version of Morgan that had asked to be unseen.

And it was calling them home.

Their body tensed involuntarily, muscles locking as a rush of emotion moved through them. Grief, yes, but older than that. Regret. The kind you don't even realize you carry until something says your true name aloud.

They wanted to deny it. Push it back. They hadn't come here to be unmade.

But the garden didn't seek to unmake them.

It sought to restore something.

Something broken.

Or perhaps stolen.

Morgan let out a slow breath, eyes still closed. "What are you?" they asked, their voice steady despite the tremor threading through their chest.

The soil beneath their fingers warmed.

And then, ever so faintly, a whisper. Not from the earth, not from the air, but from somewhere inside them.

"Not what. Who."

The words didn't belong to the garden.

They belonged to the thirteenth.

And as Morgan opened their eyes, they knew:

This wasn't a sealed spell or a hidden ward.

It was a person.

A memory. A presence. A name.

And it knew theirs.

## Chapter One Hundred Thirty-One: The Name Beneath the Lanternlight

Cassie couldn't sleep. She'd tried. Twice.

The first time, she had curled beneath the quilt Baz had mended last autumn, the one with the frayed hem she never fixed on purpose because she liked how it looked a little unfinished. But her body didn't settle. The weight of her limbs felt too present, like the bed was holding her attention instead of releasing it. Her breath kept catching. Not in fear, but in anticipation. Like the moment before a spell reacts to your hand.

The second time, she'd made tea. Lavender and clove, with a whisper of bergamot charm still clinging to the tin's lid. It had helped, briefly. The scent filled the kitchen like a memory, and the warmth gave her hands something to hold. But it didn't quiet the restlessness in her chest, that low, subtle thrum of something just outside the reach of words. The kind of sensation that didn't come from intuition alone, but attunement. The magical tether you develop when you live too long in a place that listens back.

She was standing by the window in the greenhouse now, mug warm between her palms, watching the night breathe in and out across the Hollow. The lanterns along the central path had long since dimmed, casting everything in soft indigo. The wind had gone still. Even the blooms near the windows were quiet.

But Cassie wasn't.

She could feel something moving beneath the surface. Not physically. There were no tremors, no spells misfiring, no sudden gusts of magic. But there was a shift. A weight dragging through the old threads of the land like a hand brushing against buried lace. Something subtle, deep, and recently reawakened.

And then, as if called by her awareness, the door creaked open. Morgan stepped inside.

Cassie turned before they could speak.

The moment she saw their face; her breath left her in a shallow wave. Morgan didn't look panicked. They didn't look injured or frightened. But their eyes, those steady, perceptive eyes that so rarely revealed anything before they were ready, held a shadow. Not fear. Recognition.

Cassie set the mug down on the counter. "What happened?"

Morgan didn't answer immediately. They shut the door behind them with a quiet finality, as though sealing something out or maybe sealing it in. Their fingers hovered near their chest, not clenched, but curved. Like they were still holding something that hadn't quite let go.

Cassie didn't push. Instead, she reached across the counter and retrieved the kettle. Poured a second cup. Set it down beside Morgan with gentle precision.

Only then did Morgan speak. "I went back to the garden."

Cassie nodded once. "We figured you might."

"I didn't plan to stay long. I just... needed to listen."

"And did it speak?"

Morgan's jaw tightened. "Not at first."

Cassie moved to sit across from them, her hands folded in her lap, spine straight. She didn't interrupt. She didn't offer charm or joke. She waited.

Morgan's gaze dropped to the cup in front of them. "The thirteenth memory, whatever presence it held, it's not passive anymore. It didn't try to scare me. It didn't even threaten. It just... recognized me."

Cassie's stomach tightened, but she held her voice level. "Recognized you how?"

"By name." Morgan looked up now. "Not the name I use now. The one I left behind. The name I stopped saying when I came to the Hollow. The name I thought was buried with the old self I didn't want to carry anymore."

Cassie inhaled slowly. "And it remembered that."

Morgan nodded. "And called me by it. Not aloud. But inside. As clearly as breath."

The silence between them bloomed wide and intimate.

Cassie reached forward, placed her hand over Morgan's. "That's not just memory. That's knowing."

Morgan's throat moved as they swallowed. "And it didn't just know me. It needed me to know that it knew. It wasn't showing off. It wasn't trying to manipulate. It was… asking to be remembered. As a person."

Cassie sat back, the weight of that statement settling in the room like a fog that knew all the corners.

"Then it wasn't a spell," she murmured. "Not a ward. Not a containment glyph. It was a burial."

Morgan nodded again. "But of what? Or who?"

They looked to her then, gaze steady but heavy. "Cassie… it remembered me before. I think I knew it. Or whoever they were."

Cassie blinked. The idea wasn't impossible. The Hollow held stories that ran deeper than anyone had dared to map. Morgan's magic had always been more than weaving. It was memory-bound, empathy-threaded, attuned to things that lived outside of linear time.

But still, this felt like more than connection.

This felt like history.

She stood, needing to move, and paced to the window. The night outside remained unchanged. But now the quiet felt deceptive. As if something below the garden was listening through the dirt. Cassie turned back to Morgan.

"What name did it use?"

Morgan's lips parted. For a moment, it looked like they might hesitate. But they didn't.

"Ember."

The word hit the air like a dropped stone in still water.

It was small. But it rippled.

Cassie felt her breath catch. Not from memory—she didn't recognize the name. But the sound of it belonged. Not to her. But here. To this land. To this magic. Like it had always been part of the threadline and had simply been waiting for someone to say it aloud again.

"Ember," she repeated, softer now. "That's not a spellword. That's a soul."

Morgan nodded once. "I think they were once a person like us. A weaver, maybe. Or a protector. Maybe something else entirely. But someone made the choice to bury them in memory. Not kill. Not erase. Just… contain."

Cassie's voice turned sharp with instinct. "And now that container is unraveling."

Morgan looked at her, and the truth was in their silence.

Cassie pressed her hand to her sternum. The warmth of her own charm-stitch pulsed faintly beneath her ribs.

"They're not just waking," she whispered. "They're looking for a way back."

Morgan leaned forward, hands folding around their tea at last.

"I don't think they're coming to hurt us," they said. "But I don't think they're coming alone."

They sat in the quiet together then, as the lanterns outside flickered lower, as the blooms trembled in their beds, as the Hollow, beneath root and ritual, adjusted its weight.

Cassie looked to the shelves near the door, to the bundles of unfinished sigils and half-labeled charms.

"Then we need to prepare," she said. "Because remembering something doesn't mean understanding it. And I have a feeling this memory... wants to be seen."

Morgan nodded.

"And if it was buried, it was buried for a reason."

Cassie looked up.

"But maybe not the reason we think."

## Chapter One Hundred Thirty-Two: What the Hollow Heard

It began, as many things did in Alden's Landing, with breath.

Not a gasp. Not a spell. Just breath. Taken in through human lungs and pushed past lips shaped by memory, speaking a name the earth had not heard in generations.

Ember.

The word unfurled slowly at first, brushing through the trees like a low wind that remembered its way through the leaves. It caught the edges of petals not yet bloomed, slipped between cobblestones where charms once slept, and settled in the moss-covered bones of the Hollow's oldest roots.

The land did not startle.

But it paused.

A stillness took hold. A shift. The kind of deep pause that follows the first creak of a door long rusted shut. The Hollow, which had watched quietly for so long, gathering, weaving, forgiving, tilted toward the sound.

Because the name wasn't just sound.

It was a key. And keys, once turned, open more than doors.

Beneath the garden, the soil warmed.

Not from sun. Not from spellfire. But from recognition.

The memory of Ember had not died here. It had been nested. Pressed gently into the loam by hands not cruel, but desperate. The thirteenth stone had not been meant to trap; it had been meant to tend.

A promise made not in fear, but in grief.

And the Hollow had kept it.

Until now.

The utterance of the name was a breath exhaled into a long-held ache, and the earth did not resist it. Instead, it adjusted. It listened.

Old vines near the Loom trembled, curling toward each other like hands reaching in the dark.

The spiral paths near the Threadfound's gathering circles shifted, their lines loosening as if stretching after sleep.

And deeper still, where no human foot had touched and no crafted magic dared linger, a pulse of resonance, soft and sorrowful, rippled through stone.

The Hollow did not judge.

It had seen too many versions of truth to hold one above another. It had watched wars and weeping, promises kept and broken, births beneath trees and deaths no one witnessed. It had held them all—not as history, but as weft.

But Ember?

Ember had been different.

Not powerful.

Not feared.

But remembered.

Remembered wrong.

The memory the Hollow kept was not the one passed down in story. It was not neat, nor easy. It did not fit into spells or cautionary tales.

It was a memory of sacrifice.

Of someone who had chosen to be forgotten—not because they were dangerous, but because what they held could not yet be known.

And now, someone had remembered.

Now, the weave was changing.

Near the greenhouse, a cluster of blooms that had refused to open since the last solstice finally stirred. Their petals unspooled slowly, revealing not color, but light. A pale gold that shimmered faintly as if made of dust and sighs.

Cassie's charms near the window began to hum.

Just once.

A low, clear tone.

Not warning.

Not joy.

But acknowledgment.

Inside, Morgan sat curled in a chair, eyes closed, breath held. Their name, the one they had not spoken in years, still echoed beneath their ribs. And the Hollow felt it.

Not as intrusion.

As invitation.

Near the edges of the Hollow, where threadlines laced through trees older than memory, something else responded.

The stone paths curled tighter.

The air thickened with scents of cedar, ash, and a hint of salt. Not sea salt. Tear salt.

Something that had waited began to move.

Not fast.

Not angry.

But inevitable.

The Hollow did not rejoice.

It did not mourn.

It simply opened.

And as it did, something long kept quiet whispered back:

They spoke the name.

We are no longer alone.

## Chapter One Hundred Thirty-Three: When the Ground Spoke Back

The first hum began as a vibration behind the charm wall, a subtle shift that Cassie almost missed.

She had just risen from her chair, half-focused on putting the kettle on for another round of tea, when the sound gently unfurled behind her. It was low and round, not quite a melody and not entirely mechanical. It reminded her of breath made of memory and metal, as if someone had exhaled a song too old to be sung. It moved through her spine like a name she had once heard in a dream but never managed to recall upon waking.

Morgan was already standing.

They had not spoken a word since saying Ember's name aloud. Yet now, their posture was firm and alert. Their shoulders were squared, head tilted slightly as if listening beyond the veil of sound. Their eyes were wide, not in fear, but in something closer to recognition.

Cassie stepped to their side, drawn by instinct more than conscious thought. The windows at the back of the greenhouse had fogged, but not from weather. The condensation didn't follow the usual downward trail of steam or dew. Instead, it curled upward in slow spirals, tracing symbols that looked unintentional but somehow purposeful. It was like breath on a mirror that never belonged to her.

She pressed her hand to the glass.

The mist stopped moving.

And then, with delicate precision, a petal touched the window from the outside.

"Morgan," she whispered.

But Morgan was already moving.

They crossed the floor in deliberate steps and opened the greenhouse door without pause. The night air met them with a hush. It was not cold or warm. It did not announce itself. It simply arrived, neutral and still, as if it were holding space.

The stone path ahead was lit only by the soft glow of lanterns spaced along the trail. Yet even that small light felt different. Something had changed. The blooms that normally closed their petals at dusk remained open. But they did not stretch in their usual full bloom. Instead, they curled inward in intricate spirals, like symbols written in a language neither of them had studied but somehow understood.

Cassie followed, her boots crunching gently over the gravel. There was no wind. No frog song. Not a single rustle of leaves. The entire landscape had gone still, not in fear, but in anticipation. Even the trees seemed to hold their breath.

They stopped near the largest cluster of vines where Baz's silver-stemmed bellflowers had stubbornly refused to bloom since the early days of autumn.

Now, all of them were open.

But instead of their familiar pale blue, the petals glowed with a soft golden hue, like captured sunlight woven through silk.

Morgan stepped forward. "It's responding."

Cassie nodded, her voice barely audible. "To the name?"

Morgan considered for a moment before replying. "To more than the name. To the remembering."

At their feet, the vines stirred. They moved slowly, curling not with aggression or hunger, but with familiarity. They seemed to stretch toward Morgan's boots, not to grasp, but to greet.

Cassie lowered her gaze. "It has never done this before."

"No," Morgan replied, "but it never had a reason to before now."

Cassie watched as the vines stilled once more, gently entwining with one another. The movement was subtle but full of emotion. She saw sorrow in the motion. She also saw joy. The two existed side by side, braided into one fluid gesture.

Her voice came softer this time. "Do you think the Hollow is trying to bring Ember back?"

Morgan's eyes remained on the bloom. They tilted their head, thinking deeply before responding.

"I don't think the Hollow is trying," they said slowly. "I think it already is."

The words settled between them like the air just before a storm. Not heavy but undeniably charged.

The Hollow had always held a sense of mystery. It had always felt old, deeper than maps or memories. But it had never felt cruel. There had always been a distance to it, like the town existed beside something ancient that watched but never intervened. It was a companion to magic, not a participant.

Tonight, something shifted.

Tonight, Cassie realized the Hollow was not beside them.

It was around them.

It was holding them.

Her charm pulsed softly within her sleeve, a slow and rhythmic beat against her wrist. She placed her hand over it, grounding herself in the familiarity of that touch.

Morgan's gaze had turned toward the arch that led back to Una's garden. Their expression sharpened slightly.

"We're not the only ones feeling this."

Cassie followed their line of sight. "You think it has reached that far already?"

Morgan's voice held certainty. "I don't think it spread. I think it awakened. It was already there. It just needed to be named."

They turned their attention back to the bloom.

"I think it always remembered," they said. "It was only waiting for us to say it out loud."

Cassie stepped forward and placed her palm gently on the outer petal. The bloom did not pull away or resist. Instead, it pulsed beneath her hand, not with magic, but with presence. It was breathing with her, matching her inhale and exhale.

She whispered one word. "Ember."

The garden responded.

There was no sound. No flash of light. But everything shifted. The leaves bowed slightly as though caught in a breeze that did not exist. The mist on the greenhouse windows vanished. The stones along the path shimmered faintly, as if winking back at her in quiet approval.

Cassie stepped away slowly. Her heartbeat fluttered like a bird just beneath her ribs.

"They're not gone," she said quietly.

Morgan nodded. "They were never gone."

Silence followed, but it was no longer hollow. It was not the kind of quiet that preceded danger or the kind that followed confusion.

It was full.

Alive.

The silence was presence itself.

Cassie reached out and took Morgan's hand. They stood there together, still and silent, sharing that moment without needing to fill it with anything more.

The Hollow had answered them.

Not with fear.

Not with power.

But with recognition.

And now, it was watching. And it would not forget.

## Chapter One Hundred Thirty-Four: The Garden That Remembered Differently

Una was already awake before the sky changed. She hadn't planned to visit the garden. Not that morning. Not so soon. But she had risen from bed while the stars still lingered and found her hands pulling on her boots before she could name the reason why. The kettle had remained cold. Her shawl hung forgotten on the peg. Only her satchel that was half-full of charms and clippings seemed to know where they were going.

The garden had never called her before. Not like this.

The path to it was still wrapped in darkness, the kind of deep early-hour quiet that sits between sleep and certainty. The world hadn't decided what kind of day it would become yet. Neither had Una. But the pull beneath her ribs was steady.

As she stepped through the vine-wrapped arch, the first thing she noticed was the light. Not sunrise. Not lantern.

A faint, golden shimmer laced through the dew threading along leaves, caught on web-thin moss, gathered in beads along the rim of the stone bowl at the garden's center. It wasn't bright. But it glowed. And it wasn't hers.

Not in origin. Not in memory.

The garden had remembered something new.

She stood at the edge of the ring, unsure whether to enter.

It felt different.

Not sacred. Not threatened.

Occupied.

The twelve stones remained in place. Unchanged, solid, humming with the slow resonance Baz's harmonic array had helped reawaken. But now, even they seemed… alert. They leaned, subtly, toward the thirteenth space, the patch where she had once pressed her palm and felt not welcome but witnessed.

Now, it hummed too.

Quietly. Like a heartbeat through soil.

She stepped forward.

The garden allowed it.

The moment she crossed into the ring, her senses shifted.

The air carried scents of bark, loam, something like ash, but gentler. Like something long smothered had begun to burn again, but not wildly. It was a hearth scent. A warming.

She approached the thirteenth space slowly.

There was something there. Still no stone. No sigil or sudden bloom.

Just dirt.

But the dirt no longer looked empty.

It breathed.

The soil moved in small pulses, timed to her footsteps. Not reacting to her. Anticipating her. And as she knelt before it, her body filled with a strange, aching memory…

Not hers, but familiar.

She briefly saw a flash of someone kneeling just as she was, hands pressed deep into the same soil. Not burying. Not planting. Blessing.

394

Their face was turned away. The light behind them too bright to reveal details.

But they were crying and whispering a name.

She couldn't hear it, but she felt it answer.

A name not prayed to.

A name returned to.

Una blinked and the vision was gone.

But her breath had caught. And the weight behind her eyes that pre-tear fullness that doesn't always mean sadness, held firm.

The thirteenth space had not waited to be remembered. It had waited for the world to be ready.

The garden had not just remembered differently. It had remembered forward.

She rose and moved to the bowl at the stump's center.

It had collected dew overnight, but the surface shimmered faintly. It wasn't from the sky above, but from something beneath.

She stared into it. Her reflection wavered, but not from motion. From magic.

Faint threads like root filaments coiled at the water's surface and twisted downward. Into earth. Into time. Into memory that wasn't bound by her body.

She whispered, "Ember."

The shimmer held. A breeze passed through the garden - soft, deliberate, listening. And then, from the edge of the vines, a bloom opened that had never grown in the garden before.

White-veined with gold at its heart. Still closed at the edges, but unignorable.

Una stood quietly for a long time.

The garden had changed. Not just in rhythm or in reach. In intent.

She no longer stood in a space meant to hold her past. She stood in a space being prepared for what was returning.

Not a haunting. Not a reckoning.

A becoming.

And the garden?

It was no longer hers alone.

## Chapter One Hundred Thirty-Five: The Shape of Return

The first time Ember's presence took form, it wasn't dramatic.

There was no rupture in the earth. No storm clouds above the garden. No fire blooming in the threadlines.

There was only a shape, a shimmer, rippling along the inside of a single bloom at the far edge of the Hollow. A flower too young to open. A vine too old to twist. And somewhere between their roots, something breathed.

It wasn't Ember, not fully. But it was more than memory.

It was momentum.

Morgan was the first to feel it shift.

Not in the garden. Not in the greenhouse. But beneath their ribs, where magic and selfhood entwined. They had spent their life attuning to the emotional sediment others left behind. They knew the rhythm of grief, of legacy, of silent longing.

But this?

This was different. This was mutual.

It wasn't just Ember being remembered.

It was Ember remembering back.

They knelt alone near the Looming Tree, hands pressed into soil that hadn't moved in weeks, when the pulse began. A slow wave of warmth, not from light, but from recognition. Not power. Not hunger. Just... acknowledgment.

They whispered the name again—not aloud, not even in voice, but in feeling.

Ember.

And the tree responded.

A single vine descended. Not quickly. Not with urgency. But like a hand brushing a shoulder. Like a breath finishing someone else's sentence.

Morgan closed their eyes.

For the first time, they didn't just feel for Ember. They felt with them.

Elsewhere in the Hollow, things began to... shift.

In Una's garden, a second bloom of the gold-veined white flower opened overnight, this one nestled near the thirteenth space. Not sprouting upward, but outward, like an invitation.

In Baz's workshop, a copper thread curled off its spindle without touch and wove itself into a loose spiral, not one he had planned. It pulsed with harmonic resonance that matched none of his tuned frequencies.

And in Cassie's hand - while she was wrapping a tea jar for a customer her charm line snapped.

Not from weakness.

From release.

The thread coiled twice on her palm and rested. Like a story that had finished itself without needing to be told.

Cassie didn't panic. She simply whispered, "You're close, aren't you?"

And the charm, faintly warm, pulsed once.

The town didn't change overnight.

There were no bells tolling. No official announcements. No carved runes in the sky.

But the air carried something new.

An ache, maybe. A clarity. The sense that something long overdue had begun to round the final bend. Children dreamed of golden roots. The baker's sourdough proofed in half the time. A lantern left unlit near the river glowed without heat.

And in quiet corners, people began asking:

"Who was Ember?"

No one had the answer.

But everyone felt they should.

Ember's presence didn't push into the world.

It gathered.

It coalesced.

It moved like steam around memory, taking shape where hearts were open—not to history, but to complexity. To the idea that what had been buried might not be dangerous. Might not be broken.

Might simply be unfinished.

And the Hollow responded in kind.

No longer a vessel. Now, a participant.

The vines leaned toward the town.

The threadlines shifted, no longer spirals of containment, but spirals of invitation.

And in the center of it all where Una's garden whispered, where Cassie's threads warmed, where Morgan's pulse synced with a name they once laid to rest, something bloomed.

Not a person. Not yet.

But a shape.

The shape of return.

And the story began to listen for its end.

## Chapter One Hundred Thirty-Six: Seen

It happened just after dawn, the kind of light that doesn't ask for attention, only softens the world by showing it as it is.

Morgan had returned to the garden.

Not to search.

Not to summon.

Just to sit.

They carried no tools. No threads. No charms. Only themselves, wrapped in the shawl Una had given them weeks ago, stitched at the corner with a sun that resembled a spiral. It wasn't symbolic when she made it. But now, nothing felt accidental.

The garden welcomed them.

It did not pulse. It did not sing. But it allowed.

Morgan crossed into the ring and lowered to the ground, knees tucked beneath them, hands resting palms-down in the grass. The morning air was cool. Damp with dew. The kind that makes breath visible, even when it's slow.

They closed their eyes.

Not to shut out the world. To feel it.

There was no sound of arrival.

No footfall. No whisper. No shift in the leaves.

But Morgan felt it. Like a drop in water, like the change in a room when someone enters quietly and the silence adjusts to their shape.

They opened their eyes and Ember was there.

Not standing.

Not hovering.

Just... present.

A figure, at the edge of the garden, where the thirteenth space brushed against the memory of all the rest. Not fully formed, more suggestion than solid. Their edges shimmered like dew shaken loose. Their face was half-shadowed by light, and where their feet met the earth, the grass didn't bend but brightened.

Morgan did not move.

They didn't need to.

They somehow knew that to act too quickly might startle the moment back into silence. And this was not a moment to be lost.

Ember didn't speak. Their mouth didn't move.

But their presence did.

It reached gently across the space between them, and Morgan felt something settle in their chest. Not a question. Not a command.

A memory.

Of a time before becoming.

Of threads not woven yet.

Of a person, not a myth, not a warning, who had chosen stillness over survival, hiding over harm.

Morgan whispered, "You stayed."

And in that moment, Ember smiled.

Not wide. Not bright.

Just enough.

Enough to say I see you. Enough to mean you saw me.

And that was enough.

The light shifted. A breeze moved through the trees.

And Ember began to fade—not vanish, not depart—dissipate.

Like mist stepping back from water.

But as they did, Morgan clearly and undeniably saw the eyes.

Not haunted. Not pleading.

Known.

And for the first time, Morgan didn't feel responsible. They felt remembered.

Ember did not need to stay. They had been seen.

And now, the story could end—

Not in forgetting.

But in belonging.

## Chapter One Hundred Thirty-Seven: What Bram Remembers

Bram had always kept the back corner of the greenhouse empty.

Not neglected—never that—but untouched. While the rest of the space bloomed with careful rows of herbwork, magical blooms, and experimental grafts, that single section remained a quiet arc of stillness. He told himself it was for airflow. Or utility. Or rest. But even he knew better.

Some spaces weren't left bare by accident.

They were left bare by memory.

Even when you didn't remember why.

The morning after the blooms began to glow, Bram rose earlier than usual. The sky hadn't yet softened today, and the Hollow still slept. But something in his hands refused stillness. Something in the way his palms felt warm before touching soil, in the way the air tasted like thyme and ash.

He didn't make tea. He didn't wash his face. He pulled on his boots with yesterday's socks still half-rolled inside and crossed the garden path with the rhythm of someone walking toward something he'd avoided naming for years.

When he stepped into the greenhouse, the light met him like a held breath. The eastern glass was misted with condensation, and the familiar hum of bloom-magic throbbed low along the benches. But it wasn't the familiar rows of calming root or whispering mint that pulled his eye.

It was the back corner.

Something had bloomed.

It was small, no larger than his palm. Nestled where no seed had ever taken root, no water had ever been offered.

A gold-veined white bloom, petals spiraling inward like a secret.

He stopped, but not from fear.

From recognition.

Bram moved toward it slowly, one foot at a time, knees loose with something deeper than caution. When he knelt, his knees creaked against the wood, and he felt the ache in his back he usually ignored. But none of that mattered. The bloom pulsed once, faint light, faint warmth, and he knew.

He hadn't been a weaver. He hadn't been a spellcaster.

But he had been a gardener.

Even then.

And Ember...

Ember had come to him with a single bulb, shivering, dirt-caked, already bleeding light at the root. They had placed it in his hand, no words, no instructions.

And he had known.

He'd planted it, days later, not knowing what it would become. But believing it mattered.

That was all Ember ever asked of anyone.

Not worship. Not defense.

Just care.

And when the garden they'd shared—not this one, another—was torn apart by something unspoken, something no one dared to name, it was Bram who had taken the last root. Wrapped it in waxed cloth. Hidden it behind other seeds.

And forgotten.

Not all at once, but slowly and deliberately.

Until the memory grew too heavy to carry, so he folded it into silence and built his greenhouse around the echo of that grief.

He pressed his fingers to the new bloom's edge, and it pulsed once more.

Not in magic, but in forgiveness.

"I'm sorry," Bram whispered, voice rougher than usual.

The bloom didn't reply. It didn't need to.

The light held.

The warmth stayed.

And Bram closed his eyes and let the memory of Ember—their laughter, their stillness, the weight of their trust—settle back into him.

Not as pain. But as truth.

When he stood, he didn't feel heavier. He felt returned.

Somewhere, out in the Hollow, Ember had been seen. And now, they had been remembered.

Not as myth.

Not as mystery.

But as friend.

And maybe—just maybe—Bram would be brave enough to greet them again.

## Chapter One Hundred Thirty-Eight: The Gathering of the Remembered

The invitation had no ink. No name. No time.

But somehow, by sunrise, everyone knew where to go.

It started with the vines.

Sometime during the night, they had unwound from their usual paths and arched across the central clearing in the Hollow. Not overtaking. Not constraining. Just shaping a quiet, curving threshold. They formed a ring at the meadow's heart; a natural circle lined with white-veined blooms and newly awakened mosses that glowed faintly gold.

By morning, people were already arriving.

Not in a rush.

Not in a line.

But like water, moving toward gravity.

Baz came first, shoulders stiff with anticipation, one hand trailing a thread of copper that shimmered like memory. Behind him, Una arrived with her satchel tucked under one arm, a golden petal caught in her hair. Morgan followed, their steps slow, eyes tracing the pattern of vines as if memorizing a language, they were only now beginning to understand.

Cassie came last.

She walked alone, a mug of tea in one hand, her other gently brushing the charm at her wrist that had until yesterday, refused to rest. It was still now. Quiet. Like it was listening too.

They gathered not because they were told to, but because the Hollow was ready.

And so were they.

The clearing was still. Not silent. Birds chirped in the trees, and wind stirred through the upper canopy, but held. Like the land itself had drawn a circle around the moment and whispered, This matters.

Cassie stepped into the ring first. She didn't hesitate, but she moved slowly, reverently. The ground beneath her feet felt warm. Familiar. Like a heartbeat just beneath the soil.

Morgan followed.

Then Una.

Then the others.

Even Shaw came, hovering at the edge like a question, but present.

And finally, Bram arrived, his hands stained with soil and his eyes soft. He took his place beside a stone he hadn't touched in years.

Together, they waited. There was no flash of light. No sudden appearance.

Only a shift in the air.

Like the clearing exhaled.

And when it did—Ember was there.

They stood at the center of the ring, not conjured, not summoned, but present. Fully.

Their body shimmered only slightly at the edges, like dew catching first light. They wore no robe, no sigil. Their face was quiet. Steady. And wholly, unmistakably theirs.

Cassie's breath caught.

Morgan's fingers twitched.

Bram bowed his head.

No one moved to touch them.

But everyone felt it.

They were real.

Ember didn't speak at first. They simply looked at each person in turn.

Not searching. Not accusing.

Just recognizing.

And as their gaze met each face, something passed—quiet, invisible, but deeply known. A memory shared. A grief acknowledged. A presence returned not with expectation, but with grace.

Finally, Ember lifted their hand.

Not in command, in greeting.

And the vines along the ring bloomed in full. White and gold. Soft and luminous.

The scent of ash and thyme and something older filled the clearing.

Then Ember spoke in a voice low and clear, not loud, but carried by every leaf and root. "You remembered."

That was all and it was enough.

Cassie stepped forward. Her voice caught once, then steadied. "We didn't know we had forgotten."

Ember smiled, not sad, not triumphant. Just… true. "No one ever does."

Morgan came next. "You're not just memory."

"No," Ember said. "I'm story. And you chose to keep telling it."

Bram stepped forward last. "I'm sorry."

Ember turned toward him.

"You remembered with your hands, Bram. That's more than most ever do."

A hush fell. Then Shaw stepped inside the ring.

Everyone turned.

He didn't speak. Not at first. But his eyes—once full of suspicion and tight-edged fear—softened.

"I thought I was guarding truth," he said quietly. "But maybe I was just protecting a silence that didn't belong to me."

Ember nodded once, and the vines, once tight, parted further - making space.

What happened next wasn't spectacle. It was integration.

The roots beneath the Hollow pulsed. The threadlines stitched wider paths. The air grew warmer, welcoming.

The land didn't change, but it accepted.

And Ember?

They stepped forward into the ring.

Into the town.

Into the story that no longer needed to be buried.

And Alden's Landing? For the first time in a very long time, it became a place where every name, remembered or lost, was allowed to return.

## Chapter One Hundred Thirty-Nine: What We Carry Forward

The clearing had long emptied by the time they gathered again. The light was thin with late afternoon, brushing gold across the Hollow's stones and warming the window glass of the greenhouse. Outside, vines rustled gently, more relaxed now, their growth less urgent. The gold-threaded blooms still opened here and there, but the energy had softened, like a breath finally let out after years of holding.

Inside, the kettle steamed. Cassie poured slowly, hands steady, her eyes flicking up from time to time to meet the quiet glances of the others gathered around the worktable. No one sat in a circle. No one needed to.

There was no ceremony left to perform. Only reflection.

And breath. And tea.

Morgan leaned against the windowsill; a long sprig of white-veined bloom tucked behind one ear. They hadn't said much since Ember's appearance, only small observations, like stitching together the silence. Cassie suspected the experience had shaken something loose in them, not painfully, but definitively.

Una sat nearby, sketching absent-mindedly in the margin of a charm book. Every few lines she'd stop, tilt her head, and scratch something out. She hadn't returned to the thirteenth space since the gathering, but Cassie knew she would soon.

Bram had taken his usual chair, worn at the arms, and sipped slowly from a mug that had once belonged to his grandmother. His hands looked different somehow - older, maybe. Or simply truer. As if remembering Ember had allowed his body to settle more honestly into itself.

Baz sat cross-legged on the floor; tools scattered in a careful arc around him. He wasn't working, not really, but kept them close, as if

413

the act of arranging them gave shape to the feelings he wasn't quite ready to voice.

Cassie placed her own mug down with a soft clink. "So," she said. "That happened."

The others smiled, faint and full of weight.

Morgan finally spoke. "It didn't feel like an ending."

"It wasn't," Una replied.

Cassie nodded. "But it was a turning."

Bram glanced out the window. "They were… just as I remembered. And not at all."

Baz exhaled through his nose. "I've built a hundred circuits to track intention. Nothing I've made ever lit the way that moment did."

Cassie reached for the charm thread around her wrist. "I thought I was weaving stories all this time. But maybe I was just learning how to hold them."

Silence fell again. But it was companionable.

Then Morgan said, "Do you think Ember will stay?"

No one answered right away. It wasn't a question of belief. It was a question of need.

Una closed her sketchbook and looked up. "I don't think they came to stay. I think they came to return. To us. To this place. And to whatever comes after."

Bram nodded. "Sometimes return is enough."

Baz ran his fingers along a copper coil. "And sometimes it's just the beginning of building something stronger."

Cassie leaned back, letting the chair creak beneath her. "We didn't rescue them," she said. "We didn't fix anything."

Morgan smiled faintly. "We remembered."

"And that," Cassie said softly, "was the spell."

Outside, the wind stirred again. Not hard. Just enough to shake a few blooms loose and carry them along the threadline paths.

Cassie watched as one petal drifted by the window and caught a current of air, spiraling upward.

She didn't follow it. She didn't need to.

Inside her chest, something steady pulsed.

Not excitement. Not relief.

Just presence.

Whole, unraveled and rewoven.

And quietly, the Hollow began its next breath.

## Join the Magic Beyond the Pages

I love connecting with readers and would be thrilled to visit your book club, whether that's in person (if you're local or semi-local!) or through a cozy Zoom chat across the miles. We can dive into the world of Emerdeen, swap favorite moments, talk creative sparks, and maybe share a few secrets about what's next.

If your club would like to schedule a visit, reach out to me through my website at www.melodyksmith.com. Let's make some bookish magic together!

## Book Club Discussion Questions:

1. How does Cassie's understanding of magic evolve from her first discovery in *Stirred & Spellbound* to the deeper ancestral magic she learns to embody in *Rooted & Remembered*? In what ways does this mirror her emotional and personal growth?

2. Emerdeen itself changes throughout the two books. How does the world reflect the balance between creation and decay, and how does that balance parallel Cassie's own inner world?

3. The Crafting Coven grows from a collection of individuals into a shared force for restoration. How does the group dynamic shift across the two books, and what does this say about collective healing versus solitary strength?

4. Baz and Morgan both serve as mirrors for Cassie in different ways. How do their relationships with her reveal distinct aspects of identity, belonging, and purpose?

5. Throughout the series, crafting is portrayed as a conduit for magic and memory. How do the acts of making, mending, and creating symbolize transformation across both books?

6. *Rooted & Remembered* explores duality, shadow, and integration. How does this theme reframe what readers learned in *Stirred & Spellbound* about what it means to be "light" or "good"?

7. The natural world—especially plants, rivers, and roots— serves as both setting and symbol. Which moment involving nature resonated most deeply, and why?

8. The restoration of the World Tree is a major turning point. How do you interpret its symbolism, and how does it connect to Cassie's role as a conduit of balance?

9. By the end of *Rooted & Remembered*, magic feels less like something to wield and more like something to remember. How does this shift redefine the reader's understanding of Emerdeen's power and the lineage it protects?

10. Looking at the series as a whole, what do you think Emerdeen is ultimately trying to teach about creativity, heritage, and healing?

## About the Author

Melody K. Smith is an author, dreamer, tequila lover, wife, dog mom, and bestie material.

She has spent the past three decades bringing clarity and connection to the nonprofit world through organizational strategy, social media management, employee engagement and digital communications.

A lifelong creative, Melody channels her passion for storytelling into fiction that stirs the soul and sparks the imagination. When she isn't writing, she's elbows-deep in crafts, mixed media, and curated chaos—always drawn to the magic of making something from nothing. Her home is part art studio, part sanctuary, and part tasting room, where tequila is appreciated like fine poetry and poured with purpose.

Whether on the road, at her crafting table, or beneath the stars with a good drink in hand, she's always collecting stories and living a few worth telling.